STOCKHOLM SYNDROME

STOCKHOLM SYNDROME

MIRANDA MACLEOD

Apple Blossom Press
Bolton, MA

Stockholm Syndrome

Copyright © 2017 Miranda MacLeod

All rights reserved. No part of this publication may be reproduced, distributed, or transmitted in any form or by any means, including photocopying, recording, or other electronic or mechanical methods, without the prior written permission of the publisher or author, except in the case of brief quotations embodied in critical reviews and certain other noncommercial uses permitted by copyright law.

Find out more: www.mirandamacleod.com
Contact the author: miranda@mirandamacleod.com

This is a work of fiction. Any resemblance of characters to actual persons, living or dead, is purely coincidental.

Apple Blossom Press
PO Box 547
Bolton MA 01740

ONE

CLICK-A. CLICK-A. CLICK-A.

It was the first thing Leigh heard as she regained consciousness; that constant tick-tick-ticking in the distance. The sound was rapid and rhythmic, like the persistent beat of the metronome *Fröken Olson* used to torment her with during piano lessons when she was a young girl in Stockholm.

"Snabbare. Du håller inte takten."

"Play faster. You're not keeping the beat." Her brain translated the memory into English without effort. Thanks to having an American father and Swedish mother, she'd known both languages since birth, and spoke without a trace of a foreign accent in either.

Click-a. Click-a. Click-a.

Would it ever stop? Her stomach knotted, palms sweating with all the remembered panic of lesson days when she knew she would never be able to play the first movement of Mozart's "A Little Night Music" at full tempo, no matter how many hours she'd practiced. She'd hated piano, quitting by age ten and never thinking of it again. So, of all things, why the hell was she hearing a metronome now?

More importantly, why did everything seem so dark and cramped? She shifted her body in place, which caused her head to spin. *Why does the whole world seem to be flipped upside down around me?*

Adrenaline seared her veins as full awareness of her situation kicked in and sent Leigh bolt upright from her crouched position. It was a huge mistake. With a sickening thud, her head made contact with the roof of whatever space confined her. The resulting flashes of color that burst against her retinas on impact were all that was visible in the utter blackness. She curled back into a ball and rested her cheek against the cold metal surface beneath her. *Where the hell am I?*

One arm gingerly ventured out, just far enough to brush across the surface above her head. Rough carpeting scratched her fingertips. She sniffed the air and breathed in a rubbery smell of tires with a pungency that coated the back of her throat. There was a whiff of gasoline, too—a faint, sharp smell—yet there were no sounds to indicate an idling engine.

In fact, there were no noises at all. No voices or traffic sounds—just silence—apart from the infernal clicking that had yet to cease. Synapses mired in the pea soup of her addled brain sputtered and sparked as she tried to muster enough concentration to put the puzzle pieces together.

The clicking could be from a turn signal. Maybe I'm in the trunk of a car? A car that's flipped upside down, she amended, owing to the oddness of her positioning. *But how did I get here, and is there anyone else around?*

Too many questions made her reel, and no answers seemed forthcoming. That her current predicament was somehow work related was a safe bet, given that she made her living as a spy, but when it came to the exact sequence of events that had led up to her being stuck where she was, mostly she was drawing a blank.

She'd been working around the clock for weeks, that much Leigh remembered, pulling twelve-hour shifts on Embassy Row from the back of a white-paneled surveillance van that masqueraded as a cable installer's vehicle. Her team had been tasked with identifying the boss of a Berlin-based crime syndicate, and the only solid lead her agency had turned up was a possible connection to the German diplomatic corps.

Like so many of her team's investigations in their beginning stages, it had been going about as well as a search for a needle in a haystack. How do you gather significant intel on a crime boss who has no known address, no confirmed associates, who doesn't own a cell phone, and without having so much as a single photo or voice recording of the subject on file?

Good fucking question.

But that's why the government issued Leigh a

paycheck every week, to figure shit like that out. Most people thought the spy business was all glamor and intrigue. Boy, were they wrong. Mostly, it was a slog, and often the biggest breaks came down to sheer dumb luck, like bumping into a pretty girl at a bar and sneaking a peak at her phone when she was too drunk to notice.

The bar.

Leigh groaned as disjointed memories from earlier that evening flashed in her head, like a slideshow where the frames had all become jumbled up in the wrong order. *Drinks. Scantily clad women. Strobe lights and a throbbing bass. Bright red lips. More drinks.* Her stomach lurched alarmingly. So, *so* many drinks. But the pieces were coming together enough to make out at least part of the picture.

Ladies' night at Cobalt.

It'd been her first night off in weeks and she should have gone straight home for some shut-eye, but how could she once she'd heard one of the nightclubs in Dupont Circle was hosting a lesbian night? Leigh loved nothing better than a party. Used to be that if you were looking for a little action, you could at least count on the Phase. That club was notorious for its rundown interior, too-loud music, overpriced drinks, and not enough bathrooms… *God, I miss that place.* Ever since it closed, an evening out was about as common for Leigh as watching a full eclipse of a blue moon while riding bareback on a unicorn. No way was she going home without at least making an appearance.

And then she'd recognized the woman standing at the bar—Giselle—an au pair from Paris who just happened to work for the family that lived next door to one of Leigh's prime targets. Her gut had told her it was the break she'd been waiting for. She wasn't interested in the girl, per se—though with a body like that, poured into a spandex micro-dress that was more of a formality than an actual item of clothing, it's not like Leigh would've said no—but her real target had been the girl's bejeweled iPhone.

On it, Leigh knew they might find a text to some new phone number they could add to the contact tree, or a photo snapped from the playground that would reveal someone they hadn't seen before lurking around the neighborhood. Would Giselle's phone offer such a clue? Probably not, but stranger things had happened.

Somewhere back in the van, Leigh also knew there was a file on the young French woman, along with files on every other resident of the neighborhood. She hadn't been able to recall all the details they'd gathered on Giselle, but she also knew there wouldn't be many. A name, a passport photo, and perhaps a thoroughly mundane log of all her dog walks and trips around the block with the baby. She'd have liked more. The fact that the au pair was interested in women could have been *super* helpful, for instance, if someone had bothered to make a note—but gathering what little they'd managed on so many residents had been enough of a daunting task that she could hardly expect more than bare bones.

Technically, protocol dictated that Leigh should've had that mostly useless file in hand before making a move, and more importantly, permission from her boss, Javier, too. But all Leigh had needed was to get her hands on that phone for two seconds. Waiting around for a green light on something so simple was an agonizing waste of time, and a potential missed opportunity. One thing Leigh had learned in this business was, moments like that were fleeting. Acting fast on your feet could lead to glory, and potentially the promotion to team lead she so desired.

Of course, ignoring the rules and going with your gut could also get you stuffed in a trunk when you least expected it. It was an important corollary to the gut rule that Leigh really needed to take to heart with greater conviction in the future. Assuming she had a future.

Her hand traveled back along her scalp, and was about half the distance to her neck when it hit a lump the size of a quail's egg. At least now she knew why it hurt so much. Either it was an injury she'd sustained when the car flipped, or someone had hit her to knock her out, and done a pretty thorough job of it. She leaned toward the latter explanation. On impulse, she patted her pockets. No keys or phone, so they'd likely searched her body, too, while she was out cold.

Could it have been Giselle? The sound of her quickening pulse merged in her ears with the clicking turn signal. Had she read the situation all wrong? If Giselle was a foreign agent, she could have been surveilling Leigh all along, and the encounter at the club was a setup. Or she might have been a member of the very crime syndicate they were hunting, and then Leigh was in some real trouble.

Goddamn it, Leigh, we have protocol for a reason!

It was Javier's voice, with its slight Spanish lilt, that boomed inside her cranium, ricocheting off her skull and lodging itself deep in the gray matter. *You're a spy, not a fucking cowboy!* She dug her fingertips into her temples, trying to ease the ache. Why did the memory of his voice have to be every bit as goddamn loud as the real thing, even if it did make a valid point?

Giselle an enemy agent? Preposterous. They'd flirted and had a few drinks. Okay, more than a few. But at no time had Leigh sensed danger. She'd bet money that Giselle was no more than what she appeared to be, a smoking hot au pair who giggled a lot and was obsessed with Snapchat and dancing.

Oh, god, that dancing. Leigh's loins tightened despite the precariousness of her situation as she remembered the sway of the woman's hips, and the light sheen of sweat that had shimmered between her breasts in the dim light of the club's dance floor. Ironically, a little light bondage had definitely been high on Leigh's list of ways to end the evening. She just hadn't anticipated that she'd find herself alone, fully clothed, and in a trunk.

Shit. I'm still in the trunk. She'd been trying so hard in her groggy state to remember how she'd gotten there in the first place that Leigh had almost forgotten she hadn't yet managed to escape. She drew a breath and coughed, her lungs tight with the effort. The air in the trunk had grown stale, the gasoline smell increasingly pungent, and she was starting to lose her ability to think clearly.

I've gotta get outta here before I suffocate.

She strained to detect the sound of any other people beyond the confines of the trunk, but they were just as lacking as before. Wherever she was, it was isolated, and she was alone. Given that the car she'd been abducted in was upside down, something bad had happened while she was unconscious. Either her captors had fled when the car flipped, leaving her behind, or else they were out cold in the main part of the car. If she was going to escape, now was as good a time as any, before anyone who might be unconscious woke up.

Leigh swiveled her head as fully as its aching would permit, and blinked into the darkness. It was still as black as when she'd first opened her eyes, but her hopes rose at the thought that if she looked really hard, she might spot a glow-in-the dark latch release lever. That was the easiest way to get out of a trunk, assuming the lid hadn't been crushed against the ground when the car flipped.

There was no sense getting her hopes up. Without enough open space beneath it for the trunk lid to swing open, her options would be extremely limited. She'd have to check.

Leigh made a gentle bouncing motion and the lid of the trunk moved up and down freely. It was a promising start. She bounced harder, and her hopes rose as the trunk continued to move unimpeded. If she could find the lever, there was a good chance she could open the lid enough to escape.

But her hopes were quickly dashed. Either it was an older model car that wasn't equipped with one, or else her captors had thought ahead and removed it. She fought back her rising panic, focusing instead on the skills she'd gained through her years of agency training. There were two more ways to get out of a trunk, but she'd need a clear head to carry them out.

If the backseat folded flat, that was her next best bet. Trailing her hand along the carpeted surface of the seatbacks, she sighed in relief as her fingers dipped into a break between the seats. There was no release button to be found, but Leigh's legs were strong. Pivoting until her feet were against the seat, she pulled her knees back as far as the cramped space would allow and let them fly. Nothing budged. Leigh groaned and let her head droop against the floor.

Not the floor. The ceiling. Relief flooded her. She hadn't accounted for the fact that the car was upside down. Instead of being stuck, there was a good chance she'd just applied force to the wrong part of the seat. She readjusted and tried once more. This time, her reward was a loud crack as the seatback yielded beneath her feet.

Hallelujah!

She lost no time in scrambling into position to ease her body through the opening, but almost instantly she encountered a new obstacle. Something was blocking the seat. With sweat pooling along her brow, she pushed her shoulder against the seatback until the opening was large enough to fit a hand through, but she simply lacked the strength to widen the gap any further. Fingertips tingling, she patted her hand around on the other side of the opening, sucking in her breath as she made contact with something cold and clammy.

Her hand recoiled, knowing there was only one thing that felt like that—human flesh. Steeling her nerves, she reached out once more and encountered a hand, its dangling, sausage fingers slightly curled against the car rooftop beneath it. Then a wrist, covered in wiry hair. No pulse.

She squeezed her eyes shut, trying to picture the scene that was just out of view. The victim was a man, still strapped into his seat and suspended upside down. Judging by his hand, he was large, too large to even hope to move out of the way, given her limited mobility. She swallowed roughly, trying not to think about her dry throat and the agonizing heat that had built up in the trunk, then swept her hand along again, searching for anything she might have missed. Her breath caught as she brushed against something hard and thin. *A phone!* It must have fallen out of the dead man's pocket during the accident.

Leigh grabbed the phone and drew her hand back through the crack. Fingers trembling, she pressed the button and squinted at the sudden illumination from the screen. *Locked.* Her disappointment was barely discernible at this point, having already experienced so many previous complications to inoculate her. After all, she was a spy. She could beat a locked cell phone if she had to.

As the screen went dark, her brain lit up with one final plan. The trunk release cable. It was third on the list of common ways to escape a trunk, but she'd known her chances of finding the thin cable in the dark were less than ideal. *With the light from a phone, however…*

She shimmied to the driver's side and made a sweep with the light, her heart skipping a beat as she spotted the black cable wedged along the side. Leigh let out her breath, the sudden movement of air providing fleeting relief from the sweltering heat as it swept across her damp forehead. She curled and uncurled her fingers in preparation, testing her dexterity, then wrapped them around the cable and gave a tug. A click of the latch, an almost imperceptible drop of the trunk lid beneath her, then nothing. A victory cry died on her lips. In a fit of frustration, she tossed her body back and forth, trying to dislodge the latch, but it was no use. It was stuck tight, and there was only one option left.

Though the thought of touching the corpse on the other side of the seat divide sent a wave of nausea through her, Leigh willed herself to move. With the phone on, she wedged it beneath the dead man's hand, maneuvering it until his fingertip was squarely within the circle on the screen. The phone now unlocked, Leigh quickly changed the password so she could unlock it on her own in the future, as taking the finger along was *not* an option she could stomach. Then she opened his contact page and blinked rapidly as she took in its wealth of content, while joy and despair warred within.

This is a goldmine! Despite the seriousness of her personal situation, her thought was of her case. Her gamble had paid off. Whoever this man had been, he was connected to the Berlin crime syndicate, no question. She recognized enough of the names and numbers to confirm it, but there were so many new ones, too. Any one of these could be the break they needed to finally close in on the big boss. *It's just a matter of time now.* With any luck, they'd be listening in on every one of that bastard's phone calls by morning.

There was just one problem. To deliver the goods,

she had to get out of the trunk. And that's where the despair came in, because her only hope for rescue was to call her agency's emergency line. Calling 911 was out of the question. *What am I doing locked in a trunk with a dead man's phone, officer? Please refrain from carting me off to jail and allow me to explain!* But as her finger hovered above the keypad, she froze.

Despite the trauma her head had sustained, 911 was at least a number she could remember. But the agency's hotline, the one some clueless middle manager insisted on changing more often than a pair of socks to comply with his bullshit idea of a security protocol? *Yeah, not so much.* If she'd had her own phone, the number *du jour* would have been conveniently entered under the name of a fictitious pizza delivery place. Inconveniently, the dead thug who had owned this phone had not done her the courtesy of programming her secret agency hotline into his speed dial for her.

Think, dammit!

Her eighth-grade locker combination bobbed to the surface of her brain, along with the phone number for her mother's old Stockholm flat, her shoe size, and the number of the last page she'd read in the paperback novel she'd grabbed at the drugstore to pass the time in the surveillance van. The purchase had come to six dollars and twenty-seven cents, another number that she could recall that would do her no good.

Be systematic, Leigh. Think like a spy. It was Javier's

voice, calm and soothing this time. Systematic. She'd entered the new number just a few days ago. It had to be in her memory bank somewhere. She needed to start with something she knew and hope the rest would follow. *Area code?* She took a cleansing breath, clearing her mind. Two-oh-two. The D.C. area code was two-oh-two. She closed her eyes and breathed again, focusing on letting the breath out in a slow and steady stream. *Two-oh-two, two-oh-two.*

Her eyes opened in the dark, a self-satisfied grin stretching her cheeks as she punched the number onto the keypad. She'd remembered, and just in time. Wooziness made the screen dance in front of her. The heat and lack of oxygen were taking their toll, the smell of gasoline overwhelming now. Leigh knew she had little time left to summon help. Staving off a fainting spell, she waited tensely as the phone began to ring.

TWO

STRETCHING her arms toward the fluorescent light fixture that flickered above her head, Amanda waited for the satisfying pop of stiff tendons in her neck. It was late, but her night was far from over. Around her in the call center at the greater D.C. area's most popular public radio station, rows of cubicles sat empty. It was a hopping place in the daytime, full of enthusiastic volunteers and the constant ringing of phones, but not a lot of people called in for a fundraiser after midnight, so aside from the night manager in his office, Amanda had the volunteer room to herself.

Though, technically, she wasn't a volunteer. She wasn't *that* much of a masochist to sit by herself in the world's least ergonomic chair, in the middle of the night, answering phones for no pay. No, she was an office temp—a slightly gentler form of masochism—and she was certainly no stranger to the work.

Temping hadn't been her first career choice, if you could even call it that. Not by a long shot. She'd been on the fast track to law school, top of her class at Boston College. She'd aced the LSAT, scored glowing letters of recommendation from her professors, and had all her applications neatly stuffed in a dozen thick envelopes, stamps in place. One afternoon she'd found herself in front of a big blue mailbox on Commonwealth Avenue, the envelopes clutched in a hand that was frozen above the slot.

She couldn't bring herself to do it, couldn't drop them in. In that moment she'd realized two things, that she would rather die than become a lawyer, and that after four years of college, she didn't have the first clue what she wanted to do with her life. The only certainty was that her bills wouldn't pay themselves, and temp work was a steady gig.

The phone on her desk jangled, and Amanda reached out to catch it on the first ring.

She smiled into the phone, knowing that friendliness came through in her voice better that way. Friendly voices made for bigger donations. She might be a temp, but she took pride in doing any job to the best of her ability. Not that anyone usually noticed. People paid about as much attention to temps as they did to the office furniture.

"Hello! Thank you for calling Baltimore-Washington Public Radio!"

"*Que?*"

"Baltimore-Washington Public Radio? You've called the pledge drive hotline."

"*Maria?*"

Amanda sighed, her smile fading. "No, I'm sorry. You have the wrong number."

"*Que?*"

"El numero? Uh…tiene el numero equivocado."

She heard a click as the person hung up on the other end without another word. She wouldn't have understood them, anyway. She didn't speak Spanish, but she could say "sorry, wrong number" in at least four different languages. That was a constant. After answering phones in offices all around greater metro Boston, it had arguably been her most transferrable skill when it had come time to move. She sighed. Four years spent looking for a career path that could hold her interest, and the only thing that had changed in all that time was her location.

She'd made the move south to Baltimore six months ago. Aunt Millie was the reason. *Poor Aunt Millie.* At seventy-five years old, her mother's older sister had gone from the occasional forgotten detail to exhibiting symptoms that were increasingly worrying. Still, Amanda had remained optimistic that her condition would improve with a little rest and relaxation, or perhaps some added exercise or a change in diet. But it was when her aunt had asked how her mother was doing during one of their weekly phone chats that Amanda knew she couldn't ignore it any longer, not if her aunt's memory had diminished to the point that she'd forgotten her only sister's death from cancer the year before. It was a lapse that was impossible to ignore or explain away. The time had come to take action.

With her mom gone, Amanda had no one left but Millie, and she'd been raised to believe that family came first. To be honest, she'd welcomed the change, as the mid-Atlantic was enjoying much milder weather than New England's brutal winter that year. It's not like she was leaving much behind—no career, no relationship, not even a pet. She'd simply wrapped up her last temp assignment in Boston, given her landlord notice, and the next thing she knew she was moving a few boxes into the spare bedroom at her aunt's home in the august Baltimore neighborhood of Ten Hills. She'd registered at a new temp agency when she arrived—the one and only true benefit of temping being that you could do it anywhere you went.

Her plan had been to work while keeping a watchful eye on Millie, and it had gone well enough at first. In fact, Amanda had been placed at an investment company downtown, and there were signs that it could lead to a permanent position. It still wasn't her dream job, perhaps, but as her twenty-sixth birthday had approached, Amanda had begun to see the appeal of a steady job with decent pay and benefits, and maybe a little bit of appreciation now and again. The next time a job offer came around, she'd decided she'd accept. But that prospect had evaporated when she'd arrived home one night to find the fire chief waiting at her front door. Her aunt had set a chicken to roast in the oven and forgotten it was there until neighbors called to report black smoke pouring from the kitchen window. The hard truth was that Millie simply couldn't be trusted on her own anymore.

Since then, Amanda's world had consisted of days spent in the grueling process of sorting out insurance coverage and getting her feisty aunt settled into the right assisted-living facility. They'd been through three so far, and Amanda had a sneaking suspicion they weren't quite through. That left only nights for working, and the graveyard shift options weren't exactly inspiring. The public radio pledge drive was just the latest in a string of overnight temp gigs, neither the best nor the worst she'd experienced. She'd done anything from working at an answering service to filling in at the security desk in a high-rise lobby. If she'd had trouble finding her calling before, she certainly wasn't going to find it now. She could send a trained monkey to do most of these jobs for her and no one would notice the difference. Still, it could be worse.

She glanced at the white mug on her desk, emblazoned with the station's call letters, and gave a half smile to see it filled to the brim. Her dream job it was not, but at least this assignment provided unlimited free coffee and plenty of downtime to catch up on some reading. Coffee was her lifeblood for the long nights, and more and more, the escape of a good book was the highlight of each day.

Reaching into the cotton canvas satchel that sat by her feet, Amanda pulled out that evening's reading options and plopped them on the desk in front of her. She'd brought two books with her tonight. One was a paperback, its pages dog-eared and the cover torn. It was a classic spy novel and arguably her favorite book of all time. The other was larger and brand new, its glossy cover pristine and without a single crease. This book was filled with logic puzzles, which the author claimed had come directly from secret tests administered by the Soviet Union to would-be spies at the height of the Cold War. A careful observer might detect a theme to her choice of reading materials, and for good reason. When it came to anything dealing with espionage, Amanda was obsessed.

She studied her options, weighing which was a better fit for her mood. *Puzzles, for sure.* Temp work could be a mind-numbing experience, and puzzles were the best way she'd found to stay sharp. She rubbed her palms together, giddy at the prospect of diving in. Her spy skills were formidable, if she did say so herself. She was a natural talent.

Now that *would have been the perfect career for me.*

An incredible longing swept over her for a time period that had so cruelly come to an end just before her birth. She would have made a kick-ass spy, if only the Iron Curtain hadn't been a mere memory by the time she was a kid. Now, real spies were a relic of the past, and she was stuck wasting her talents night after night for barely more than minimum wage.

Most people thought her obsession with espionage was weird. Her Aunt Millie was the one person who understood. In fact, the puzzle book had been a recent gift from her aunt, who had signed the title page with best wishes for her twenty-fifth birthday. Of course, Amanda had actually been turning twenty-six, but the fact her aunt had remembered at all had brought tears to Amanda's eyes. It was the perfect gift, and proof that even in her impaired state, her aunt was there for her like no one else.

Amanda had just extended her arm to scoop up the book when a shadow fell across her desk. Her body tensed, ready to pounce, until she heard the familiar voice of the night manager.

"Hey, Amanda. Pretty dead in here tonight, huh?"

She took a deep breath to compose her nerves before swiveling in her chair to face him.

If I had a stiletto strapped to my ankle right now, you're the one who'd be dead. She didn't say that out loud, of course, knowing instinctively that a temp who talked about knife-wielding at work didn't tend to get her contract renewed. And with bills piling up for herself and her aunt, she kinda needed the job. Instead she plastered the same pleasant smile across her face that she used to answer the phone. "Hey, Adam. Yeah, it's really quiet tonight."

"Someone must have locked up the cell phones at the White House, 'cause there hasn't been a single outrageous tweet all day to keep listeners glued to the news past their bedtimes."

"Thank god for that." Though she usually kept her opinions to herself, she'd found it was hard to do at a twenty-four-hour news station. Luckily, she and Adam shared similar political views, and she'd enjoyed having a like-minded companion to talk with during the long nights. "Sometimes it's nice to go a full day without being terrified by current events, you know?"

"What, Russian plots and white supremacist rallies aren't your idea of fun?"

Amanda laughed good-naturedly, sneaking only the quickest sideways glance at her book. She longed to start reading, but it would have to keep until Adam was done. *I wonder how long that will be?*

His expression grew serious. "You know, you've been here a couple of weeks now and I wanted to talk to you about something."

Butterflies fluttered in Amanda's stomach. *Is he going to offer me a job?* She'd exceeded the fundraising targets almost every night since she'd arrived. Maybe he'd actually noticed? She thought once more of the stack of bills at home. Assisted living wasn't cheap.

This wasn't her dream job, but she was competent at it. And it was nice to be acknowledged for her hard work. *Maybe it's worth considering…*

"Amanda?" Adam was staring at her, and she realized she hadn't responded.

"Sorry. Please, go ahead." She looked at him intently, waiting for him to resume but becoming puzzled as the tips of his earlobes grew alarmingly pink.

"It's just that, well…Amanda, I was wondering…" He stopped mid-thought, gulping as if swallowing the rest of the words.

Amanda's lungs tightened, suddenly sensing what was coming and dreading it. *This isn't about a job after all.*

The rest of his words tumbled out in a rush. "Anyway, it's so quiet tonight, and I just kicked up a recorded news program from the BBC that's going to run another hour, so I was thinking that no one would miss us if we ducked across the street for a coffee, you know?"

Damn it. He's asking me out.

It wasn't the first time something like this had happened while on a temp assignment. She supposed she was attractive enough, in a nonthreatening, girl-next-door kind of way. When she was young, her mother used to say it was Amanda's smile that made people stop and take notice, her teeth in particular. She'd said they sparkled like a girl in a chewing gum commercial, and that was why all the boys couldn't help falling head over heels. Alas, the older Amanda became, the more she realized she had little interest in all those boys, and the sad fact that her teeth had never had anywhere near the same magical power of attraction when it came to women, had always felt like one of life's more spiteful jokes.

She drew her lips in, trying to minimize the effects of her stupidly mesmerizing teeth. "That's really nice, Adam, but I just made myself a cup." She lifted the mug and took a sip to emphasize this point, hoping perhaps the dark brown liquid would dull her shiny smile in the process. "Plus, if we got caught..." He opened his mouth, the set of his jaw making it clear he intended to plead his case, and her heart sank as she realized that subtlety was going to be lost on him. "Look, Adam, the truth is that the only thing that might entice me to risk losing this gig is if you told me you were taking me across the street to meet your really hot sister, okay?"

He blinked, then his jaw snapped shut, lips pressed into a pout, as the meaning of her words sank in. "Oh. Huh. Another time, maybe."

Despite the rejection, he whistled a little tune as he walked away, and Amanda was relieved to see him taking it so well. One of the major drawbacks of temp work was how often she got to repeat this conversation as she flitted from office to office. But Adam returned to his desk without further incident, and

Amanda felt reassured that the remainder of her time at the station would be business as usual, even if a permanent position was unlikely. She shrugged. It was just as well. Working in the call center of a public radio station full time would have been as good a fit for her as going on a date with Adam—so uncomfortable she'd probably have broken out in a rash.

Someday I'll find the right one.

Whether she was thinking of a career or her love life, it wasn't entirely clear.

The hands of the clock were moving backward. Amanda would swear to it. Her coffee was gone and she was fading fast.

Recalling her stack of books, Amanda once more reached for the one with the shadowy Soviet spy on the cover. The phones had remained quiet all night, and Adam would need some time to lick his wounds before being worth much in the conversation department. A good brain teaser was just what she needed to keep her awake. As she thumbed through the table of contents, a thin envelope fell to the desktop. Amanda frowned as she picked it up and broke the seal with her index finger. Inside was a sheet of letterhead and a full-color trifold brochure.

Spy-ventures Academy of Espionage, the front of the brochure read, with the word 'spy' printed inside the outline of a magnifying glass to really drive the theme home. Amanda snorted. *What is this, some sort of Hogwarts letter for spies?*

She squinted at the brochure photos of smiling men and women wearing an assortment of stiletto heels and trench coats as they engaged in martial arts, and shook her head. *No self-respecting spy would actually dress like that!*

The brochure promised a comprehensive assortment of spy classes and true to life make-believe missions, perfect for every budget—though the price range they advertised was enough to make her eyes bug. *People pay that much money for nonsense like this?* And yet, the more she read, the more her curiosity was piqued. What she wouldn't give to enroll in just one of their basic courses, if only to see what it was like. But unless she won the lottery, it wasn't meant to be.

She pushed the brochure aside, but her eyes were drawn to the letter, which remained folded and unread where it had fallen. Curious, Amanda picked it up, her heart pounding ever faster as she read. *Dear Agent Amanda Princeton*, it began, and already it had her full attention. A personalized letter? That wasn't exactly standard practice for a mass marketing campaign. *Congratulations on your acceptance to Spy-ventures Academy of Espionage.*

Her fingers trembled. Acceptance? But she'd never applied! Where had this come from? She glanced around, half expecting to see an owl after all. *Or maybe owls are just what they send for wizard school letters. Spies would probably use carrier pigeons.* But there were none of those, either, and she nibbled on her lip, deep in thought, until the answer came to her. *Aunt Millie, of course!*

The letter had been tucked into her birthday present, after all, and it was exactly the type of gift her sweet, quirky aunt would think to indulge her with. In fact, her aunt had bought her things like this before, if not quite so elaborate. She was always ordering her spy books or subscriptions to surveillance magazines, and a few times had even purchased her spy-themed mail-order mystery kits where a mystery had to be solved using a series of clues that arrived in packages in the mail. A training course at an honest-to-goodness spy academy had Aunt Millie's name written all over it. She'd probably put the envelope in the book to surprise her, and then forgotten all about it by the time Amanda unwrapped it.

Imagine me going to spy school…it's too much! And yet she knew she couldn't give the gift back, and only partially because her aunt wouldn't let her. The truth was, she was dying to see what this academy of espionage was all about. She grabbed up the brochure again, this time grinning from ear to ear at each picture, which inspired feelings of glee instead of envy or derision now that she knew she'd soon be joining their ranks. *Although if they try to make me wear high heels or a trench coat, I'll have a few choice words for them.*

She was lost in a world of shadowy operatives when the sudden ringing of the phone on her desk made her jump. She stared at it in confusion for a moment before answering, having forgotten where she was in her excitement. "Hello," she said in her most professional voice, grinning broadly and forcing her thoughts to focus on doing her job. "Thank you for calling Baltim—"

A woman's voice, hushed and urgent, filled Amanda's ear, cutting her off mid-sentence. *"This is Agent Vesper, delta omega, requesting passphrase authentication."*

"Oh…kay."

Amanda stifled a sigh against the phone's mouthpiece. *Another crazy person.* Along with wrong numbers, crazy people were something a temp could count on when answering phones. Since starting at the station, there'd been at least one nut each night, plus half a dozen in a single shift when there'd been a full moon. Still, even a crazy person might have a credit card and want to make a donation toward quality programming, so she'd better do what they were paying her to do.

Plus, this woman's voice was super sexy, all husky and breathless. She wouldn't mind hearing it some more, even if its owner *was* certifiable. "We appreciate your call. If I could just get your details?"

"Repeat, this is Agent Vesper, delta omega. Make me a drink?"

Well, isn't that forward of you, Sexy Voice Lady? But the way the stranger spoke, so confident and commanding, sent a shiver of desire right down to Amanda's toes, which were curling inside her sensible black flats as if ready to spring into action and fulfill the woman's every demand.

Amanda's lack of control over her physical response to the woman's voice rapidly filled her with a fierce indignation, all but obliterating the initial attraction. She scowled at the phone. *What's up with this looney tune?* She was about to hang up when the envelope from Spy-ventures caught her eye. *Agent Vesper?* She tapped one finger against her lips, suddenly certain she'd overlooked an important explanation for the weirdness of this call.

Could this be part of their spy game? *Is this my first mission?* The receiver slipped against her suddenly slick palms as she brought the phone back to her ear. "I'm sorry. You were saying something about making you a drink?"

There was a muffled, guttural sound on the other end of the phone that hinted of frustration, but when the woman spoke, her voice was all business. *"You must be new. It's the first half of the passphrase. You need to authenticate with the other half."*

Amanda grinned triumphantly. *A riddle.* It was just as she'd suspected. *A drink. A drink…spies and a drink…*There was James Bond, of course. That had to be it, but what phrase would be the code? *Shaken not stirred?* Amanda shook her head. *Too easy.* If that turned out to be the answer, she'd be so disappointed. It was no challenge at all. *Think. Agent Vesper wants a drink.*

Amanda chuckled as the answer came to her. *Of*

course! The Vesper Martini. It was the martini invented by double-oh-seven himself, the recipe enshrined in the pages of *Casino Royale*. Like the devoted fan she was, she knew the passage from memory.

"Just a moment," Amanda recited. "Three measures of Gordons, one of vodka, half a measure of Kina Lillet. Shake it very well until it's ice-cold, then add a large thin slice of lemon peel. Got it?" She tensed, waiting for the woman to respond. They were, word for word, the directions given by Bond to the bartender. It just *had* to be the right answer.

"Well, it's about time. I thought I'd suffocate waiting. I need an extraction. Give me a secure line where I can send my coordinates."

Amanda bristled at the woman's rudeness. For the money her aunt had paid this operation, their employees could be a little more polite. Still, she supposed the urgency made it feel more authentic. She rattled off her cell phone number.

"And that's a secure line?"

Amanda rolled her eyes. "Yes, of course it is." *A secure line. Geez. Talk about taking this game a little too seriously.* A moment later, her satchel vibrated with the received text. "Okay, got it."

"Please hurry." The woman's voice had grown faint and breathy, as if running out of air.

Amanda frowned. "You mean, right now?"

"Uh, yeah." Despite her breathlessness, a barb of sarcasm gave renewed strength to her words. *"I'm trapped in a trunk and there's a dead body in the backseat. Now would be preferable."*

The line went dead and Amanda's brow furrowed as she replaced the phone in its cradle. Her shift wasn't over for another three hours, and ducking out early to play a make-believe spy game was just as poor an excuse as grabbing a cup of coffee with a date, but something about the conversation left her jittery. *It felt so real.* She knew it wasn't, but no matter how many times she repeated that fact to herself, her spirit remained troubled. Finally, she stood and approached Adam's office.

"Hey, Adam?"

He looked up from his desk, a hint of leftover embarrassment shadowing his features. "Uh, Amanda. What can I do for you?"

"It's just, I'm not feeling so well." She wrung her hands, feeling guilty over shirking her duties. "And it's so quiet tonight…"

Adam waved his hand. "Go on, go home. I can handle any calls."

Amanda felt her cheeks begin to stretch into a grin and stopped them short. *No sense torturing the poor man with my wretchedly perfect teeth, now that he's being so accommodating.* She nodded instead. "Thanks. I really appreciate it."

With her books stuffed back into her satchel and the coordinates plugged into her GPS, Amanda was out the door and behind the wheel of Aunt Millie's

Mini Cooper in a flash. Her hands, even sweatier now than they'd been on the phone, gripped the steering wheel tightly.

Am I really doing this?

But there was really no question that she was. How could she not? With the worry over her aunt's illness and trying to earn enough to make ends meet, it had been way too long since she'd been able to just let loose and have some fun. She needed a little escape, and a spy fantasy was just the thing. Besides, she could tell her aunt all about it when she went to visit the next day.

She started the car and navigated the mostly deserted streets of Baltimore with ease. Muggy night air streamed through the rolled down windows, and there was the smell of impending rain from a summer storm. As she headed toward an unknown location well outside the city limits, unsure of what she would find at the other end, she couldn't remember the last time she'd felt so excited to be alive.

THREE

DIRT CRUNCHED beneath her tires as the Mini slowed to a crawl. Amanda eyed the glowing GPS screen suspiciously, increasingly convinced it had led her astray and was about to send her plummeting to her death down some unmarked ravine that lurked just beyond her headlights' reach. She'd been to the middle of nowhere before, and it hadn't been half as remote as this place. But she'd checked Agent Vesper's coordinates three times. This had to be it.

Thick clouds from the evening's brewing thunderstorm parted overhead and the glinting of a moonbeam off something in the distance caught her attention. There was an outline of a hulking shape that sat roughly five hundred feet dead ahead in a clearing at the edge of dense woods. *A car?* But it was all wrong for that. Amanda's nerve endings buzzed as she tried to process what she saw. If it was a car, it was flipped over, wheels pointing to the sky. Her breath caught as she imagined the caller with the sexy voice trapped inside. Her foot twitched, itching to press the gas pedal to the floor, but she reined in the impulse. *She's not really trapped, dummy, remember? None of this is real.* She was still uncertain of the safety of the road ahead, and there was no sense getting herself killed for a game.

She engaged the brake and sat motionless, taking a minute to let her eyes adjust before scanning every detail that the car's high beams revealed. Now that she'd had a chance to study it, she concluded that the mystery shape was definitely a car, probably a large sedan. Though its topsy-turvy state still filled her with unease, its very presence at eye level instead of in a ditch reassured her that the road might be safe enough to continue along, though slowly. She shifted into first gear and pressed the gas just enough to work her way back up to a crawl.

A breeze rippled through the trees, bringing a sudden stench through the open car windows that burned her nostrils. Amanda tensed and stopped the car, pulse ticking faster as she recognized the scent of gasoline. She gave a thin laugh at her response. *God, that feels real. A little too real.* Though she knew it was just a special effect, the combination of the flipped vehicle and the terrible smell inspired caution. She shut off the engine and decided to approach the rest of the distance on foot. Outside the car there were no sounds other than a cacophony of crickets and the occasional rumble of thunder.

The moon hid behind another patch of clouds, and a moment later her foot caught on the uneven ground, causing Amanda to stumble in the inky darkness. She cried out as her ankle wrenched painfully to one side, cursing herself for not leaving on the headlights. But she was almost to the vehicle, and as the moon once more peeked out, she could see well enough that it seemed pointless to walk all the way back. *Or hobble,* she thought, sucking in her breath as she attempted to place her full weight on the injured foot.

"Shit, that hurts!" she exclaimed. *Maybe this was a mistake.*

"Hello?" A muffled voice called out. "Is someone there?"

Amanda froze in place, recognizing the same sultry voice she'd heard over the phone now emanating from the inverted trunk. Her pain momentarily forgotten, she closed the remaining distance with a purposeful stride.

"Yes, I'm here! Agent Vesper?"

There was a shuffling sound as the trunk bobbed, followed by a muffled groan, then the woman answered. "Yeah. It's me. Think we can skip the pleasantries until after you spring me? I can barely breathe."

"Of course." She choked on her words, the air so thick with fumes that Amanda flipped up the collar of her shirt as a makeshift mask. "Can you pull the trunk release?"

"Gee, if only I'd thought of that myself." The agent's words dripped sarcasm.

Amanda's cheeks burned at the snippy response. But of course, she should have guessed that Spyventures wouldn't make the mission that easy to complete, not after going to the trouble of staging such a convincing scene. "How about the backseat? I can climb through the rear passenger door and release the seat latch."

"Sure. If you don't mind disposing of the lifeless body of that two-hundred-and-fifty-pound goon suspended from the seat belt."

Amanda squinted through the rear passenger window, jumping involuntarily as lightning flashed and she made out the shape of a body, exactly as Agent Vesper had described. Thunder cracked. *Holy shit!* She pressed one hand to her chest, trying to calm her racing heart. *It's only a game!*

Frankly, from the brochure, she'd expected the Spyventures' experience to be a little bit cheesy. But this was a high-quality mission, she'd give them that. For a crash test dummy in a suit and wig, that body was convincing as hell. She shivered despite the night's lingering heat. No way was she going to touch that thing, fake or not.

Amanda's mind raced, trying to remember the details of a video she'd watched of ways to escape a trunk in case of a kidnapping. It was the type of thing she watched for fun, and probably just one reason of many why she still found herself single at the age of twenty-six. "Okay. How about the release cable?"

"Do you think I skipped basic training, or something?" The woman in the trunk sounded beyond peeved. "I already did that, but the latch is stuck half open, and no amount of moving has dislodged it. You're gonna have to pry it open."

Her words dissolved into a wracking cough that made Amanda wince with sympathy pain. Though obviously simulated, the gasoline fumes in that small space had to be torture. Her own lungs burned, and she shook her head as she searched around on the ground for something to help pry the lid loose. *Whoever was in charge of setting this scene got a little carried away.* She'd give them high marks for authenticity on the course evaluation, for sure, but the fake gasoline smell was a little too much. The part of Amanda that had planned to become a lawyer couldn't help but think that Spy-ventures was setting themselves up for a lawsuit, either from a sensitive customer or a worker's comp claim.

There was nothing useful to be found on the ground, so with some reluctance, Amanda picked her way over the rough ground back to the Mini, popped the trunk, and lifted the carpet to reveal a toolkit. There was a curved tire iron, and she pried it up, gritting her teeth as her short nails scraped against the metal.

"Okay, I've got something," she announced when she'd made it back to the car.

"Then what are you waiting for?"

Amanda glared at the license plate from behind which the make-believe spy kept making her rude comments. "If your full weight is on that latch, I could work at it all day and it won't budge. *That's* what I'm waiting for."

"Oh."

"Yeah." Amanda gave a smug nod in the woman's direction. *That will teach you to underestimate me.* "So, if you could lift yourself off the lid, even for a few seconds, I think that would give me the best shot."

The woman responded with a weary groan. "Okay, but I won't have the strength to hold it for long, so don't mess around. On the count of three, give it all you've got."

Amanda shut her eyes and blew on her hands to dry the dampness from her fingers before choking up on the tire iron like a miniature baseball bat. "Okay. Here I go. One...two...THREE!"

The clanging of metal hitting metal shook the night, and with a deafening squeak of rusty hinges, the trunk lid came free, followed a fraction of a second later by the thud of a body falling onto the lid before rolling to a stop at Amanda's feet. Still clasping the tire iron, Amanda laughed nervously. It reminded her of the piñata she'd had at her fifth birthday party, only instead of candy, her prize was a woman.

Best. Piñata. Ever.

Amanda giggled.

"I'm glad you find this funny." The agent's voice hardened. "What the *hell* were you thinking, hitting the trunk like that? I said to *pry* it for a reason. Metal on metal? One spark and this whole thing could've blown."

"I…" Amanda's mirth evaporated as the stranger pointed out her mistake. Had that gasoline been real, she could've killed them both. *What a careless mistake.* On the other hand, it wasn't real, and they both knew it, so this fake spy needn't have scolded her quite so harshly. Amanda stiffened. "You also said you were too weak to hold yourself up for more than a second, if you recall."

Seemingly mollified by her retort, the stranger growled as she attempted but failed to blow the shaggy blonde mop from in front of her eyes. She looked ridiculous, and Amanda started to giggle again. *Serves you right, you grump.* But as the rescued spy raked her fingers through her hair, revealing a strong jawline and pert, upturned nose, Amanda's laughter died away for a very different reason this time, and her heart skipped a beat.

From the deeply resonant voice over the phone, Amanda had expected someone larger, but the woman sprawled in the dirt appeared to have a more compact, athletic build. It was hard to tell, but Amanda guessed she'd be maybe five foot three, five foot four, if standing. Though too dark outside to make out their color, the fire in the woman's eyes was unmistakable, and sent a corresponding jolt of heat through Amanda's insides.

The woman cleared her throat. "You just gonna stand there, or were you planning to help me up."

Amanda shook herself back to the present, her cheeks ablaze. She held out a hand. "Sorry." But as she hoisted the woman to her feet, indignation over the woman's rudeness replaced embarrassment. *Is it too much to ask to be appreciated every once in a while?* "You could try saying thank you, you know."

"Maybe I'd be more inclined to, if my ears weren't still ringing from you waling on the trunk like some kind of Lars Ulrich wannabe."

Amanda glared. "I don't know who that is, but if he's so great, maybe you should've called him to rescue your sorry ass from that trunk instead of me."

The woman's jaw dropped. "Jesus, seriously? Lars Ulrich is the drummer from…you know what, never mind." She took a deep breath, brushing her hair away from her face again with one hand. She held her gaze steady, drawing Amanda in until she felt wobbly inside. "Thank you…Sorry, what was your name?"

"Uh…" Amanda paused, forcing her tongue to cooperate with every ounce of concentration. "Amanda. My name's Amanda."

"Pleasure to meet you."

Amanda nodded, unable to speak through the sudden lump in her throat. She coughed, then shook her head. "Those gas fumes are bad. And I think you may have hit your head when you fell out of the trunk. You know, if conditions are always like this, you might think about suing."

The woman held her arms across her belly, letting out a hearty laugh, as if Amanda had told the world's funniest joke. "Lawsuit? Good one! Now, do you think we can get out of here?"

The fake spy's shirt had ridden up as she clutched her sides, and Amanda stared at the exposed skin of her abdomen, taut and toned. She gulped and nodded again, feeling like a fool. *What the hell is wrong with me right now?* Finally, she managed to cock her head in the direction of the Mini. "My car's over there."

The woman lifted one eyebrow so saucily that Amanda wobbled on her feet. "Nice ride. Agency issue?"

Amanda pressed her hand to her lips, stifling a maniacal giggle. *Get a hold of yourself!* "It's my Aunt Millie's."

The woman nodded appreciatively. "Your Aunt Millie has good taste. I love the racing stripe."

Amanda responded with a toothy grin and this time it was the stranger's turn to look muddled.

"I…uh…" The woman gulped, looking off-balance.

"Has anyone ever told you what an amazing smile you have?" She began to sway alarmingly.

Amanda's hand shot out to steady her, her breath catching as electricity pulsed up the length of her arm on contact. "I think that bump on the head was worse than we thought. Let me help you to the car."

The woman shook her head and pulled away, looking frazzled. "No, I'll meet you in a minute. I have one last detail to attend to."

Brow furrowed, Amanda headed to the car alone, turning every so often to see what the woman was doing. But the darkness had returned and her motions were obscured by shadow. *Probably just calling Spyventures to let them know we're done.*

She'd sat herself in the car and started the engine, the windows rolled up and the air-conditioning blasting, by the time the woman returned.

The agent flopped into the passenger's seat and shut her eyes. "All right, then. Let's get out of here before it blows."

Like it's really going to explode. But instead of rolling her eyes, Amanda trembled. The deep, authoritative tone of the woman's voice shook her to the core, and she put the car into gear without a word. Slowly, she turned the car back in the direction from which she'd come.

"Where to, Agent Vesper?"

"D.C. And you can call me Leigh. Smith."

Amanda's eyebrow arched at the undeniably fake

last name, but she didn't challenge her on it. "Nice to meet you, Leigh Smith." She turned her head and flashed a broad smile. Despite the lack of light, she could have sworn she saw Leigh's cheeks flush even darker than Adam's had earlier that night.

As the car rolled toward the highway, there was a bright flash of light followed by a golden glow just visible in her rearview mirror. An image formed in her mind of flames licking at the overturned car, but she dismissed it as absurd. What she'd seen was a flash of lightning from the storm, nothing more. Even the best spy school wouldn't set fire to their props for the sake of authenticity, and as real as it felt, tonight's adventure was only a game. Still, she couldn't help but hope that Leigh would be her guide for the rest of whatever else Spy-ventures had in store. And that it would be soon. Her pump was primed and she was ready for more.

FOUR

"HERE YOU GO, BOSS." Despite her rough night, Leigh summoned maximum swagger as she strutted into Javier's office and slapped the dead goon's cell phone down on the desk with a loud plunk. "That should make last night's adventure worth the hit to the agency budget."

Javier looked up from his desk, the confusion plain to see in his dark eyes. "You look like shit, Leigh. And what the hell is this?"

"That, my friend, is the intel that's gonna crack our case wide open." Leigh bit the insides of her cheeks, trying to remain cool and not dissolve into a smug grin. "Guaranteed to be linked to the Berlin syndicate, and there's at least fifty new numbers on that mother, too."

Javier's eyebrows shot up as he reached for the cell phone. "I…"

"Speechless, huh?" This time, Leigh allowed herself a crooked smirk. "So, I guess that more than makes up for the cost of rescuing my sorry ass, right?" *Sorry ass, isn't that what the agent from the extraction team said last night?* Her smirk went goofy at the memory. *Amanda.* Such a fiery personality, and Leigh was positive she'd never seen anyone with such sparkly teeth.

"Rescue?" Javier reached for the cell phone, turning it over in his hands as he examined it. "From what, too much gin?"

Leigh laughed. "See? That's what I'm talkin' about. Extraction team? What extraction team, am I right?"

The lines crisscrossing Javier's brow deepened. "What the fuck *are* you talkin' about? *Extraction team?* I haven't heard anything about an extraction team."

Funny one, Javi, you old joker. They'd known each other almost five years, since Leigh's rookie days, and had been partners in the field until his promotion, so she knew he couldn't resist a well-timed prank. But Leigh frowned as she studied her boss's face and saw no trace of joviality. "Javier, I was abducted last night, remember? I called the agency hotline, around midnight." Her stomach fluttered as his face remained stony. "They sent an agent out to bring me in. They didn't tell you?"

He shook his head as his fingers flew across the keyboard on his desk. "Not a word. And there's no record of your call in the logs, either."

But…the girl with the teeth…she'd been real, right?

Growing light-headed, Leigh lowered herself into a chair opposite Javier and massaged the spot on the back of her head that still throbbed from where she'd been knocked out. "I don't get it. Why wouldn't they log the call?"

Javier let out a long breath as he clasped his hands behind his head. "I think you better start from the beginning."

Gut twisting in anticipation of his response, Leigh told the story in detail, starting with the chance encounter in the nightclub and ending with the rescue after calling the emergency hotline. When she'd finished, Javier's face was grim.

"Goddamn it, Leigh, we have protocol for a reason!"

Leigh cringed. His voice was every bit as loud as it had been in her head. "Yeah, I know. I'm a spy, not a fucking cowboy," she muttered.

Javier's jaw clamped tight as she stole his line. "Yeah, well maybe not for long. Another unauthorized mission, Leigh? You may be considering a career change after the paperwork it takes to straighten out this latest breach of protocol."

She gave her blunt fingernails obsessive scrutiny as she shifted uncomfortably in her chair. She'd defend her instincts as an agent any day of the week, but this wasn't exactly the first time she'd found herself in a pickle as a result of following what those instincts had told her to do. "It was worth it, though, right? I got the intel."

"Annoyingly, yes. You always do, which is what makes being your manager such a challenge. It would be a hell of a lot easier for you to learn a lesson from these incidents if they didn't keep earning you commendations. You know, I haven't been here much longer than you, and I never got anywhere near your clearance rate on assignments. You ever wonder why you're still just a field agent and not heading up your own team, like me?"

"I assumed it was because the director thinks you're prettier than me. But who says I even want to head up a team?" she challenged.

"Your personnel file, for one." The look he gave her was still firm, but there was an understanding in his eyes. "I know you've tried for a few promotions, but you're never going to get one unless you learn to follow every rule, no exceptions."

Leigh shrugged, pretending the truth didn't bother her as much as it did. "That's just not my style."

"I've noticed. But it's mine, and now I have to deal with this whole mess of the emergency call not getting logged, on top of everything else." He rolled his eyes skyward. "You sure you even dialed the right number?"

"Come on Javi, now you're just trying to be a jerk. Of *course* I'm—" Leigh stopped abruptly, her bravado fading as she recalled those brief moments of confusion over the phone number. "I mean, I'm reasonably certain…"

"*Reasonably* certain?" Javier's cheeks puffed up like a balloon, the air whistling through his lips. "That's not good enough."

"It's just, you know how they're always changing it. It used to drive you crazy when we were out in the field together. But, yes, I dialed the right number."

Unmoved by her assertion, he picked up the prize from her mission. "You used this phone to call?" When Leigh nodded, he handed it to her. "Can you unlock it?"

Leigh entered the password she'd set, then scrolled to the recent call log. "Here it is, right here. It's the last number on the list." She handed the phone back to Javier with a triumphant flourish.

"That's not the hotline."

"What? Of course it is. Or else, how did I get out of that trunk?"

Agitation turned her boss's face beet red. "I don't know who the hell you called, or why the hell they rescued you, but it wasn't us."

"But, that's not…"

"I swear to god, Leigh. There's screwing up and then there's screwing up. How could you forget the hotline number?"

"The same way you always did as a field agent. The pencil pushers upstairs changed the number three times just this week, Javi, so cut me a little bit of slack."

"Slack? Not this time, Leigh. In case you've forgotten, I'm one of those pencil pushers now, and unless I do some major damage control, we're both in serious shit."

Javier began pounding furiously on his keyboard, making her ears ring. *Shit, he's right. This could be bad.* Bending the rules to get critical intel was one thing. But a wrong number? The agency frowned on stupid mistakes, even if their own policies *did* help cause them.

He continued typing and Leigh figured by this point he was probably writing up her transfer orders to the worst assignment he could think of. She shut her eyes to concentrate on the clicking, hoping it would calm her nerves and straighten out her head. It had the opposite effect.

Click-a click-a, like Fröken Olson's metronome. Her mind raced over the events of the previous evening, and there was one question that caught hold of her and wouldn't let go. *Who the hell got me out of that trunk?*

Finally, the clicking came to a halt. "Huh," he said as he took in the information from his screen. He shook his head as if in disbelief but didn't give any clues as to what he had discovered.

"Huh, what?" Her heart raced, a million possibilities flooding her brain, each more awful than the next.

"Javier, give it to me straight. What happened to me last night?"

"You've been in the surveillance van the last few weeks, right?"

"Yeah…" Leigh answered tentatively, uncertain where he was headed with this line of questioning.

"Been listening to the radio a lot?"

If he was drawing this out to torture her, it was working. Sarcasm, her first line of defense, crept into her response before she could stop it. "What do *you* think? You keep scheduling us for twelve-hour shifts."

"We're shorthanded." Javier held her gaze steady, and despite the gravity of the situation, there was a look in his eyes that resembled amusement. "I'll bet you've been listening to the news on public radio a lot. Tell me, have they been doin' one of their fundraisers?"

Leigh snorted. "When aren't they? You remember how it was. But what are you getting at, Javi? I don't see what this has to do with anything."

"What I'm getting at, Leigh, is you dialed the number for the goddamn public radio pledge drive."

"I did *not!*" Leigh shut her eyes and tapped her fingertips together as she tried to recall the number she'd dialed the night before. *I know I got it wrong, but there's no way I made such a boneheaded mistake as that! Let's see…Two-oh-two…oh, shit.* Her indignation fizzled, replaced by the deep red heat of mortification. "So maybe that *was* the number I dialed."

Javier chuckled, his mood lightening. "Public radio. I can't wait to write up *this* report."

But Leigh grew more troubled as she realized her biggest question remained unanswered. "But who was the chick with the gorgeous smile who got me out of the trunk?"

Javi rolled his eyes. "Some sorta groupie from the nightclub, knowing you. Probably followed you, trying to get your number."

He'd meant it as a joke, but Leigh's alarm increased. "I swear to you, I'd never seen her before." Her stomach lurched, that same feeling in her gut that always meant trouble. "You don't think she's allied with the Berlin group, do you?"

A cloud passed across Javier's face. "Damn it, Leigh! Just when I'd started to relax. I honestly hadn't considered it from that angle before, but now that you've said it, I don't think we can rule it out just yet. Don't you know anything about her at all?"

Leigh closed her eyes again, searching her memory. "Average height, long brown hair, gorgeous smile."

"Yeah, you mentioned the smile before. Twice."

"No, I mean it was…" Leigh shook her head, the memory of the woman's smile defying description. "Javi. Seriously, you don't understand how hot she was with that smile."

"Uh huh." Javier rolled his eyes. "So, did Miss Hottie have a name?"

"Amanda." Her brain continued to whir, searching

for any forgotten detail. "Oh! She drives a Mini, black with one of those checkered racing stripes along one side. She said it belonged to her aunt…Mollie?" Leigh frowned. "Muffy? It was something like that."

Javier gave her an exasperated look. "Five years as an agent and that's the best you can do? You've gotta remember more than that."

"I'd been hit on the head and was asphyxiating on gasoline fumes, Javi. Besides, I thought she was from the agency. I didn't think I needed to commit the entire encounter to memory."

"Nah, just the smile," Javier quipped. "Right, well, that's enough to get an agent started, anyway. In the meantime, I want you to sit right there and write down absolutely everything you can remember from last night. No detail's too small." He handed her a blank notebook and a pen, chuckling when she groaned. "You know the drill. I told you the paperwork would be enough to make you rethink your occupation."

With all the stoicism she could muster, Leigh took the book back to her desk and began furiously scribbling every bit of minutiae she could recall out of the fog that was the previous night.

Normally she would have jotted down the license plate of Amanda's car, the perfume Giselle had worn at the club, and a million other details with ease, but today she fought for every single one. Though feeling better after a few hours of sleep, the lump on her head still smarted and had left her with memories that were hazy at best. When she squeezed her eyelids shut to concentrate on recreating the scene as she always did, it was no use. Only one detail was crystal clear—Amanda's smile. *Damn Javier for being right about that one.*

Dazzling white teeth framed by lusciously plump lips. No lipstick, but a hint of gloss. Maybe strawberry flavored. Leigh had noticed it in the car as they drove, once the stench of gasoline had faded away, that sweet berries and cream smell that she would forever associate with her childhood and the mega-packs of Bonne Bell lip gloss that her father would bring back to Stockholm for her from the airport gift shop after one of his trips to the States. She could almost feel the tube between her fingers, gliding it along her lips like she'd loved to do as a kid. It had tasted delicious, too. It would have made Amanda's lips so soft and sweet…

Cool it, Leigh, you're in the middle of a job, not a Katy Perry song! If she didn't manage to remember something more pertinent than that woman's smile, Javi would kill her. She'd been poring over her notebook assignment for over an hour when Javier stood in front of her desk and gave a triumphant shout.

"Ha! I think we may have found her." He held up his tablet so she could see.

Leigh's pulse pounded as she took in the image of the familiar face. "That's her." Her insides flipped. It was definitely her rescuer, but who was she? What might they be about to discover? *Please, don't let her be working for Berlin.* Leigh's job was on the line if she was, but that wasn't why she was praying so fervently. The thought that Amanda might be the enemy stung much more than it should, like a personal betrayal. "Who is she?"

"Amanda Princeton, age twenty-six as of a few weeks ago," Javier replied. "She's a temporary office assistant at Baltimore-Washington Public Radio, working the night shift. She lives with her aunt, Millie Rodgers, over in the Ten Hills neighborhood."

"*Millie,*" Leigh said, smacking her palm to her forehead. "I was close."

"Yeah, well, it's good you remembered the aunt, because that's where it gets interesting. They ran Ms. Rodgers's credit card, and a charge came up from an operation called Spy-ventures. It's some sort of make-believe spy academy."

"*Spy* academy? You're kidding me."

"Nope. Dead serious. As far as I can tell, they offer a bunch of totally bogus programs to teach people how to be Hollywood movie spies. Ms. Rodgers purchased one of their packages for her niece's birthday."

Leigh's eyes grew wide and she laughed with relief. "So, this woman came to my rescue last night because she thought it was part of a spy-themed birthday present?"

"Maybe."

Though her insides had relaxed considerably at the

news, her mood deflated considerably at his continued, "Maybe?"

"In addition to the radio station, her file also says she used to temp in dozens of major companies, most of them with lots of overseas clients. That would make a great cover for getting access to sensitive information for Berlin."

"But it's such a coincidence, surely—" Leigh's throat constricted as she recalled how knowledgeable the woman had been about escaping from trunks. In her experience, normal people didn't know those types of things.

"Tell me, which one is harder to believe, that the Berlin syndicate has agents all over D.C. and you got hold of one of them by mistake, or that your call happened to go through to a grown woman who enjoys spy stories so much that she thought she'd pretend to live in one for a few hours in the middle of the night?"

Leigh weighed the options and frowned. Both were preposterous. "But, Javi, you can't really think she's an enemy operative. I mean, if for no other reason than she let me go. Why would she do that?"

"Maybe she put a tracker on you. Maybe she liked your smile as much as you liked hers." He shrugged. "Bottom line, she's probably not involved in all this."

Leigh let out a relieved breath. "That's what I was trying to say. So maybe we can just leave all of this out of the report?"

"Hell no. Protocol is protocol. Besides, if she is involved with Berlin and we guess wrong, people could die. We need to be sure, and I think I've got a plan." A wicked smile teased his lips. "You're going to be her handler."

"Her what?"

"Her handler, from the Spy-ventures Academy of Espionage. I'll get one of our guys to erase her aunt's purchase from their records, then you'll show up and take her over to the agency training course instead."

"What, you figure if she passes the course too easily, we know she's a spy?" Leigh scoffed. "If she floats, she's a witch?"

"No, smart-ass. You take her through some obstacle courses, sure. Put her at ease, get a feel for whether she's legit if you can. But more importantly, you keep her busy for several hours while we send a team to sweep her place and get to the bottom of this. If she's really some civilian who wants to make-believe she's a spy, I'm sure you'll give her her money's worth, and she'll never know the difference."

"And if she's not?"

Javier's gaze was unwavering. "You know the answer to that, Leigh. If she's working for Berlin, this doesn't end well for either one of you, or me either, for that matter. Reassignment for both of us, at the least, maybe a forced retirement for you."

Leigh shifted uncomfortably, not liking either

option. Unbidden, Amanda's sweet smile once more flashed inside her head. "And what about her?"

"What do you think?" Javier's eyes were cold and hard.

A shiver ran through her at the thought of Amanda's fate if it turned out she was more than she appeared. The most beautiful smile in the world wouldn't save her if she was in bed with Berlin. Though it shouldn't matter to her one way or the other, Leigh found herself saying a silent prayer that her rescuer was just an average, all-American girl with a thing for spies.

FIVE

THE MORNING SUN had already burned away the last of the predawn coolness when Leigh pulled into the parking lot of the agency training course that would play the role of the Spy-ventures' school that day. It was a small facility, and seldom used in the hotter months. By pulling a few strings, Javier had managed to secure the whole place for her use under the guise of a department team-building exercise. It was a little white lie that went against her boss's usual by-the-book style, but they'd both agreed that until they determined Amanda's true loyalties, the less the higher-ups at the agency knew about any of this, the better.

Frankly, it was no wonder to Leigh that no one else had booked the course that day. Even in the relative coolness of her car, sweat already dribbled down her back. The prospect of spending a whole day on an obstacle course in the sticky mid-Atlantic heat made her grumpy. Even after years in the States, her Scandinavian blood preferred the more temperate climate of her birth. She thought longingly of the surveillance van where she would otherwise be spending her day. At least it had air-conditioning, which made it a plum assignment by comparison. If Javier had been sadistic enough to plan a real team building exercise on a miserable day like this, she'd probably have quit on the spot.

Leigh stopped the car and looked around the nearly deserted lot. Only one other car was there, the familiar black Mini with its checkered racing stripe along one side. Its owner stood nearby, one leg propped up on the front bumper as she gave her calf muscle a deep stretch. Heat swamped Leigh's body from head to toe as they made eye contact, and though she might tell herself otherwise, her response had almost nothing to do with the weather.

Leigh scowled as she swung her legs out of the driver's side door, unable to account for the intensity of her attraction. There was no excuse for it. It's not like Amanda had made any efforts to look sexy. She was dressed for a day of physical activity, in a pair of bulky cargo capris and a loose-fitting sports tank, neither of which did anything to enhance her figure. Her brunette hair was pulled back into a utilitarian ponytail, except for a few tendrils that had escaped confinement. *Sun-streaked tendrils.* Her eyes refused to look away from the lovely, golden blonde wisps that framed the woman's soft face in the most distracting way.

Stop ogling, Leigh scolded herself. *She's probably an enemy agent, remember?*

"Good morning, Leigh! Nice to see you again!" Amanda's voice rang with an enthusiasm that suggested the hellish heat didn't faze her one bit.

"Uh, good morning." A thousand-watt smile had accompanied Amanda's greeting, and Leigh battled to keep her voice detached while her knees buckled under the onslaught of that glossy grin. Even from several feet away, she swore she could smell strawberries, like a fresh pie baking in the sun. "I guess you found the place okay?"

Amanda nodded. "I must be the first one here. I suppose everyone else will be here soon, though?"

Everyone else? Leigh took a long sip from her water bottle to buy herself time to think. In their haste to pull this mission together, neither she nor Javier had taken into consideration that Amanda was expecting to be part of a full-fledged class today. Not that it would have mattered. With the rest of the team pulling up outside Amanda's house that very minute to search it with a fine-tooth comb, they could hardly have spared any agents to pose as students. But *that* wasn't exactly an explanation she could give to Amanda for why she would be flying solo today.

Instead, Leigh flashed a disarming smile. "Oh,

didn't your aunt tell you? You have one of the deluxe packages. It comes with a private lesson."

"Private?" A shadow crossed Amanda's face, and for a moment Leigh feared she wasn't buying the story. "Aunt Millie really can't afford that! She shouldn't have spent so much on me."

Though she didn't want it to, Leigh's heart melted on the spot. The woman's genuine concern for her aunt touched her deeply. She had a soft spot for old folks herself, her own elderly grandparents in particular, and so Leigh quickly moved to reassure her. "I'm pretty sure she had a coupon. You know, for a reduced-price upgrade."

Relief at the news brought out Amanda's smile in full force, and Leigh's head went a little woozy from the sweetness of it. The response was completely unprofessional and unbefitting a seasoned agent. *For all you know, Aunt Millie is just a ruse,* she reminded herself with as much force a she could muster. *She's probably working for Berlin, too.* But it was next to useless. As long as Amanda was armed with those lush lips and sparkly teeth, Leigh feared she would be outmatched, no matter how solid her agency training might be.

"Oh, before I forget," Amanda said, holding out an envelope, "here are my forms and photos, all filled out."

Refocusing on the task at hand, Leigh nodded as she took the packet. She managed to refrain from a massive eye roll on the grounds that doing so would blow her cover, but of all the ridiculous things she would be required to do in the name of 'spy school' today, she thought this one might take top prize. Every Spy-ventures' graduate received an assortment of fake passports and other essential undercover documents as part of their package. Of course, as a bona fide member of the intelligence community, Leigh had never actually possessed anything of the sort. But as Leigh had discovered in her research, there was nothing genuine about any part of the Spy-ventures' program. Fictional spies in movies always seemed to have stacks of fake documents at their disposal, and the Academy of Espionage was essentially one massive spy movie stereotype brought to life.

She tossed Amanda's documents into her trunk, where Javier would collect them later in the day. No doubt he'd pass them off to one of the rookies left behind in the office, some unfortunate team member who wasn't field-rated yet and got stuck doing the really shit jobs. Their department didn't exactly specialize in forgeries, but it hardly mattered. The examples from the Spy-ventures' website mostly looked like they'd come from a beginner's Photoshop class. It would be hard for even the greenest newbie to get it wrong.

Awaiting her in the trunk was a brown paper shopping bag containing the props and supplies she would need for the day. Recalling the activities ahead of her,

Leigh's cheeks burned crimson and she revised her earlier opinion that the forged documents were the most embarrassing thing she would face that day. That was just the tip of the iceberg.

Trench coats and fake guns…For god's sake, I'm a highly trained professional!

Having to recreate all of the ridiculous Spy-ventures' curriculum wounded her pride. But it was the only way to maintain her cover, so she reached past the jumble of genuine intelligence gathering paraphernalia that she always kept on hand in the back of her car and reached instead for the juvenile assortment of fake guns, knives, and other spy toys that would be her teaching tools for the day, all the time wondering if Spy-ventures had been founded by a couple of twelve-year-old boys.

Once they'd entered the grounds, they began with some warm-ups, then as many trips through the obstacle course as they could manage. Leigh was stalling, hoping to have word from her team before being forced to begin the more humiliating portions of the curriculum. But by the third time through, the mugginess had become oppressive, and Amanda looked as much on the brink of melting as Leigh felt. Back at Amanda's empty house, the rest of Leigh's team should've made good progress in their search by now, but there was still no word on what they'd found.

Leigh snuck a glance at Amanda as the woman drew a sip of water from her plastic bottle, so blissfully unaware of what was going on back at her home, or how dire the consequences could be, depending on what they found there. The sheer innocence of her appearance was a weight on Leigh's chest, though she knew it shouldn't be. Appearances could be deceiving, as every good spy knew.

Still, no word means they haven't found an obvious smoking gun. That's a good sign, right?

Either way, she had a few hours left to kill before the team would finish its sweep. With a sigh, Leigh knew it could be put off no longer.

"Okay, come right over here," Leigh said, leading Amanda to an open area near the obstacle course and setting down the bag that she'd hoped to ignore. "Let's try something new. Time for a little hand-to-hand combat training." Leigh reached into the bag and rummaged around in disgust, finally pulling out a pair of red stiletto heels and a long beige trench coat while struggling not to wrinkle her nose at the sight.

"Seriously?" Amanda's face reflected Leigh's own feelings of disdain perfectly. "I was really hoping we could do a little better than that."

"Well, it *is* part of the standard course, but..." Leigh frowned, then stuffed the coat and shoes back in the bag with relief. "Since this is a private lesson, I suppose I could bend the rules."

Amanda's smug expression would've been annoying under most circumstances, but her lips were pursed in such a way, with the sun glinting off a thick layer of strawberry gloss, that annoyance was the furthest thing from Leigh's mind. At the forefront was a particularly vivid memory of an epic gun battle from one of the many spy movies she'd watched to prepare for the day. Like real doctors who can't stand watching medical dramas, Leigh almost never indulged in the genre. They were too much fantasy for her taste. But picturing herself in the role of Brad Pitt, shooting the bad guys while wrapped around a badass Angelina Jolie—well, that was one fantasy she could wholeheartedly embrace, so to speak.

Leigh dug into the bag once more and emerged with four plastic guns, fighting back a wicked grin. She knew exactly what her lesson plan would be. Despite the fact that in real life, without head protection and facing fifty armed assassins, those fools would have been dead in half a second, that scene in the film had been sexy as hell. She'd watched it a dozen times, learning the choreography by heart in the process, and she was more than happy to reenact it now with the lovely Ms. Princeton. Her job had to have a *few* perks. Besides, with her hair pulled back the way it was, Amanda made a very convincing Angelina Jolie.

"Take these," Leigh said, handing Amanda two of the props. "Now we'll start out side by side, and I'm going to walk you through an active shooter simulation."

Her chest puffed up just a little, pleased with how official she'd made it sound. *If I weren't already a spy, I'd make a kick-ass fake spy instructor.* Amanda raised an eyebrow as she took one plastic gun in each hand, but refrained from making any comment as she fell in beside Leigh.

"We're in a store, and there are several armed men just beyond us, out there. Now we'll step out, like this." Leigh took a step, pointing one gun forward and one to the side, and Amanda followed suit. "Good, now back-to-back, one gun in each hand, firing to the side." Leigh snuck a peak behind her to admire Amanda's graceful movements. "You're doing great!"

Amanda's cheeks flushed at the praise. "Now what?"

"Okay, they're returning fire, so now we both duck. Now pivot so we're front to front." Leigh swallowed roughly as her chest made contact with Amanda's sports bra-bound breasts, which were deceptively shapely despite their restrictive covering. A light coating of sweat along Amanda's bare collar bone glistened in the sun, and the scent of strawberries was intoxicating. For a moment, Leigh lost all sense of time and place.

"And now?" Amanda prodded helpfully.

Leigh blinked and let out a breath. "Um, yes. Now I fire at the targets behind you, and you do the same behind me."

"With my arms like this?" Amanda asked, wrapping them to each side of Leigh with all the comfort of a warm embrace.

Her eyes were level with Amanda's mouth, and it was taking every ounce of concentration for Leigh not to pull her close enough to taste those strawberry lips. This wasn't at all how it had happened in the movie. *Damn it. I forgot how short I am.* Leigh lacked the height advantage of the average leading man, and in fact, Amanda had a good three inches on her. *This was a bad idea. Better hurry through the rest.*

"Uh, yep, that's about right. Now pay attention, because the next part goes quick. We're going to pivot, backs together, shooting assailants on either side, then to the front. Now a one-eighty spin. You duck," Leigh pushed down on Amanda's back as she spoke, forcing her into a crouch, "and I'll shoot over there."

"And now I toss you the other clip?"

"Exactly. Now you—" Leigh frowned as she realized that was exactly what happened next in the film. "How did you know that?"

Amanda blinked slowly, the faintest smile tugging at her lips. "*Mr. & Mrs. Smith* is one of my favorite movies, too."

Leigh's whole body burned scarlet. "Oh."

Amanda chuckled. "Even if they both would've been dead the second they burst out of the shed, with fifty assassins and nothing covering their heads."

Embarrassment forgotten, Leigh's heart skipped a beat. "Right? Totally unrealistic."

"Completely," Amanda concurred.

She patted Amanda across the back with one arm. "Wanna go shoot some real guns?"

It had been a knee-jerk impulse, the type of thing she might have said on a date. But this wasn't a date, it was a mission, and Leigh sucked in her breath as she realized the seriousness of her slipup. There was a primitive shooting range on the other side of the facility, and Leigh happened to have the key, but had she honestly just suggested giving a real weapon to a possible enemy agent? *What the hell is wrong with me?*

But it was too late to back out now. The suggestion had been made, and Amanda seemed more than eager to give it a try. This was one time Leigh needed to hope her gut instincts were right. Otherwise her hormone-fueled blunder might've just sealed her fate.

SIX

AS THEY WALKED toward the enclosure that housed the shooting range, Leigh prayed that at that exact moment, her team was finding mountains of evidence that would clear Amanda of all suspicion. And it wasn't just because she didn't want to end up getting double-crossed and shot when her back was turned. The woman had gotten under her skin, and if she wasn't being whisked away to a secret government detention facility at day's end, Leigh had half a mind to ask her out. Not that she had any reason to expect that Amanda would accept. In fact, she'd probably only watched that movie because she liked Brad Pitt. But then again, Leigh had been surprised before.

"So, big Brad Pitt fan?" she asked, just to put the matter to rest once and for all.

"Sorry, what?"

"You know, *Mr. & Mrs. Smith*. I assumed you watched it mostly for him."

"Nope. Not particularly." A coy look passed Amanda's face. "Not my type."

"Oh really?" Leigh's heart picked up speed. She scanned Amanda's face for additional clues, but she'd pressed her lips into a tight line and clearly had nothing else to offer on the matter. Even so, what she *had* said spoke volumes, and hope made Leigh's feet feel lighter on the path the rest of the way to the range.

The building was narrow and long, with a solid gray gun safe on one end and a paper target pinned to the far wall. As Leigh surveyed the thick metal safe behind which were kept actual guns and ammunition, she came back down to earth with a thud. Until proven otherwise, Amanda was a potential threat and had to be treated with the utmost caution. Handing her a loaded gun could be suicide. As Amanda stood waiting, Leigh continued to stare at the safe and ponder alternatives.

"Isn't this the part where in a movie, a suave, seasoned agent would take advantage of the situation by cuddling up to teach the newbie how to shoot?" Amanda teased, with an expression that hinted she was hoping that was exactly what Leigh had planned.

Frustration clouded Leigh's thoughts. Of course, Amanda would choose now, of all times, to start flirting. As if it wasn't enough of a challenge to be practical and focus on the risks involved instead of giving herself over completely to the undeniable magnetic attraction she felt.

Wait. Did she just call me suave?

Suddenly, she felt like James Bond, whom she knew for certain would never let a minor inconvenience like a beautiful woman possibly being an enemy agent get in his way. To hell with practical. She was going with her instincts on this one. She cocked an eyebrow and gave her best Sean Connery impression. "That's a service I'd be happy to provide."

Amanda giggled. "That's a terrible Bond impression."

Leigh stiffened. "It isn't! My Bond impressions are legendary."

"I'm sure they are. In your own mind."

"Fine." Leigh's eyes narrowed. "Just for that, I'm not giving you any guns."

Amanda's jaw dropped. "What? For teasing you?"

Leigh grinned, thoroughly enjoying the situation which was made sweeter by the fact that her flash of temper had led her to such a perfect solution to her dilemma. "That's right. No guns for you, princess. But if you behave yourself, I might let you touch my knife."

"I'll bet you say that to all the girls. Does it ever work?"

Touché. Amanda's lips were arranged in a pout, but behind it, Leigh was fairly certain Amanda was highly amused. Playful banter aside, it was still a foolhardy plan. When it came to weapons, knives were just as deadly as guns, and almost as easy to use. It didn't take much training to figure out that the pointy end goes into the other person. But knives were Leigh's weapon of choice, her specialty, and she trusted her reflexes to get her out of danger from all but the most skilled opponent. Amanda had surprised her in many ways, but she doubted she would be a match for her in this.

Raising the hem of her pant leg, Leigh revealed a narrow strap a few inches above her ankle that held in place a small ebony-handled knife with a folded blade. "Have you ever thrown one?"

"A knife? No, but I've always wanted to." The thrill in Amanda's eyes was evident as she eyed the weapon. "Only, that just looks like a regular pocketknife. I thought you needed special ones for throwing."

"What good would that do you?" Leigh shook her head, all the while soaking in Amanda's admiration. "When you're out in the field, you have to be prepared. You never know what kind of knife might be around when you need it. Why limit yourself to just one? That's *my* motto."

"Oh really?" Amanda shut her lids, reopening them languidly as she held Leigh's gaze. "Is that your motto with everything?"

"*Absolutely* everything," she said, a wink accompanying her best James Bond voice. It was a killer line.

There had to be at least a dozen different ways Amanda could interpret it, and Leigh meant every single one of them.

Retaining her composure, Amanda gave a thoughtful nod. "Smart. I always dreamed of having a knife like that to carry, although I pictured having it strapped a little higher up."

Leigh shook her head vigorously, back to instructor mode. "No. Any higher up than mid-calf and it gets caught up in the hem of your pants."

Amanda shrugged casually, but there was a mischievous glint in her eye. "Yes, well, in my dream, I was wearing it under a slinky red dress, with a slit up to about here." She drew a line with her finger at a spot on her thigh so obscenely high up that Leigh's throat went dry just picturing it.

"You have a lot of dreams like that, do you?"

"Oh, you have *no* idea how many."

And then Leigh sort of swallowed her tongue and made a few choking sounds while Amanda giggled like a naughty schoolgirl. The image formed in Leigh's mind of Amanda *as* a naughty schoolgirl, and the whole process repeated itself with a lack of dignity that was completely unbecoming to a world-class spy.

There was only one way to save face. Grasping the knife by the hilt, Leigh hurled it at the target that hung from the far wall. It hit dead center with a loud *thwack*, its sharp tip buried deep.

Amanda's head swiveled as the knife made impact, her mouth falling open. "Damn."

Leigh strutted down to retrieve the knife, then handed it to Amanda. "Your turn."

Amanda eyed the weapon with uncertainty, her earlier bravado gone. "I wouldn't know where to begin."

"Just give it your best shot." Leigh cringed as Amanda chucked the weapon clumsily and her prized knife clattered to the ground several feet short of the target. "That's going to need some work."

Though they'd joked about it before, Leigh nonetheless took full advantage of the situation now, standing close behind Amanda as she guided her body into the correct formation. One arm held Amanda steady just above the waist, and she could feel the rise and fall of Amanda's breath against her palm, her own breathing quickly falling in synch. As Leigh positioned Amanda's fingers around the hilt of the knife, she allowed herself to linger just a moment longer than was strictly necessary, and she could feel the hitch of Amanda's breathing in response.

"You need to find the balance. Can you feel it? Now aim and throw," Leigh whispered just beside Amanda's ear, and felt the woman's breath catch again.

If this were a spy movie, Leigh would've fully expected Amanda to hit the mark this time. But this was real life, and so the most she was anticipating was that, under her instruction, the knife might make contact with some portion of the wall, or at least graze the surface on its way to the ground. Instead, the blade sank deeply into the paper target's surface, just a finger's width outside the center circle. A chill swept over her.

"Wow! I can't believe I hit it! Talk about beginner's luck." Amanda clapped her hands in glee, seemingly genuine in her surprised delight at hitting the target, but a cold lump settled in the pit of Leigh's stomach. She wasn't buying the act. Not this time.

Leigh stepped infinitesimally backward, seeking to put distance between her body and Amanda's without raising undue alarm. Whoever Amanda was, she had to be more than she seemed. She'd managed to guess the second half of Leigh's passphrase all on her own, after all. And made her way flawlessly through a complicated set of weapons maneuvers, even if she had seen it before in a movie. Now she'd gone from clumsy incompetence to nearly throwing a bull's-eye in the space of a single throw.

Leigh had been taken in by her flirtatiousness and that damned smile, but this was no normal office temp. Her hands trembled as she reached for her phone. Had she made a serious miscalculation in going with her gut and letting her guard down?

Status update?

She typed the text surreptitiously, concealing the phone in her palm as she went to retrieve her knife with what she hoped was a worry-free, ambling gait.

They had to be nearly finished with the sweep by now, and she prayed Javier would get back to her before her nerves were shot. Or she was.

She glanced at the gun safe on her way back and thanked her lucky stars she'd chosen not to open it after all. Even so, perhaps hanging out with a safe full of weapons a few feet away wasn't such a smart idea. For all she knew, Amanda might count safecracking among her impressive list of skills.

"Time's almost up," Leigh said after she'd stowed her knife safely back beneath her pants leg. "Maybe we could head back outside?"

Amanda gave a shrug and headed toward the door. As Leigh followed, watching intently, careful not to turn her back on the woman for a second, her phone vibrated with Javier's reply text.

All clear.

Leigh frowned, truly taken aback. Having convinced herself the moment the knife hit the target that Amanda was guilty as sin, she'd expected an order to tackle her to the ground and put her in handcuffs on the spot. She could almost see the team arriving to cart Amanda off to some secret prison. *All clear?* Were they absolutely certain?

"Hold on a sec, Amanda," she said once they were both outside. "I just need to make a quick call to the office."

Amanda shrugged again and busied herself with examining the contents of one of her cargo pockets.

Despite having given them a sneaky yet thorough pat down hours ago, and just having received the all clear, Leigh remained on high alert for a weapon. She would not be fooled again.

"Javi," she said softly into the phone when her boss answered, "are you sure?"

"Yeah. Good news, Leigh, the place was clean."

"No chance you missed something?"

"Trust me, we went over everything twice. There's no way this woman's anything other than a temp with a quirky old aunt and a weird thing for spies."

Leigh frowned. "You're absolutely sure?"

"Why?" Her boss's voice, which had been carefree before, turned cautious. *"Did something happen?"*

Leigh thought of the knife-throwing incident, but dreaded the coal-raking she'd get for letting a suspect handle a weapon. She already knew she'd been making mistakes like it was her first day on the job ever since Amanda arrived on the scene. She didn't need it pointed out to her, or recorded in her personnel file. "It's just, she seems very skilled."

"Well, Aunt Millie's given her a bunch of gifts like this one over the years. Target shooting at the police academy, some martial arts lessons, even a simulated boot camp for her college graduation. I'm not surprised if some of it stuck."

"Yeah, maybe that's it." *Could that explain the knife?* She desperately wanted to believe it, which meant she probably shouldn't. Not yet.

"Leigh, she's a temp. A pretty little temp with a killer

smile, who you will not have to kill with your bare hands in the parking lot or detain her while a team comes to bundle her off to a secret prison. Okay?"

Leigh snorted. Javi knew how her mind worked. "Okay."

"Look, she's not working for Berlin. We'll have to put you on desk duty for a few weeks until we can establish whether the incident the other night means that your cover was blown, but as long as you lie low, there's no immediate danger. You can relax a little now. We all can."

"Lie low?" Leigh frowned. Her life was all about work, twenty-four seven. With the exception of hanging out at a nightclub, which was clearly off the table for the moment, she wasn't sure she knew how to lie low. "Relax?"

"If you wanted to ask her out for a drink sometime," his teasing tone came through loud and clear, "something tells me she'd say yes."

Man, he really does know me. "Yeah, why's that?"

"Because guess who discovered Amanda was the treasurer of the campus LGBT group when she was in college? That's right. Your favorite boss."

Leigh rolled her eyes at his gloating tone, but refrained from telling him she'd already gleaned this piece of intel on her own. "Nice job, Javi. But if you really wanna be my favorite boss, you'll fill in for me tonight on my surveillance duty so I can ask her out right now."

"No can do. I just put in a twelve-hour shift in that fucking thing while the team searched her house."

She'd been joking, and his answer was hardly a surprise, but now that she'd said it, taking Amanda out would be smart, and not just because she found her ridiculously attractive. Her department heads might be satisfied that Amanda was completely on the up-and-up, but Leigh wasn't prepared to agree with their assessment just yet.

"Come on, Javi. You just told me I had to lie low and relax until you determine the status of my cover. You'll have to assign someone else. That's protocol." She tried not to gloat over her flash of brilliance in invoking protocol.

"To hell with protocol. We wouldn't be doing any of this if you had remembered nine simple digits, now would we?" But then he paused and sighed, and Leigh knew she was about to get her way because Javier really wasn't the type to say to hell with protocol so easily. *"Damn it. There's no way I can work twenty-four hours straight, but I can't send you, either. I guess I could send Toni. She's not officially field rated yet, but she's eager and it's an easy assignment."*

Leigh grinned. "Thanks, Boss!"

"Don't go thanking me. Your slipup the other night has caused a major headache and as soon as you're cleared for duty again, I'm going to make sure you pay for it, you hear me?"

"Absolutely. Hit me with your worst. I look forward to it, sir." Leigh let out a breath as she ended the call.

She had no doubt that Javier would find plenty of ways to make her pay. She probably deserved it, too. She was a good agent, and though she sometimes played fast and loose with the rules when it came to bypassing red tape, she was humble enough to admit that she'd screwed up big this time and deserved a reprimand. A few weeks of desk duty would be a good reminder to her that she needed to balance her gut instincts with caution and a level head.

If being assigned to temporary desk duty for her screwup also happened to free up the evening for drinks, she wouldn't look a gift horse in the mouth.

Leigh trotted over to Amanda, tempering her excitement at asking the woman out with the constant reminder that she could still turn out to be a double-crossing enemy agent. "So, it looks like I'm off duty the rest of the night. I was wondering, would you like to go for a drink?"

With a flash of mischief in her eyes that set Leigh's heart racing, Amanda replied, "I don't know. I'm not in the mood to go out, but maybe…"

"Maybe what?" Intrigue made her heart pound harder.

"Well, you're a spy, right?" Amanda giggled. "I mean, not a real spy, but you play a convincing one, which I'll admit I kind of like. In fact, I've always *dreamed* of inviting a spy over."

"I'd really like to know more about these dreams of yours."

"I bet you would. So, use your spy skills to figure out where I live. No cheating, though. You have to give me a five-minute head start. If your mission's a success, maybe I'll invite you in for a little something when you get there."

Without waiting for a reply, Amanda turned toward the parking lot. The sway in her hips as she walked left little doubt what sort of something she had in mind, and it wasn't just a martini.

By now, Leigh's heart had nearly escaped the confines of her chest. *Oh, the mission will be a success, all right.* Leigh already knew exactly where she lived because in addition to the fact that the rest of her team had been camped out at the woman's house all afternoon, Leigh was a real spy. And Amanda was…what? Just a temp, or something more nefarious? Leigh wasn't sure. But as she watched the woman get into her car and drive away, a thrill that was half lust and half sheer terror tore through her.

Whatever she is, I'm sure as hell gonna enjoy myself finding out.

SEVEN

AMANDA GUZZLED down the last of the water from a bottle she'd left in the car that morning, hot drops spilling carelessly over her lips and down her chin. She tossed the empty bottle onto the floor beneath the passenger's seat and gripped the steering wheel with both hands as she willed her breathing to slow.

Oh, god. Did I really just do that?

She had no idea what had possessed her to behave so boldly. Not that she was a prude. She'd had her fun in college, though she'd experienced a dating dry spell after graduation, mostly self-inflicted, as she bounced from assignment to assignment, trying to figure out her future. Considering she'd never been successful at that, it sometimes felt like a waste that she hadn't let loose a little more often, but there was no going back to change things now.

Besides, she'd still managed to go out now and

then, even if it had been mostly to the touristy bars in Quincy Market after work. Even in the straightest of establishments, she'd still managed to get lucky every so often. But since arriving in Baltimore and taking on responsibility for Aunt Millie, sex and dating had been the furthest things from her mind. Until she'd met Leigh.

What on earth came over me? But she knew the answer. She was a sucker for a sexy spy.

Coming to rest at a traffic light, Amanda closed her eyes and pictured Leigh, all suave and confident like a female double-oh-seven come to life. The character's sex appeal was legendary, and Leigh had it in spades. Amanda knew her keen interest in espionage was an oddity, seen by most potential partners as something to be tolerated rather than shared and embraced. But considering what she did for a living, Leigh could be the rare person who would fully appreciate her quirks. Hell, they might even share a lot of the same fantasies.

I guess I'm about to find out.

Sure, given that she was only a 'fake spy,' there was a good chance the woman might turn out to be less than a real go-getter when it came to motivation. Then again, as a temp who mostly answered telephones on the graveyard shift, Amanda knew the same could probably be assumed about her. It wasn't a crime to be a little lost in life sometimes.

Shit. Lost. What if she can't find the house?

The light had just turned green and Amanda's foot

was poised lightly on the accelerator when that terrifying thought crossed her mind. *She's not a real spy, after all. You just said so yourself.* But no, Amanda reasoned, thinking back on their class, Leigh had genuine skills. And she'd seemed confident as hell when Amanda issued the challenge. Surely, she wouldn't act so cocky if she couldn't follow through. *Right?* She'd damn well better have some skills. That was the foundation of Amanda's attraction to her. Amanda intended to make the trip worth her while, but Leigh would have to earn it first.

Pulling into her driveway, Amanda turned off the engine and sat for a moment, perfectly still, as the sudden quiet rang in her ears. *This is nuts.* She could still change her mind, pull back out of the driveway and go. There were bars nearby, or coffee shops. She'd meet Leigh there—that was assuming the woman was even following her. Maybe she wasn't. But if she was, Amanda would just laugh it all off as a joke. It had just been a little game, she could explain, one last fantasy to end their day of make-believe.

But no. She tugged the key from the ignition and marched herself up the driveway to the kitchen door, resolute. Amanda knew enough about fantasies to know that wasn't how this one was meant to end. This one was special. It deserved to play itself out to the end.

She flipped on the outside light, and left the door open as she went inside, wide enough to make it clear that Leigh should come in that way, too. She paused again, a shiver creeping down her neck and shoulders. The open door worried her, being a woman alone. It wasn't safe.

It will be fine, you scaredy-cat. After all, if she were even half the tracker her ego implied, Leigh was probably only a few minutes behind. In fact, there wasn't much time to get ready, to set the scene the way she'd pictured it in her imagination so many times.

What she wanted was to be wild for once, to throw caution to the wind and live like a character in one of her books, the sexy Bond girl who captures the heart of the spy. And why not? She could pull off 'sexy' if she tried. Probably. Leigh had seemed to think so, anyway, at least enough to ask her out for a drink. Who knew when she might have an opportunity like this again? She might as well make it memorable.

Reaching her bedroom on the second floor, Amanda opened a drawer in her dresser, removing a pair of shiny silver handcuffs wrapped in pink fur. They were a novelty pair, a gag gift left over from a bachelorette party she'd gone to for a coworker in Boston. It had been held at one of those really awful clubs where straight girls liked to go and make the bride-to-be dance around with a hat made out of condoms on her head. Why so many women thought that was funny—that, and cakes shaped like penises—Amanda could never figure out. Sometimes straight girls were a real mystery. The party had also featured a stripper cop, hence the handcuffs as a prize. They were cheap and a little bit tawdry, not unlike the party they'd come from, but Amanda figured they should work just fine for what she had in mind...

STATELY OLD TREES lined Amanda's street, which was mostly filled with solidly built brick and stucco houses of the English cottage designs that had been so popular in the Ten Hills neighborhood during the early twentieth century. They were spacious, but not overly grand, telegraphing a century's worth of middle class respectability.

The sun still burned bright, as it always did in June, but Leigh knew it was later than it seemed. She was used to that, having come from a land of midnight sun. A glance at the dashboard clock revealed it was well past six. Though the sun wouldn't set for another two hours, outside the neighborhood was mostly deserted at this point, with bicycles left on front lawns and cars parked in driveways in a way that suggested their occupants had returned home for the day and would probably just be sitting down to dinner inside.

The house where Amanda lived, which Leigh knew from her file actually belonged to her Aunt Millie, was a two-story cottage, with bare brick peeking through the white plaster here and there in an artfully deliberate manner. It was on a road named for a far-off

English town, like most of the streets in the area. There was a brick walkway leading from the street to a rounded front door of heavy wood, and a smaller path off the driveway that appeared to lead to a side entrance. The black Mini Cooper sat in the driveway, and the side entrance had been left open, its outside light switched on.

Leigh frowned as she chose the smaller path, her body tensed and on guard as both her gut and her head told her to take it slow. She scoped out the quiet neighborhood as she approached the open door. It looked safe, but that didn't mean much. Lots of places looked safe that weren't. She stood before the open door, tapping her fingertips together as she tried to assess the risk. Had Amanda left the door open for her, or had someone else forced their way in, and were now waiting inside?

She unsheathed her pocketknife from its ankle strap, the heft of the ebony hilt against her palm calming her nerves. If someone inside meant her harm, she was prepared. Cautiously, she entered the house, visually clearing each room as she made her way through a small country-style kitchen and formal dining room toward the front of the house. Despite her best efforts at stealth, aging floorboards groaned beneath her feet as she went, and her heart clenched at each sound, every creak betraying her presence to any intruder who might lurk beyond her view.

She made it through the house without incident,

until she found herself in the front entry, where an oak staircase led to the second floor. If anyone else were in the house, including Amanda, they'd have to be up there. Chances were that it was *only* Amanda upstairs, who'd carelessly left the door unlatched, and nothing more. Even so, Leigh's senses remained on high alert, as years of training demanded.

She suppressed the urge to call out and announce her presence. It was such a natural thing, to let Amanda know that she'd arrived, that it almost felt wrong not to. There was no reason to suspect anything was amiss now that Amanda had been thoroughly cleared by her agency. But deep down was that nagging worry, what if they'd gotten something wrong?

Maybe it was the aftereffects of having screwed up so monumentally that night at the club, but tonight Leigh intended to play everything by the book, and then some. Aside from the danger of an intruder, there could be an ambush of Berlin syndicate thugs awaiting her just beyond the second-floor landing. Amanda could be in on the whole thing, or a hapless victim. The possibilities for danger were endless.

Almost as endless as my out-of-control imagination, mocked the part of her that hadn't entirely bought into Javier's by-the-book lectures, recent events notwithstanding. *Come on, get a grip on yourself!*

She crept silently up the stairs, keeping her weight to the edges of the treads to avoid squeaks. There was no one in the upstairs hall, and Leigh let out the breath she'd held during her ascent. A hallway mirror reflected the interior of a bedroom at the far end—a pale face, dark hair loose around white shoulders, motionless, showed in the streaked glass. When she saw it, she gasped.

A deeply buried memory surfaced of a different face, its beauty frozen in a death mask, cruelly streaked with blood. *Natasha.* Her stomach twisted violently. She'd been a rookie then, thought she knew everything—though some might argue she still did. She'd made a bad choice, and the error had cost an innocent woman her life, and changed the course of her own forever. Her pulse raced. *Have I done it again?*

She shut her eyes tightly and when she opened them, the woman in the chair was clearly Amanda, though the resemblance to Natasha from that angle was striking. She hadn't noticed it before. As she looked closer, Leigh realized with a start that Amanda's body was bound to a chair in the middle of the floor. Her field of vision narrowed until Amanda was all she could see—Amanda, another innocent woman who was in danger because of her.

Please don't let me be too late this time!

Caution yielding to panic, Leigh rushed in, grabbing the back of the chair and spinning it so she could get a closer look. She registered a startled face, eyes wide, and very much alive. She quickly searched the room and found it empty. Relief swept over her. Whoever had done this, it was going to be okay now.

She'd gotten there in time. "Amanda, what happened?"

Amanda's eyebrows twitched as she bit her lip, looking undecided how to answer. "I won't tell you!" she declared, her voice strong. "Not even if you torture me."

Leigh swayed between bafflement and alarm. "I don't understand." Her nerve endings tingled as all at once a horrifying possibility presented itself, the only one that made sense. *Betrayal.* Amanda wasn't the victim after all, but a traitor.

"Is this about the Berlin syndicate?" Leigh whispered, already dreading the answer.

"Yes!" Amanda's face lit up enthusiastically. "Oh, that's a good one! Yes, exactly. The Berlin syndicate."

"My god. You're working with them, aren't you?" Leigh let go of the chair and stumbled backward, feeling gutted. How could her whole team have been so blind? *Amanda's working for the enemy!*

She backed away toward the door, patting her pocket for her phone while not letting her eyes leave the traitor's face for a second. *This is a setup.* She wasn't certain who had tied Amanda up. Not the agency, that much she knew. Perhaps another faction at war with Berlin? Whatever had happened, she needed to call it in, get backup now before someone else came to finish her off. Her body froze as something bumped into her from behind. *Oh god, I didn't clear the rest of the upstairs!* But it was just the doorframe. She stared at Amanda, uncertain how any woman could be so calculating and cold.

Leigh paused, phone in hand, confusion rocking her. Far from revealing fear or anger, Amanda looked… perplexed. And slightly miffed.

"What are you doing?" Amanda inquired, her voice shockingly calm for a woman whose evil plan had just been blown out of the water.

"What do you think I'm doing? I'm calling it in."

"Calling it…But…" Amanda's brows drew closer together, her face a study of consternation. "Aren't you even going to *try* to get the information out of me first?"

So that was her plan, to keep Leigh talking while her coconspirators came to Amanda's rescue and did away with her. *Ruthless bitch.* "I'm not falling for that. Interrogation's above my pay grade, Ms. Princeton."

Now the woman looked positively dumbfounded, which made no sense at all under the circumstances. "It's just, there's a whole drawer of lovely interrogation tools, right over there." She said it in a strange sort of stage whisper, her head simultaneously bobbing in the direction of the dresser that stood against one wall, as if providing Leigh with a useful hint.

Leigh didn't trust a thing the woman said, but she'd still have to check it out, find out what was inside. Approaching the dresser while still keeping watch on her prisoner, Leigh glanced inside the open center drawer. She did a double take. *What the hell is this?* Time stood suspended as she struggled to make sense of the jumble of dildos, vibrators, nipple clamps, and other assorted paraphernalia inside, most of them still new in their boxes.

"This is a drawer of sex toys," Leigh said, her tone flat. She squinted, taking a really good look at Amanda, who was nodding slowly and giving her the indulgent look usually reserved for a village idiot who finally got an answer right. "A lot of them."

"There was a sale."

Leigh's eyes traveled from Amanda's face downward, her mouth going dry as she suddenly noticed that Amanda's confining sports bra and loose tank had been replaced with a plunging v-neck top. *How did I miss that before?* "Did you change your clothes?"

"Of course. The other ones were hardly appropriate."

Still perplexed, she circled Amanda's chair, stopping in her tracks as she got an unobstructed look at the back. "Do those handcuffs have pink fur on them?"

"Well, er…"

"They're not even attached to the chair! If somebody tied you to the chair they sure did a crap job of it. Why are you still sitting there?"

"You're kind of ruining the atmosphere, here." Amanda's face was wrinkled, and she was clearly put-out. "I mean, it started out okay with that Berlin thing, but this isn't exactly how it was supposed to go."

Leigh gaped. "How it's supposed to go? How exactly is being tied up *supposed* to—oh..." The truth struck her between the eyes. *I'm such an idiot.* "This is some sort of a role-plaything, isn't it?"

"Well, obviously." Amanda's pouty look morphed into one of self-doubt. "At least, I thought it was obvious. I mean, with the whole dream conversation earlier, and…yeah. But it probably wasn't very clear, now that I stop and think about it. I'm really sorry about that."

"No, no. It's my fault." Leigh covered her eyes with one hand, feeling like a fool. For a super spy, she could, on occasion, be remarkably dense. Usually when women were involved.

"No," Amanda insisted, "I should have given you more of a heads-up ahead of time, worked out some of the storyline more. It's just, you seemed to be catching on so quickly in the beginning, and it's always been sort of a fantasy of mine, to, you know…"

"Er…" Leigh's brow furrowed, her heart filled with regret at the disappointment reflected in Amanda's eyes. *Oh, man, I really screwed up.* The worst part was, if she'd known what this was going in, it would have been such a turn on. *Fuck!* There had to be a way to fix this. "Okay, I know. Maybe I should go out and come back in, and, um, we could start over?"

Amanda shrugged as much as her bound hands would allow. "I mean, only if you want to. I understand if you don't. You must think I'm a crazy person."

Only if I want to? Oh, yeah. Leigh wanted to. "I don't think you're crazy. I'm the one who was acting insane. So, what do you say, one more chance?"

Amanda grinned, rocking Leigh to the core. "Okay, let's start over."

"Just so I have this straight, I'm supposed to be the spy, and you're the possible enemy operative, and I'm trying to figure out if you've betrayed me?"

"Yeah, that's pretty much it."

Talk about art imitating life. Leigh hesitated at the door, knowing she needed to make this right, redeem the situation after she'd bungled it so badly. She'd have to come up with something really special. "You know, I've got a change of clothes in my trunk that might look more the part."

"Not the trench coat and heels?"

"No, not those." Leigh laughed at the thought of donning those awful props. She had something much better in mind. "I could use a quick shower, though. It was pretty sticky out today, and you look so nice and clean. And was that perfume I smelled?"

Amanda blushed. "Yeah, just a little. I put it on when I changed my bra."

"Yeah." Leigh's gaze traveled back to Amanda's newly exposed cleavage, where a hint of red satin showed above the t-shirt's edge. "That's a really nice bra." She stared a little longer before remembering the mission at hand. "I should, uh…" She turned to leave, but the red satin had reminded her of something and she looked back. "I don't suppose—" she stopped, a sudden onset of bashfulness stealing her words.

"Suppose what?" Amanda encouraged.

"Well, you know that dress you described earlier today, the red one with the, uh…" She drew a line across her thigh, her throat too dry to continue. "You don't really have one like that, do you?"

Amanda's eyes sparkled with mischief. "Actually, I do."

"You don't think you could…"

"Help me get these cuffs off."

"What?"

"The cuffs. I can't change clothes with my hands tied together. The key's on the dresser."

Dashing to get the key, Leigh snapped the cuffs open. She frowned as she looked at the pink bits of fur, which, though silly novelty cuffs, had a very real lock on them. "Amanda, what if I'd gotten lost and hadn't shown up. How were you planning to get out of these?"

Amanda's nose wrinkled as she contemplated the scenario. "I guess Mrs. MacGregor next door would have had a very interesting story to share with her bridge club next week."

Leigh snorted. "I'm glad I made it, then."

"Yeah, me too."

The words held such anticipation—along with an underlying tenderness not usually associated with this type of scenario, at least not in Leigh's experience—

that she was left breathless. It was alluring, yet alarming. Amanda's eagerness was plain, but beneath that was a hint that she was open to the potential for their encounter to be more than the simple fulfillment of a fantasy. She might want to see Leigh again. Leigh's heart fluttered at that proposition, and her physical response warned her that she might be more receptive to that prospect than she'd like to admit. It was a red flag that she knew she should heed. A spy's life was safest without emotional entanglements.

"So, fifteen minutes?" she asked, because she sucked at heeding red flags.

Amanda's teeth shone through her perfect smile, erasing any doubt that she'd be worth the risk. "Perfect."

EIGHT

AMANDA STARED at her reflection in the mirror and was relieved to find that the woman staring back didn't look especially crazy or desperate. In fact, she looked like the best version of herself that she'd seen in months, someone who was in control and decisive, like the woman she'd always assumed she'd be well on her way to be being by now. Perhaps she would have been like this all the time if she hadn't bailed on law school, or lost her mother, or spent the past six months dealing with her aunt's illness. Then again, perhaps not. Either way, she took it as a good sign that maybe just a little recklessness was exactly what the doctor ordered for right now.

Discarding the clothing she was wearing, she slipped on a pair of thigh-high stockings that were hidden deep in the recesses of her lingerie drawer, then retrieved the famous red dress, all sparkling and sequin-covered, from her closet. Like the stockings, the dress was left over from that time she'd gone as Jessica Rabbit to a Halloween party on campus her senior year, back in the days when she knew how to have fun and did so regularly. She donned the dress and thanked her lucky stars that it still fit, still revealed all that it was meant to reveal, and clung in all the right ways.

She was studying the result with satisfaction when she noticed the way the top of one stocking peeked through the dress's generous slit. She hadn't been kidding when she described how high cut it was, and it gave her an idea. Being a regular person and not an actual enemy agent, her bedroom was fresh out of deadly knives, but she had a slender metal nail file on the dresser top, so she slid it into the top of the stocking to mimic the real thing. Next, she grabbed the handcuffs, considered them briefly, but then tossed them aside. They no longer felt quite right, and tying herself up again would keep her from getting what she wanted most at that moment—a good, stiff drink.

Soap-scented steam wafted from the bathroom as Amanda headed toward the stairs. Showering would keep Leigh busy for at least a few minutes longer, not to mention changing into whatever it was she'd retrieved from her car. A discarded paper bag sat at the base of the stairs, the horrible trench coat and heels in a wad at the bottom, but it offered no clues as to Leigh's intended attire. Nerves fluttered in her belly as she tried to think what it might be, but her imagination drew a blank. Her lips stretched into a grin anyway as she plucked the heels from the bag. They were atrocious, but they were her size and roughly the same bordello red as the dress—which made them perfect for tonight—so she put them on and tottered into the living room.

She appraised the contents of the drink cabinet, pondering what to make and chuckling as the answer presented itself. Vesper martinis. Leigh would appreciate that, at least, she was fairly certain she would. Her insides fluttered again, this time in acknowledgment of just how little she knew about the woman who currently stood naked in her shower. It gave her pause, the fact that Leigh was a stranger, but not nearly as much as it probably should have. After all, it was the fictional spy version of Leigh in whom Amanda was most interested tonight, and she knew everything there was to know about those. They could get to know each other for real some other time, perhaps.

"Amanda?" Leigh's voice called out from upstairs, sending rivulets of alcohol over the edge of Amanda's glass as she jumped.

"Change of venue," Amanda called back, flicking her tongue along the glass to catch the spill. "I'm in the living room." She downed half the contents of the glass in one large gulp, squelching the last of her nerves with a deluge of gin.

Amanda's heart raced at the sound of footsteps on the stairs. The figure who appeared moments later was almost unrecognizable, her golden hair darker, still wet from the shower and slicked back from her face. She wore a crisp white tuxedo shirt and black dinner jacket, and her black trousers were the formal type, with a satin stripe up the sides. Though a simple enough disguise, the transformation was astonishing.

"You had *that* in the trunk of your car?"

"I have a lot of things in the trunk of my car. You never know when you'll need to go incognito."

Wow. Sexy. Amanda stared dumbly for a second, then managed to blink. "Drink?"

Leigh took the martini glass from her hand and took a deep whiff. "A Vesper martini," she said, slipping into a James Bond accent. "So, you know who I am, then?"

Amanda felt a thrill as Leigh assumed her character, and with a nervous bite of her lip, she tried to follow suit. "Perhaps."

Leigh stepped closer, examining the slit in her dress. Amanda might as well have been naked, the way the appraising look seemed to strip her bare. Impossibly close now, Leigh ran her hand along the silky stocking, grinning as she came into contact with the point of the nail file. "Just as I suspected. You intended to betray me."

Amanda's chest puffed in mock outrage. "I would never! I was just being prepared."

"Don't be coy. Give me the, er…" Leigh stumbled mid-thought, her eyes glued to Amanda's heaving cleavage. "The, um…"

"The nuclear codes?" Amanda suggested helpfully.

"Yeah, those."

"I don't have them."

"I don't believe you. I think you're hiding them somewhere under that dress."

Amanda laughed, then gasped as Leigh lunged in and kissed her.

"I love your laugh," Leigh said in her regular accent as she broke character. "Has anyone ever told you what a beautiful smile you have?"

"Several," Amanda admitted. "Just usually not the right people."

Leigh traced a finger along her lip. "Your teeth…"

She giggled as butterflies tickled her insides. "Funny, my mother always said it was the teeth."

"Hmm." Leigh's other hand inched its way up the outside of her thigh toward her hip, the dress riding up with it.

"I never believed her, though," Amanda babbled as the fingers of both of Leigh's hands firmly gripped the indent of her waist. She melted into another kiss that lasted an eternity.

"Sorry, what were you saying?" Leigh asked as one hand resurfaced from beneath the dress, seeking the closure at the back and yanking it down with a loud zip.

"I can't recall." The dress skimmed the length of Amanda's body on its way to form a puddle of sparkling crimson on the floor, raising goosebumps on her bare flesh. Her breath made a hissing sound as Leigh's hand swept inside the cup of her bra, her toes digging into the floor to stabilize her body as it began to sway. She cleared her throat. "Still looking for those nuclear launch codes?" she asked, maintaining some semblance of the fantasy.

"Yes. I'm very thorough."

Mmm, nimble, too. While the first hand continued to caress her swollen nipple, the other made its way around her back, freeing the row of hooks on the red satin band in no time at all. Almost without Amanda noticing, the bra joined her dress in the pile at her feet.

She was naked now, except for stockings and those ridiculous shoes. She'd skipped panties, which she hoped made her seem more daring, though in truth, she hadn't done laundry in several days and had been unable to locate anything but some cotton granny panties that were hardly a worthy accompaniment to the red push-up bra. It was her special occasion bra, and it deserved a match or nothing at all.

Nearly lost in a sea of sensation, a faint voice in the far recesses of Amanda's brain struggled to remind her that she was in the middle of a game. She couldn't give in quite so soon. What fun was that?

Think. What would a real enemy agent do?

Run.

And so, she did, just as quickly as the thought entered her head. She ran, heels clicking on the bare wood, just for the thrill of running, the look of genuine surprise on Leigh's face as she did so just adding to the enjoyment. She wanted Leigh to chase her, and after a moment of startled confusion, Leigh did exactly that. Amanda reached the stairs several steps ahead of her pursuer, stopping a fraction of a second to consider her options—stairs or front door?

You're naked, remember? Don't be an idiot.

It would be a fatal move for a real enemy agent, as there was nowhere to go when she reached the top. She was sure to get caught. Then again, wasn't getting caught the whole point? Besides, the alternative was to run into the front yard and risk giving Mrs. MacGregor a heart attack. She planted one pointy heel on the first step and took them two at a time.

Her sights were set on the bedroom, but as Leigh closed the gap to just a hairbreadth behind her, the ultimate betrayal occurred, and it was perpetrated by the remnants of her own costume. Within inches of being in the clear, she caught her stupid borrowed heel on the top riser of the staircase and stumbled onto the landing, skidding to a halt on her blessedly well-endowed derriere. Leigh was on top of her in a second, pushing her back. One leg pressed between her thighs, igniting sparks of pleasure that twinkled like stars behind her eyelids. She stretched her arms above her head, angling her pelvis to maximize contact, when she felt something close around her wrists, and heard *snap! snap!* in rapid succession.

Amanda's eyes flew open. "You handcuffed me to the staircase!"

"Of course, I did," Leigh replied, clearly enjoying herself. "I have no intention of chasing you around the whole house. I have more important things to do."

"You'll never find what you're looking for," Amanda protested, fighting desperately to retain the thread of their role-playing.

Leigh arched an eyebrow. "Oh, I know exactly what I'm looking for, and where to find it."

And indeed, she did.

Leigh's body pressed against Amanda's breasts, feeling impossibly soft beneath the smooth, crisp cotton of her shirt. The unexpected coarseness of her wool trousers tickled Amanda's legs delightfully as Leigh positioned herself so that their bodies were in perfect alignment from head to toe. Amanda noted a bit absentmindedly that the dinner jacket had disappeared somewhere between the living room and here. She regarded the top button of Leigh's shirt studiously, almost reverently, trying to remember if there had once been a bow tie. If there had been, it, too was gone. She longed to reach for that button, yank it with her fingers until she felt the fabric yield and part. But her hands were cuffed to the sturdy oak newel post on the edge of the landing, and she doubted Leigh would allow them to be set free any time soon. Instead she nipped at the tiny pearlescent button with her teeth whenever it came close enough to try. She'd get what she wanted eventually.

Beneath her, the polished wooden floor was hard and cool against Amanda's bare skin, providing sweet relief to the intense heat that radiated from above, even as the shock of so many contrasts—hot and cold, soft and coarse—stoked her internal fires to a dangerous degree. She wanted to feel everything, lose herself in touch and smell and taste. Leigh nuzzled her neck, her lips searing the sensitive skin just above her collarbone and unleashing a current of pure lust that she rode like a wave. She pressed her thighs close around Leigh's hips, rocking her pelvis. She traced her toes along the silky ribbon that ran down the length of the formal trousers. The entirety of her awareness was reduced to the scorching heat of Leigh's body between her legs and the scent of soap that wafted from her lover's still-damp hair.

She gasped as Leigh's mouth claimed her breasts in bruising ecstasy, first one and then the other. Bound as she was, she had no choice but to submit, not that she'd have chosen to move a single inch. In complete surrender, she gave herself over to the experience—to the drag of a tongue across her breasts, and fingers exploring and stroking her dampened folds—until she was completely lost to anything else. The sound of her own voice crying out shocked her back to her senses.

She would have sworn it came from someone else, a sound that was completely foreign to her ears.

"My turn," she huffed once she'd caught enough of her breath to speak at all. "Undo the cuffs."

"Not a chance," Leigh replied with a grin. She shifted her body away, the sudden absence of heat making Amanda shiver despite the evening's warmth, making her strain to recapture its comfort. "I'll be right back."

Amanda watched Leigh retreat down the hall, still clothed and much less rumpled than expected. She should have felt self-conscious now that the intensity of the moment had passed, all sprawled out and naked on the floor, but she was too busy trying to figure out what Leigh had in store next to give it a passing thought. Then Leigh reappeared, carrying one of her dresser drawers. Amanda had no doubt which one it was.

"Planning to torture me?" Amanda asked, trying to recapture her character, even as her body tingled in anticipation. *Such exquisite torture.* "What do you have in mind?"

"So many choices," Leigh said, running a hand through the contents of the drawer. She held up a hot pink vibrator, fixing Amanda with a look that sent her melting into the floorboards. "This might be a good start. But as I always say, why limit yourself to just one?"

NINE

LEIGH STRETCHED her back and limbs in the darkness, sporting a wide grin and nothing else, her clothing having ended up—somewhere. It had been stripped away in record time when she'd finally unlocked the handcuffs. Over the course of several hours, they'd made it from the hallway to the bedroom, and worked their way through the contents of Amanda's special drawer, too, until they'd eventually collapsed—spent and exhausted, though thoroughly satisfied—onto the bed. Amanda had fallen quickly into a deep and silent sleep, but Leigh was wide awake.

As Amanda slept, Leigh watched her chest rise and fall, entranced by the simple, rhythmic beauty of its motion. This was the point in evenings such as this when she would usually slip away to avoid the awkwardness of morning, but unaccountably, she had no desire to do so this time. Amanda had been a surprise in bed, both in terms of enthusiasm and skill, but if she were honest with herself, it wasn't just the prospect of more sex that made her linger. She simply didn't want to go—a dangerous desire for a spy determined to be alone.

Maybe it was the woman's sharp wit, or her wickedly playful streak, but something about Amanda told Leigh she'd found a kindred spirit. Bottom line, she didn't want the evening to end. Instead, she longed to drape her arm across Amanda's waist, pull her so close that she could feel the echo of Amanda's heartbeat against the walls of her own chest, and allow her fingers to trace lazy circles around the woman's navel as she slept. She desired it so much that her arm ached from wanting. She wasn't sure what to make of that.

Acting on her impulses, she lifted her arm and reached out through a shaft of moonlight that fell across Amanda's sleeping form. Inches from her goal, Leigh's fingertips already warming from the anticipation of body heat, a deafening buzzing sound pulled her up short. The noise emanated from the bottom of a pile of discarded clothing beside the bed—*ah, so that's where they went!*— a vibration coming from deep within the pocket of her black dress trousers, where she'd placed her phone. Rolling away from Amanda with a sigh, Leigh dug the phone out from its hiding place and glared at it like a pesky intruder. But when she saw the message that had appeared on the screen, her blood ran cold.

She stared at the message, willing the words to change, or disappear entirely. But they remained, as if etched on the screen.

Initiate Stockholm Protocol.

It had to be a joke. It was Javier, the eternal prankster. After being forced to give her the night off, he just couldn't resist yanking her chain. That had to be it, a small taste of that punishment he'd promised. Honestly, she'd probably have done the same thing to him if the situation were reversed. Besides, it couldn't be anyone else. He was the only one in her department who knew anything about her past, and certainly the only one with security clearance high enough to have details about the Stockholm Protocol. As that realization sank in, she felt a tightening deep in her gut. *Get real, Leigh. Even Javi wouldn't joke about that.*

A string of numbers followed the words, an authorization code that changed daily and which Leigh would need to match to her own key to verify that the order was real. With jittery hands, she located the corresponding code. It was a match.

The second she entered confirmation, the phone shook with an incoming call. It flew from her unsteady fingers and sailed over the edge of the mattress. She tumbled after it, scurrying to retrieve it as it skittered across the floor. Once back in her grasp, she crawled into the hallway so that she could talk without disturbing Amanda's sleep.

She tensed as she answered the call, not knowing what, or whom, to expect on the other end. "This is Agent Vesper. Message received. What the hell's going on?"

"Leigh, it's me, Javi."

Her lungs deflated in a rush. "Jesus, Javi! So, it's a prank after all? You scared the crap out of me with this!"

"Leigh, it's no prank." His somber voice left no doubt. *"Toni's dead."*

Toni? Her brain whirred, trying to place the name. "Toni the newbie?" She shut her eyes, heart clenching as she pictured a young, eager agent with short hair and compact build similar to her own. She'd barely known her, but any time an agent was lost, it was a tragedy. "What do you mean she's dead?"

"She was filling in for you tonight in the van, Leigh."

"Jesus. How did it happen?"

"Best we can tell, they saw her getting into the van and thought it was you. About an hour after her shift started, she went silent. The outside of the van had been sprayed so full of holes, they probably never knew they'd hit the wrong target."

"They...surely you mean someone from the Berlin syndicate, coming back to finish whatever they'd started when they kidnapped me the other night? Why trigger the Stockholm Protocol?"

"I didn't, and it wasn't Berlin. The order came straight

from Henrik in Stockholm. Anatoly Vasiliev was behind this."

Natasha's father. Leigh winced at the mere mention of his name. "But Vasiliev's been in jail for almost five years. It can't be him."

"I'm sending you a picture of the crime scene now. You can see for yourself that this has all the hallmarks of the Russian mob."

The photo arrived and, fighting back a wave of nausea, Leigh studied it closely. *Shit. That's the Russians, all right.* A hail of bullets had turned the van's sides to Swiss cheese, and poor Toni's body into little more than a raw, bloody lump. Typical Russian mobsters, too much testosterone and no appreciation for moderation.

Leigh shuddered, wracked with equal parts guilt and revulsion. "I see what you mean. But why now, after all this time?"

"No idea, and no time to find out. We're getting you on a plane to Stockholm tonight, before they realize their mistake. I'll meet you at the airstrip with all the documentation."

Despite the horror of the circumstances, or maybe because of it, Leigh was taken by an overwhelming urge to laugh. After five years with the agency, she was finally getting her very own set of fake documents like a real movie spy. "Tonight?"

"ASAP. You'll meet with Henrik when you get there, and see if he can shed some light on what's going on."

Henrik was an agent with Säpo, the Swedish Security Service, which was her birth country's main intelligence gathering agency. He was the one who had recruited her into intelligence work just after college, after her mother's untimely death had brought her back to Stockholm, aimless and mad at the world. He'd been her mentor, and he was intimately familiar with the details of the Vasiliev case, the one that had broken her heart and sent her running back to the States.

Henrik will have answers. Her tension abated slightly with this silent reassurance.

All through the conversation, Leigh had been sweeping over the crime scene photo, over and over, looking for a clue. It was what she did best. In the brief silence, her eyes landed on a familiar looking folder, spattered with blood.

"Javi." She struggled to speak through a throat that had tightened with tension. "Javi, is that Amanda's file?"

"Where?"

"On the floor of the van, in the photo." She fought to keep the desperation from her voice as all of the possible implications sank in. "Was Amanda's file in that van, Javi?"

"Fuck. Yeah." Clearly, he knew what it meant, too, without her having to spell it out. *"I gave it to Toni to put together some Photoshop stuff for that stupid Spy-ventures thing. Shit. We'll send an agent to check on her immediately."*

"No need," Leigh snorted softly. "She's sound

asleep, about ten feet from me."

It drove home just how serious the situation was when Javi failed to tease her mercilessly about that revelation. Instead, his tone remained grave. *"Your call, Leigh. What do you want to do?"*

"Take her with me." The answer was immediate, an impulse straight from the gut, but she knew it was right.

This was all her fault, another innocent she'd brought into harm's way just by spending time with her, but she would be damned if Amanda was going to end up like Natasha. There was no time for hesitation or second guessing. If the Russian mob knew about Amanda, then she was in danger. Vasiliev was a cruel bastard. His goons could be on their way to the house right now, just to wrap up loose ends.

Leigh's brain whirred, already planning. "Can you get together papers for her in time? Real ones, I mean, not the bullshit Spy-ventures' stuff."

"I'll have 'em in an hour. What will you tell her?"

Leigh considered in silence, weighing her desire to be truthful with her knowledge that too much truth could be deadly. Quickly, she hit upon a workable solution. "We'll tell her that it's all part of the Spy-ventures thing. A new deluxe package we're testing out, like a focus group, and she's along for the ride."

"Got it. I'll follow your lead. See you at the airstrip."

She regretted the need for subterfuge, but the sooner they were on the plane to Stockholm, the safer they both would be. It would be okay. Leigh trusted Javier with her life, though when it came to Amanda's safety, she trusted no one but herself. It was imperative that Amanda not leave her sight.

With a troubled sigh, Leigh returned to the bedroom and perched on the edge of the bed, stealing a moment to allow her fingers to trail along the curve of Amanda's bare hip before giving her body a gentle nudge. Electricity danced beneath her fingertips, the simplest touch stirring up Leigh's desire once more, though it was hardly the time for it. Right now, Leigh just prayed that her new lover could be talked into joining her on one more adventure that night, of a very different kind than anything they'd shared before, and one that Leigh wished with all her heart wasn't necessary.

THEY STOOD in the middle of a clearing in the dark, Amanda's hand curled lightly around the handle of her carry-on suitcase. Beside her, Leigh held one, too. It was apparently one of the many props she carried around in the trunk of her car, which made Amanda wonder anew what life as a make-believe spy was really like. It didn't seem to be at all like the cheesy costumes and unrealistic classes she'd pictured. If whatever this thing was between her and Leigh worked out, maybe she'd ask about job openings.

The night was muggy and still, and the field where they waited smelled heavily of freshly cut grass. With only the light from the moon, she could see nothing but the outline of trees in the distance. It reminded her of that night earlier in the week when she and Leigh had met at the fake crash scene, and she wondered somewhat idly how many fields like this the Spy-ventures folks owned. What an odd business model they followed, bringing people out to empty fields in the dead of night to play make-believe. And yet, somehow it worked. She was having a blast.

Beside her, Leigh shifted from foot to foot nervously. Amanda noted a stiffness to her demeanor, and wondered whether the sudden restraint she detected had anything to do with the utter abandon they'd exhibited together earlier that night. To call the sex mind-blowing wasn't an exaggeration, though as good as it had been for both of them, it had crossed her mind as she was falling asleep that Leigh might not be there when she awoke. The woman seemed the type to make a stealthy exit, to avoid entanglement. It had pleased Amanda immeasurably to be proven wrong, and yet she had to admit that standing side by side in a field in the dead of night, suitcase in hand, was a twist in the progression of their relationship that she hadn't seen coming.

"Javi will be here soon." Leigh's voice felt booming as it shattered the quiet, though in reality she barely spoke above a whisper.

"How is this going to work again?"

Leigh had explained it at the house as Amanda packed, but she'd still been half asleep. Now that she was fully awake, the whole thing didn't make a lot of sense. Something about documents and a plane, and needing to hurry. Amanda's insides gave a sharp twist as she was forced to admit that she had no idea what she'd signed up for. She wasn't certain whether her response was more the result of excitement or worry.

"Like I told you, it's an extraction adventure," Leigh replied, as if that explained everything perfectly. Amanda's silence must have clued her in to her continued confusion however, because after a pause, she added, "It's a new VIP package we're trying out. We're pretending to be spies who've been burned, and we need to escape to safety."

Amanda nodded thoughtfully. "So, we're going to get on a plane—wait, not a real one?"

"Yes, it's real."

"But it won't really fly."

"Well, actually—"

"You must be joking!" Her stomach clenched again. *That's insane!* "The liability insurance alone on something like that must cost a fortune. Plus, the fuel, and the pilots—" She stopped mid-thought, recalling that she was going to be an actual passenger on this plane. "They are *real* pilots, right? They're not just pretending, like we are?"

"Of course, they're real pilots. As for the cost, like I

said, it's a VIP experience. It's amazing what people are willing to pay for. That's why I couldn't let you miss out on a chance to try it out for free."

Recalling the price list on the Spy-ventures' brochure, Amanda nodded. "I appreciate it, really I do." She suspected an experience like this one would blow the brochure's standard package prices out of the water. Leigh's explanation had cleared up most of her questions, but one detail troubled her. "The luggage. Why did I need to pack a suitcase? I mean, we're just going to take off and circle a few minutes, right?"

"Authenticity. We're in the fantasy business, and it only feels as real as you make it, right?"

Thinking back on their role-play fantasy of a few hours previous, Amanda raised an eyebrow. "You can say that again." She giggled with evil delight as Leigh, catching her meaning, sheepishly looked away.

"Oh, look," Leigh pointed excitedly, cutting off any other questions. "There's Javi now."

Amanda's head swiveled in the direction of Leigh's finger and gasped. Two rows of lights had snapped on, illuminating the surface of the grass, and between them was a plane—an honest to goodness plane—rolling slowly between the glowing lines. It came to a stop, a door opened, and a set of stairs folded down. The figure of a man, reduced to a dark outline against the brilliantly lit cabin, descended the stairs and headed across the field toward them.

"How did that get there?" Amanda gaped, and

didn't even try to hide the awe that filled her words. "Did it land there?"

"On the grass?" Leigh gave an amused chuckle. "We would've heard it right above our heads. Besides, it's a little too big for that."

It was a much larger aircraft than the tiny, crop-duster style plane she'd expected, although a good deal smaller than a commercial jet. Of course, it couldn't have landed without them noticing. Amanda's cheeks tingled. "You could use some fog," she pointed out in an attempt to forget her foolishness.

"What?"

"Fog. You know, that fake fog juice they use on stage. It would really set the right mood, like a scene out of Casablanca."

"Having a real plane appear out of thin air in the middle of the night wasn't impressive enough for you?"

"I thought you wanted my opinion on how to improve." Amanda crossed her arms in front of her chest. "I'm just saying, fog would add to the experience."

"Right. I'll pass that along." Leigh reached for Amanda's hand. "It's time to board. Come on."

Amanda's suitcase bumped across the uneven grass as they closed the distance between themselves and Javi, Leigh's Spy-ventures colleague. Once again, the oddness of packing a bag tickled at her subconscious, but Amanda's brain was brimming with too many new questions about the evening's adventure to pay much attention to any one thing in particular. Her jaw dropped as they drew close enough to the plane for her to truly appreciate its size. "It's much bigger than I expected. How are we going to take off from this field?"

A deep laugh from the mysterious Javi was her reply. "You weren't kidding, Leigh. She really is a quick one," he said. His voice was soothing and melodic, betraying just a hint of a Spanish accent, and immediately made Amanda feel at ease.

She also felt as tickled inside as if she'd received a great compliment. *He actually recognizes that I have a brain—in fact, they both do!* She'd grown so accustomed to being underestimated in her working life that the glow of recognition was a feeling she'd nearly forgotten. She wondered again if Spy-ventures was looking to recruit new talent.

He held out his hand. "You must be Ms. Princeton. Pleasure to meet you."

"Likewise," she said, giving his hand a firm shake. "So how, *exactly*, is this going to work? Your coworker's been a little vague." She shot Leigh a look of mild exasperation, though it was obvious she was teasing.

"You'll get aboard, have a few drinks, and we'll whisk you away to a safe location. Easy-peasy."

"And we're really going to fly in this plane? Or was Leigh making that part up?"

"No, it's real. There's a service road at the end of the field, just past the lights. It's long and flat with no traffic, so it makes for a perfect runway. No need to worry. We're all highly trained. So, are you ready?"

Amanda inhaled deeply, considering. It was crazy, but for some reason she trusted his and Leigh's assertions that she'd be safe, and her sense of adventure outweighed any remaining concerns. She grinned. "I'm ready!"

"Geez, you were right about the smile, too," he said to Leigh, who replied with an 'I told you so' shrug. "Here, before I forget, you'll need these," he added, holding out two small booklets.

Amanda examined hers in the light from the plane and was able to make out a red cover with gold print. Inside was her picture, one of the ones she'd given Leigh that morning at the training course, along with the fictional identity of a Swedish national. She looked at Javi, impressed. "A Swedish passport? Wow, it looks way more authentic than I expected."

"Well, it should," Javi deadpanned. "I picked it up from my contact at the Swedish embassy an hour ago."

Amanda started to laugh but Leigh quickly cut in.

"Javi," Leigh said, her tone unaccountably sharp, "stop clowning around. Our graphics department does a really good job on the premium packages, don't you think?"

Javi pulled his phone from his pocket, his brow furrowing as he studied the screen. Amanda marveled at the realistic look of concern on his face, and made a mental note to give his acting extra high marks on her evaluation when they were done.

"We're running out of time. Ms. Princeton," Javi said, motioning toward the plane. "Why don't you go ahead and board while I take your suitcase and go over the last few details with Leigh."

Her body humming with anticipation, she ascended the short staircase to the plane and was greeted by a flight attendant, looking ultra-sharp in a crisp blazer and skirt of navy blue, with a matching uniform cap perched jauntily atop her chestnut curls. The attention to detail by the Spy-ventures wardrobe department was perfect. She handed Amanda a glass of champagne with a bright smile, and ushered her to her seat as Amanda looked around the plane's interior with unconcealed admiration.

"Wow."

It was like nothing she'd ever experienced, or even imagined could exist. Instead of rows of seats like a commercial jet, there was a room with an L-shaped sectional and reclining chair upholstered in rich, creamy leather, with a softness that invited you to sink right in and never get up. Amanda sighed as she snuggled into the sectional's corner seat and propped her feet onto the generously padded ottoman that also served as a coffee table. The bubbles from her champagne tickled her nose as she sipped, and she soon stifled a yawn as her body tried to remind her that it was the middle of the night and she'd been woken from a sound sleep.

Finally, Leigh appeared in the cabin and settled onto the cushion beside her. "How's the experience so far?"

"No complaints." Amanda grinned, then guzzled down the rest of her champagne so she could set the glass down and slide closer to Leigh. "That Javi guy is really convincing as a secret agent."

"Uncannily so." Leigh nodded toward the empty glass. "Would you like another?"

This time Amanda couldn't reign in her urge to yawn. "I'd better not. I won't be able to keep my eyes open, and I don't want to miss anything."

"Go ahead and rest," Leigh said, her voice soft and soothing. "It'll be a few more minutes before we get started."

"It's so exciting, though." Amanda's eyelids fluttered shut and she struggled to force them open again. "You won't let me sleep through it?"

"I promise." Leigh's arm slid behind Amanda's back, her hand firm and comforting as she urged Amanda's head to rest against her shoulder. "I'll wake you up when it's time."

With a slight nod, Amanda allowed her lids to shut more firmly, breathing in the spicy clean scent of Leigh's short, shaggy hair until she'd drifted into a welcome sleep.

TEN

HARSH MORNING SUN streamed through the window and Amanda's eyes flew open. Her cheek was pressed against something incredibly warm and soft, but it wasn't Leigh. She blinked and recognized the buttery leather of the plane's upholstery as it came into focus mere millimeters from her face. Beyond it was the interior of the plane's cabin, rotated ninety degrees as she was now stretched out horizontally across the sectional. Her eyes grew wider as she looked around and realized that Leigh was nowhere in sight. She was all alone.

She sat up with a start, the pounding of her heart joining the muffled hum that filled her ears. It was the sound of the plane's engines, and even before daring to look out one of the windows, she knew what she would see—fluffy clouds below, and a brilliant blue dome of sky above. They were airborne, and much higher in altitude than Leigh had led her to believe they'd be. The glare of daylight told her that several hours had passed, and this added to her alarm. *Where am I, and where's Leigh?*

With sickening dread, it came to her what this was. *I'm being sex trafficked.* It was exactly the type of thing Aunt Millie always warned her about, being too trusting and getting whisked away by a human trafficking ring. The old woman swore she'd seen it on the news. Amanda had never believed her dotty aunt, but now here she was. This is what happened when you gave into fantasies with reckless abandon. Of *course*, she was being sex trafficked, after that sample of her skills that she'd given Leigh the night before. What had she been thinking, inviting a strange woman into her home like that?

Just as her panic was reaching a peak, the flight attendant entered, balancing a silver tray with a coffee pot and mug. Her navy-blue uniform was just as freshly pressed as it had been the night before, her dark curls just as bouncy, and Amanda felt rumpled and sloppy by comparison.

"*Välkommen till Stockholm, Fröken Princeton.*"

Amanda frowned, her panic turning to confusion. "I'm sorry? I didn't understand." The flight attendant hadn't spoken the night before, and she realized now it was probably because she didn't speak English. Agitation seized her as she wondered how to make the woman understand. "Please, where's my companion?

Do you know what I'm saying? Where's Leigh, and where are we?"

"I said welcome to Stockholm." The low, gravelly voice was familiar, all trace of an accent gone, and it sent the same shock of desire through Amanda's body as it had the first time she'd heard it over the radio station phone, despite the fact that Amanda now suspected the voice's owner of being part of a human trafficking ring.

"Leigh?"

"Yes, Amanda. It's me."

Confusion mounting, Amanda fixed the flight attendant with a long, hard stare, then gasped. It *was* Leigh, but she'd never have recognized her. She'd changed into the same uniform that the other woman had worn, her short, flaxen hair hidden beneath a curly brown wig. Amanda blinked hard, and now that she knew what she was looking for, Leigh's features shone through, but it was remarkable how thoroughly she'd been transformed by this simple disguise.

Her eyes narrowed into tiny slits as she puffed herself up with as much bravery as she could manage. "Be honest with me. Am I being sex trafficked? Are you selling me into a life of sexual bondage against my will?"

"My god, you have the kinkiest fantasies." Leigh grinned naughtily. "But this is hardly the time or the place. Maybe we can revisit this little scenario later, though, after we land? I'm really curious where you're going with it."

It wasn't exactly the answer Amanda had expected, and heat flared as, for just a second, her mind wandered over the many possibilities that 'little scenario' presented, but she quickly stopped herself. As Leigh had said, it was neither the time nor the place. If nothing else, though, she was fairly sure their exchange had confirmed that she wasn't about to be sold as a sex slave to some depraved billionaire, and relief at that fact buoyed her, but it didn't last for long.

"Leigh, what the hell is going on? Why are we still up in the air, and what are you talking about with this whole Stockholm thing?" Leigh opened her mouth to reply, but Amanda wasn't quite finished. "Come to think of it, since when can you speak Swedish like that? If I didn't know better, I'd swear you weren't American at all! When are we going to land, and how long did you let me sleep?"

Leigh blinked twice, slowly, waiting. "You done?"

Amanda pressed her lips together tightly, not saying another word.

"Okay, then. Just hear me out, without interrupting, and I promise I'll explain. Will you do that?" After Amanda gave a curt nod, Leigh continued. "To answer your first question, we're currently about an hour outside of the Arlanda airport in Stockholm. The pilot's beginning the initial preparations for landing, which is why I came in, to make certain you were buckled."

"Landing? In *Stockholm*? For real?" Though she'd promised not to speak, Amanda couldn't help it. She hadn't been expecting *that*. Her agitation returned with a vengeance. "Jesus, Leigh, are you Spy-ventures people out of your minds? I mean, I know you said it was a VIP experience, but I didn't know it would be something like this. I can't just waltz into a foreign country. I don't even have a passport!"

"Yes, you do," Leigh said mildly. "Javi gave it to you last night."

"Are you nuts? I can't enter a foreign country with a fake passport. It's illegal."

"It's not fake. Javi picked it up from his contact at the Swedish embassy last night, just like he told you. And that's the other thing, Amanda, we're not pretending. We're actually spies."

Amanda's eyes widened as a fresh wave of panic engulfed her. "Oh, my god. You *are* nuts. What have you done, Leigh? You've kidnapped me! You've taken me to a foreign country against my will. I may not have gone to law school, but that's gotta be a federal offense."

Calmly, Leigh poured coffee into the empty mug and handed it to Amanda, who took it with trembling hands. "Technically, I guess I am working a little off the books. But I didn't kidnap you. You got on the plane yourself, even if I didn't tell you the whole situation, and whether *that's* a federal offense is the least of our concerns right now. Amanda, you're in danger. We both are."

"Yeah, I'd say we're in danger," Amanda scoffed, barely allowing the gravity of Leigh's words to penetrate. "We're about to present foreign officials with fake passports and get sent to the gulag, or wherever it is they send criminals in Sweden."

"Pretty sure the gulag is Russia. And once and for all, your passport isn't fake. Take a look at it yourself."

Amanda took the booklet from her pocket and examined it, biting her lip. It certainly did look convincing. "Real or not, I guess it's a good enough replica. But it says I'm Swedish. Unlike you, I don't speak Swedish. It may not be fake, but they're going to know immediately that I am."

"That's the beauty of it. We got you a diplomatic passport, and we're arriving on a private flight. The passport agent will meet us at the gate and look at it for about half a second before waving you through, no questions asked. It's standard procedure."

Amanda downed another swig of coffee, though she doubted it would improve her jittery nerves. "And what about you?"

"I have a crew ID, so same thing. Why do you think I'm dressed like this?"

"God only knows. I'm hardly the only one around here with kinky fantasies." Amanda rolled her eyes. "I thought you were her, you know, the flight attendant from last night. I really didn't recognize you."

Leigh laughed. "I always know my disguise is a real success when the woman I just slept with doesn't recognize me a few hours later."

"Oh, you *always* know that, huh? So, I guess this is just a typical date for you, then." Amanda glared, squirming at the memory of being so intimate with someone who had clearly been lying to her at every turn. "Where is she, anyway, that flight attendant? Did you steal the uniform from her?"

"First, I don't think last night counted as a date. We didn't actually go anywhere. Before this, I mean. And steal is such an ugly word. I prefer procured. And the less you know about any of that, the better."

A chill shot down Amanda's spine. Physical intimacy aside, the Leigh she'd thought she'd known was a lie. Who knew what this woman was capable of? "Oh my god, you didn't kill her, did you?"

Leigh's eyebrows shot up. "Kill her? Of course not. I'm a government agent, Amanda! I don't just go killing people like I'm in some Hollywood action movie. It's just safer for you if you don't know every detail."

Amanda shifted in her seat and fiddled with the handle on her mug, feeling foolish at her rash accusation. "So, what, Spy-ventures is a front for a government agency or something?"

"Nope."

Amanda set her cup down and fixed Leigh with a steady stare. "I know you don't want me to know the details, but you're gonna need to do better than that if you expect me to go along with whatever this is when we get to the gate and not tell the agent my passport's a fake and I'm being held against my will."

"You wouldn't."

"Oh, you're damn right I would."

Leigh sighed and shook her head. "I should have known you were going to cause problems. Even in handcuffs, you were bossy."

"I didn't hear you complaining about it last night." Amanda raised her eyebrows challengingly. "So, tell me about Spy-ventures."

"Fine," Leigh snapped, her jaw hardening under the humiliation of defeat. "Spy-ventures is exactly what they say they are, a fake spy school for people with more dollars than sense."

As a customer, Amanda knew she should take offense, but she found it difficult to argue with the assessment. "Then why do you work for them?"

"I don't. I work for a government intelligence agency that conducts surveillance of foreign nationals on U.S. soil who are suspected of links to organized crime. A week ago, while following up on a lead, I was hit over the head and stuffed in a trunk. I tried to call my agency's emergency hotline to come rescue me, only I...uh...was connected to you instead. And you basically know the rest."

"Connected to me instead…" Amanda frowned. "You mean that night when I was at work, you dialed the wrong number?"

"Hm." Leigh's cheeks flushed as she studied her fingernail intently. "And now a situation has developed that has put us both in considerable danger, and we're on our way to Stockholm so I can keep you safe while I sort it out."

"You dialed a wrong number." Amanda cocked her head to one side. "You're saying I'm in danger and need to trust you with my life, and you couldn't even remember your own agency's telephone number?" Amanda's head felt like it was spinning. *How can any of this be real?* She started to laugh, the situation too bizarre to do anything else.

"It changes, okay? And it's not like I ever have to use it, and…" Leigh's eyes narrowed and her lips formed a slight pout. "Go ahead and laugh, but you'll be thanking me when you get home safe and sound."

"Oh?" The word dripped with a sarcasm tinged with fury. "And when exactly is that going to be?

Leigh's shoulders slumped, the fight seemingly going out of her. "I don't know."

Shaken by the honesty of the admission, Amanda turned toward the window and stared at the unfamiliar coastline below. There was a whir and bump as the landing gear locked into position, and a cold lump formed in Amanda's stomach as reality sank in. When she spoke again, her voice came out thin, almost timid. "Seriously, what am I caught up in, Leigh?"

Leigh's response was equally grave. "An agent was murdered last night. I asked Javi for the night off so I could take you for a drink, and he'd assigned her to take over my shift. They thought she was me."

"That's terrible!" The revelation hit Amanda like a shockwave, and she pressed a hand to her heart. "But how does it put me in danger?"

"Those photos and paperwork you gave us, the ones for the fake IDs. They were in the van when she was killed."

Amanda's blood ran cold as the potential dangers that could create presented themselves one by one, but then she paused. It was all too much to believe. "Oh, come on," she said in a tone she hoped would make Leigh understand that she wouldn't tolerate being made a fool of. "You're making all of this up. This is some sort of elaborate joke."

Silently, Leigh pulled out her phone and turned the screen to face Amanda. On it was a photograph of a woman, clearly dead, blood splattered all around. "See that folder next to her, covered in blood? That's your folder. Whoever's responsible for this knows who you are."

"That's...that's not just a prop, is it?" She knew it wasn't, but she had to ask. "It's real?"

"It's all real, Amanda."

Tears stung her eyes as the impossibility of her

situation struck her full force. "I can't go home. I can't see Aunt Millie. Wait, what about my phone?" She patted her pocket but it was empty. "Where's my phone?"

"I'm sorry, but it wasn't secure."

"Then I can't even call to tell her I'm okay?" Tears burned Amanda's eyes. "All she wanted was to get me a birthday gift, and now I might never see her again!"

Leigh reached out a hand, an expression of helplessness on her face. "Amanda—"

"I wish I had never heard of Spy-ventures," Amanda spat, her anger and frustration boiling over. "I wish we had never met, and you'd just managed to dial the *right* number the first time, and left me the hell out of this mess!"

"Yeah, well, me too," Leigh replied, with just a touch of frost. "Especially since that insecure line of yours was probably how they tracked me down in the first place, when I sent you those coordinates. If *this* is the attitude I'm going to have to put up with, believe me, it was hardly worth it for a mediocre roll in the sack."

"Mediocre?" Incensed, Amanda leaned forward until she was inches from her erstwhile lover's face. Leigh's left eye twitched almost imperceptibly, and as if realizing Amanda had noticed, she squeezed both eyes shut as she shifted to put distance between them. Amanda stifled a laugh. She'd heard that even the best poker players had a tell, and if that was true, she was almost certain that she'd just discovered Leigh's. *Mediocre roll in the sack, my ass. That twitching eye tells me otherwise.*

"Putting aside the fact you would have been gunned down in the back of a surveillance van tonight if you hadn't been rolling in the sack with me, I'd lay odds it was the best night of your entire life."

Leigh glared, then stood. She shoved a folder into Amanda's hands. "Your cover story. Memorize it, just in case. We'll be on the ground in under thirty minutes." Leigh walked stiffly toward the far end of the cabin. "And as for that bet? You'd lose."

"I doubt it." Her chin jutted out defiantly. She glanced at the folder that had been thrust into her hand and the reminder of the colossal lie she'd soon have to pull off dampened her fiery spirit, but she wasn't about to let Leigh see that she'd been shaken. "Admit it, Leigh. That was the best sex of your life. Too bad you'll never have me again."

Her bravado lasted until Leigh was out of sight. Then with hands shaking, she picked up the folder that housed the details of her false identity. *I'm on the run with a spy.* Spies were real, her life in jeopardy, and everything she'd believed to be true had changed in an instant. Like it or not, Leigh might be her only hope to make it home alive.

ELEVEN

"YOU LOOK VERY..." Leigh swallowed the rest of her thought as she took in the simple black dress she'd loaned Amanda with an appraising eye. Usually demure in cut, with a sensible hem and a bateau neckline designed to graze the collarbone, it felt shockingly revealing on her counterpart. Amanda's extra height made the hemline skimpier, her broader torso causing the fabric to cling and stretch across her breasts in a most revealing way. Leigh cleared her throat as she forced her eyes upward. "Um, nice. Appropriate, I mean. It should work fine for the meeting. And that short black wig suits your features."

Amanda sucked in her cheeks in that way she had of expressing her annoyance without uttering a word. Leigh had seen a lot of that look today. The fact that she deserved it didn't make it any more pleasant. "This dress is two sizes too small. If you'd told me where we were going, and what we were going to do when we got here, I might have packed more of my own *appropriate* clothing and wouldn't have needed to borrow yours, you know. Plus, this stupid wig itches. I don't see why I couldn't have just put on a hat or something, if it was really so important to be disguised."

Leigh held her tongue, making a mental note to add more options to her stash of disguises if at all possible. It was an impressive collection, especially given how quickly she'd pulled it together, but it was heavily dependent on wigs. Leigh liked wigs. With her short hair, they were simple and effective, and surprisingly comfortable. But they'd both need to change their appearance daily, as remaining unrecognizable was essential to moving around undetected by Vasiliev's men. So maybe she'd find a few hats. She sure as hell wasn't going to listen to Amanda whine about an itching head the whole time.

As they made their way along the cobblestone streets through Gamlastan, the heart of Stockholm's medieval city, sunlight reflected off the ancient buildings, turning their stone façades a deep honey-gold that was warm and inviting. However, the distance between Leigh and Amanda as they walked side by side, coupled with the muttered complaints that continued to punctuate the journey, chilled the mood. In part, Leigh couldn't blame her for being angry. This whole thing had come as a shock to her, finding herself on the run in a foreign city, let alone discovering her pseudo-date was a real-life secret agent. But it's not exactly like Leigh had been expecting their evening to turn out the way it had, either.

As for real shock value, try finding out someone's trying to assassinate you! Sure, television shows would have everyone believe that spies dealt with life-threatening shit like that every day, but Leigh spent most of her time tucked safely away in a van. *A van!* The biggest danger she faced most of the time was rush hour traffic. The way Leigh saw it, Amanda might try being a little more understanding about what *she* was going through.

"There's the restaurant, over there," she said, placing a guiding hand on Amanda's shoulder. Her companion's muscles stiffened at her touch, prompting Leigh to push with even more deliberateness as she ushered her through the age-worn front door. *It's not fair to blame me. It was for your own good.* But she didn't hold out much hope that Amanda would see it her way any time soon, and the frustration of that reality was eating her up inside.

It was early for dinner, at least by Swedish standards, and the main dining room was mostly empty when they arrived. Here and there, a few couples occupied sturdy farmhouse chairs and pored over menus atop the linen-

draped tables, sipping snaps from small fluted glasses that twinkled with a combination of candlelight and the evening sun that still streamed through the ample windows. It was one of the oldest eating establishments in the city, every inch of it steeped in culinary tradition. Normally Leigh would have relished the chance to sit and sample the fine Scandinavian dishes of her youth, but under the circumstances, the gnawing in her belly was more from nerves than hunger and the thought of eating left her queasy.

Once inside, Amanda paused to look around, but Leigh shook her head and took her by the hand. "Not in the main room. Henrik will be waiting in a private room downstairs." She tugged Amanda toward a narrow staircase, gripping her fingers tightly so as not to give her the chance to argue.

Leigh really should have learned her lesson by now. After a few fumbling steps, Amanda dug in her heels and refused to budge another inch, and Leigh, trained operative that she was, found herself unable to do anything about it but stamp her foot. "Amanda, cut it out!"

"I will *not!*" Amanda's voice raised an entire octave and several decibels on the final word, and Leigh's eyes darted around the room in alarm.

"Amanda, *please,*" she hissed. "You're making a scene."

"Not until you let go of me, stop trying to drag me around, and instead actually explain what we're doing here, and I mean all of it this time."

"Fine." Leigh dropped her hand and Amanda

crossed her arms tightly in front of her chest. "But I've already explained everything I can. We're meeting with Henrik, an agent with the Swedish special police."

"And he's your handler?"

Leigh tilted her head back and forth, so-so. "He was, several years ago. He was the one who was responsible for recruiting me into intelligence work, and he oversaw my first case."

"And that case is related to why someone pumped the van they thought you were in full of holes last night, and why you kidnapped me, and we're now on the run?"

"See? I told you I'd already explained everything."

Amanda rewarded her attempt at humor with a derisive snort. "Yeah, right. I still don't know what that case involved, or why an American agent was being recruited by Swedish police, not to mention what you hope to find out from this Henrik guy tonight. You know, I may be just a temp, but I'm not dumb. If you tell me everything, I might be able to help."

"I can't tell you." Despite knowing she spoke the truth, the evident disapproval on Amanda's face filled Leigh with dismay. It wasn't like she relished keeping her in the dark, but it was necessary for her safety. "I'm really sorry, Amanda, but I can't. All I can do is tell you that it's imperative for both our sakes that you sit quietly while I speak to Henrik, and go along with the cover story we worked out."

Eyes shut tight, Amanda drew in a breath, considering. "So, tell him I'm an American colleague helping you with a case, and then keep my mouth shut."

"Exactly. You don't even have to say that much. Javi's already briefed him about why you're supposedly here, and I'll introduce you. Just…just don't contradict what I say, okay?" She cringed inwardly at the pleading in her tone, but Amanda's cooperation was essential to getting the information out of Henrik that she needed, and an angry associate made for a loose cannon. "Please, Amanda."

Amanda sighed. "Fine. But I'll walk in there on my own. I'm capable of that much. And I don't want your hands on me."

You sure have changed your tune since last night. Leigh bit her tongue, knowing a flippant remark would sink any chance of a cease-fire. She clasped her hands behind her back to prove they would cause no further offense. "Deal."

"Where are we going?"

"Down those stairs," Leigh said, keeping her hands together and motioning with her head. "You first, though. I won't touch you, but I'm not turning my back on you, either. You're not the only one who isn't dumb."

The room at the bottom of the stairs was a wine cellar, its short, domed ceiling and rough walls reminiscent of a cave, though a coat of bright white paint saved it from feeling oppressive. The floors were red stone, polished to a high shine by centuries of wear. A gentleman with close-cropped blond hair and a beard turned reddish with age occupied the only table in the room beside a fireplace where a trio of candles burned jauntily.

The man stood as they approached the table, opening his arms wide. *"Linnea! Hur mår du, min kära vän?"*

Leigh fell into his welcoming embrace. *"Du vet väl Henrik. Det har ju varit svårt."*

"Indeed, I do know how it has been, my dear," he replied in Swedish as they took their seats around the table. "A most difficult time. And your colleague, she's okay with us not speaking in English?"

Leigh glanced at Amanda, relief warming her as her reluctant guest smiled amicably and gave a slight nod. She knew Amanda hadn't understood a word they'd said, and Leigh marveled at her instincts for subterfuge. It was exactly the right move, keeping the unknown third party guessing as to just how much you knew or understood. In her momentary admiration, it was almost possible for Leigh to forget how frustratingly stubborn the woman could be, and it occurred to her not for the first time how, under a different set of circumstances, Amanda had the natural potential to be trained into a very good spy.

"See?" Leigh replied, still speaking in Swedish. "It's fine. Now tell me, what's going on?"

Henrik's hands formed a steeple, his fingertips

tapping against his lips as he passed a moment in thought. "Ah, Linnea, where to begin? I'm sure you won't be surprised to hear that your government isn't the only one to have experienced the influence of certain far-right groups lately."

"They're everywhere these days, aren't they?"

"Hmm," he nodded in agreement. "And the United States isn't the only place in the west where Russia is hoping to get a warmer reception than they have in the past."

A cold lump formed in her stomach at the confirmation of her fears. "So, this *is* the Russians, without any doubt?" The lump doubled in size as Henrik nodded in the affirmative.

"Anatoly Vasiliev was released from prison last month."

"Last month?" Air whistled through her teeth as she breathed in, as if the news had caused her physical pain. "But he was never supposed to get out! I was assured of that when I testified."

"Oh, my dear, I know how awful this must be to hear, but he really is free." His hand grasped her fingers, which had grown clammy and cold. "I can't tell you everything, but suffice it to say the political climate has shifted rapidly and the Vasiliev family have suddenly found themselves with a lot of powerful friends."

"But he's a lowlife mobster!" Leigh looked at

Henrik incredulously. "The entire family stinks with ties to organized crime, and everyone knows it."

"Oh, they stink all right, but it's amazing what can be overlooked when people like Anatoly and his comrades are so good at what they do. And it's not just here where they have friends. I hear they're connected at the highest levels back in Moscow."

What had started as a lump now sat like a boulder, weighing down Leigh's insides. "And he's personally issued a kill order against me, because of Natasha." A slight tilt to Henrik's head and a raise of the eyebrows gave her the answer. "Then I'm as good as dead, unless Säpo has a plan to protect me like you promised they would." Leigh glanced at Amanda, who was still listening with an intent look on her face, and her heart sank. "And her, as well. It's my fault she's been dragged into this."

"We'd like to help you both, of course. It's why I initiated the protocol to bring you back, just as I always said I would if Vasiliev surfaced again."

Wait, he'd like to? Leigh couldn't help but catch the cageyness of his assertion. *There's going to be a catch to this, the old bastard.* He was her mentor and almost like a father to her, but he was also a spy, and business was business. "Like to? That's not quite the same as *will*, though, is it?"

"If it were up to me…" He shrugged as if to punctuate the fact that it was not. "There are some in Säpo who don't trust you, Linnea. They think you held onto information during the case, kept back some pertinent details."

"The laptop," Leigh supplied, her voice as cold as her insides. "I told you I don't know what happened to it. I was in shock over finding Natasha's body like I did. I was hardly paying attention to the computer hardware."

Henrik waved his hand as if to dismiss the topic. "Of course. I believe you. And when I head back to the office tomorrow morning, I'll see what I can do to get a full security detail assigned to you right away. But you know how these things sometimes are." He fixed her with a level gaze and the message was clear. Deliver the goods, or take your chances with the Russian mob boss who wants to see you dead.

A sharp cramp in her insides made Leigh shift uncomfortably in her seat. The stress of the past twenty-four hours was getting to her, amplified by the fact that, contrary to what she'd just told her beloved old friend, she knew exactly where the information was that he had asked for. But Anatoly Vasiliev's stolen laptop was her safety net, her single trump card. Had the time really come to turn it over? Only if there truly were no other options.

She stood from the table, a pleasant smile on her face to hide the turmoil inside. She looked from Amanda to Henrik. "If you'll both excuse me a moment," she said, this time switching to English for Amanda's benefit. "Nature calls."

The excuse was half true. As topsy-turvy as her insides felt, a trip to the restroom wasn't the worst idea she'd ever had. But more pressing than that was the chance for a moment alone. She needed to clear her head before making one of the riskiest decisions of her life. *Do I turn it over, or not?* She couldn't afford to get it wrong, both for her own sake as well as Amanda's. If she played her cards wrong, they'd both end up dead.

"*HAR DU BESTÄMT VAD DU SKA BESTÄLLA?*" Henrik asked, gesturing toward her menu.

Amanda glanced at the leather-bound booklet in her hand and felt her cheeks burn. "To be honest, I can't make heads or tails out of this thing."

As one eyebrow arched, the copious age lines in Henrik's forehead deepened. "So, you don't understand Swedish after all, Ms...I'm sorry, we haven't been formally introduced. I'm Henrik." He held out his hand and gave Amanda's a firm shake.

"Amanda," she replied. "Amanda Princeton."

"Ms. Princeton. You must trust Linnea very much if you're willing to let her speak to a foreign agent for so long without you understanding a word she's saying."

Trust her? Incredulous laughter bubbled in her chest, threatening to erupt. *I'm being held hostage by that woman, and I didn't even know her real first name until just now!* Amanda wanted nothing more than to let the truth spill out, to confess exactly what was going on and beg for this man's help to return home, but the words lodged in her throat even as she opened her mouth. There was something about his demeanor that made her suddenly wary, an overeager spark in his cool blue eyes. It's what he wanted her to do, she realized, to let everything come tumbling out in an unguarded moment. *He suspects her of something, and he wants to know if I'll betray her.*

She swallowed and met his eyes. "Of course, I do. We're partners."

"Yes, partners. Professional or romantic? Or maybe both?" It was clear he was betting on the third option.

So, he's aware of all that, too? Amanda hesitated, unsure of the best response. "I don't see how that's any of your business," she answered, opting for mildly indignant.

"My apologies." A faint smile teased his lips, but she still wasn't sure if she'd passed his test. He glanced up and raised his hand into the air. "*Ursäkta!*" he called out, and a waiter quickly appeared. "Could we get an English menu for the lady, please?" Henrik turned his eyes to Amanda once more. "Have you ever tried Swedish snaps?"

"Not that I recall. This is my first time in the country." She cringed as it occurred to her that it was a stupid admission to make, seeing as how she was traveling on a Swedish diplomat's passport. On the other hand, if he was already in touch with Javier as Leigh had claimed, he must know at least some of the truth surrounding her identity, and it would be easy enough for him to confirm for himself that she didn't speak the language.

"Of course. Well, then, you're in for a treat." He grinned and held up three fingers to the waiter. "*Tre stycken Bäska Droppar, tack.*"

When the waiter left, he refocused his attention on Amanda in a rapid fire of words. "She'll be back any moment, and before she returns, there are a few vital things you should know. Five years ago, your partner offered testimony that was responsible for putting a very prominent Russian businessman, Anatoly Vasiliev, behind bars for what we all assumed would be a life sentence. Instead, he's just been released. We believe she is in possession of an old laptop computer, one that she stole from Vasiliev's house the night he was arrested."

Amanda drew a shallow breath but remained composed. "I see. And I assume you've asked her about it?"

Without dignifying her question with a response, Henrik continued. "There are two other things you should know. First, the same night Vasiliev was arrested, his daughter, Natasha, was killed in the raid. She and your partner were lovers, and he blames her for his daughter's death. This vendetta of his is personal. I'm sure you can guess what that means for her, and anyone who is associated with her. Second, the only way my agency can help protect both of you is if she produces the laptop. It has all the evidence we need to bring his organization down, for good this time."

"And if she's telling the truth and doesn't have it?"

"She has it. She just needs some convincing to do the right thing and turn it over. *You* need to convince her, Ms. Princeton." Amanda opened her mouth to protest, but Henrik shook his head, cutting her off. "You must. Here's my number. If you see or hear anything, anything at all, contact me."

After a moment's hesitation, Amanda took the card he offered and tucked it inside her bra. Leigh might search her belongings if she had the opportunity, but Amanda felt confident the contents of her bra would remain off limits. She'd made it fairly clear that if Leigh touched her again, she risked losing a hand.

Moments later, Leigh returned to the table, looking only slightly less ill at ease than she'd been when she left. Just behind her was the waiter, three narrow glasses balanced on a tray in one hand. As Leigh sat down, the waiter placed one glass in front of each of them, the caramel liquid sparkling invitingly in the candlelight. Amanda grasped the glass and brought it to her lips.

"Amanda, stop!"

Her hand jerked as Leigh shouted the warning, the contents of the glass sloshing down the front of her dress. Blood pulsed through her temples, making her head spin, as she stared at the glass. *My god, was Henrik trying to poison me?*

Across the table, Henrik chuckled. "See what you've done, Linnea?"

"What..." Amanda stammered, "what exactly is going on?"

Leigh rolled her eyes at Henrik, though it was clear she did so with affection. "He was trying to play a trick on you. That drink he ordered is—well, it's an acquired taste, to say the least. It's one of the strongest, most bitter snaps you can get, the type of thing young boys think it's funny to make unsuspecting tourists drink, although *most* of them outgrow it long before his age."

With a hand that still shook from adrenaline, Amanda set the half-empty glass on the table. The pool of snaps in her lap had soaked through her dress, making her crotch unbearably damp. She glared at Leigh. "Is that all? The way you reacted, I assumed he was trying to kill me."

"Nothing so dramatic, Ms. Princeton," Henrik said, "though if someone wanted to, I trust you see how easy it could be."

It was a thinly veiled warning, a reminder of her vulnerability if Leigh's Russian mobster decided to make a move. But if Henrik was trying to scare her into compliance, he'd gravely miscalculated his approach. Swiping Leigh's glass from the table, she tossed her head back defiantly and splashed the entirety of its contents down her throat.

Holygodalmighty!

Amanda's throat constricted at the assault, her stomach seizing as if to refuse admittance to what might possibly have been the nastiest concoction she'd ever had the misfortune of tasting. But Amanda refused to be defeated. She swallowed hard, blinking once to force back tears, and set the empty glass down, smiling as if she didn't have a care in the world. Henrik could take his warnings, and Leigh her protectiveness, and both could shove them up their asses. Just because she wasn't a real spy like them, she wouldn't be treated like she was of no consequence.

"Not bad," she said to Leigh with a casual shrug. "Too bad mine spilled."

Leigh snorted. "Yeah, on *my* dress. We should get you back to the room and get you cleaned up."

Amanda frowned, her tummy rumbling. "Now? We haven't even ordered."

"You can't be comfortable, sitting there all wet."

Like you care. Leaving is convenient for you. "We haven't eaten yet, and I'm hungry."

"We'll get something from room service." Leigh stood and pushed in her chair. "I'm sorry, Henrik, but I need to get Amanda out of those wet clothes."

"Indeed." Henrik's smirk brimmed with innuendo, but he didn't look overly surprised by the sudden change of plans. "I'm sure we'll be in touch again soon. Enjoy your evening, ladies."

Leigh cupped Amanda's elbow, signaling her to stand. Amanda flinched, but rose and allowed herself to be directed up the stairs. Once outside, she paused at the edge of the cobblestone street, crossing her arms and stamping her foot. "What the hell was that all about? I wasn't kidding about being starved."

"I couldn't get a signal in the wine cellar, and I'm waiting on a confirmation text from Javier."

"Gee, well I'd offer you my phone to try, but you stole it from me. You couldn't just go back to the bathroom and wait for the text there?" She wasn't positive, but she assumed that's what Leigh had been doing when she left the table the first time.

Leigh snorted. "And leave you to plot with Henrik about how to betray me?"

"I have no idea what you're talking about. All Henrik and I talked about while you were gone was what looked tastiest on the menu. But I guess I'll never know." She said it more peevishly than she'd intended, but her hunger was genuine and the shock of the day was wearing on her.

"Bullshit. He told you about Vasiliev and the laptop, and gave you his card to call him as soon as you had any information, which you stuffed in the left cup of your bra." Leigh laughed. "Don't look so surprised, Amanda. I'm a spy, remember? Besides, that dress is so tight, I can see the outline of a business card through the fabric, clear as day."

Despite herself, Amanda flushed with heat at the knowledge that Leigh had been looking at her breasts closely enough to notice. "Fine. So now what?"

"Now we go back to the hotel and order dinner, then get a good night's sleep. We'll be heading out first thing in the morning."

"Out? You mean back to Baltimore?"

Leigh shook her head. "No. To retrieve the laptop."

"Then you do have it?"

"Of course, I do. And as soon as the sun's up, which I'll warn you is very early this time of year, we'll be heading north to get it."

A rush of excitement overtook her given the fact that Leigh had let her in on that detail. Even though she wasn't a spy, perhaps Leigh would start to appreciate her value and treat her more as an equal from now on. If they were going to travel together, Amanda wanted to be a partner in the adventure, not a piece of luggage that got dragged from place to place without a choice. Being treated with respect would certainly improve her temperament.

TWELVE

"YOU BARELY TOUCHED YOUR DINNER." Leigh's nose wrinkled at the sight of cold meatballs swimming in slightly congealed gravy on Amanda's plate. True, they weren't as good as the ones at the restaurant would've been, and they didn't hold a candle to her grandmother's secret recipe, but the hotel's version was still better than anything you could get in the States. Letting them go to waste seemed almost criminal.

Perched at the edge of the bed beside the room service tray, Amanda pouted. "They had jelly on them."

"Those are lingonberries." She looked at the tiny, luscious berries and salivated at the memory of their tart tanginess. Leigh recalled somewhat idly that Amanda had had a pleasing tanginess to her, as well, but the memory held marginally less appeal at the moment since the woman had spent most of the evening acting like a spoiled brat.

Amanda shrugged peevishly. "Whatever you call it, it looks like something you'd put on a sandwich. I can't eat meatballs with jelly. I still don't see why we had to rush out of the restaurant in such a hurry."

Leigh sighed. "I already explained as much as I could. And you know, the restaurant's meatballs would have come with jelly, too. It's just how they do it here. And it's delicious," she added, feeling the need to defend the cuisine of her birthplace.

"Yes, well if you'd let me order them for myself, I could've asked them to leave it off."

"If I'd let you order them yourself…Is that why you're mad? The room service girl barely spoke Swedish, let alone English. Who knows what you would've ended up with if you'd ordered for yourself. Besides, I couldn't risk you trying to explain to her that you've been kidnapped and are being held against your will, now could I?"

Amanda clenched both fists at her sides, and her face took on the look of one those characters in a cartoon who's about to have steam come out of their ears. "You don't think I'm competent and you clearly don't trust me, so why the hell did you drag me along?"

"Because you're much too pretty to let Russian mobsters shoot bullets at." She'd meant to flatter her with a compliment, but as peace offerings went, this one fell well short of the mark.

"I'm more than that, you know." Amanda spoke with controlled anger. "If you told me what's going on —like where we're going, and who might be following, and what's on this laptop we're after—I could help. Not that you deserve it."

"I can't let you help, Amanda. You're a civilian."

"So now you're going to start playing by the rules, huh? It's okay to take a civilian hostage, but heaven forbid you tell her what's going on, because *that* would be against the rules."

"You're not a hostage."

"So, I can go home?"

"No."

"Can I at least have my phone back?"

"No." Leigh squirmed. This was starting to sound a little hostage-like.

"Then, if you're not going to let me in on the mission, explain to me how I'm not basically a prisoner."

"I'm protecting you."

"I didn't ask you to. If you'd told me what was going on back at my house instead of lying to me, did it ever occur to you that I might have come along of my own free will?"

"There was no time!" Leigh fumed as somewhere deep in her brain a little voice was saying that Amanda had a point. Instead of acknowledging it, Leigh doubled down. "You would've fought me on it. I mean, look at you. You can't even eat a plate of meatballs without turning it into a debate."

"I guess we'll never know." Amanda's voice squeaked as she ended the sentence in a yawn, sounding like a little mouse, and Leigh wondered how it was possible for someone so infuriatingly stubborn to be so goddamned adorable in the process. It wasn't fair.

"Come on, Amanda, you're exhausted, and so am I. It's making us both testy." Leigh made a move toward the bed, which though small, occupied most of the tiny bedroom that was typical for a downtown Stockholm hotel. Defiantly, Amanda stretched her limbs to claim the space and Leigh scowled. "Scoot! This is half mine."

"Uh-uh. No way." Amanda's jaw hardened. "I'm not gonna budge. Find your own place to sleep, because you're not sharing with me."

"Seriously? I'm paying for this room, in case you'd forgotten."

"Because you kidnapped me, in case that slipped your mind."

Will you stop saying that? Every time she said it, it felt a little more true.

Despite overwhelming fatigue, Leigh decided to give reasoning with her one last shot. "Amanda. Please. I can barely see straight. Unlike you, I did not get a full night's sleep on the plane."

Amanda blinked, unmoved. "Not my fault."

Leigh snorted. "Actually, it is. Your snoring kept me up."

Amanda's eyes narrowed menacingly. "I don't snore."

"I beg to differ."

Amanda's argumentative posture slipped away and she looked at her frankly and with a touch of confusion. "Seriously, Leigh. I don't snore. I've even had a sleep study at my doctor's office and they told me as much. I never snore, unless I've taken a sleeping pill." Her eyes widened as a realization seemed to strike her. "You drugged me! Oh my god, you didn't just kidnap me, you drugged me!"

"Hush!" Leigh lunged toward the bed. "These walls are paper thin."

"Like I care!" Amanda's eyes flashed wildly. "I don't care if the whole hotel hears me!" There was a loud snap as, with a single deft movement, Leigh straddled Amanda and snatched the fuzzy pink cuffs she'd grabbed from Amanda's bedroom in case of emergency and used them to secure one of Amanda's wrists to the bed railing above her head.

"Shh," Leigh soothed, clamping her other hand over Amanda's mouth with just enough force to stun her into momentary silence. "Amanda, will you please calm down and listen to reason?"

A hairbreadth from her hand, Amanda's nostrils flared. "Mmm, hmm hmm," was her response. The words didn't need to be recognizable for Leigh to gather that her request had been denied.

When she finally seemed calmer, Leigh shifted her weight off her companion, though she kept one hand over her mouth, just in case. As she moved, her thigh grazed Amanda's crotch. It hadn't been intentional, but despite the precariousness of their situation, she nearly laughed out loud as Amanda responded by clasping her legs around Leigh's body and pulling her closer. *For heaven's sake, I think she's enjoying this, the little tart!*

"Easy, princess," she said dryly. "This is hardly the time or the place."

"Mmm, hmm mm hmm!"

Leigh slowly lifted her hand just enough to allow Amanda to speak. "I don't know what you're talking about," Amanda denied, while failing to release her legs, and in fact wiggling beneath Leigh in a way that, though probably completely unconscious, did little to lend credence to her claim.

Leigh regarded her with one eyebrow raised. "Admit it. You are *so* turned on right now." Searing pain as teeth sank into the flesh of her palm was the only response.

Fine, I deserved that.

Leigh removed her hand, but though she'd given her back the ability to speak as freely as she wished, Amanda's lips were pressed into a thin, angry line and she said nothing, just accused her with her eyes.

"I didn't drug you Amanda. I would never..." *After what happened with Mom?* She wouldn't go into it, not now, but it was true. "It wasn't me, Amanda, but someone at the agency may have slipped a pill into your drink. I don't control everything they do."

Something about Amanda's expression suggested she believed Leigh, but she just didn't seem able to let go of her anger. Instead, she lashed out anew. "That's supposed to convince me you're innocent in all this? Real convincing, when you've got me handcuffed to a bed, ready to take advantage of the situation."

"Take advantage...oh, please." Leigh had had enough. She extricated herself from Amanda's pretzeled legs and rolled to the far side of the bed, which regrettably wasn't all that far on such a minuscule bed. "I have no intention of taking advantage of *anything* tonight except a flat surface, trust me." She stood and brushed her rumpled clothing smooth, then made a move toward the door.

Amanda frowned, looking perplexed and a little perturbed that Leigh was backing down from a fight. "Where are you going?" she demanded.

Leigh's shoulders slumped. She would not give into the temptation to reengage. "I told you, I'm exhausted. I'm going to see if I can find a lounge chair by the pool to catch a few hours of sleep."

"What about me?" It came out as sort of a whimper, and Leigh felt a little sorry for her despite herself.

"The bed's yours, fair and square."

Exasperation showed on Amanda's face so clearly that Leigh nearly started to laugh. "I meant, what about the fact that you've handcuffed me to the headboard?"

Leigh couldn't help feeling amused. "Well, we both know this is hardly the first time you've found yourself handcuffed to something, so spare me the outrage. I suggest you spend your time wisely, and quietly, getting some shut-eye. If a concerned neighbor calls the police, they'll have more than a few questions about that diplomatic passport in your purse." The knob turned with a satisfying click in Leigh's hand as she relished the look of subdued frustration on Amanda's face as the full scope of her situation sank in. "Good night, Amanda. I'll be back in the morning."

Heading down the hall in search of the pool, Leigh let out a low chuckle. *You'll never have me again*, that's what Amanda had said to her on the plane that morning. The words rang in her ears again now, as her skin still tingled from their accidental encounter. Even while at each other's throats, the magnetic attraction between them was almost impossible for her to resist, and she knew Amanda felt it, too. *Never? We'll just see about that.* But not tonight. Until Vasiliev's laptop was in her possession, too much was at stake to risk distraction.

THIRTEEN

AMANDA'S TEETH clattered together as Leigh shifted their rental car's gears with a grinding lurch. "Jesus, my Aunt Millie's a better driver than you are. Didn't you ever learn to drive a stick?"

"Yes, I know how to drive a stick." Leigh shot her a defensive look. "It's these back roads. The highways are in much better condition, but we're too conspicuous there."

"Roads look just fine to me," Amanda muttered, turning her head to look out the passenger window. The mention of her aunt made her heart heavy. "She'll be worried about me, you know."

"Your aunt?"

Amanda nodded. "I visit her at least three times per week, especially with her trying to adjust to this latest facility. She'll wonder where I am."

"I thought she had dementia or something."

"It doesn't mean she doesn't know I'm there," Amanda snapped. *Why do people always assume that she doesn't know?*

"No, of course not," Leigh's tone was contrite, but it wasn't enough to completely mollify the anger her comment had sparked. Amanda had just about had it with people thinking the energy she put into her aunt's well-being was a waste.

"She's my only family, Leigh. How would you feel if you had to put your family through worrying like that? If you even have any family," she added doubtfully. "Do you have family?" Leigh remained silent and Amanda kicked at the floor mat in frustration. "Right, I guess that's one more thing you can't talk about."

Leigh sighed. "Of course, I have family, Amanda. They think I'm an analyst for the Department of Agriculture, and that I travel all over the place gathering soil samples for the lab. And if they had any idea what I really do for a living, they'd be worried sick all the time, which is why I don't tell them. And it can be damn lonely sometimes, keeping that secret, but I do it to keep them safe."

Leigh paused and Amanda felt herself softening toward her companion after the unexpected frankness of her admission. But instead of responding, she sat quietly and continued to watch the road, not quite ready to forgive.

"Look, I'm sorry if your Aunt Millie's worried. I

didn't mean for that to happen. I'll have someone from the agency check in on her tomorrow."

With this genuine show of concern, the last of Amanda's anger evaporated—which annoyed her. *Companion? She's my captor!* But the fiery indignation she'd kept burning the day they'd arrived in Stockholm had mostly fizzled overnight, to the point that even she wasn't really buying her argument anymore. As her anger had faded, Amanda had begrudgingly been forced to admit that she couldn't come up with any better solution for keeping them both safe than what Leigh had done. Under the circumstances, what choice did she have but to take Amanda with her, no questions asked. As much as her methods sucked, she'd done the best she could with an impossible situation. Amanda prayed to never have to admit that out loud.

"God, how did you even end up here?" She'd mostly been musing to herself as she pondered their situation, and hadn't expected an answer, but after a brief silence, Leigh opened her mouth and began to speak.

"You mean in Stockholm? I was born here."

"No, I meant how did you end up a spy. Espionage is thrilling in a book, but this shit's real." Leigh downshifted and the car lurched violently, throwing Amanda against the back of her seat. "Ow! Wait a minute. You're really claiming you're Swedish? I don't think I believe you. I've never met a European who was this bad at driving a stick shift."

"*Half* Swedish. My father's American and I learned how to drive when I moved to Rhode Island as a teenager."

"Oh, well that explains it. Maybe you should just tell me where we're going and I'll drive."

"Nice try."

Seconds ticked by as silence once again filled the car, made more agonizing as Amanda realized how much more of Leigh's story she wanted to hear. "So, that's it?" Amanda asked when she couldn't wait any longer for Leigh to resume. "That's all you're going to tell me about how you ended up a spy?" Her appetite had been whetted and she didn't bother to hide the disappointment behind her words.

Leigh sighed. "No, I guess I can tell you more. But I'm going to need a cup of coffee and a snack before I do." Leigh slowed the car and put on her turn signal as they approached a roadside café. "Let's stop in here."

The 'here' Leigh was referring to was a roadside café, housed in a small building with wooden siding that was painted the deep red color ubiquitous in the region. The parking lot in front held only a couple of cars, but even so, Leigh pulled around to the back of the building before choosing a spot.

"Harder to see from the road," she explained.

Inside, the decor was a blend of rough wood plank walls and moose antlers alongside sleek Scandinavian light fixtures and furniture that created a charming juxtaposition of old and new. There was a long counter with food, and plenty of chairs and tables filled the room, but they were currently all empty in this out of the way place and the cars they'd seen out front appeared to belong to the staff. Leigh motioned Amanda to find a table while she went to the counter, and returned shortly balancing steaming cups of coffee and a plate of cinnamon rolls topped with a generous sprinkling of pearl sugar.

"They don't have icing on them, like American ones," Leigh informed her as she slid the plate in front of Amanda. "I figured I'd warn you in advance, since you threw such a fit over the meatballs last night."

Amanda knew Leigh was poking fun at her, but surprisingly she didn't mind. She knew she'd been insufferable, though she'd stop short of apologizing for it unless tortured. "It's a lot harder to ruin a cinnamon roll," she said as she grabbed one from the plate. She took a grateful bite, rolling one of the lumps of sugar around her mouth with her tongue before swallowing. "They taste wonderful." She sipped the hot coffee cautiously, closing her eyes in bliss as she savored the rich brew. "Coffee's good, too."

"Amazing. Two for two? I should mark this day in my diary."

Amanda rolled her eyes even as she allowed Leigh a moment to gloat. "I believe you were in the middle of a story?"

Leigh took a bite of her own cinnamon roll, then chased it down with two big swigs of coffee before she spoke. "So, yeah. I moved back to Sweden the summer after college."

"And you went to college in Rhode Island?"

Leigh confirmed Amanda's guess with a nod. "Yep. My dad's alma mater. I could've gone for free in Sweden, but it meant a lot to him for me to go there and I thought an American degree might open doors in more places when I looked for a job."

"But you ended up back in Sweden. Why?"

Leigh bit her bottom lip, looking uncomfortable. "Family shit. I'd rather not get into it."

Amanda nodded, willing to allow her some space. "And Natasha—how did she figure into all of it?"

Leigh stared thoughtfully at her coffee. "All that family shit I mentioned? She's the one who got me through it."

"But I thought Henrik said she was Vasiliev's daughter. Didn't you start dating her as a cover to spy on her family's business?"

Leigh laughed. "Hardly. I had no idea who her father was, other than a Russian immigrant who'd started a successful business and became something of a philanthropist."

"You had no idea he was involved in organized crime?"

"Not a clue! I mean, he was on the board of the foundation where Natasha and my mother worked. I was shocked when Henrik approached me, asking me to be an informant."

"An informant, but not an agent?"

Leigh shook her head. "No. I never actually worked for Säpo. Henrik just wanted me to do a few simple tasks that I could carry out because I had access to the house through Natasha. In exchange, he promised that when her father was taken down, she wouldn't get caught up in the fallout."

"There's always a catch with him, isn't there?"

"You noticed that too, huh? It's the nature of the business, I guess."

"But she ended up dead." Amanda detected an expression of pain flit across Leigh's face when she said it, and immediately felt remorse for the bluntness of her words. "I'm sorry, I mean…"

"You're right, she did." Leigh was businesslike once more, all trace of emotion carefully tucked away. "It was all a big mistake, but because of her death and the fact that my role in all of this put the head of a powerful criminal organization in prison, I was pretty much a walking target in Stockholm."

"So, you left."

"Henrik pulled some strings on my behalf. He had contacts in an organized crime unit in D.C., and he talked up my skills to them and arranged for me to get a job with the agency."

"An agency you still won't tell me the name of."

Leigh regarded her for a moment with a mixture of weariness and just a touch of regret. "It's safer for you if I don't say. But take your pick of initials, they're all similar."

Amanda nodded, no longer feeling the need to press the point. "And that's when you started using an alias?"

Leigh frowned. "An alias? Oh, you mean Leigh? No, it's just short for Linnea, but my dad was the only one who used it. My mom hated how American it sounded, but I loved it, so when I moved that's what I started using."

So, you told me your real name, after all. Amanda warmed at the confirmation that at least something from their initial meeting had been true. It felt strangely meaningful that not everything had been part of her cover. Well, except for Smith. That had clearly been a lie, but once again, Amanda felt generous in allowing Leigh some secrets.

Leigh called out in Swedish to the woman behind the counter, who quickly came over with a refill of coffee. Leigh raised an eyebrow as she lifted her fresh cup. "So, what about you? Now that I've told you my story, you have to tell me yours."

"Me?" Amanda felt her cheeks tingle as Leigh studied her unblinkingly. "There's nothing to tell. Besides, you're the spy, I'm sure you already know everything there is to know."

Unable to deny it, Leigh just shrugged. "Maybe. But there are a few things that've been eating away at me."

"Like what?"

"How did you throw the knife so close to the bull's-eye?"

"Pure dumb luck."

"Bullshit."

"I swear to God."

Leigh shook her head, clearly not convinced, though Amanda spoke the truth. "Okay, then. That night when I accidentally called you at work, how did you know the passphrase?"

"What, you mean the vesper cocktail thing?" It was Amanda's turn to shrug. "I guess it was just kind of obvious."

"Obvious? Hardly," Leigh scoffed. "That's even less believable than the knife. Out of a hundred people, ninety-nine of them would have answered 'shaken not stirred' or had no clue at all. Hell, maybe one in a million would have thought to answer something different than that, and even then, they'd have needed a minute to look it up. But not you. You just rattled off the answer like you had it in front of you the whole time."

Amanda dropped her gaze to her lap, suddenly bashful. "I read a lot, and I guess I just have a good memory." She ventured an upward glance, and the look of open admiration on her companion's face sent a fresh flush to her cheeks, even as it emboldened her flirtatious side. "Wait a minute, does that mean you think I'm one in a million?"

Leigh chuckled but didn't look away. "Talk about something that should be obvious. I mean, I wouldn't just kidnap *anyone*, you know. If I'm going to take you on the run with me, I must think you're pretty special."

The heat from Amanda's cheeks traveled the length of her body, causing even her toes to tingle. "I see. So, does that mean you can tell me where we're headed? You know, since you trust me now and everything."

Leigh had turned her head as Amanda was talking, and her eyes were now fixed on two men, their backs turned to them as they placed an order at the counter. One was tall and wore a brightly colored leather motorcycle jacket. The other wore a tank top that exposed muscular arms covered in tattoos. Amanda studied the inked designs, noting that some of the writing appeared to use the Cyrillic alphabet.

Finally, Leigh turned back, still looking distracted and looking a little rattled, and answered Amanda's question. "North, someplace safe."

Amanda fixed her with as stern a look as she could manage, not willing to let her off too easily. "You said as much before. An agency safe house?"

"Yes, it's a safe house."

Leigh's left eye twitched as she said it, immediately recalling the time she'd called the sex they'd had mediocre. Amanda knew she'd been lying then, and that what she was saying was a lie now, or at the very least that there was something important Leigh was leaving out. Under her continued gaze, Leigh pressed a hand to the top of her cheek, belatedly conscious of her tell-tale tick.

"So, where's the laptop?"

"Hidden behind a tree in a meadow. We'll retrieve it tomorrow. It'll be another long drive." She swiveled her head toward the counter as she spoke, and tapped the tabletop nervously with the blunt nail of her index finger as she watched the two men, who still stood facing away from them. "In fact, we should probably get back on the road."

Amanda sensed the answer was a half truth at best, but she let it go. She was keenly aware of the sudden urgency in Leigh's voice, and she too now had her eyes on the two strangers at the counter. She downed the last of her coffee. "Yeah, let's go."

They walked casually but quickly toward the door, and Amanda noted how careful Leigh was to keep her body turned in such a way that if the men at the counter turned, they would not be able to see her face. Once they were out the door, Leigh doubled her pace the rest of the distance to the car. Popping open the trunk, she tossed her wig and outer jacket into the back and urged Amanda to do the same.

"Who were they?" Amanda asked as she fumbled with the pins holding on her wig. "Vasiliev's men? I noticed the one had tattoos in Russian."

"Yeah, me, too. I don't know who they are, but we're better off to lose these disguises and put some distance between us in case they're trying to follow. Their bikes are parked right out front, so I don't think they saw the car way back here, unless they were really looking."

Leigh held the passenger door open for Amanda, who passed through close enough in her haste that she accidentally brushed her hip along the length of Leigh's extended arm. Despite the tension of the moment, she grinned as she heard Leigh's sudden intake of breath. She resisted glancing up to catch the look on Leigh's face. She knew if she did that it might send one, or both of them, over the edge, and this was hardly the right time for flirtation when Russian mobsters might be hot on their heels.

Besides, her resolve not to sleep with the woman again hadn't changed just because they'd had a nice chat over coffee. Even if she'd wanted to reconsider it in theory, she wasn't about to make the mistake of getting involved with a secret agent on the run. Judging by her vast knowledge of books and movies on the topic, those types of things never ended well. But it didn't mean she couldn't enjoy having the power to elicit a response like she had from a simple touch, right? And there was nothing wrong with experiencing the corresponding tingling of her own body. It was completely natural, and didn't have to lead to anything more—although if she were honest with herself, she'd have to admit that it did make her want to brush up against Leigh again and again, just to see what would happen.

Amanda looked behind their car as they pulled out onto the road, and saw no signs of being followed, but she couldn't be sure. "Are they following us?"

"I don't think so." Leigh's voice wobbled just a bit, making Amanda wonder whether it was from the prospect of a chase, or if she was still feeling off-balance from the way their bodies had touched.

They drove for another hour, mostly in silence. The road stretched endlessly with little else but fields and farmland to catch her interest, so Amanda amused herself by every so often resting her hand close enough to the stick shift that her fingers brushed against Leigh's hand when the car hit a bump. Her reward was the flustered way Leigh bit her lip and clenched her fingers more tightly around the stick shift each time they made contact. Amanda figured she was just doing her part to ease the tension. It was harmless fun, and a great way to keep them both from worrying about being tailed by Vasiliev's men. Every so often, Amanda would imagine Leigh's fingers squeezing her knee instead of the stick shift, though she'd definitely deny it if asked.

Eventually they turned onto an even less populated road than the one they'd been on, and soon pulled up in front of a farmhouse, its little cluster of buildings painted in deep reds and yellows. Leigh stopped the car, then walked around to Amanda's side to help her out. Leigh had just opened the car door and offered Amanda her hand when a gray-haired couple emerged from inside the house. When Leigh caught sight of them, her hand tightened around Amanda's fingers like a vise and she cursed under her breath.

"Shit. What are they doing here? They were supposed to leave for the cottage in Nynäshamn weeks ago."

Leigh's alarm caused Amanda, too, to tense, as she wondered if the old couple worked for Vasiliev, too. "Who are they, Leigh? Are we in trouble?"

Instead of answering, Leigh dropped Amanda's hand. "Stay there! I'll go deal with them."

Amanda eyed the old couple with mounting dread. Given their age, they would have experienced the worst of the Soviet regime. God only knew what sort of butchery they might be capable of. As she watched Leigh march toward the house and its occupants, and whatever unknown dangers awaited her there, Amanda's heart raced, and she whispered a prayer that Leigh would make it back unharmed.

FOURTEEN

LEIGH'S STOMACH flip-flopped as she approached the elderly couple in the doorway. *How am I ever going to come up with an excuse for what I'm doing here?* One look at their beaming faces and she knew she didn't stand a chance. Trained operative though she was, there were a handful of people she'd come across who could see right through her lies no matter what she did to hide them. As it turned out, Amanda Princeton seemed to be one of them. Her grandparents were the other two.

"*Hej, Mormor! Hej, Morfar!*" She enveloped her grandmother in a hug, hoping her enthusiastic greeting would distract them from the inconvenient questions they were just dying to ask. It didn't.

"Linnea!" After returning her embrace, her grandmother held her out by the shoulders, her expression a blend of joy and confusion. "What are you doing here?

We had no idea you were coming to Sweden this summer."

Leigh shrugged nonchalantly. "It was a last-minute trip. For work. I thought I'd surprise you."

"You work too hard, my dear," her grandfather replied as he took his turn clasping her firmly against his chest. "We never see you anymore since you went to America. It's been almost five years!"

She grimaced into the fabric of his shirt, partly out of discomfort from its coarseness against her cheek, but mostly from guilt. She'd promised to come many times, but never followed through. She told herself it was for their safety, but that was only half the story. The memories were too painful.

"Well, I'm here now," she murmured into his chest.

Her grandmother frowned, suddenly looking suspicious. "Yes, but why come here, to the farm? You know we're always at the cottage this time of year. We've never missed a summer! In fact, we'd be there now except your grandfather was waiting on a part for his boat that got delayed and we're running a few weeks behind. You know how he prefers to work on it here in the workshop."

"Like I said, it was a very unexpected trip," Leigh answered, deciding to stick as close to the truth as she could to avoid being caught in a lie. "I honestly didn't expect you to be here, and just thought I'd stay in the guest room overnight. I was going to call later, once my work was done."

To Leigh's relief, her left eye remained tick-free. While she hadn't made specific plans, she'd like to believe that she wouldn't have gone back to D.C. without popping down to the cottage for at least a quick hello. What kind of person would it make her if she hadn't? As such, it wasn't technically a lie.

"I've told you before, that room is your room, any time you need it." Her grandmother tousled Leigh's hair affectionately, and she was at once immensely relieved she'd ditched the wig from her disguise earlier in the day, as that would have been a very difficult accessory to explain.

"Thanks, Grandma."

"Of course, dear. You know you're welcome any time, although we're heading down the coast in the morning. But perhaps you'll join us? You *and* your girlfriend, of course. My, isn't she lovely? What a beautiful smile!"

Leigh snapped her head around to see that Amanda had left the car and was already most of the way to the house. She'd been so caught up in seeing her grandparents that she'd nearly forgotten she wasn't alone. "No, no, Grandma. She's just a coworker, helping with the, uh, soil samples." *Fuck*. She felt the nerve near her eye spasm like it was signaling her dishonesty in Morse code.

"Mm hm," was her grandmother's diplomatic reply. "Well then, why don't you and your 'colleague' take your bags inside and then meet us in the kitchen for dinner?"

The room where they would stay was in a separate building just across from the main house, on the second floor of what was the property's original eighteenth-century farmhouse. Some previous owner had long ago built a bigger house that better suited the needs of modern families, but it was a rare Swede who would waste a perfectly good building, and so the tiny structure had remained intact and was now used as an office and place for guests. It even boasted that most Swedish of amenities—a sauna—to make the long winters cozy and warm. The staircase to the guest room had steps so narrow that they had to be taken with feet sideways, and so steep that though the women had managed several trips through a CIA-designed obstacle course just two days prior, they were both thoroughly winded by the time they reached the top.

"Safe house, huh?" Amanda asked between gulping breaths after plopping her suitcase in the middle of the hallway like it was made of lead. "I *knew* you weren't telling the truth."

"Oh, come on, Amanda. It's a very safe house. My grandparents' house is one of the safest places I know."

She said it jokingly, but an unpleasant apprehension dampened the humor. This *had* been one of the safest places she could think of, a nondescript farmhouse in the middle of nowhere, but that was when Leigh thought her grandparents would be hundreds of miles away. The possibility that she'd compromised their safety by coming here was too awful to contemplate. It truly was the primary reason she'd never come to visit since her involvement with the Vasiliev case. Her presence posed too great a risk to the people she loved.

Grabbing hers and Amanda's suitcases, she tossed them through the guest room's open doorway with barely a glance inside and little concern for where they'd land. Even without looking, she knew the floor would be clear except for an oval braided rug, the room laid out exactly as it had been for decades, with a single dresser in the corner and a bed piled generously with down-filled duvets. The room was always ready for her return, though until now it had sat disappointed.

She moved toward the stairs and motioned for Amanda to follow. "We'd better head down. It's not a good idea to keep my grandmother waiting when it comes to meals."

Though the house was modern, the kitchen was as traditional as they came, with bare wooden beams in the ceiling, open shelving piled high with a mishmash of crockery that went back generations, and an ancient cast-iron stove whose bundles of fresh firewood proved that Leigh's grandmother still put it to use daily. A rod suspended from the ceiling held dozens of thin, wobbly rounds of *knäkebrot,* the traditional crispbread that had been rolled out by hand with the special pegged pin her grandfather had carved. Leigh knew, too, that the holes in their centers had been cut with a juice glass that her own mother had once drunk from as a girl. Nothing here had changed.

The delectable aroma of food was heavy in the air, and the tears that had gradually been building since their arrival reached the brim, stinging Leigh's eyes as the overwhelming sense of comfort, and the pain of loss, overwhelmed her. Though she rarely allowed herself the indulgence back in her D.C. apartment, just the thought of her grandmother's cooking could set off a wave of homesickness like nothing else. In the rare times she did think of her past, distance allowed her to pick and choose, to compartmentalize. Here, it was impossible. Memories came in a rush, like waves knocking her down, threatening to hold her under until she drowned.

On the long farm table, Leigh's grandmother had prepared a feast worthy of a Christmas smorgasbord. There was a platter of sliced ham and a steaming bowl of small boiled potatoes. Four different types of pickled herring in glistening sauces sat beside a full wheel of white Swedish cheese and a pile of the same homemade crisp bread that hung from the ceiling, only these were broken into pieces and nestled inside a linen-lined basket. There were vegetables, too—two types of cabbage, and beet salad, along with fresh cucumbers from the garden—and perhaps best of all, a heavy skillet filled with perfectly browned meatballs, their surfaces shiny with oil. Though it had become a trend among the more health conscious to bake the meatballs in the oven, Leigh knew it would never occur to her grandmother to do anything of the sort, and she loved her all the more for it.

"Are you positive she didn't know you were coming?" Amanda whispered, her eyes wide as she surveyed the spread.

Leigh laughed. "No, this is just how she is. She can prepare a five-course dinner at a minute's notice with nothing but the contents of her pantry. It's like a superpower."

Amanda nodded as she took a seat in the ladder-back chair that Leigh held out for her. "Aunt Millie's the same way. She came to visit me in Boston once and made an entire dinner when I could have sworn my refrigerator was completely empty."

Leigh refrained from comment, and instead busied herself with filling her plate to the brim, but it struck her how similar she and Amanda were when it came to family. Neither of them had much, and those closest to them were aging rapidly. Leigh saw the evidence of it now in the cautious way her grandfather lowered himself into his chair, and though her grandmother was still as ambitious in the kitchen as ever, her pace had slowed noticeably since Leigh's last visit. It was no wonder Amanda had displayed so much concern about her Aunt Millie. But the same circumstances that had brought Leigh the joy of seeing her grandparents, had taken Amanda from her aunt, and the burden of this fact weighed heavily on Leigh.

Amanda, on the other hand, seemed to have little thought at the moment for anything but food.

"This is amazing!" Amanda closed her eyes as she savored the remnants of a meatball that she'd mostly demolished in one bite.

"Try it with the lingonberries, dear," Leigh's grandmother encouraged, pointing to the dish of deep red, jellied berries.

To Leigh's surprise, Amanda dutifully spooned some berries onto her plate and scooped them up with another meatball.

"Heavenly!" This time Amanda's eyes were wide with wonder. "I had no idea!"

"That's because you refused to listen to me in our room last night," Leigh muttered, and could've sworn she saw her grandfather smirk. There was no way either one of them was buying her 'just friends' story after that little slipup.

Ignoring her, Amanda smiled broadly at Leigh's grandmother. "I can't thank you enough for your hospitality. This is the most amazing meal, Mrs..." Amanda's smile faded, replaced by a furrowed brow. "I'm sorry. I'm not sure what to call you."

Leigh's grandmother, who had just risen from the table to retrieve a cake from the oven, turned back to face them. "Sorry, what was that? My hearing's not what it once was."

"Never mind," Leigh interjected before Amanda had a chance to repeat herself. She winced as Amanda's elbow made contact with her rib. "Hey!"

"Why'd you do that?" Amanda whispered. "I have to call them something, and do you realize I don't even know your last name? Because I know it isn't Smith."

"Yes, I'm aware of that."

Amanda glared. "What, so even *that's* need to know?"

"As a matter of fact, it is. It's safer for everyone if you don't know my full name, or theirs. But more importantly, it's pretty obvious my grandparents think we're dating, so can we stop discussing this? It would be beyond awkward for me if they realized you didn't even know my last name."

"Oh, well, okay. I'll just call them 'hey, you!' We wouldn't want things to be awkward."

"Ha ha. Look, they're very informal, so just call them by their first names, Olle and Ulla." Though the rest of her words were said with her usual American accent, she pronounced each name exactly the way she would in Swedish.

Amanda stared blankly. "Uh-lee and Uh-lee? Your grandparents have the same name?"

"No." Leigh frowned. "Listen again. Olle and Ulla." But even as she said it, she realized that the names, which sounded so distinctly different to her ears, would be nearly indistinguishable to a non-Swedish speaker.

Amanda gave it another shot. "Oh-lay?"

Leigh's lips puckered as she bit back a laugh. "Pretty sure that's either a face cream or something a Spanish bullfighter says."

"I swear," Amanda said with a pout, "if I didn't see their names right there, I'd think you were making this up to torment me."

Leigh glanced at a spot on the wall where a cross stitch sampler commemorating her grandparent's wedding was displayed. "See? Not my fault. They've had these names since way before I was born. Just try your best. Or mumble, or something."

"You're no help."

"So, Amanda," Leigh's grandmother said as she returned to the table, "did you grow up on a farm, as well?"

"A farm? Nope. Baltimore, born and raised."

"Oh. I was just wondering how you and Linnea—oh, sorry, Leigh," her lips twitched with obvious distaste at her granddaughter's preferred nickname, "came to be working together."

Leigh's stomach clenched as she saw the confusion on Amanda's face. They hadn't prepared a cover story since she'd expected the house to be empty, and Leigh had no idea how Amanda would respond. But she needn't have worried. In seconds, Amanda's look of confusion cleared as she worked out what was going on.

"At the Department of Agriculture, you mean? Luck of the draw. I was sent there on a temporary assignment, but I guess I did a good job because they just snatched me up," Amanda gave Leigh a pointed look, "and wouldn't let me go, no matter how much I begged."

"A temporary assignment?" Leigh's grandfather asked somewhat gruffly, as Leigh knew he had little patience for young people who lacked ambition.

"Yes, I was an office temp. Not a solid career choice, I know, but my Aunt Millie—that's my mother's sister—became ill and I had to move back to Baltimore to care for her." Amanda concluded by flashing her brightest smile in his direction.

"How admirable," he said, and it was clear that the old man was thoroughly charmed. "Does your mother live in Baltimore, too?"

"Grandpa," Leigh said in a warning tone. "You don't need to give her the third degree."

"It's all right. I don't mind," Amanda replied. "Sadly, no. My mother passed away last year. It's just Millie and me now."

Leigh's grandmother clasped her right hand to her breast. "Oh, my goodness! You poor dear. You know, Leigh's mother—"

Leigh cleared her throat loudly, interrupting her

grandmother's train of thought. She'd begun shifting uncomfortably in her chair as soon as she registered the look of compassion on her grandmother's face. She could guess where this conversation was headed, and it was the last place she wanted it to go. There were certain things that were private, that needed to stay private, so that Leigh could maintain the emotional distance necessary to keep doing her job. She stood from the table before her grandmother could remember what she'd been about to say. "Time to get to bed, I think."

Amanda looked at her in surprise. "Bed? It's still light out!"

"Of course, it's still light out," Leigh replied. "It's Sweden. This far north, it barely gets dark."

Leigh's grandmother nodded. "That's true. Even I sometimes forget, and I've lived here my whole life." She glanced at her watch and clucked her tongue. "It's already after ten o'clock, can you believe it? As much as I was enjoying our visit, we've all got a long day ahead of us tomorrow. You girls should get some sleep."

Before Amanda could protest—and Leigh had already learned enough about her companion to know that the look her face was currently sporting meant that was exactly what she was about to do—Leigh strode to the kitchen door and straight through to outside, with Amanda trotting behind her to keep up. Leigh felt a twinge of regret. The evening had been going so well, and Amanda's mood was likely to suffer from this abrupt shift in gears, but there was no helping it. There were certain boundaries she would not allow to be crossed.

"Come on," she encouraged, thinking of an incentive that she hoped would lessen Amanda's inevitable burst of outrage over the way dinner had ended, "if we hurry, we'll have time to go in the sauna before we go to sleep."

FIFTEEN

AMANDA STOOD at the bottom of the guesthouse stairs, arms crossed. "Are you going to make a habit of that?"

Leigh paused halfway up and turned to look back with an expression of feigned innocence. "Of what?"

"Dragging me away from my meals, that's what. This is the second night in a row. At least this time you let me eat something first."

"My grandmother's too good a cook, it would've been cruel not to let you eat. Besides, she would've killed me if we hadn't stayed at least long enough to have seconds."

"It *was* good." The memory of dinner took the edge off Amanda's mood. "Hey, where are you going? I thought we were going in the sauna."

"It's still warming up. I thought I'd look for some old swimsuits in the dresser upstairs, unless you'd rather go naked?" Leigh arched one eyebrow suggestively and Amanda felt her toes tingle.

"In your dreams," she teased, though she was fairly sure she'd be seeing *that* look again in *her* dreams that night.

They changed quickly and when they arrived back downstairs, the small wooden sauna was piping hot inside. Leigh spread two thick white towels on the bench, and took a seat on the one closest to the hot stones. Amanda settled onto the other, careful to position herself far enough away in the close space so that their bare skin wouldn't touch, then closed her eyes as the heat relaxed the tension from her muscles. It was the first time since this whirlwind of an adventure had begun that Amanda had had a chance to stop and unwind, and soon her body felt limp and drained to the point of exhaustion.

"You okay?" Leigh asked, her voice softened by concern. "Do you want me to put some water over the rocks?"

Eyes still closed, Amanda gave a weak nod and soon heard the sizzling splash of water hitting stones, and felt the sudden moisture envelop her like a fluffy cloud. "I feel like we've been on the run forever. How can it only have been a few days?"

Leigh sighed. "I'm really sorry, Amanda, for dragging you into this. Please believe me."

She knew she could stretch this out, make Leigh suffer a little, but was surprised to find that doing so held no appeal. "It's okay. I know you didn't have a choice."

She opened her eyes and caught a faint smile play across Leigh's features. What a contrast she could be, so serious and secretive about her work, so genuine and caring toward the people she loved. Seeing her with her family this evening had come as a real surprise, and added a layer of depth to Leigh's mystery. Emotions roiled within as Amanda struggled to come to terms with her conflicting feelings for this woman she hardly knew, so irresistible, and yet completely untrustworthy. She shouldn't want to have anything to do with her, and yet the prospect of waking up and getting to spend another day together would be enough to keep her tossing and turning in sleepless excitement half the night. *What is wrong with me?*

They sat in silence for several minutes, the heat of the sauna sapping them both of the energy to do much of anything except sit and allow beads of sweat to form, glistening, on their skin. Finally, with a yawn and a stretch, Leigh stood and wrapped the towel around her body, though not before Amanda had the chance to sneak an admiring glance at her shapely legs and firm, bare stomach, along with all the other lovely parts of her that the old swimsuit she'd found upstairs did very little to conceal. The resulting jolt of attraction simply added to Amanda's inner turmoil, leaving her head muddled.

"It's going to be an early morning," Leigh said. "I think I'll jump in the shower and then head up to bed."

Amanda blinked several times and gave her own limbs a stretch, but remained seated on the bench. "I'll be up in a few minutes."

Leigh nodded. "Just switch the heat off when you're done. I'll leave a nightshirt in the bathroom for you."

The sauna door clicked shut, and she was alone. Amanda drew a shaky breath, rubbing her temples to clear her head. *She's left me alone.* In a flash, Amanda realized that she could escape right now if she wanted to, just sneak away, taking advantage of the fact that Leigh had left her unguarded. Never mind that she was exhausted and wearing nothing but a bathing suit. She could still get away, hot-wire the car—she'd seen a video on it once and was sure she could manage it— and drive until she reached Stockholm. She could call Henrik and tell him where Leigh was in exchange for safe passage back to the States.

She should *want* to do all of that, immediately, while there was still time. And yet in bewilderment, Amanda realized that it was the furthest thing from her mind. In fact, what she truly wanted was to stay, to help Leigh and be a part of the adventure that lie ahead.

Since they'd arrived at the farmhouse, it had been easy enough for Amanda to forget the truth of their situation. With a satisfying meal and a relaxing session in the sauna, it felt like she was on a vacation. She'd long since stopped thinking of herself as a hostage, long since forgiven Leigh for tricking her onto that plane in the middle of the night. It was simply part of the package when you were in the company of a spy. *Hell, we're on the run from mobsters!* Despite the obvious danger she was in, the thought made her smile a huge, goofy smile. In the morning, she, Amanda Princeton, would be part of a secret mission to retrieve a laptop that belonged to a Russian crime boss.

Electricity zinged down her spine, as it struck her that her entire life she'd been preparing for a moment like this. Every book she'd read, or martial arts class she'd taken, every spy movie she'd watched, or video on lock picking or escaping trunks or all the other things that had earned her a hefty share of ridicule from most of the 'normal' people in her life—maybe it had all been for this purpose. Had she finally found her calling? It was a real possibility, but she'd have to stick around and see this through if she wanted to find out.

Wrapping the towel around herself, Amanda switched off the sauna, rinsed in the shower, and headed upstairs, her bare arms and legs turning to gooseflesh beneath her skimpy nightshirt in the relatively cool air. In the bedroom, the shades had been drawn and it was nearly dark, with just a faint glow around the edges of the window to remind her that it was still not quite dusk outside. Leigh had changed into a t-shirt for sleeping, too, and was already under the covers of the room's only bed. Amanda hesitated, remembering her own unwillingness to share the hotel bed the night before.

As Amanda silently worked up the nerve to grovel for space, Leigh scooted to one side of the mattress and lifted the sheet beside her in invitation. Amanda quickly slid beneath. She rested her head on one of the downy soft pillows, and clutched the top of the sheet tightly to her chest before Leigh had the chance to change her mind.

"Thanks," she said, her voice quiet. "I probably don't deserve it, after yesterday."

She felt the bed vibrate as Leigh chuckled softly. "Yeah, well, I'm feeling generous."

Leigh's hand rested on the sheet hem, barely an inch from hers, and Amanda reached out a finger until she made contact. She smiled as Leigh's finger wrapped around hers. Despite what they'd gotten up to with their fantasy role-playing a few nights before, and the fact that at this moment not a single other bit of their bodies touched aside from their linked pinkies, the intimacy of the moment was overwhelming. It was like warm honey flowing through her veins and filling every nook and cranny. Amanda's eyelids fluttered shut, bliss overtaking her.

"Get some sleep," Leigh whispered in that resinous alto voice that Amanda could feel in the marrow of her bones. "We'll be leaving with my grandparents for the coast first thing in the morning."

Amanda rolled onto her side by way of acknowledgment, keeping a firm hold on Leigh's pinky so that her whole arm followed, draping over Amanda's shoulders and allowing their bodies to curl into a spoon. She snuggled closer, her eyes growing heavy as Leigh's rhythmic breathing told her that she'd already drifted off to sleep.

And then it hit her.

Leaving for the coast in the morning? Amanda's eyes flew open. *What about the laptop?*

She remained motionless as her heart threatened to pound its way out of her chest. The only way they could leave in the morning was if there was no need to retrieve the laptop. That meant that Leigh already had it, or it was very nearby. And yet she'd described the location in detail—the meadow and the tree where they would search for it—and her eye hadn't twitched at all. *How could that be?*

For whatever reason, Leigh had been dishonest with her about the laptop, just as she had been with pretty much everything else from the moment they'd met. Amanda's blood boiled, the forgiveness she'd extended to her companion earlier quickly evaporating. The weight of Leigh's arm across her shoulders was like an anchor as she bided her time, waiting for her to fall into a deep enough sleep that Amanda could slip away. And then? She'd search until she found wherever Leigh had really stashed the laptop. What she'd do after that, she wasn't sure, but at least she'd have the upper hand.

WHERE'S SHE HIDING IT?

Amanda stood beside the bed, studying Leigh's sleeping form, an odd numbness inside. There was no time to feel hurt over the woman's betrayal. She could do that later, once the laptop was safely in her possession. Right now, she needed to get inside Leigh's head, to think the way she did, so that she could figure out the hiding place. It had to be near, probably in the guesthouse. Leigh would want it close. Plus, if her grandparents hadn't been home, the main house would've been locked tight. Leigh would want it more accessible, somewhere easy to slip in and out unseen. The guesthouse was the obvious place to start as it had probably been hiding here all along.

Could it be under the bed?

Dropping to her knees, Amanda looked beneath the bed, but though shadows hid all but the outer perimeter from sight, Amanda quickly dismissed the location. The space between the frame and the floor was wide open, not even a dust ruffle to conceal it, and so while it appeared well hidden in the darkness of night, all it would take was the flip of a light switch to reveal anything underneath. Leigh would never be so careless, even if she were stowing something in a hurry.

Inside the dresser?

The top two drawers were much too narrow to hold even a small tablet, let alone an older model computer, but the bottom three had potential. She held her breath as she eased the first one open, inch by agonizing inch, so as not to let the wood squeak. It was empty, and she let out her breath in a burst of disappointment. She repeated the process twice more, but turned up nothing except a few woolen blankets and a change of clothing in such a juvenile and outdated style that they must have come from the closet of a teenage version of Leigh. Thwarted again, Amanda left the bedroom and crept down the stairs to explore the rest of the guesthouse.

The sauna was a definite 'no'. Even if there had been a suitable hiding place inside, the fact they'd cranked up the heat and steam earlier eliminated it. No way would Leigh take a risk like that with a sensitive piece of electronics. Similarly, Amanda ruled out the small bathroom, which had been built in the Scandinavian style where the shower drained directly into the middle of the floor instead of having its own enclosure. A few minutes of hot water and every inch of the space would be dripping with humidity, rendering a laptop useless. With those rooms eliminated, only the first floor office remained.

As Amanda surveyed the decades of junk that filled

the space, her spirits fell. While every other part of the main house and guesthouse bore the stamp of Leigh's neat-as-a-pin grandmother, this space was her grandfather's domain. Apparently, the elderly gentleman had never met anything he deemed worthy of throwing away. It would take hours to search the room, and that was time she didn't have. Her eyes swept over pile after pile, looking for a promising place to begin, but nothing stood out until her gaze was halted by a painting above the desk. Its generous canvas depicted a bucolic scene of a peaceful meadow with a massive oak tree in the middle.

Hidden behind a tree in a meadow. Leigh's description of the laptop's location played back in Amanda's head as she studied the scene. That had to be it. How else could she have lied so effectively, without her usual tell? Lies were harder to detect when they were mostly true. Every spy knew that.

Amanda grasped one side of the painting's solid frame in each hand, its deeply carved designs digging into her palms as she hoisted it high enough to dislodge it from its hook. She lowered it to the ground, and stifled a whoop of satisfaction at the sight that greeted her—a large metal safe, firmly embedded in the wall.

Bingo.

It was exactly the type of safe that one expected to find hidden behind paintings such as this after years of watching spy movies. And if those movies were to be believed, cracking it should be a breeze. Amanda searched her memory for the most common ways to go about the task. *Dynamite?* A great option for the special effects team of a major motion picture, but not the best solution in real life. Aside from the fact that she was unlikely to find sticks of TNT on a remote Swedish farm, she was trying to break into the safe quietly, not blow up the house. Drilling and freezing the lock were equally impractical. She'd need to figure out the combination.

First, she'd need something to listen with. *A stethoscope?* Again, not the most common tool to find lying around, but then again, any listening aid would do. It didn't need to be fancy. Leaving the safe for a moment, Amanda ran into the bathroom and returned with a water glass. She held it up to the safe, pressed her ear against it, and gave the dial a spin. An onslaught of rapid clicks filled her ear, like a playing card stuck in a bicycle spoke. She frowned and spun it again, this time a little more slowly.

What the hell am I trying to hear?

She'd read an article once about safe cracking, and it had sounded easy enough. The first step was to listen for clicks and determine the combination length. She needed to hear two clicks close together. Goodness knows the spies on television managed it in the blink of an eye, so maybe she just needed to concentrate a little harder. She closed her eyes and pressed her ear against the glass once more, turning it slowly.

Nothing.

Amanda set the glass down on the desk and scowled at the safe. Why couldn't real life ever go as smoothly as it did in a movie? Spy flicks and Internet articles aside, she didn't know the first thing about how to carry out this task. She could listen all night and it wouldn't do her any good because she had no clue what she was doing. And figuring out the length of the combination was only the first step. Even if she managed it, she'd never be able to hear the subtle sound changes that provided hints to the magic numbers. It was pointless. There had to be another way.

Think. How can I guess the combination?

A combination was like a puzzle, and if there was one thing Amanda excelled at, it was solving puzzles. Even without verifying by hearing the clicks, it was a good guess that the combination had three numbers. Most basic models did, and this didn't look like anything particularly high-end. It was likewise a safe assumption that the numbers chosen would be significant. That's just how people worked. They chose combinations that they could remember. *So, what is significant and has three numbers?* Amanda smiled. *A date.*

It might be a birth date or some other meaningful date. Leigh's birth date was the perfect choice, but of course Amanda had no idea what that might be. She didn't even know how old Leigh was, she realized in a huff, before putting her hurt feelings over that fact aside to nurse at a more convenient time.

She glanced around the room, taking in the filing cabinets in their disarray. A search through the files might help her narrow down the options, but she didn't have a lot of time. The sun, which had never truly set, would be up again soon. Amanda squeezed her eyes shut, forcing her brain to think harder. Wasn't there anything she could try? The image of a cross stitch sampler came into focus on the backside of her lids.

What was the date on it? December something, nineteen-fifty-six. So, twelve and fifty-six were two possible numbers, but she still needed the third. *Eight?* She was almost sure that was it. Fingers trembling, she reached for the dial and gave it several rapid turns, then slowly lined up the notch with the number twelve, then eight and fifty-six. She pulled the latch, but it failed to open.

European dates and American dates are written in a different order.

She shook her head at her mistake, then tried again, but still no luck. Unwilling to admit defeat, she put the numbers in yet another order, and this time when she tried, the latch gave way and the heavy metal door swung open. Inside was a chunky black laptop.

Amanda slid the laptop out of its hiding place carefully, almost reverently. It was the key to her safety. *And Leigh's, as well.* She squared her shoulders, trying to ignore that inconvenient truth. Why should it matter to her what happened to Leigh? The woman had lied to her, kidnapped her, dragged her into this whole mess...*and by doing so has shown me the type of adventure and excitement I've dreamed about my whole life.*

Amanda clenched the laptop to her chest. Taking the laptop to Stockholm, calling Henrik and turning it over—that was a sure thing. He might be a scoundrel at times with the way he'd demanded they retrieve this laptop to earn his protection, but he was also a government official working on behalf of the Swedish special police. There were certain responsibilities that came with that, like holding up his end of a bargain. He'd promised to get her home safely if she turned over the evidence he required, and by virtue of his position if nothing else, she trusted him to keep that promise.

Could the same be said for Leigh? She was a habitual liar. She'd barely kept her own agency in the loop on what she was doing, and mostly she seemed to be flying by the seat of her pants. What reason did she have to believe that Leigh would keep her safe? For that matter, *could* Leigh manage to keep her safe, assuming she was so inclined?

Yes.

Despite every reason to doubt, Amanda believed that she could. She believed in Leigh, even though she probably shouldn't. She closed her eyes, reliving the sensation of Leigh's arms wrapped around her. Had she ever felt safer? She knew so little about the woman, but even so, Amanda was certain she'd never felt such a strong connection with anyone before. It wouldn't be easy to turn her back on that. And it would hurt like hell.

Damn it, I'm falling for her.

Amanda knew that her emotions should play no role in this decision. Wasn't that the central lesson of every spy novel ever written? Giving into feelings had been the downfall of even the very best spies since the genre was invented. If James Bond could give her one piece of advice right now, it would be to go. She should take the laptop and leave. Now.

But can I really double-cross her? She clenched her eyes tightly shut. *Enough. You know what you need to do.*

Determined, Amanda tucked the laptop under her arm and slammed the safe door shut. It gave a satisfying thud before bouncing back open. Amanda glared at it but refrained from giving it another try. She needed to act quickly, before she lost her resolve. Laptop firmly in place, she strode out of the guesthouse and into the already brilliant sunshine of early morning, heading for the car.

SIXTEEN

LEIGH WAS AWAKE IN AN INSTANT, sensing even before her eyes flew open that she was alone in the room. The space where Amanda had lain beside her was empty, the sheets cold to the touch. Leigh frowned as she hefted her body upright in bed, wishing she could stay just a little longer. It had been the best sleep she'd had in several days, snuggled into the familiar mattress in her childhood room, with Amanda's warmth and sweet scent surrounding her.

Despite her best intentions, Leigh let herself flop backward on the bed, turning her face into Amanda's pillow and breathing deeply. It didn't smell of strawberries this time. In their hasty departure from Baltimore, Amanda had forgotten to pack her lip gloss and Leigh wondered idly whether they could stop into a store on their drive down to the coast and buy her some more. But even without that signature scent, there was something about the way the pillow smelled that was uniquely Amanda, and the merest whiff flooded Leigh with an intoxicating cocktail of emotions—comfort, desire, and something more that she couldn't quite define.

She stretched her arms above her head and felt something pop. She wanted nothing more than to find Amanda and take her back to bed for a few hours more. She'd been so tired the night before, much too exhausted to do anything but lean into Amanda's warmth as they spooned on the bed, but it hadn't escaped her notice that something had shifted between them in the hours since Amanda had met Leigh's family. There'd been a different kind of connection between them. It had felt a little like forgiveness, and maybe the beginnings of trust. She nuzzled the pillow and breathed in again. At least she could hope. She wasn't certain what she wanted where Amanda was concerned, but forgiveness and trust were both steps in the right direction.

Tearing herself away from the pillow, which she would absolutely not admit to having been snuggling like a toddler with a favorite teddy bear, Leigh sat up again and forced herself to her feet. They had a mission to accomplish, and lingering in bed any longer was a luxury she couldn't afford. She needed to retrieve the laptop from the safe downstairs, and then figure out a way to come clean to Amanda about the lie she'd told, and break the news that they wouldn't need to go searching for the device after all, since it had been just inches away from them this whole time.

She wasn't even sure why she'd lied about that, except that it was what her training told her to do. It was stupid, really, since Amanda could see right through her to the point that it was hardly worth the effort trying to conceal anything from her. But still, Leigh was a spy and deception was part of her nature. Aside from Henrik, Javier, and a few close associates at work, Leigh trusted no one, and yet she couldn't help but wonder if it might not be time to let Amanda in. The woman's instincts, after all, were spot-on. She'd be an asset. Should Leigh share the entirety of her plan, and treat Amanda like the partner she'd come to think of her as more and more over their days together? Or was it risking too much?

Where is Amanda, anyway? Leigh strained to hear the sound of running water from the shower, but there was nothing but silence. Amanda's clothing from the night before was gone, though her suitcase with the rest of her belongings remained. A flutter of unease tickled her insides as Leigh pulled on her clothes and headed for the staircase, wincing as her still-tired muscles registered their complaints at the steepness of the descent. Leigh peered through the glass in the sauna door, but the bench was empty, and the bathroom door was open wide to reveal a similarly empty space.

In the tiny entryway, brilliant sunlight streamed in

from the outside through a crack in the front door, and Leigh realized someone had opened it and failed to shut it all the way. Squinting at the strip of light, Leigh remembered the effect that the early morning sun sometimes had on visitors, how hard it could be to sleep through near twenty-four-hour daylight when you weren't used to it. Perhaps Amanda had woken up early and gone for a walk around the farm? But as she took a step toward the door, she glanced into the office, and her blood turned to ice in her veins.

The framed painting of the meadow with its giant oak tree was on the floor, leaning against the wall. The safe it had concealed was exposed, its door ajar. Approaching it, Leigh knew what she would find inside. *Nothing.* Her sweet, warm, trustworthy Amanda had double-crossed her! With a heavy heart she looked inside anyway, hoping she was wrong, but she wasn't. The safe was bare, and her only hope of safety for herself and her family was gone.

She raced across to the main house, noting as she did that their rented car was gone, too. That confirmed it. Amanda had betrayed her, no question about it. With each step, the pain in her chest, right around the spot where her heart was, grew more pronounced. Though they'd known each other only a week, the loss of Amanda's companionship left her bereft, like losing her mother. Like losing Natasha. By the time she reached the main house, she was completely blinded by her unshed tears. *How could life be so cruel again?*

Which was why she was so stunned when she wrenched open the kitchen door and saw Amanda seated at the long farmhouse table, chatting with her grandmother while gobbling down a stack of thin Swedish pancakes as if she didn't have a care in the world.

"Good morning, Leigh." Amanda smiled, but it wasn't the usual one that sent a tingling jolt of desire down to the tips of Leigh's extremities. It was a smile that hid a secret, the face of a woman who knew she had the upper hand, and a look that sent a trickle of ice down Leigh's spine.

"Oh, good morning dear!" Her grandmother bustled to the stove when she saw her granddaughter and immediately began fixing her a plate, seemingly oblivious to the electric current that passed between the two younger women. "How would you two like to take your breakfast out to the table in the back garden?"

Not entirely oblivious, then, Leigh corrected, *but she's mistaken the tension as a romantic one and thinks we just want to be alone.* Though that was the furthest thing from her mind, Leigh seized on the opportunity her grandmother had offered and expressed an unbridled enthusiasm for al fresco dining. She needed to be alone with Amanda, all right. She needed to get to the bottom of whatever foolhardy thing the woman had done, and then decide whether or not to throttle her for it.

Once they were outside and out of view of the kitchen window, Leigh grabbed Amanda roughly by the elbow.

Amanda gasped. "Hey! What's that all about?" She had the audacity to sound as if her feelings were hurt.

"What the hell do you think it's about?" Leigh countered, barely able to contain her rage. "What did you do with it?"

A smile teased Amanda's lips, leaving no doubt that she knew exactly what Leigh was talking about. "It's somewhere safe."

"Oh, really? And the car, too, I suppose?"

Amanda gave a small shrug. "Both safe. So, shall we talk about this now, or do you want to eat your pancakes first? They're really good."

"Good? Of course, they're *good*. My grandmother's the best fucking cook in Scandinavia, so it doesn't surprise me that they're *good*." Leigh was seething with anger, her entire body clenched. "What does surprise me is that you have the guts to sit there and eat them, right at her table, after what you've done. You've put their lives in jeopardy, and ours, too."

"I haven't done anything," Amanda replied calmly. "Not yet."

"Oh, not yet? Not *yet*? Then what are you waiting for?" Leigh pressed her lips into a thin, hard line as she awaited Amanda's response.

"I'm not sure. It would've been easy, you know, to take the laptop and the car and go. I've been up for three hours. I'd probably be halfway to Stockholm by now. But I couldn't go through with it. Not without at least giving you a chance."

She'd expected a list of demands, an attempt at blackmail, not an olive branch. Leigh's brow furrowed at this unexpected turn. "A chance to do what?"

"To treat me like I'm part of whatever this plan is that you've put together, and not just a detail to be dealt with. You lied to me, Leigh. Looked me right in the face and lied, which I actually didn't think you'd be able to do. In fact, you've lied to me from the very beginning, and shut me out, and made decisions that impacted me without asking for my advice, and frankly, I'm a little tired of it."

Though she'd already been thinking along similar lines to this when she woke up—although in her version, she seemed to remember coming across in a much better light—hearing this list of her shortcomings from Amanda now made Leigh squirm. She *had* done all of those things, yet through it all, Amanda had mostly been a very good partner, and only occasionally a pain in the ass—which upon reflection, Leigh had to admit she'd deserved as often as not.

She pressed her lips together, then mumbled, "You're right."

"I am? I'm sorry, could you speak up? I'm not sure I heard you."

Leigh gave a grunt, then forced herself to speak more loudly. "I said you're right. And I'm really sorry."

Amanda's eyes and mouth twitched, and it was her turn to be surprised. "Really? You're sorry?"

Though it was as uncomfortable as an itchy sweater, Leigh continued. "I am. I shouldn't have kidnapped you, or dragged you to my grandparents' house without telling you where we were going, or lied about where I'd hidden the laptop. I should have shown you more respect, and included your input." She could tell Amanda was studying her left eye for that tell-tale twitch, but she wouldn't find it. This time, Leigh was being absolutely sincere.

"Well, yes. You should have." It was clear that Amanda had the wind taken out of her sails by Leigh's apology. She paused to stuff some pancake bits into her mouth, and she seemed to be digging through her brain for anything else she could be upset about while she chewed. She soon found something. "And why *did* you lie about the laptop?"

Leigh squirmed uncomfortably under Amanda's accusatory tone, her own mouthful of pancake suddenly dry enough to choke her. "I'm…not sure."

"Really?" Amanda scoffed, shaking her head. "I don't believe that. You know why I think you did it? I think you were planning to drive out on your own, pretending you were going for the laptop, and ditch me. By the time I realized you weren't coming back, you'd have been hours ahead and I'd have no idea where you'd gone."

"Amanda, that's not—" Leigh bit back her denial as

she could already feel the first signs of twitching in her eye. *Damn it!* She'd trained with some of the best agents in the world to keep that tell under control. She could pass any lie detector test, fool the agency's top experts, and yet when it came to Amanda, she was as useless as the greenest rookie. She might as well never have gone to a single day of training for as much good as it did her. "Okay, fine. That was *one* of the options I was considering. I hadn't decided. And for the record, I wouldn't have just ditched you. I would have sent someone from the agency to escort you safely home."

She tensed in anticipation of Amanda's response, but instead of anger, Leigh was surprised to see a look of satisfaction on Amanda's face.

"There. That wasn't so hard, was it? Now, why don't you explain to me why we're actually going down to the coast with your grandparents today. Because as much as this little family reunion you have going on is super heartwarming, I know you wouldn't risk being around them any longer than you had to if there wasn't a really good reason."

Leigh gaped. This woman's deductive skills were uncanny at times. "There's someone I need to see in Nynäshamn. An old friend with a knack for technology. This laptop has been the biggest safety net I've had to keep Vasiliev's organization at bay, but I don't know exactly why. I desperately want to know what's on it before I turn it in."

Amanda nodded, holding her steadily in her gaze. "So, you don't trust Henrik."

Leigh shook her head. "No, I do. At least, as much as I trust anyone. It's just a precaution. Once I hand it over, I'm not stupid enough to think that Säpo won't shut me out. Or my own agency, either, for that matter. All I know is whatever's on that hard drive is damaging enough to Vasiliev's organization that they've left me alone all these years to avoid having it released. I just need to know what we're dealing with."

Amanda grinned, and despite herself, Leigh's knees got wobbly in an instant, her body flush with warmth.

"What is it?" Leigh asked, trying to keep her skyrocketing pulse under control.

"You said 'we.' Did you mean it? We're really in this together now, you and me?"

Leigh tried not to grimace as she confirmed the truth of it. "I guess so."

"No more secrets?"

Leigh shook her head, and this time it seemed less painful to her to give honesty a try. "I promise to try."

"Good enough. And you'll let me drive us to the coast?"

"Absolutely not."

"But I'm a much better driver. And I'm the one who knows where the car is," Amanda added when Leigh failed to yield.

"Doesn't matter. I drive at least halfway, or I get

out those fuzzy pink cuffs of yours when you least expect it and you ride the rest of the way in the trunk."

"You do remember that I know how to escape a trunk, right?" Amanda blinked slowly, clearly waiting to get a rise out her. "I'm a lot better at it than you are, in fact."

"Yeah, maybe." Leigh grinned, her humor restored by this banter between them, the perfect antidote for anything that ailed her. "But can you do it while going full speed on a highway? Actually, I might enjoy watching you try."

"I'm sure you would." Amanda rolled her eyes. "Fine, we'll each drive halfway. But I'll be counting the miles."

"I'd expect nothing less."

As Leigh followed Amanda to find the hidden car, a surge of affection warmed her through, but worried her, too. Leigh needed to be careful. Emotions could be dangerous in her line of work, let alone falling in love. And if she was reading them correctly, every sign indicated that she was well on her way to falling hard.

SEVENTEEN

AMANDA SURVEYED the exterior of the house dubiously. Though its red paint and white trim were identical to the rest of the houses along the row, there was an air of neglect to this one that stood in contrast to the others. It had a creepiness about it that made Amanda shiver. Or perhaps she was just projecting her own worries about what they'd find on the laptop when Leigh's friend managed to get a peek inside. "You're sure this is the right place?"

"Positive." Leigh seemed thoroughly unconcerned, though it was difficult to know for certain. They'd had to give up their more elaborate disguises so as not to alarm Leigh's grandparents, but Leigh had still insisted they do the best they could with regular street clothes. Until they knew for certain that Vasiliev's men weren't tracking them, it was best if they were difficult to spot, and so today Leigh wore a wide-brimmed hat and dark sunglasses, with the collar of her shirt turned up high. The combined effect was a face shrouded in deep shadow, only her lips visible. But her lips, at least, appeared completely at ease with the current situation. "I've known Max since we were kids."

Amanda removed her own sunglasses and examined the small porch where they stood. A straw mat sat in front of the door, printed with the word *välkommen* in bold letters and decorated with a red Swedish horse. It would have looked significantly more welcoming if it hadn't been caked with what appeared to be half a century's worth of grime. There was a doorbell which—though screwed on somewhat crookedly—looked like it might be in working order, and yet Amanda noted that Leigh had yet to press it. "Should we ring?"

"No need. It would just scare him, so I texted when we left the cottage. Besides," she added, pointing to a spot under the eaves where Amanda could just make out the lens of a webcam, "I'm sure he already knows we're here."

As if to prove her correct, the door swung open the moment she said it, rusty hinges letting out a tortured squeal as if they'd gotten so out of the habit of guests that they weren't sure what to make of being put to work. A tall, skinny man who looked to be in his mid-thirties stood in the doorway. His skin was the shocking white of a Scandinavian who hasn't ventured out into the sun in quite some time. On his chin was a scraggly blond goatee, his unkempt hair yanked back into a short ponytail. His expression was almost menacing at first, and it was clear that he was as unused to greeting guests as were his front door hinges, but when he saw Leigh, his eyes lit up and his face was transformed with a warm smile.

"Leigh!"

"Max!" Leigh wrangled the man into a bear hug, which left him looking slightly startled, but not displeased. "So good to see you again. And this is my colleague, Amanda."

Max nodded but did not reach out a hand, perhaps having already had his fill of human contact from Leigh's hug. "Nice to meet you, Amanda."

Amanda smiled politely. "Thank you for letting us come by."

"Of course. Anything for Leigh. Please, come in."

They entered the foyer and kicked their shoes off into the corner as was the custom, though Amanda regretted it immediately when she saw the state of the place. They stepped into what was probably meant to be the living room, but was in reality a room furnished almost entirely with a blend of electric keyboards, recording equipment, and computers. There was little in the way of seating except for a couple of mismatched wooden chairs, some sort of fancy ergonomic thing behind the desk that was obviously intended for Max's use alone, and a single, rumpled-looking sofa. Picking her way across the piles of cables and stacks of paper that littered the floor, praying the whole way that her bare feet would survive intact, Amanda chose a seat on the sofa. Leigh remained standing while she dug through a quilted floral tote bag she'd borrowed from her grandmother to carry the laptop in.

"This is it?" Max asked. He took the heavy computer with both hands, then expertly navigated through the flotsam around him to set it on the single bare spot on his desk. Given the general disarray of the room, Amanda suspected he'd been busy clearing enough space for it just before they arrived. He hooked in a few cables, then turned on one of the monitors and peered at the glowing screen. "Let me kick off a few diagnostics to see what's going on inside."

He and Leigh began chatting in Swedish, and since she was unable to make out what they were saying, Amanda relaxed into the surprisingly plump pillows of the couch and tuned them out. There was a rustling behind her as one of the sets of thick curtains that kept the room shrouded in semi-darkness shifted to reveal a furry black feline face with long whiskers and bright green eyes. The cat balanced two paws heavily on Amanda's shoulder, then pounced into her lap, spun rapidly in a circle, and began the vital task of kneading her thigh. The kitty had just settled into a sleeping pose and closed its eyes when Leigh and Max came to join her.

"You made a friend." Max studied the cat with a

bemused expression on his face. "Minerva doesn't usually like people."

Amanda gave the cat a little tickle beneath her chin and was rewarded with a strong head butt against her palm, demanding more. "Could've fooled me." She looked with interest at the assortment of equipment around the room. "So, Max, what is it exactly that you do?"

"I'm a composer," he answered, pulling up one of the wooden chairs for himself as Leigh took the remaining space beside Amanda on the couch.

"He's a hacker," Leigh added blandly.

Amanda's eyebrows shot up. "For real?"

Max shrugged. "It pays better than composing. But I'm not like one of those anonymous guys with the masks and stuff, if that's what you were thinking."

"No, of course not," Amanda said, though that was precisely what she'd been thinking.

"Max gets hired by companies to try to break into their systems, and then tell them how they can eliminate their vulnerabilities," Leigh explained. "He's a good musician, too, though."

"And how do you know each other?" Amanda asked.

"His mother was my piano teacher."

"Oh?" Amanda took a break from petting the cat to give Leigh her full attention. "I didn't know you played piano."

"She doesn't," Max answered with a wry grin.

"Worst student my mother ever had."

Leigh rolled her eyes but didn't argue. Instead she reached her hand over to stroke the cat, who immediately arched her back and hissed in protest, then jumped to the floor, leaving both Amanda's and Leigh's hands suspended side by side in midair. Without thought, Amanda wrapped her fingers around Leigh's as both hands drifted down to rest just above Amanda's knee. She only realized what she'd done as ribbons of heat radiated up her thigh, and she glanced in the opposite direction so as not to call too much attention to it, though she didn't for a moment consider letting go.

"Oh!" she exclaimed, spying a familiar book on the end table beside the couch with a shadowy spy figure on its cover. "I have this book at home." She reached out her free hand and picked up the book of Cold War–era spy tests, the very same one her aunt had given her for her birthday.

"Really?" Max regarded her with renewed interest. "Have you done them all yet?"

Amanda shook her head. "No, I just got it and I'm afraid I didn't get a chance to do many before our… business trip."

"You work at the agency with Leigh, then?"

Before Amanda had a chance to concoct a reply, Leigh chuckled. "No, I kidnapped her," she explained. "We were sort of in the middle of a date at the time."

He glanced down to where their intertwined fingers

had settled into the space between Amanda's thighs. "Looks like you still are," he remarked, not seeming the slightest bit surprised by Leigh's kidnapping confession.

"Technically, it wasn't a date. You said so yourself." Heat rising in her cheeks, Amanda pulled her hand away from Leigh's under the pretense of giving the book a closer look. "We didn't go anywhere, remember?"

Max pointed to the book. "Have you done number four yet?"

Amanda flipped to the puzzle he'd mentioned, but it didn't look familiar. "No, I don't think so."

"Why don't you give it a read now and tell me what you think."

Amanda scanned through the exercise, which was a story involving a diverse group of people in a train station where a suspicious package has been found. After giving multiple clues, the reader was asked which person was their prime suspect for having smuggled in the package. Lacking paper to make notes, Amanda closed her eyes and visualized the scene, incorporating every detail. Finally, she opened her eyes and sat up straight in her seat. "The barrister," she said with confidence.

One eyebrow arched slightly upward, but otherwise Max's face registered no change. "Interesting. Not the businessman?"

Amanda shook her head fiercely. "Too obvious."

"Oh, watch out, Max," Leigh said, "she has a real thing about riddles being too obvious."

"So, am I right?" Amanda flipped through to the end of the book where the answers were printed. Her face fell when she saw 'businessman' as the answer for number four. "Well, that's a disappointment."

"Yeah, I thought so, too," Max said, "and so I called the publisher's number that was listed on the title page of the book and confronted them about it."

Amanda regarded him with interest. "Really? What did they say?"

"They asked if I wanted to apply for a job."

Amanda frowned. "With the publishing company?"

"No, the KGB. Or whatever it is they're calling themselves these days. Or maybe NSA, FBI, CIA…"

"They're basically all the same, anyway," Leigh opined, seemingly unimpressed.

Amanda's jaw, however, had dropped, and she was about to launch into about a dozen more questions when a beeping noise from the direction of Max's desk stopped her. "What's that?"

"Diagnostics are done." Max rose and retrieved the laptop, returning with a look of consternation etched across his face.

"Uh, oh. Bad news?" Leigh asked.

"Not good," he replied, scowling at the laptop. "Not good at all. It wouldn't even run. Hold on, let me check something." He typed furiously onto his keyboard, his expression darkening. "Shit."

Leigh's brow furrowed as she stared intently at the laptop. "What is it, Max?"

"It's password protected, which of course we already knew. The thing is, usually at the very least you could hook it up and run a script that would keep trying combinations of passwords, and eventually you'd crack it. Brute force. That's the first thing Säpo would do, certainly."

"Sounds time consuming," Amanda said.

"Yeah, but it gets the job done. The thing is, you have to be able to connect it to another machine to do it. This one won't even connect to my keyboard. I'm going to try using the laptop keyboard." This time he typed directly onto the laptop and the screen lit up to show a red circle with a password prompt inside. Max's face fell. "Fuck."

Leigh cringed. "Do I want to know what you found?"

"I recognize the logo, that red circle. It's a sort of fail-safe, a security program to prevent that type of blunt attempt I told you about. That's why the keyboard wouldn't work. The program blocks any peripherals until the password is manually entered directly onto the keyboard."

"So that you can't hack into it remotely?" Leigh guessed.

"Yeah. But also, after a certain number of attempts, you're done."

"Locked out?" Leigh asked.

Max shook his head. "That's for amateurs. No, with this program, the hard drive will self-destruct. Totally wiped."

Leigh's eyes widened. "How many attempts?"

This time Max shrugged. "Not sure. It's user preference, so it varies. Probably not more than five. Maybe just one. Depends how paranoid the owner was."

"Pretty fucking paranoid," Leigh muttered. "So, that's it, then? There's no way to break into it?"

Max took a deep breath, exhaling slowly. "There are a few things I can try. I'll start by opening it up, popping out the hard drive and cloning it so we can have more leeway to make a mistake."

He pried a screwdriver out of the mountain on the desk and went to work loosening the screws on the computer's bottom panel. Amanda clasped Leigh's hand lightly, hoping to provide some reassurance as they watched and waited.

"Whoa!" Max stared at the inner workings of the laptop like he'd just encountered one of the seven wonders of the world.

Leigh squeezed Amanda's hand. "Is that good, or bad?"

"It's...something I've never seen before in a machine this old. The SSD is soldered directly to the motherboard."

"SSD?" Amanda asked.

"Solid state drive. It's the hard drive," Max

explained. "Jesus, who was this guy?"

"Russian mobster," Leigh answered.

"Not KGB? Because between this and that security program, there's some pretty high-level shit going on here."

Amanda could feel the growing tension in Leigh's body being telegraphed into her hand.

"Can you still do it, Max?" Leigh's voice was shaky.

Max let out a breath and shrugged. "How long do I have?"

Leigh bit her lower lip. "We're supposed to meet with Henrik in three days for the handoff."

Max snorted. "Then, no. Three days? I'd need at least three weeks. Minimum."

Amanda's mouth fell open. "Three weeks?"

"At least. I could take it apart in less, but if you want it back together so you can hand it off undetected, well…" His hands began to gesticulate as he spoke. "First, I'll have to unsolder the hard drive, then put it on a clean board. We'll have to clone it, crack the password. I mean, if you're lucky that will take a few days, but it could be more."

Leigh shut her eyes. "How much more?"

"Days, weeks, months. Depends what the password turns out to be."

"Months?" Leigh opened her eyes, wide. "I had no idea it could take that long."

"I thought you were a spy," Max scoffed. "How do you not know that?"

"My job's just to find the stuff. Once I turn it over to our computer forensics team, my part's done. How the hell do I know what they do with it?"

"Well, I know they show it all lightning fast in Hollywood movies, but in real life, these things take time. Plus, I have to carefully solder it back onto the original board. Assuming I don't break a pin."

"And if you do?" Amanda asked, Leigh seeming to still be recovering from the prior bad news to seek any more.

Max drew a finger across his throat and made a face. "Toast."

Amanda's face fell. "So, that's it, then."

"No, not necessarily. But we'd need to have a much better idea what the password was before I'd be willing to try. Unless we have that, though…" His shoulders slumped as he put the cover back in place. "I'm really sorry, ladies."

He walked with them to the front door and handed the computer back to Leigh. "I wish I could be more help."

"It's fine," Leigh reassured him, though Amanda could see by the slight twitch in her eye that it really wasn't, not that it was Max's fault. He'd done his best. But she could tell that her companion's stress levels had gone off the charts with this news. She made her way down the porch steps slowly, heading in the direction of the road as if she were dragging a heavy weight.

"Thank you," Amanda said, this time holding out

her hand so that he couldn't dodge giving it a shake. "Hey, Max? Do you really think those people at the publishing company were recruiting spies?"

"I don't know." He gave a half smile. "Maybe you should give them a call and find out for yourself."

Amanda glanced toward the garden gate where Leigh waited. "I don't know about that."

"You've got a real knack for it."

Amanda chuckled. "I think I've got my hands full as it is, just trying to keep up with the spy I've already got. But thanks for the compliment."

"Sure. Well, look, if you two think of anything that might bring us closer to guessing the password, you give me a call, okay? Leigh's got the number."

Amanda thanked him again, then paused halfway down the walkway to wave to the black cat in the window before joining Leigh at the gate.

"What did Max have to say? I've never seen him so chatty with someone he doesn't know."

Amanda waved her hand dismissively. "It was nothing. Just to call him if we have any new leads."

The rest she kept to herself. She doubted that Leigh would show much enthusiasm for Max's suggestion that she might make a good spy. In fact, Leigh would probably laugh at her over it, and Amanda knew that she'd probably be right. Even so, it didn't stop Amanda from daydreaming about what could happen if she worked up the nerve to call that number in the book once she got back home, just to see.

EIGHTEEN

AT THE FAR end of the backyard where the grass ended in a sudden slope to the water's edge, Leigh and her grandfather were hard at work, putting the finishing touches on the boat. Amanda wasn't exactly sure what that meant. The boat had been lowered into the water when they arrived and was still floating now, so as far as Amanda could tell, everything must be pretty much in order with the vessel. However, both the old man and his granddaughter had seemed to be of a different opinion on the matter, and they'd set to work on a long list of tasks the second Leigh had walked through the door that afternoon.

Outside it was a perfect summer evening. A refreshing breeze swept through the open window—a far cry from the sweltering heat back home in Baltimore—and once again Amanda could nearly have convinced herself that she was on vacation, if it hadn't been for the worry that had begun churning in the pit of her stomach ever since their visit with Max. Every time she thought about the password, her sense of helplessness grew. Amanda suspected that for Leigh, working on the boat was a therapeutic way to deal with the blow that had been dealt by Max's assessment. Amanda had no such escape, and so as each hour brought them closer to the moment they'd have to hand over the laptop, her agitation grew.

That laptop was Leigh's insurance policy, and hers, too. Whatever was on it was important, and as long as they had it, they could expect some level of protection from Henrik and his agency. But Henrik expected them at a meetup in Gotland in three days. If they handed it over without the chance to look inside first, Amanda knew it wasn't just the computer they'd be losing. They'd also surrender any hope of maintaining the upper hand.

There was the issue of pride, too. It was an impossible puzzle, and Amanda desperately wanted to be the one to figure it out. She'd even run up to the store earlier and bought a notebook to start making a list of possible passwords, or at least the types of things people commonly based them on—birth dates, names of loved ones, schools attended. Most of the lines remained blank, though she'd been able to glean some of Vasiliev's information online and could probably find more with time.

After an hour of work, she'd ended up with a

massive list of possibilities, but no solid leads. Amanda held no illusions. The amateur skills she'd used to open Leigh's grandparents' safe were hardly in the same league as what would be needed for this job. She'd made a really lucky guess with the safe combination, and it had still taken three attempts to get it right. Based on what Max had told them, three attempts might be enough to fry the hard drive for good. Her brain chased itself in circles, hoping for a break, as she stared blindly out the window.

"Beautiful, isn't it?" Leigh's grandmother came to stand beside Amanda. Unaware of her inner turmoil, she likely assumed Amanda was admiring the view.

Amanda was startled by her sudden appearance but tried to hide it with a casual nod. "Yes, very." Whether by 'beautiful' the woman had meant the boat, her granddaughter, or the sparkling water of the Baltic Sea that lapped against the edge of the grass, Amanda wasn't certain, but all three were lovely in their own ways.

"Do you know anything about boats?"

"No, not at all." Amanda shook her head. "Leigh seems to, though."

"Yes, she's been around them since birth. It's been a few years, but it's not something you forget."

"So, you've had that boat a while?"

"Oh, my, yes! We've had a few different ones over the years, but that one's special. It's a Pettersson, one of the most famous Swedish boat builders. It belonged to Olle's father. It's as old as Olle is. Actually, just a little bit older. About nine months, in fact." The old lady laughed as Amanda tried to puzzle out her meaning. "Those boats have a reputation for their tight sleeping quarters. Olle's parents spent a whole summer aboard just after they got married, cruising around the archipelago. Lo and behold, little Olle came along the following April, so you can imagine what they might've been up to."

"Oh!" Amanda's cheeks tingled as hot blood rushed to turn them red. She tried to think of a reply, but the revelation had left her dumbfounded and she wasn't certain she'd ever be able to look at the boat in quite the same way again.

"Would you give me a hand setting the table?" Leigh's grandmother asked, as if their previous conversation had been as run of the mill as asking for someone to pass the sugar.

"Yes, of course." Amanda was grateful for the distraction.

"I've made moose for tonight, with a forest berry tart for dessert. Do you like moose?"

"Moose? I don't think I've ever had it." Amanda pondered this curious menu item, and thought how life with Olle and Ulla Whatever-their-last-name-is seemed like something out of a Swedish fairytale. *Roasted moose and forest berry tarts?* She could get used to eating this way. "Honestly, I'm not sure the grocery stores back home in Baltimore carry a lot of moose."

"Oh, we have it here all the time." Her words flowed without ceasing and Amanda could tell that the woman was in a chatty mood, but she didn't mind. She enjoyed Leigh's grandmother's company and was relieved to have something other than their password troubles to occupy her mind. "Olle hunts it himself, you see, and it keeps nicely in the freezer for quite a while. Maybe I could send some home with you. Leigh's always loved it, and honestly, I think she's getting too thin. Is she getting enough to eat?"

"I…uh…" *How should I know? We've only just met!*

"I know, I'll send you home with some recipes, too. Maybe you could try to fatten her up a little? Do you know how to cook?"

"I know the basics." Amanda frowned at what the question implied. "You know we're not a couple, though, right?"

"Leigh did say something like that, yes." She gave Amanda a knowing look that suggested she wasn't buying it. "I guess I just have a feeling about it, Grandmother's intuition. All she needs is a little patience, what with the loss she's experienced."

Amanda nodded solemnly. "Natasha, you mean?"

"Her ex?" Leigh's grandmother's face registered mild surprise. "No, no dear. I meant her mother. You can't imagine what a relief it is for me to know she's found someone who really understands what she's gone through, losing her mother so young."

"Oh, of course." Amanda hoped her tone didn't

betray the shock she felt over this revelation. Leigh had never said a word! "I hope you don't mind," she continued, seizing the opportunity, "but she's never shared the whole story…" *Or any of it.*

"Oh, it was such a shock," she launched in, clearly enjoying having company to talk to. "It was right after the end of her senior year in college when it happened. Jenny—" she pronounced the name in the Swedish way, *yen-nee,* and her expression became melancholy, "—that was my daughter. She'd been so stressed at work and was having trouble sleeping. She'd never been one to take pills, but it's so much worse to have insomnia in summer with the long days, you see. It was almost certainly an accident."

"Yes, I'm sure it was," Amanda assured her, though the woman's hesitation over the word 'almost' had not escaped her attention.

"Leigh flew home right away, but of course her mother was already gone. I don't think she ever quite forgave herself for that."

Amanda nodded silently. *So that's the family trouble Leigh had alluded to.* But never once had she so much as hinted at the loss they had in common. "And then Natasha."

"Oh, yes. That Russian girl. I'll give her credit that she helped Leigh a lot in those first few months, though I'm not convinced I'll ever completely approve of finding a date at a funeral."

"At the funeral?" Amanda's jaw dropped, too

shocked over this latest piece of information to give much thought to the casual way in which Leigh's grandmother referred to her granddaughter's slain girlfriend as merely 'that Russian girl'.

"Natasha and Jenny worked together at the Swedish Heritage Foundation. It's an organization that helps immigrants, and I guess Natasha's father was an immigrant so that's how she'd gotten involved in the cause. But then she went back to Moscow and left Leigh in quite a sad state."

"You're saying that Natasha went back to Moscow?" Amanda struggled to keep her tone level. *Does she not know that Natasha's dead?*

"Yes, just up and left. And then poor Leigh decided to go back to the States for a fresh start right after that. I guess I can't blame her, but we've barely heard from her since she left. I'll admit, I *do* blame Natasha a bit for that."

"My goodness." It was all she could think to say as it sunk in that Leigh had never told her grandparents the truth of what had happened with Natasha and Vasiliev. *Spies and their secrets.*

"Now that I've brought this up," Leigh's grandmother said, walking across the kitchen to a small desk, "I wonder if there's something you could do for me. I've been holding onto these for a while, meaning to give them to Leigh, but I know she doesn't want to see them and I've always been afraid she'd refuse." She reached into a drawer and pulled out a packet of papers tied up in a string. "They're to do with her mother. Maybe you could give them to her, when the time seems right?"

"Of course." Amanda's hands trembled as she took the packet and tucked it into the back of her notebook, overwhelmed with the task she'd agreed to perform for a woman whom she'd come to care for greatly, yet barely knew. "Thank you, Ooh-la...I'm so sorry. I know I got that all wrong."

"Oh, that's all right. Why don't you just call me *Mormor*, like Leigh does. It's Swedish for Grandma."

"No, I couldn't," Amanda replied, shaking her head. "It wouldn't be right. That's for family."

"Of course, you could. I insist! I have a feeling about you two, remember? Grandmother's intuition. Now, Leigh tells me you're heading to Gotland on Thursday?"

"Uh, yes. That's right." Amanda was still so awash in emotions that the sudden change in topic caught her off guard, though whether it was intentional on the other woman's part or she was unaware of the impact her offer had made it was hard to say. "We're taking the ferry."

"Such a romantic island—the medieval city of Visby, with all those Gothic ruins to explore, and the wonderful outdoor cafés." Leigh's grandmother sighed happily. "And don't think for a minute I believe this is part of your business trip. There's nothing on Gotland that could possibly be of any interest to the US Department of Agriculture."

"Well…" Amanda stalled, not sure what cover story Leigh had already told with regard to this diversion.

"It's okay. Your secret's safe with me." She chuckled. "Oh, I have such fond memories of that place. Olle and I went there on our honeymoon, you know. Sailed there on that very boat out there."

"Is that right?" Amanda looked at the boat in alarm. Remembering the intimate details that had already been shared with her about Olle's parents' honeymoon on said boat, Amanda prayed she wasn't about to be regaled with any tales of a similar nature about Ulla and Olle's time onboard.

"I suppose the ferry's faster, though, even if it is crowded this time of year. Such a shame, as traveling in your own boat is much nicer company. At least you won't be leaving for a few days. I was down by the ferry terminal today and the place seemed to be absolutely crawling with Russian tourists."

There was a clatter behind her and Amanda jumped, turning to see Leigh in the doorway to the kitchen, bent over to retrieve the items that had tumbled out of her hands. Amanda knelt down to help and Leigh leaned in close to whisper in her ear. "Did she say Russians?"

"At the ferry terminal," Amanda whispered in return. She turned to Leigh's grandmother and spoke at a normal volume. "Russian tourists?"

"I suppose it's not so unusual," she replied with a small shrug that was at odds with the possible importance of what she'd seen. "Probably just a tour group heading back across the Baltic. They looked like they could have been a motorcycle club."

"So, you're an expert on Russian motorcycle clubs, now?" Leigh asked with a laugh that Amanda knew was intended to hide her mounting concern.

"Well, I don't know. They looked a little rough. At least one of them had on a motorcycle jacket despite it being a warm day, and another was completely covered in tattoos."

Amanda and Leigh exchanged a look. These men from the terminal fit the description of the men they'd seen in the café up north. It couldn't be just a coincidence.

"*Mormor*," Leigh said, looking pointedly out the window toward the water, "I think you're going to have to go drag *Morfar* in from the boat for dinner. I told him it was time, but you know how he is." After her grandmother had bustled herself out of the kitchen to retrieve her husband and had left them alone, Leigh turned to Amanda, her eyes flashing with urgency. "Go upstairs after dinner and make sure your bag's packed. As soon as they've gone to bed, we're heading out."

Amanda's heart began to race as the seriousness of the situation set in. "Can we catch a ferry tonight?"

Leigh shook her head. "Too dangerous. If they're

looking for us down by the terminal, we're bound to get caught. No, we'll take the boat."

Amanda stared out the window at Leigh's grandfather's antique boat, it's deep red mahogany nearly glowing in the evening sun from all the cleaning and polishing they'd done. "*That* boat?"

"It's our only choice." The expression on Leigh's face was a perfect mirror of the anxiety Amanda felt. "I'll leave a note to explain, and we'll have it back good as new in a few days."

Amanda swallowed roughly, her throat suddenly dry. "And if something happens?"

Leigh gave a humorless laugh. "Well, then the Russians might as well kill us, because if they don't and anything happens to that boat, my grandfather probably will."

STEALING her grandfather's boat had been the easy part. The thirty-foot motorboat was equipped with a single mast toward the bow, and so she'd used the sail to slip silently away from the house until they were far enough away that the sound of a boat's motor wouldn't alarm her sleeping grandparents. The guilt that would come from her actions would be more difficult to handle, but that would be much later, when she was safely through this predicament and had time to reflect. If there was one thing being a spy had taught her, it was how to compartmentalize. For now, Leigh's biggest challenge was choosing a destination to plot into her navigation app.

Gotland was their final destination, but heading straight there was too obvious. There were several islands in the vicinity that were popular vacation destinations with young people. Any of them would probably do as a decoy, but Leigh wanted to choose one that Vasiliev's men were less likely to search. Preferably one with a bar. The islands of the archipelago were mostly known for beautiful nature and outdoor sports, but at this point what Leigh really wanted was a drink, and her grandfather hadn't yet replenished his usual onboard stash for the season. She was poring over the nautical charts, narrowing in on a choice, when she was distracted by Amanda stealing glances at her from behind her notebook.

"What?"

Given the unintended snappishness of her tone, Leigh thought Amanda might bury her face back inside her book, but instead she set it down in her lap and held her gaze steady. "How do you do it?"

"Do what?"

"Make yourself look so different. I've seen you in a dozen different disguises, and I'm fooled every time."

Leigh held out an arm and studied the linen coat she'd thrown on as they left. It belonged to her grandfather, along with the Swedish sailor's cap that covered her short hair. As disguises went it wasn't elaborate, and so Leigh couldn't really explain the transformative effect except that when she wore it, as with any disguise, she inhabited it completely. It was this complete dedication to the illusion, rather than any particular costume choice, that best explained her skill with disguises.

"Well, how about you?" Leigh plucked at the sleeve of the floral dress she'd grabbed from her grandmother's closet for Amanda. "I'd say you look pretty different right now."

"Oh, this?" Amanda responded wryly, shifting the fabric to show it off to best effect, while patting the garish scarf that covered her hair and completed the look. "Do you like it?"

They both laughed. The dress was at least twenty years out of fashion and Leigh doubted even her grandmother would be caught dead in the thing. The combination of that and the scarf transformed Amanda from an attractive woman in her twenties to a color-blind, middle-aged Swedish housewife most effectively. Neither disguise would hold up to a close examination, there just hadn't been time, but it was Leigh's hope that anyone watching their boat from a distance would see nothing more suspicious looking than a Swedish man and his wife out for an evening cruise. They'd change when they got to their destination, which Leigh now chose at random by letting her finger fall on the map.

"So, what's with the notebook?" she asked once

she'd charted their course in her app. "Writing a memoir of your life as a spy?"

"No. I'm making a list of password ideas for Vasiliev's laptop. Most people—even mobsters, I'm sure—choose passwords with significance so they can remember them. I thought if I knew enough details about the guy, I might have a better chance of figuring it out."

"Like what?"

"Birth dates for him and his family, where he was born, names of pets—anything, really. Some of it I was able to find online while you were working on the boat, but I still have a lot of blanks."

It was Leigh's turn to be impressed with her companion's skills. "That's a solid plan. You have a real knack for this, Amanda."

In the fading light, Leigh saw Amanda's face grow flush. "I don't know. I doubt it will do any good. There are too many possibilities, and we just don't have the time."

"Maybe not, but I admire your diligence. Half of succeeding in the intelligence game is just not giving up."

Amanda's expression turned thoughtful. "Do you really think I'd make a good spy, Leigh?"

There was an earnestness in her tone that made Leigh's stomach tighten nervously. Amanda was serious. Leigh chose her next words carefully, so as not to crush her but not to encourage her, either. "You're young and smart, and you have a lot of stamina. Those are all things our recruiters like to see. I think that with the right training, there's no reason you wouldn't do well as an agent. But it's not an easy life, Amanda. You end up with few friends. You give up your family."

"I hardly have friends or family now, honestly."

"There's your Aunt Millie." Leigh's nerves were soothed by the pensive look on Amanda's face when she was reminded of her aunt. *That struck a nerve.* "What would she do without you, Amanda?"

"What she's doing right now, I suppose," Amanda replied, but she didn't sound convinced.

"Right now, you've only been gone a few days, and we have an agent stationed at her nursing home to watch over her. If you were an active agent instead of a civilian who's gotten caught up in this mess, that wouldn't be the case."

Amanda sat quietly, mulling over Leigh's words. "So why do you do it?"

Leigh sighed. "I'd say it was because I love my country and want to make a difference, but you'd know I was lying. You always do. The truth is, after Natasha's death, I was angry at guys like Vasiliev. I had a score to settle. At that point, I felt like I had nothing left to lose."

"And because of your mom?"

Leigh froze at the unexpected mention of her mother. "Why would you say that?" It was a connection she'd made in her own mind, that her mother's death, though unrelated to what came after, had been a catalyst for everything else, but it wasn't something she'd ever shared.

"There's something I should tell you." A shadow flitted across Amanda's face. "Your grandmother told me about what happened to her, with the overdose. I'm really sorry."

This admission was a stab to Leigh's gut, and the look of genuine empathy on Amanda's face just drove the pain deeper. "My grandmother talks too much."

"She's definitely chatty," Amanda agreed. "Look, I know what it's like, Leigh. I've been through it, too."

"This was different." Leigh swallowed, her throat suddenly thick.

She knew that Amanda meant well, but their situations weren't the same. Everything in Leigh's life had changed irrevocably that summer, and her mother's death had started the dominoes falling. Meeting Natasha, being recruited by Henrik, Natasha's death, and joining the agency in the States—they were all deeply connected in her psyche. She'd used it all to strengthen herself, to become the best agent she could be, then stuffed the details and emotions from that summer deep inside herself and sealed it up. It had made her who she was, but she couldn't talk about it, couldn't share how she felt, for fear that if she ever did, she'd come apart at the seams.

"Leigh, please. I can see how much pain you're in right now. You can talk to me."

Amanda was reaching out to her on the most basic emotional level, and never had Leigh wanted so badly to let someone in. But she couldn't. If Amanda wanted to know what it was like to be a real spy, this should be her first lesson. Closing off your emotions, not allowing yourself to connect. It had been the first thing Henrik had taught her, too, after Natasha died. Attachments are dangerous. They cloud your judgment and can get people killed.

Leigh took a deep breath, composing her face and steadying her nerves. "I'm okay, really. It was just unexpected to have it brought up like that. I'll be fine." With every fiber of her being, she managed to keep the nerve in her eye under control.

Amanda studied her silently for a moment, as if unconvinced, but eventually gave a nod. "Okay, if you say so."

They rode the rest of the way in silence, Leigh giving her undivided attention to the nautical charts while Amanda continued making her lists. It was past ten o'clock when they arrived at their destination, and as they were no longer so far north as Leigh's grandparents' farm, the sun had nearly set for the four or five hours that would pass for night. There were several other boats at the marina, and lots of people milling about on the shore. Seeing this, Leigh felt relieved. She'd made a good choice. With simple shorts and t-shirts, they could blend in easily here among the rest of the vacationers, and slip away unnoticed in the morning.

Leigh maneuvered the boat into an empty slip and hopped onto the dock to search out an attendant to pay for the spot. A bored but pleasant young man sat in a kiosk, taking payment and offering tourist brochures. Leigh paid him for the night but declined a list of local hotels. There was no need, as they'd stay onboard the boat that night.

"Bicycle rentals, kayaks?" The man offered, holding out more brochures.

"No, thank you."

"What, not the outdoor type?" he joked. "How about a party? There's free admission at the dance club tonight."

"Dance club?" As she said it, Leigh could make out the low, throbbing pulse of music in the distance. The beat drew her in, as did the promise of a fully stocked bar. She'd never been one to say no to a party.

"Yeah, just up the hill." The young man pointed in the general direction of the music and Leigh nodded her thanks.

As she headed back to the boat, Leigh's spirits began to lift. She'd been troubled ever since the conversation about her mother, and she knew Amanda had been feeling it, too. She couldn't let Amanda in too deep, but she didn't want to fight, either. Without something to distract them, they'd both sit and stew in their own juices all night and it wouldn't do either one of them, or their mission, the least bit of good. A quick change of clothes and they'd be safely unrecognizable and ready for an evening out to erase the tension.

"Amanda?" she called as she approached the boat. Her companion looked up from her notebook, her face brightening in response to the cheerfulness of Leigh's expression. As always, the sight of Amanda's smile rocked Leigh to the core, and so she forced herself to study the woman's hideous scarf to avoid looking directly at it, like one would avoid staring directly into the sun. "Come on, let's get changed. We're going out."

NINETEEN

THE ISLAND'S most popular nightspot played a variety of the techno music commonly heard in European dance clubs, each song pulsing with the same monotonously enthralling beat that went on and on, seemingly without a beginning or an end. Some people didn't like it, but Leigh found it invigorating, the music so all-encompassing as they entered the building that she could feel her heartbeat shift in time with the rhythm. Once through the doors it was exactly the type of scene she craved—dark and hot, and filled with enticingly bare and sweaty bodies. She'd have preferred if there hadn't been such an even mix of men and women, but she couldn't exactly complain. Lesbian clubs were hard enough to come by in D.C., so it's not like an island the size of a postage stamp in the middle of the archipelago would have one. It didn't matter, anyway. It had the most important thing, an atmosphere that invited all thoughts and cares to be cast aside for another time. Leigh was more than willing to oblige.

Her lifestyle demanded the ability to distance herself from her emotions, and this was how she did it. This was how she put the things that troubled her into their boxes, with parties and alcohol and fun but meaningless hookups. The agency shrink might not think it was the healthiest coping mechanism, but it worked for her, and thanks to Amanda's well-intentioned prying, Leigh had a hell of a lot of shit to stuff back into its box tonight. With her intuitive, deductive leaps and that caring way about her that promised she'd understand everything if Leigh just opened herself up to her—well, the woman had proved to be quite the Pandora.

She made a beeline for the bar, pulling Amanda along by one clasped hand. It wasn't a romantic gesture, but rather was prompted by fear that either one of them might easily get lost in the crowd. The chances that any of Vasiliev's men would bother to look for them in this remote spot were slim, but there were other dangers. Spies and mobsters weren't the only threats when you were two attractive women in a room filled with drunk vacationers, after all. Not that that would stop Leigh from imbibing a little herself. *Hell no.*

There was a full display of hard liquor on offer, but in deference to the heat, Leigh ordered two hard ciders. The delightful Scandinavian beverage was nearly impossible to come by back home, and it offered sweet refreshment while packing a deceptively powerful punch. She went with the classic pear flavor, but there were others, too, and she'd eventually work her way through all of them that night, if she had her way.

"Do you want to dance?" Her voice rang in her ears but Amanda squinted at her with the confused look of a person who couldn't quite hear what had been said. "Dance?" Leigh repeated, this time leaning so close that she could feel the moisture from her breath against her own lips as it formed an invisible cloud between her mouth and Amanda's ear. Before she could stop it, an image formed in her mind of sinking her teeth into the plump skin of Amanda's earlobe. She yanked her head back before she could follow through on the impulse.

"Sure!" Amanda yelled back. "Let's dance."

The ease with which she'd been convinced caused Leigh a mild ripple of shock. Considering how things had been running so hot and cold between them on the boat, she'd anticipated more of a fight. A quick glance at the bottle of cider in Amanda's hand offered one possible explanation. It was already nearly empty. With one last swig, Amanda drained it and set it on the bar before taking Leigh's hand and leading her to the dance floor. *Look who's in a take charge mood,* Leigh mused, not at all unpleasantly.

They made it a few feet from the bar and onto the edge of the packed dance floor, then stood in place and swayed with the music. The crowd was so large that they were pressed up not only against each other but against half a dozen strangers, too. Though it was all straight couples surrounding them, no one seemed to pay them much mind. That was one thing about her birth country, people were much more likely than in America to just mind their own damn business. As the music shifted to a softer melody, Leigh finished off her drink and took advantage of the opportunity to plant one hand on the small of Amanda's back and pull her in tight. She was rewarded with Amanda's arms draped around her shoulders. The intimacy was intense, but it still counted as dancing, which meant it didn't need to be acknowledged or analyzed. For the span of one song, maybe they could both simply exist in this space together and not have to mean anything by it.

It took mere seconds for the slow sensuality of the dancing to take its toll. This close to Amanda's body, she could almost smell strawberries and cream. It was an illusion, of course, since they'd never had a chance to replace that long-lost lip gloss, but subconsciously that scent represented for Leigh everything about this woman that she craved. Her mouth watered at the merest thought of Amanda's lips. *Why?*

Wanting sex was a natural instinct, and to be expected in a place like this, but that wasn't what Leigh was experiencing. It was more than that. She shut her eyes and could see the smile that would light up Amanda's face the moment she figured out something that had been puzzling her, so pleased with herself and the world. Of all her smiles, Leigh thought that one was the best. And she could see, too, the expression Amanda had worn when she'd brought up the topic of Leigh's mother. Her response had been a visceral one the moment she saw it, the complete certainty that when Amanda claimed to understand her, she really did in a way that no one else could.

This is all wrong. Nothing's going back in its box at this rate.

Still holding Amanda against her, Leigh concentrated as hard as she could to conjure up one of Amanda's flaws. *God knows she has plenty!* She recalled the restaurant in Stockholm where they'd met Henrik, the way she'd dug in her heels so stubbornly and refused to move. *Infuriating! Except…how can she be so annoying and so hot at the same time?*

She scanned the room for someone else to dance with, the usual cure for when things threatened to become too intense. It was no use. It wasn't some random hookup Leigh wanted. Only Amanda. It had been years since she'd felt that way about anyone. Not since Natasha.

No, you're not supposed to be thinking of Natasha right now, or your mother, or Henrik, or the laptop either. Leigh reminded herself that she'd come here to forget all of that, to hit the reset button so she could carry out the looming handoff to Henrik without getting herself or Amanda killed by Russians in the process. That was what mattered right now, not anything else. And besides, she reasoned, there was no reason to think Amanda felt anything for her in return except a friendly concern. She'd already sworn in no uncertain terms that they would never have sex again. *You kidnapped her, and you've lied and shut her out at every turn. Grow up, Leigh. She's not going to give you another chance at anything more than a casual friendship, at best.*

The slow song came to an end, the beat picking up immediately, and no longer having a valid excuse to hold her close, Leigh let Amanda slip from her arms. She headed immediately for the bar and grabbed two more drinks. A couple was just leaving a u-shaped booth in a corner and Leigh snagged it without hesitation. It would be quieter there and she suddenly felt the need to escape the noise and crowd she'd thought she wanted. Amanda followed, saying nothing. After sitting for a full minute, Amanda still had not spoken, and Leigh grew agitated. Neither her companion's silence nor the noise of the room was helping one bit. For the first time in her life, she wasn't in the mood for a party.

"Are you not having fun?" Leigh asked, finally

breaking the silence. "Do you want to go back to the boat?"

Amanda looked at her in genuine surprise. "Go back? Are you kidding? I can't remember ever having a night like this in my life!"

"Are you sure? It won't hurt my feelings if you want to go back." It occurred to Leigh that what she'd really rather be doing at that moment was sitting with Amanda back at the boat, working on her list of passwords. Maybe if they worked on it together, they could crack the password after all. Maybe there was still time to find out why the information on the laptop was so important before it was out of their possession for good.

But Amanda laughed. "How could I not be having fun? I think I'm just so overwhelmed that I don't know how to process it all."

Leigh frowned. "Overwhelmed by what? It's just a club."

"Maybe an international secret agent is used to being on the run in foreign countries and spending the evening in dance clubs on vacation islands, but up until a week ago, I was just an office temp. This is all incredible!" She tipsily downed the rest of her drink and Leigh wondered exactly how much she'd had.

What concerned Leigh even more, though, was the star struck look on Amanda's face. She'd seen it before, on overzealous rookies during their first weeks at the agency. Agents like Toni, the one with hair the same color as Leigh's who'd been assigned to the surveillance van. She'd been so eager to do field work, she'd practically begged Javi to let her go. And then she'd ended up dead. This life Amanda romanticized wasn't a fantasy. It was time she made Amanda see that.

"Amanda, being a spy isn't as glamorous as people think. It's a lot of paperwork—"

"And clandestine meetups on foreign islands—"

"And sitting in vans for hours while your butt goes numb and you listen to the news on public radio for so long that it's the only phone number you can remember."

"Well, look how well that turned out." Amanda flashed her amazing grin, and the rest of Leigh's arguments fizzled on her tongue, but her expression must have betrayed her misgivings because soon Amanda cocked her head to one side and gave a her a long, steady look. "Fine, I can see *you're* not having fun. How about one more round of drinks and another dance before we go?"

Leigh eyed the empty bottle of cider next to Amanda's hand. "Are you sure that's a good idea? We've already had a few."

"Absolutely! These are delicious."

With a shake of her head, Leigh settled the tab at the bar and returned with two more bottles. "Last ones. Now let's start on that dance, because it'll probably take at least two songs to make it across the floor from here to the exit."

As luck would have it, they'd only reached the midpoint when the tempo once more shifted and a slow song began to play. At the sound of the music, Amanda draped herself over Leigh, the bottle of cider still clutched in one hand. As before, a whiff of strawberries tickled her nose and this time Leigh wondered if it might be the cider. Whatever was causing it, she found it more intoxicating than any drink. As the song played on, Amanda nuzzled her head sleepily into the crook of Leigh's shoulder, her lips brushing the sensitive flesh just beneath Leigh's ear, sending a ripple through her like the flutter of a hummingbird's wings. *It's still just dancing*, Leigh assured herself. But only just.

When the song had finished, Leigh took advantage of the brief lull in the music to make a dash for the door, dragging a startled Amanda in her wake. They walked back down the hill toward the boat without speaking, and Amanda continued to sway the whole way as if the music from the club was still playing in her head. While Amanda was unsteady on her feet, the cool air had cleared Leigh's head and misgivings were piling up in her head as she contemplated just how much she'd let her defenses down that night. She could feel the effects of the emotions coursing through her the same as Amanda was experiencing her overindulgence in cider. But this wouldn't just be a hangover in the morning. It could take weeks to fully recover her control, and that was time she didn't have.

They reached the boat and Leigh climbed on first, holding out her hand to steady her companion. It could be a tricky maneuver to get from a dock to a boat when completely sober, and in her current state, Amanda stumbled wildly in the process and ended up coming down firmly onto her rear in the middle of the deck. Try as she might, Leigh couldn't help but find the spectacle charming, and she cursed herself for it as she busily straightened out the charts that they would need in the morning to navigate to Gotland. Now that she was safely on the boat, Amanda could fend for herself.

A few minutes passed and Amanda, still not having budged an inch from where she'd landed, called out to her. "Leigh?" With a sigh, Leigh turned back around to find Amanda swiveling her head around in obvious confusion. "Leigh, where are we supposed to sleep?"

Without saying a word, Leigh opened a nondescript door in the panel beneath the wheel, and revealed a sleeping compartment that stretched out to fill the space beneath the bow. Opening the door automatically turned on an overhead light in the compartment, which revealed two narrow bunks covered in red velvet and topped with mountains of silky throw pillows.

Amanda squinted at it dubiously. "Huh."

"What?"

"It's very fancy."

Leigh cocked an eyebrow, uncertain if the statement had been a compliment or a rebuke. "It's a fancy boat."

"Yeah, but, well, I wasn't expecting there to be so much red. And gold." Amanda's words slurred together and her eyes struggled not to cross as she shifted her gaze from the sleeping space to Leigh. "You don't think it's a little gauche?"

"Hey," Leigh bristled. "Don't criticize the boat."

"Sorry," Amanda made an attempt at a sorrowful face that soon dissolved into giggles. "It's a really nice boat. Your grandmother's going to change her mind about me once she finds out I helped you steal it." Only half the words were intelligible, and she seemed to be talking nonsense, so there was no way Leigh could hold a grudge.

Leigh shook her head indulgently. "It's late. Let's go to bed."

It was too low to stand in the sleeping compartment, so Leigh crawled in first and chose the bunk on the left. Amanda followed but stumbled partway, knocking out the light on her way down. She ended up in a jumble with half her body along the empty bunk and the other half across Leigh. The unexpected contact set fire to Leigh's insides.

"Amanda!" She gave her a nudge, but Amanda responded by shifting toward her instead of away, so that the bulk of her weight rested on top of Leigh. "Your bunk's over there, princess."

Amanda wiggled into a more comfortable position. "I like this one better." Her fingers plucked clumsily at the hem of Leigh's t-shirt. "And I like it when you call me princess, even if you think I don't."

With Amanda's fingers now halfway up her bare torso, Leigh summoned all her power to bring the woman back to her senses before she lost hers. "Hey, I thought you said you never wanted to have sex with me again, remember?"

"I may have changed my mind."

She leaned forward, her lips meeting Leigh's with a skill and determination that was at odds with her impaired state. Instead, it was Leigh who felt intoxicated by the kiss. As her tongue swept across Amanda's lips, the taste of strawberries overwhelmed her. There was no way it was just her imagination.

"Did you buy new lip gloss?" Leigh managed to ask between kisses.

"Mmhmm," Amanda answered, not bothering to stop. "When I went to the store for the notebook. I wondered if you'd notice."

With a hand on each shoulder, Leigh gave Amanda a gentle upward push, freeing her lips. "Have you been planning to seduce me all along?"

Amanda gave her a sheepish look. "Spies aren't the only ones who like to be prepared." Her admission sent heat coursing through Leigh's veins.

Amanda struggled against Leigh's palms, trying to get close enough to resume where she'd left off. It would have been so easy to let her. Every inch of Leigh's body longed for it, and with their bodies intertwined as they were and the gentle, rhythmic rocking of the boat, it wouldn't have taken long at all for both of them to be over the edge. And then she'd be falling and falling, and there'd be no turning back, and she wouldn't want to even if she could.

This is a mistake. You'll end up getting her killed.

The quiet voice of reason in her head came as a shock to Leigh, as did the sudden burst of strength needed to resist. Gently, she rolled Amanda onto the other bunk.

"I can't do this, Amanda."

Amanda let out a long breath, and the hurt she was feeling was like a knife in Leigh's belly. "Why not?"

"There's too much at stake. I have a mission to complete."

"Then what was the whole idea of getting me to go out tonight? Are you claiming you weren't trying to get me into bed?"

"I..." Leigh knew denying it would be a lie. Amanda would see right through it. "I let myself get caught up. But this isn't like before. It's not a fantasy. It would end up being a liability."

"I realize it isn't a fantasy." There was a hint of pleading in her voice, and something else that had more of an edge, like exasperation or anger. "Why does everyone have to underestimate me? Do you think I don't know what's at stake? Haven't I proved myself enough yet? I'm *not* a liability!"

"That's *not* what I meant! Amanda, please…" *I meant me. I'm the liability.* Leigh's voice trailed off, all her energy spent.

There was silence on the boat, and Leigh's muscles, so relaxed just moments before under Amanda's caresses, had grown hard and tense. Still, Amanda remained quiet, but Leigh thought she could feel the resentment radiating from where she lay on her bunk just a few inches away.

"Amanda, are you angry?"

With a noncommittal harrumph, Amanda flipped onto her side, her back to Leigh. It sent up a wave of strawberry scent in the confined space that was intensified by the fact that Leigh could still taste it on her lips.

"You need to get over it, compartmentalize," Leigh said it out loud, but she was talking as much to herself as to Amanda, perhaps more.

"Oh, really?" The sarcasm oozed through Amanda's reply. *Fuck. She's definitely mad.* "Is that what all your fancy spy training has taught you?"

Leigh sighed heavily, sensing another fight hanging in the balance and knowing she lacked the strength to see it through. "Actually, yes."

"Fine, oh Great Master of Espionage, how exactly do I do that? Because this is kind of killing me right now."

"I don't know," she admitted. She was having a hard enough time of it herself. "Just think of the least sexy thing you possibly can."

After a moment of silence that made Leigh brace for an onslaught, Amanda spoke. Her voice was surprisingly calm, almost conversational. "Did you know your great-grandparents got this boat for a wedding present?"

Leigh frowned into the darkness at the unexpected change of topic. "Yeah, I guess so."

"Your grandfather was conceived on this boat."

"What?"

"Yep. Possibly right there on that velvet cushion."

"Uh…" Leigh's stomach gave a sudden jolt as she processed the words into an image. Perhaps she'd had a little too much cider tonight, too.

"Of course, it could have been this one, I guess. Or out on the deck if the weather was nice."

"Uh, Amanda, that's enough—"

"Your grandparents probably fooled around right here, too," Amanda continued, and now Leigh thought she detected a note of evil glee in the words. "In fact, probably everyone in your family has had sex in here. I mean, it explains why it's decorated in red velvet and gold cushions, like a Parisian brothel."

"Enough." Leigh shuddered. "I think that did the trick."

"See how quickly I can learn?" Amanda's smirk

was almost audible in her tone. *Oh yeah, that's definitely evil glee.*

"Thanks to you, Amanda, I may never have sex again."

"Happy to oblige. Good night, Leigh."

At least, Leigh reflected as she closed her eyes and tried not to picture any of her relatives having sex, *she doesn't sound angry at me anymore.*

TWENTY

WHEN LEIGH AWOKE, the bunk beside her was empty. As she opened the doors to the deck, Leigh wondered whether Amanda was still angry from the night before. Perhaps she'd gone outside to sleep. But when she looked, Amanda wasn't there. Worry nudged Leigh's insides. *Where has she gone?*

Thinking Amanda might have left a note, Leigh began to search the boat, but there was no sign of anything to explain her absence. Her worry intensified to a low panic as a hundred terrible scenarios presented themselves for Leigh's consideration. Stumbling overboard. Kidnapped by Vasiliev's men. She doubled her efforts in searching for something to go on.

Beside the seat where Amanda had been sitting the day before, Leigh spied her notebook. She'd just snatched it up when the sound of a foot hitting the wooden deck made her spin in place. Leigh sank into the seat as relief washed over her. There on the deck was Amanda, looking a little disheveled and wearing dark sunglasses that Leigh doubted had anything to do with trying to be in disguise. *Holy hell, what a hangover she must have.*

"Where have you been?" Leigh demanded somewhat roughly. As her initial relief subsided, it was replaced by a trickle of anger at having been made to worry.

"I brought breakfast." Somewhat awkwardly, Amanda held up a brown paper sack like a peace offering. "It's crispbread and some cheese, and just whatever else the lady at the little store in town suggested I buy. Some coffee, too."

Forgiveness came at the mention of coffee, and Leigh cleared a spot for breakfast without any further scolding. She grinned as she spread out the contents of the bag. It was a simple Swedish breakfast, but in her hunger, it seemed like a feast, and the large blue and yellow tube of caviar paste was an especially welcome touch.

"Oh, yum! I loved this stuff as a kid." Leigh screwed off the cap and squeezed some of the paste onto a piece of crispbread.

As the fishy smell of the paste filled the air, Amanda's nose wrinkled. "What the hell is that?"

"Salty, squished up fish eggs," Leigh answered, suppressing a laugh as Amanda gagged. There were more appetizing ways to describe this particular delicacy, but Leigh wasn't above exacting just a small measure of revenge for Amanda wandering off and making her worry. Then she frowned as a concern wriggled its way into her consciousness. "Where did you say this came from?"

"The store down in the main part of town."

Leigh set down her crispbread and did some quick mental calculations. "Amanda, how did you pay for all this?"

Amanda nibbled her lower lip, looking sheepish. "I took your wallet. I would have asked," she quickly added, "but you were asleep."

A key detail poked at Leigh's brain, demanding attention. "Yeah, asleep on my back, with my wallet in my back pocket."

Amanda gave a nonchalant shrug as she cracked a hardboiled egg and started to peel it. "I watched a pickpocketing video on YouTube once."

Leigh stared in disbelief.

After a few more bites of food, Amanda looked up and waited to speak until Leigh had made eye contact. Her expression was both earnest and contrite. "Look, Leigh, I'm really sorry."

"About the wallet?" Leigh waved it off. "Don't be. If anything, I'm impressed."

"No, about last night." Amanda's shoulders slumped a little and her face grew pink in obvious embarrassment. "I was out of line, and really tipsy, but that's not an excuse. I just wanted you to know that I get it. This is just another job for you."

Leigh pondered. "I wouldn't necessarily say that."

"You don't have to be nice. You've been a spy for five years, so I know it's just part of the routine. But for me it's the biggest adventure of my life, and it's given me just a little validation to know that maybe I could keep up with someone like you."

Leigh's brow wrinkled. "Was that ever in doubt?" *Keep up?* Leigh was embarrassed to admit it, but sometimes it seemed that this woman ran circles around her.

Amanda looked unconvinced. "Do you know what I've been doing for work since I got out of college? I go to a new company every week, and each time they assume I'm an idiot. Do I know how to answer a phone? Can I manage putting the files in alphabetical order?" She rolled her eyes. "I mean, please. But I'm always having to prove myself, and by the time I settle in, I move on and once again no one thinks I can do anything because I'm just a temp." She sighed. "Four years of that shit. How pathetic. No wonder you aren't interested in me."

Not interested? Leigh gaped. "I thought you understood me last night, Amanda. It's not you, it's me."

Amanda gave her a look that said she wasn't buying it. "That's what everyone says."

"No, I mean it! Do you honestly think living like this could ever become routine? This is just how I get through. No attachments. I haven't dated anyone—actually gone out on a real date, not just sex—since I joined the agency. It's the only way I know how to function."

Amanda retained her skeptical look. "You haven't had a girlfriend since Natasha?"

Leigh thought for a moment, then shook her head. "Nope."

"What about a partner at work?" Amanda pressed. "I assumed you guys always had to work in pairs. You've been close to someone there."

"I'm on a team, but I haven't had a partner since Javi was promoted."

Amanda regarded her for a moment, then gave a quick nod. "I guess that explains it, then."

"Explains what?"

"Why you're so rough around the edges," she said in between chews, having resumed her breakfast with a large bite of cheese.

Leigh stiffened in her seat. "Now, hold on. I wouldn't say that."

"Oh, no. It's true." Amanda continued to chew. "And you can be very arrogant."

Leigh's mouth dropped open. "Oh really? Then why were you trying so hard to get into my pants last night?"

Amanda's lips twitched. "Well, did you see yourself in them?" She pulled the sunglasses down to the tip of her nose and gave Leigh an appraising look, her eyes sparkling in amusement. "Besides, I don't mind the arrogance so much. You clearly think you're a great spy, and you sure as hell have the skills to back it up. So why not be a little arrogant? It's justified. If I had skills like that, I'd be arrogant, too."

Leigh scoffed. "*If* you had skills? What, like cracking open a safe? Hot wiring a car? Stealing the wallet of a highly-trained agent? Skills like that?"

At first, she seemed pleased, but soon a look of doubt clouded Amanda's face. "I don't know. I mean, it's pretty clear you don't think I have what it takes."

Leigh leveled her gaze. "Amanda, I don't doubt you have what it takes. I just don't think you should put yourself at risk when there are so many other ways you could use your talents. And trust me, you have talents." Spying the notebook she'd set beside the chair, Leigh picked it up and gave it a shake for emphasis. "This notebook? It's genius, Amanda."

"It's pointless. Guessing the code is an impossible task."

Amanda's eyes were downcast and Leigh was gutted to realize how genuine was her lack of confidence in herself at that moment. "Amanda, listen to me. The team I'm on, all we work on is impossible tasks. And we do it pretty much like this. This list you made is as good as anything I've ever seen anyone at the agency produce." As Leigh gave the notebook another wave, a packet of papers bound with string fell onto the shiny mahogany deck. Leigh frowned. "What's this?"

Amanda's hand flew to her chest. "Oh, I forgot! Your grandmother wanted you to have those." Amanda drew in a breath and seemed to hesitate. "They're something to do with your mother, but she said you might not be ready to look at them yet."

Though the words hit her like a physical blow, Leigh forced herself to pick up the packet. "It's been five years. I really need to stop letting myself be afraid of them." But she knew Amanda could sense the fear.

"I could look if you want," she offered, reaching out a hand for the papers. Her voice was the same gentle, caring one that had cut Leigh to the quick the last time the topic of her mother had been raised. "I can read them first and I'll tell you what they are."

It was tempting, but one look at the letters and Leigh knew it was a no-go. Instead of handing her the papers, Leigh took Amanda's hand and gave it a squeeze, lingering for a moment before letting go. "Thanks for the offer, but they're in Swedish. I guess I have to do it myself."

Her fingers nearly numb, she fumbled with the knot and released the letters. As she perused the one on top, her concern was replaced with a rush of warm sentimentality as she realized what they were. She held one up wonderingly. "They're love letters."

"From your mother?"

"No, from someone else, written to her." Leigh

flipped through several more and confirmed they were all similar.

"She had a boyfriend?"

"I had no idea." As Leigh spoke her throat grew rough and her eyes stung with unshed tears. "She had so much life left to live. Why would she kill herself?" The words she'd never dare speak echoed in the air around her as the tears slipped down her cheeks unchecked.

Get a hold of yourself.

Leigh drew a ragged breath and shuffled the letters, hoping the distraction would help her regain control, but her hands trembled badly and several pages dropped and scattered at her feet. Before she could react, Amanda had picked up one, a photograph, and as she held it up for a better look, her eyes grew large.

"Amanda?" Leigh's pulse throbbed in her neck. "What is it?"

"Leigh," she said, her voice impossibly quiet. "you need to see this picture."

A lump of dread formed in her gut. "Why? Is it something bad?" Amanda didn't answer for the longest time, and Leigh couldn't take the tension any longer. She made a stab at a joke to lighten the mood. "Please don't tell me it's a sexy picture. I had quite enough of picturing my relatives having sex last night, thanks to you." But still, Amanda didn't say anything. She just nibbled on her lower lip and stared off into the distance. "Amanda come on, what is it. You're worrying me."

"It's Henrik."

Leigh swiveled her head, adrenaline racing through her as she looked in the direction Amanda was facing, expecting to see him coming onto the boat. But there was no one there. She turned back to see Amanda holding out the photo. A wave of cold washed over her as she held it up to see. It was Henrik, all right, with his arm draped around her mother. That look on her mother's face; she'd never seen her look at anyone like that except maybe her father when Leigh had been very young, years before their marriage fell apart, when they were still madly in love.

Full comprehension dawned. "It was Henrik who wrote the letters. He was the one who was dating my mother."

Apprehension creased Amanda's brow. "Did you know that he knew her?"

Leigh shook her head. "Not a clue. He never said a word."

They were clearly in love, and yet he never mentioned it. And if he never said a word about this, what else has he kept from me?

At that moment, the turmoil of just seconds before suddenly went dormant, replaced by a calm determination. Perhaps it was that Leigh's training finally kicked in, or maybe it was the touch of Amanda's hand as she silently clasped Leigh's fingers within her own. She knew she should question it, ask herself what this relationship meant to her, and what she thought she was doing, and a million other vital things that needed to be addressed. But there were only two questions that Leigh cared about answering now. The first was, what exactly were they about to walk into when they arrived in Gotland? And the other was, what did she need to do to keep Amanda safe?

AMANDA STOOD BLOCKING the doorway of their hotel room, one hand firmly planted on each hip. "I'm not staying here. I'm coming with you."

"Absolutely not." Leigh was equally resolute as she tried to push past her to the door.

"Come on, Leigh." Sizing up their current impasse, Amanda decided to try a different approach. "It's my first visit to Visby and I haven't seen a thing!"

It was true, and considering the picturesque spot in which they now found themselves, it was worthy of at least a minor complaint. Through the open window, Amanda could make out the light stone towers topped with dark, ornately carved spires of Visby Cathedral. A strong floral scent wafted into the room from the abundance of flowers in the gardens that had lined their way, and she could hear footsteps and the murmur of voices as people passed by on the well-worn pavers of the narrow, winding streets. Being forced to stay indoors was cruel.

The pent-up adrenaline that had built throughout the day was making Amanda stir-crazy. They'd left for Gotland that morning just after discovering Henrik's photo, staying only long enough for Leigh to leave a message for Javier and apprise him of the development. Though she'd mostly remained out of contact during their time in Sweden, discovering a romantic connection between her mother and the Säpo agent who had recruited her into intelligence work was big enough news that Leigh had felt compelled to share.

They'd cruised at top speed, arriving at the port in Visby in just over four hours. Leigh had booked a room in Almedalen, the medieval portion of the city, and a quick glance upward at a handful of step-gabled buildings as they raced at top speed up the hill to the hotel had been the only thing close to sightseeing that they'd done. Not that it was a vacation—Amanda understood that—but they were a full two days early for the meet. That had to have bought them a little time to take a breath, right?

Amanda glanced at her watch and gave Leigh her most beseeching look. "It's one o'clock. That means it's only seven in the morning back home. Javi's not even in the office yet. But it's lunchtime here and I'm starving. I can see the umbrellas from three different cafés from our bedroom window. Won't you at least let me come with you long enough for us to get something to eat? I'm beginning to feel like a hostage again."

Leigh let out an exasperated breath, but Amanda could see by the shift in her expression that she was about to give in. "Fine. Lunch."

They went to a restaurant down the hill with tables set up in an outdoor courtyard. Along one side was an ancient stone wall dripping with wisteria. A light, misty fog had started to form around the branches, making the purple blossoms stand out even more against the ghostly white that surrounded them. Amanda was happy to sit and study flowers and enjoy her meal, but Leigh looked up from her food every few seconds and scanned the foot traffic along the street, then did the same to the restaurant patrons. Every time she did it, a new crack appeared in Amanda's illusion of peaceful contentment, until she felt compelled to say something about it.

"Leigh, do you think you can focus on eating for a minute? Your soup's going to get cold."

Leigh blinked. "It's gazpacho."

"Oh. Well, also, it's driving me bonkers. Every time your head snaps up, I expect to see Henrik racing toward us, leading a charge with an army of Russian mobsters behind him."

"Welcome to the club," Leigh muttered. "We should've gone somewhere else. This courtyard is too exposed."

"We looked at every place between here and the

water," Amanda pointed out, trying to soothe her. "This was the best option, remember?"

Ignoring that, Leigh pulled her phone from her pocket and scowled. "No signal. Damn it! With this fog rolling in, the hotel room has been the only spot where I had decent service." She started scanning the crowd again, and Amanda could see she was in a rapid spiral that would do neither of them much good.

"Hey." Amanda gave Leigh's foot a playful kick from underneath the table. That caught her attention enough for her to set the phone down and stop spinning her head. When they'd managed sustained eye contact for more than two seconds, Amanda continued, "You've been checking nonstop. No one's going to sneak up this fast. What is it that's got you so worked up?"

Leigh squeezed her eyes tight. "That I'm going to fuck something up and get you killed, that's what. I should be scouting the island, or getting intel from Javi, and instead I'm sitting here eating cold soup."

"No, you're not," Amanda said gently. "You're moving it around with a spoon and not touching a bite. Leigh, relax. I have no intention of getting killed. I can take care of myself."

Leigh's eyes flashed wildly. "You don't understand. It's happened before!"

Amanda nodded slowly. "Natasha?"

The guilt on Leigh's face said it all. "I had one job. All I needed to do was keep her from going to her father's house the night of the raid. Instead, she ended up dead."

The pain in Leigh's eyes touched Amanda to the core. "What happened?"

"She was supposed to stay with me that night. Henrik thought I should warn her about the raid to be certain, but I went with my gut. I didn't want her to know the role I'd played in getting her dad arrested, and I thought it would be safe enough."

"But she went back to the house?"

Leigh nodded, looking weary. "I woke up in the middle of the night alone. I raced back to her father's house and found her body sitting in a chair in the office, already dead. And I've never forgiven myself for that."

Amanda felt moved to tears by the account, and closed her eyes trying to picture how it all had played out. A detail caught in her mind. "Leigh, how did you end up with the laptop, if the raid was already over?"

"The laptop was hidden in a compartment in Natasha's closet and they'd missed it. I took it and never admitted it, but of course they suspected. But none of it was worth losing Natasha, and nothing would be worth losing you, either."

"Hmm." Amanda shook her head slowly, sadness for Leigh's loss weighing her down even while the phrase 'losing you' somehow gave her hope. She held out her hand, knowing what she needed to do. "Give me your phone."

Leigh frowned. "Why?"

"Because this lunch is a bust. I'm going back to the hotel room to wait for Javier's call where there's a strong signal, and you're going to scout the island like you're champing at the bit to do."

A light flickered in Leigh's eyes, as if she couldn't quite believe how easily Amanda had given in. "Are you sure? You're not going to argue and hit me with a bunch of your witty remarks until I give in and we do this your way?" Despite the fact she'd won, there was a touch of disappointment in her tone.

A smile tugged at Amanda's lips, even though it was really no laughing matter. It was just that she'd started to think of the back and forth between them as something akin to foreplay, and it seemed that Leigh did, too. "Not this time. I promise I'll make it up to you later." When Leigh's face flushed all the way to her forehead and earlobes, Amanda laughed out loud. *Definitely foreplay.*

Once she'd left the restaurant, it didn't take long for the message to arrive. Leigh's phone was already vibrating with an incoming text by the time she'd reached the front steps of the hotel. Amanda plucked it from her pocket the minute she'd made it into their room. When she saw the message, her heart stood still.

Henrik is on leave from Säpo. They have no knowledge of Stockholm Protocol. What the hell is going on?

TWENTY-ONE

AS AMANDA STARED at the phone, a call came in. After a moment of hesitation, she answered it and heard a familiar voice with a slight Spanish accent on the other end of the line, saying Leigh's name.

"No, Javier. It's Amanda."

"*Amanda?*" His voice sounded strained with worry. "*Where's Leigh?*"

"She's gone out to survey the island before the handover. The cell reception's spotty, so I was supposed to wait for your call."

"*When's she due back?*" It was clear by this question that he didn't intend to tell her anything, and the lack of confidence pricked Amanda's pride.

"She'll be back when she's back." Amanda's tone was testy. Neither one of them had time to waste. "She didn't really say. Why don't you just tell me what's going on, and I'll let her know?"

For a moment Amanda thought he was going to argue, but then he changed his mind. "*Okay, I talked to a contact at Säpo this morning, and here's what I know. Henrik's been on a leave of absence since May 26th, the day a Russian mobster named Anatoly Vasiliev was released from prison. Apparently, he has a special interest in the case.*"

Amanda gave a grim laugh. "You could say that. No one in your agency knew he was on leave?"

"*No. In the event that they ever needed to call Leigh back to Stockholm, Henrik was supposed to be the main contact.*"

"That's the Stockholm Protocol?" Amanda guessed.

"*Yeah, that's right. Only when I talked to Säpo, they said they'd never initiated it. Henrik's the only one who could've done it on his own.*"

Fear for Leigh's safety gripped her. "We're supposed to meet with him in two days, and it's possible he's already on the island. Leigh's out there looking for signs of him now, along with Vasiliev and his gang of thugs. Can we trust him?"

"*I don't know. My agent spoke highly of him, so he may just be trying to cut through some red tape and investigating on his own, but to be safe, I think we need to assume the worst.*"

Oh, she was assuming the worst, all right. "I need to go find her and warn her."

"*Amanda, no. That will just put you in danger, too. You need to hold tight and wait for her to come back.*"

Amanda's first instinct was to accuse Javier of underestimating her, but she bit her tongue and stayed quiet. Deep down, she knew he was right. Even if she'd been a fully trained agent, going out there now without a solid plan would just give Henrik two targets. Until they knew for certain what his objective was, anything she did could put both Leigh and her at risk. "Okay. Fine."

It was a little after two o'clock when she hung up the phone, and though they hadn't discussed it, she assumed Leigh would be back by evening. For the next few hours she paced back and forth in the room as the sun inched its way lower in the sky. Time seemed to stand still, the daylight never ending, and Amanda grew more agitated the longer Leigh was away. *When will she get here, and why is it never night in this place?*

By seven o'clock, hunger pangs were gnawing at Amanda's belly. It had been six hours since she and Leigh had eaten lunch at the café, which meant it had been just as long since Leigh had ventured out on her own. And still there was no word from her. The combination of lack of food and her pins-and-needles nerves were making her shaky, and by half-past, Amanda decided to venture downstairs to the lobby to see if she could find a snack. She was halfway there when the phone alerted her to an incoming text. When she saw what had arrived, her head began to spin so severely that she feared she would faint, and had to reach out with her free hand to steady herself against the whitewashed stucco wall of the hallway.

She raced back to the room and sank into a chair

before pulling out the phone again. On the screen was a photo of Leigh, seated with her hands and legs bound and mouth gagged. Around her neck was a sign that read:

> *Midnight*
> *St Olof's Church*
> *Bring the laptop*

Amanda stared at the picture so long that she thought it must have been burned into her retinas. There was a smudge on the screen that obscured part of Leigh's face, and at one point she wiped it away with the tip of her index finger. She regretted it immediately. Without the smudge covering them, the look in Leigh's eyes was unmistakable. She was afraid she was going to die. A look like that could only come from one thing. Vasiliev had captured her during her reconnaissance mission, and now he planned to lure Amanda in, too.

We're both going to die.

Once Amanda handed over the laptop—because of course she would, what other choice did she have—the most likely scenario was that both she and Leigh would end up at the bottom of the Baltic sea. The laptop, and whatever information it contained, would be lost forever.

If only I could guess the password, maybe it could save us.

Amanda retrieved her notebook and looked at the

list she and Leigh had compiled of possible passwords. It stretched three pages long, and they'd only just begun. They'd been cautious before, when they thought the device would be turned over to the proper authorities for analysis, but what about now? Would it really do any harm if Amanda started plugging in passwords? She might guess right, and if not, did she really care if the bad guys got a laptop with a melted hard drive? The worst they could do is kill her, and she'd already determined that she was as good as dead.

She grabbed the laptop and set it on the coffee table, her insides churning as she weighed her options. Midnight was about four hours away. The thought of opening the lid and typing in passwords made her so queasy that she pressed her hand to her mouth to keep herself from throwing up. The smell of fish overwhelmed her and she pulled her hand away.

Why does my hand smell like fish?

Gingerly, she ventured a second sniff, though her stomach begged her not to. The smell reminded her of the fish paste they'd had at breakfast. She turned her index finger one way and the other, and then suddenly recalled using it to wipe Leigh's screen. The smudge that had covered the photo over Leigh's face must have been fish paste.

Then her brain began to whir in the way it sometimes did when there was a puzzle to be solved, and Amanda had the strongest sense that there was something else, something she needed to figure out that she just couldn't quite see. She closed her eyes and took a deep breath. She saw the smudge on the screen in her mind, and in that same location she recalled seeing the button to end a call. That answered one question. The paste must've gotten there that morning off of Leigh's finger when she'd placed her call to Javier.

Amanda breathed in again and set her mind free, letting it wander wherever it might. The image of a computer keyboard came to her, with some of the letters smudged with peanut butter. It had been at an assignment a few months back, when she'd filled in for a guy who ate peanut butter like he was some sort of junkie. He'd gotten the stuff everywhere, and she was constantly getting it on her fingers from his messy keyboard when she typed. As a temp, she'd seen variations of that kind of thing constantly. Each time she sat at a new desk, the keyboard would be a little different with certain keys dirty or scraped because they were used more often. The letters 'e' and 't' were well worn on any old keyboard, but if the paint had chipped off of the 'z' then it was almost a guarantee that the person who sat there had a 'z' in their name. Noticing things like that helped Amanda pass the time.

Amanda reached for the laptop and carefully opened the cover, curious to get a look at the keys. She frowned when she saw it. Despite the somewhat chunky appearance that older computers often have in retrospect, this model was very small, with a tiny screen and cramped keyboard that even Amanda, with her relatively small fingers, would've been loath to use. She didn't know for certain, but she'd pictured Vasiliev to be a larger man. Mobsters were always big, burly men in the movies, right? Surely, he was at least as big as an average size woman, and if that was the case, she couldn't imagine he would've been comfortable typing for very long.

What had Leigh said about Vasiliev's office the night of the raid? The laptop had been missing from the docking station. And a docking station meant a separate monitor and keyboard. But when they'd brought the device to Max, he hadn't been able to make any of his peripherals work. Not until after he'd entered a password, he'd said. Which had to be done directly onto the laptop keyboard. Amanda's pulse quickened as she realized what that meant.

If Vasiliev only used the laptop keyboard to type his password, those are the only letters that will show any signs of use!

Amanda turned on the bright overhead light and studied the keys, but none of them looked particularly worn. Still, they'd have some sort of oil on them, or fingerprints, maybe? Amanda glanced at the time and realized that she now had less than four hours until the meet. She needed to hurry.

What would James Bond do?

Amanda rolled her eyes. James Bond would have some sort of special super-secret spy device. Like a laser beam or a radioactive mist, that would illuminate the fingerprints and save the day. James Bond was a world-class secret agent, and therefore not the best role model in this instance. Amanda was more like an amateur sleuth.

Think, Amanda. What would Nancy Drew do?

She snorted. The famous girl detective would probably pull her makeup compact from the handbag that perfectly matched her shoes, and use the powder inside as a makeshift fingerprinting kit. Which wasn't such a bad idea, except this wasn't the nineteen thirties, and so she wasn't carrying a handbag, and besides which, Amanda was a somewhat typical lesbian in that the only makeup she had much use for was strawberry lip gloss. And even James Bond could not turn strawberry lip gloss into a fingerprinting kit.

She clasped her hands together, squeezing them tight. There had to be another way. Soon her fingers were tingling from the lack of circulation, but she still had no solution. She unclasped them and watched the blood race back into her fingertips, but grew puzzled as she noticed that the tips on one hand remained white, as if they'd been coated with a layer of talc. She hadn't noticed it before, and she racked her brain trying to think where it could've come from.

The whitewashed stucco in the hallway!

Amanda raced into the hall until she reached the spot where she'd been standing when the photo of Leigh had arrived. Now that she was looking for it, the patched section of bare plaster was easy to spot, as it had a dull finish that was different from the surrounding area. They'd clearly fixed a crack or hole and hadn't had a chance to paint. When Amanda rubbed the area with the blunt tip of her thumbnail, the plaster flaked off in a fine white powder that drifted to the floor. It wasn't a large spot, but Amanda figured it was more than enough for what she'd need.

Cupping one hand beneath, Amanda scraped at the wall until she had a small pile of white dust in her palm. Back in the room, she found a package of three cotton swabs in the bathroom next to the guest soap and travel-size shampoo. Dipping the swab into the plaster dust, Amanda dabbed each letter on the laptop keyboard.

Nothing happened.

The entire row of numbers along the top yielded nothing. So it was, too, when she got to the 'q', the 'w', and the 'e'—none of them showed any trace of oil or dirt. Only the fact that the 'e' came up empty encouraged her to continue. If the keyboard had been used regularly, that most common letter would have been caked in grime. When she rubbed the swab over the next letter, the 'r', a dark white dot grew visible in the middle of the key. Amanda's triumphant laughter rang out in the empty hotel room. *Success!*

A minute later, she'd identified a total of eleven letters. She should have been ecstatic, but instead she was mired in despair. This was because she'd realized when she reached the eighth one that her list of potential passwords would be useless. They were all in English, and yet Vasiliev's laptop was a Swedish one and the eighth letter she'd identified, which looked like an 'o' but had two dots on the top, didn't appear in any English words. Vasiliev's password was in Swedish. She should have anticipated that, but in her eagerness to compile her list, it had simply never occurred to her.

Fuck.

If Leigh had been there, she might have been able to help with a translation, but Leigh was bound and gagged to a chair right now, and Vasiliev was going to kill her if Amanda didn't deliver this laptop in—Amanda nervously checked the time—three hours and fifteen minutes. But if she delivered the laptop without a bargaining chip, like knowing what it contained, they'd probably both be dead in three hours and twenty minutes. There had to be someone else who could help.

Max!

She should've thought of him before. If anyone could help her solve this puzzle, it had to be him. Grabbing Leigh's phone, Amanda found his number and placed the call, praying he would pick up. On the third ring, he did.

"Max, it's Amanda. Leigh's friend. We're in trouble."

"Yeah, I'd say so," Max replied. *"Olle and Ulla went out early this morning and guess what? No boat. All of*

Nynäshamn's heard about it by now. I think Olle's planning to skin Leigh alive, and probably you, too."

Amanda sucked in her breath. "Shit, I'd forgotten about that, but that's not what I meant." She briefly explained what had happened since they'd left Nynäshamn in their stolen boat. "So now I have a list of letters, but I don't know any Swedish so I'm at a dead end."

"Okay, read me the list."

"R, O, S, D, H, K, L, Ö, Ä, C, V."

There was silence on the other end of the phone while Max went to work. Amanda tapped her fingers against her knee while she waited, her stomach tied in knots. She was almost grateful she hadn't managed to eat, as by now with all the stress her insides had been put through, there'd almost certainly be nothing left.

Just as she was about to give up hope, Max let out a whoop! *"I've got it!* Svärd och Sköld. *It's the name of an old Soviet movie about a Russian agent during World War II who goes to Germany and helps the resistance. When they released it in Swedish theaters, it was called* Svärd och Sköld. *Sword and shield."*

Amanda gasped. "Oh my god. The sword and the shield. Max, that's the emblem for the KGB." Her heart raced as the pieces fell into place. "I think you were right. What if Vasiliev isn't just into organized crime. What if he was somehow connected to the KGB?"

"If he was, then he probably still is. I don't think those guys just quit."

"Then he's definitely going to kill us."

"Not if we can get into the laptop and make a copy of the files. Before I was thinking bank account numbers or something, but now I'm thinking it could be names of other agents, or something even more secret. Whatever they are, he clearly doesn't want them public, right? So, let's enter the password and have a look. I'll set up a secure cloud account and you can transfer the files using a VPN. If anything happens to you or to Leigh, I'll send the files directly to Säpo."

Amanda thought for a moment. "Yes, send them to Säpo, but not to Henrik. We don't know for certain if we can trust him."

"I'll send it straight to the director general. We've worked together before. But you still have to enter the password, so we can get the files. Are you up for it?"

Amanda turned on the computer and waited for the login screen to appear. "Okay, ready. Can you spell the words for me?" Max did, and Amanda carefully typed each one. She held her breath and hit the enter key. The computer made a low *bonk!* sound and Amanda's heart fell as she knew immediately that they'd gotten it wrong. "That wasn't it. Max, that wasn't it. Now what?"

"Is there a fingerprint on the shift key? Maybe it's capitalized."

"Um, I didn't check." Amanda grabbed the swab and dusted the shift key, nearly shouting into the phone as a smudged fingerprint appeared. "Oh, holy shit. That was it. Give it to me again."

"*Wait, I just thought of something. Check the space bar, too.*"

Amanda's hand trembled as she dabbed the swab all along the space bar. "Nope, nothing. So, what do I do?"

"*If it were me, I'd capitalize the two 'S's'.*"

Amanda's fingers hovered over the keys, but doubt suddenly paralyzed her. They were so close, but she couldn't screw it up. "But why both, or why not the 'o', too? Max, I'm really scared. It could be anything. He could just randomly capitalize a letter."

"*True, but this is a movie title, remember? It's not random. I've just looked it up and that movie inspired a whole generation of Soviet men to join the KGB in the late '60s. That's how it would've been in the title, and given what I've just told you about the film, that's definitely what he was referencing with the password.*"

As Max spelled the words again, Amanda held her breath and pressed the keys. This time when she got to the enter key, the screen went black and the computer began to whir. She let out a little cry as she looked for smoke or other signs that the hard drive was self-destructing, but soon the screen changed to the familiar series of standard scripts that indicated the computer was booting up.

"Max, it worked!" Tears ran down her cheeks as the home screen came up and icons of file folders populated the page. At least there was now a chance that she and Leigh might escape tonight with their lives.

Max walked her though the process of loading the files onto the cloud server. The hotel's Wi-Fi connection was slow, and by the time the last file was complete, it was eleven thirty. She had only thirty minutes to walk from the hotel to St Olof's church, and the map they'd picked up at the tourist center indicated that it was a twenty-minute walk.

"Thank you so much for your help, Max. I've gotta run."

"Wait, there's one more thing. *You need to clean the log. It'll only take about fifteen minutes.*"

"Fifteen minutes? I don't have time. Why do I need to do that?"

"*It's just so you don't leave a record of what you did.*"

Amanda pondered this. "But don't I want him to know what I did? They can't trace where the files were sent by looking at that, can they? Or get to them and erase them?"

"*Umm…no, probably not. It's just something I always do for security, but you're right, you want him to know you got in, and that's your proof. Just skip it and turn the machine off. And good luck.*"

Tucking the laptop under her arm, Amanda raced out of the hotel and onto the street. It had finally become dark now, and the crowds from earlier in the day had thinned so that only one or two people were out on the narrow, cobbled road. The light coating of sea mist that had begun rolling in earlier in the day had grown to a thick fog such that, though the scent of roses was heavy in the air around her, Amanda could no longer see the gardens from whence it came. As she made her way toward the spot on the map where St Olof's church was meant to be, she could see little ahead of her except the occasional glow of a gaslight, the fog forming a halo around it that seemed to keep the light from reaching the ground. The only sounds she could hear were the shuffle of her own feet along the stones, and the sound of her heart pounding in her ears.

TWENTY-TWO

THE BUILDING in front of her was little more than a heap of stones, and Amanda checked her map again. It was the right place, but what she hadn't realized until now was that St Olof's was not an active church, but a ruin. There were numerous ruins on the island, and so it shouldn't have come as a surprise, but the sight of the abandoned and decrepit spot sent a shiver down her spine.

There was little left of the great church that had once stood there other than a single tower, and even that had been reduced to an outcropping of masonry nearly drowned in ivy, with a massive canopy of ancient trees where the roof had once been. A flagstone terrace paved the way to the door where a wooden gate barred Amanda's entry. Peering through the slats, another set of gates did the same on the opposite side. She could just make out that the floor was bare earth. The fog covered everything else.

"In here!" It was a man's voice that called out, that much Amanda knew. The voice was low and he spoke in English but with an accent. It was impossible to make out anything else as the words echoed in the enclosed space of the ruins to the point that even the words themselves were difficult to discern.

She gave the gate a push and was surprised that it swung easily on its hinges. She'd expected the creaking of rust and age, but they'd been recently oiled. Perhaps Vasiliev and his men used this place frequently for clandestine meetings. Amanda took a hesitant step into the darkness of the old church's interior, every muscle on high alert as she fought to steel her nerves. While Russian mobsters might be used to this sort of thing, it was Amanda's first clandestine meeting and she wasn't sure what to expect.

"Did you bring it?" Again, the voice called out, and this time Amanda thought there was a hint of familiarity to it, but she was far from sure.

"Yes, I have it." Amanda cringed at the weakness in her tone and volume. She tensed her abdomen as she'd learned in a drama class years ago and tried harder. "Just so you know, I've made a copy of the files! If anything happens to either one of us, they'll be released."

"Have you really?" Incredibly, the man's voice

sounded almost impressed, which succeeded in rubbing Amanda the wrong way. Even the Russian mob underestimated her.

"Yes, really," she snapped. "Now, where should I bring it? I can't see anything. Where are you, and where's Leigh?"

"Step inside."

Wrapping her arms around the laptop, Amanda hugged it to her chest as though it were a life preserver as she took a few more steps toward the center of the space. She moved slowly enough that her eyes could adjust, and after a few seconds she was able to make out patches of light that filtered in through the dense foliage that had formed a de facto ceiling high above her head. In the largest patch of light was a chair, and in the chair sat a woman with shaggy blonde hair and a petite but powerful build.

"Leigh! Are you okay?" Amanda tucked the laptop under her arm and rushed the rest of the distance between them until she was kneeling beside Leigh's chair. She spoke in a hushed voice under the guise of checking Leigh over for injuries. "Do you still have your knife in the ankle strap?" Her hopes fell as Leigh shook her head.

"Don't bother looking for the knife, Ms. Princeton." Now that it was closer, Amanda was almost certain she recognized the voice, and the realization caused her heart to clench.

Henrik.

Amanda spun around, searching the shadows until the figure of a man emerged, confirming her suspicion beyond a doubt. "Henrik! How could you do this?" Her fear was forgotten for a moment in the heat of her anger. "She considered you her mentor. How could you betray her like this?"

"I didn't betray her, Ms. Princeton. Please, just allow me to explain."

Amanda gave him a scornful look. "If you didn't betray her, then why do you have her tied up and gagged on that chair."

Henrik sighed. "You've spent quite a bit of time with Linnea. Can you honestly imagine that she'd sit there quietly and cooperate if I hadn't tied her up?"

He had a point. Still, Amanda remained unconvinced. "But why is she here at all? We were already planning to bring you the laptop in two days and hand it over without any fuss. Why kidnap her and hold her hostage when we would've just given it to you free and clear?"

"Because we didn't have two days. Vasiliev and several of his men are already on the island and they're looking for all three of us." He cleared his throat and looked Amanda directly in the eyes. "I did not mean to kidnap her. I came across her and simply wanted to talk, to warn her about the Russians. This was a last resort."

Amanda had to admit that it sounded plausible, but something about it still bothered her. "Why send me the ransom photo, and not tell me what was going on? I thought you were going to kill her."

"I had no plans to kill her, or you for that matter," Henrik assured her. "But I had to get you here with the laptop and this was the fastest way." He smiled warmly and stretched out his hands. "So, do you believe me now? Will you hand over the laptop so we can all be on our way?"

Amanda searched Leigh's eyes, which were the only thing she could see because of the gag, but she wasn't certain what message she was meant to get from them. Without Leigh's direction on something this important, Amanda was lost. "Henrik, the only way I'll ever consider handing over the laptop is if you untie Leigh and she tells me it's okay."

Henrik nodded curtly and untied Leigh's hands and feet. When she didn't struggle, he removed her gag, as well. Leigh glowered at him from the chair, but didn't try to scream or run.

"Well, Linnea? Is it okay for your friend to give me the computer now?"

Her jaw stiffened in response. "You'll need to answer some questions first, Henrik." He drew a breath as if he'd expected as much, and waited. "First, how did you meet my mother, Jenny Lundgren?"

There was a shift in his expression at the question,

a softening around the corners of his eyes at the mention of her name. "Your mother was working at the Swedish Heritage Foundation, which I happened to be investigating because of its ties to the Vasiliev family." He turned his head to address Amanda specifically. "You may not know, but that's an organization that is involved with helping immigrants assimilate into Swedish society, and they also publish case studies on their work that are used by aid organizations worldwide. Natasha, Vasiliev's daughter, worked there as a researcher, and Anatoly Vasiliev had given large sums of money to the foundation over the years." Once again, he addressed them both. "I suspected he might have been using the foundation as a money laundering operation."

"So, what, you used my mother as an informant like you did with me?" Leigh's eyes narrowed. "Only instead of luring her with the promise of a career in intelligence, you just slept with her."

"No, not at all." He shook his head vehemently and Amanda was inclined to believe his denial. "I was sent to speak with your mother on her request. She'd gotten a hold of a new batch of case studies, and was concerned with the results."

Amanda frowned. "So, she called the police?"

"It may sound extreme, but yes, essentially. She'd been involved with the cases in question and felt the data were being grossly misrepresented to skew the conclusions a certain way. These studies were used by agencies around the world to determine policy and funding, so she was rightly concerned, but she wasn't sure where to report it. I think she called every government agency in Stockholm before she finally got to me." He chuckled at the memory, but there was sadness in his eyes.

"And then you started screwing her," Leigh stated bluntly.

"We started dating," he corrected. "And we fell in love."

"If you were so in love, why weren't you there with her when she died?" Leigh's tone was harsh and accusing.

"I've asked myself that every day." There was a hitch in his voice, and it was clear to see he was crestfallen over it. "If I'd been there, I believe she'd still be alive."

Leigh must have been moved by his response because she sat quietly for a moment, considering. When she asked her next question, it was filled with hesitance. "Do you think she did it on purpose?"

"Your mother did not commit suicide." Henrik's tone left no room for question. "And I don't believe it was an accident, either. Jenny hadn't needed those pills in months, not since we started seeing each other. Someone else gave her that overdose."

Leigh's face was overtaken by a look of physical pain, and Amanda reached out to take her hand. "You mean you think that Leigh's mother was murdered?" Amanda asked when it was clear that Leigh was unable to speak.

"Yes, because of her interest in those reports," Henrik confirmed.

"Vasiliev." Leigh said the name as a statement, not a question, but surprisingly, Henrik was slow to confirm.

"Perhaps," he replied, giving a reluctant nod. "All I could ever uncover in connection with it was a code name, Mulåsna."

"Mule? Clever, like a Moscow Mule. Then it has to be Vasiliev." Leigh was firm.

"Yes, most likely," Henrik conceded. "You can see why, when I found out Jenny's daughter, whom I'd never met, was dating Natasha Vasiliev—frankly, I was taken aback. However, I couldn't pass up the opportunity to have an inside source that could shed light on both the Vasiliev crime organization, and also on who at the Swedish Heritage Foundation might have wanted Jenny dead."

"That's all?" Leigh asked when Henrik fell silent.

"Hardly. That's just the beginning, but we don't have time right now. We've been in one place too long as it is." He reached into a pocket and pulled out a card. When Leigh took it, Amanda could see numbers handwritten on the back. "Go to your boat tonight. Leave Gotland immediately, or Vasiliev may find you. Tomorrow at noon, I'll be at those coordinates in my own boat. Meet me there, and I'll explain the rest."

Leigh studied the card for a moment, then slowly nodded.

Henrik looked pointedly at Amanda. "May I have the laptop now?"

Amanda looked to Leigh, who nodded her consent. Amanda held the laptop out and Henrik took it quickly from her hands and tucked it away. He turned to go, but then looked back at Amanda.

"Did you really crack the password and copy the files?"

It took her only a fraction of a second to decide how to respond. "No. I didn't." Amanda looked up into Henrik's eyes, her chin jutting out almost defiantly. "I thought Vasiliev was the one holding Leigh and would kill us both, so I made up a story to try to save us."

"Smart." His disappointment was evident, but he held out his hand for Amanda to shake. "That was well played, Ms. Princeton. If you'd been up against Vasiliev, I think it might have worked." As he left the ruins, the glow from his approval warmed Amanda from the inside out.

"Liar," Leigh said when Henrik was gone.

Amanda frowned in confusion. "Sorry?"

A crafty smile played across Leigh's lips as she stood from her chair. "I said, that was a complete and utter lie. You cracked that laptop wide open and copied the files before you came here."

Amanda looked at her in shock. "How...how did you know?"

Leigh laughed. "It's written all over your face."

"It isn't," Amanda shot back, crossing her arms in a huff as she walked beside Leigh to the wooden gate that barred the church door.

"Oh, it is." Despite the ordeal she'd endured that day, or perhaps because of it, Leigh let out a hearty laugh. "You wanna know how I know?"

Amanda stopped and put her hands on her hips, ready to stand rooted to the spot until Leigh revealed her tell. "Tell me."

"Well, I'm not going to tell you what it is you actually do, because that would spoil it." She laughed again as Amanda glared. "But I will tell you this. You had exactly that same look when we landed in Stockholm, right as you were telling me that you never wanted to have sex with me again." Leigh smirked. "And we both know that was a goddamned lie, don't we?"

Leigh stepped outside into the night. The fog had cleared while they were with Henrik in the ruins of St Olof's church, and there was a faint tint of pink at the horizon where the sun was already making its way back into the sky. The whole thing combined with the moon shining down on the medieval city of Visby was a sight worthy of a postcard, but Amanda didn't give it a second glance. She was too busy fuming over the fact that Leigh was so obnoxiously right.

LEIGH SLOWED the boat's engine and squinted into the sun as she detected a shape bobbing in the distance amid the sparkling water. Henrik's vessel, a larger and more modern motorboat than hers which had been built for spending days or weeks out at sea, was exactly where he had promised it would be. Leigh breathed a sigh of relief. It was well past noon, and Henrik was not a man known for his willingness to wait around.

"See. I told you he'd still be there." Amanda was annoyingly nonchalant in her tone. "Whatever he has to tell us is too important for him to blow us off for being a few minutes late."

This newfound smugness didn't suit her, but ever since Henrik had complimented her cunning lie about copying the files from the laptop, she'd been insufferable. Even when Leigh had reminded her, repeatedly, that it hadn't in fact been a lie, it'd had little effect. The only thing that had finally worked was when Leigh teased her about discovering Amanda's tell. Truth be told, she'd probably be willing to put up with Amanda's smugness a good long while if it meant she could keep rubbing *that* in. Their charged banter was better than any foreplay.

"You don't know how he can be," Leigh pointed out, also not for the first time. It was Amanda's fault they were running so late, and Leigh had taken every opportunity she could to point out the likely consequences. "I've known him for five years and I'm telling you we're lucky he didn't leave an hour ago. He's not a patient man."

Amanda shrugged. "We needed to eat."

The fact that it was true was the only thing that kept Leigh's mouth shut. They'd both been starving by the time they'd made it from St Olof's to the boat, and there hadn't been a speck of food on board. It was the first time in living memory that Leigh had ever seen the small pantry bare. It was a point of pride with her grandmother to keep her kitchen fully stocked even at sea. The only reason it hadn't been this time was because Leigh had stolen the boat before she'd had a chance to stuff every nook and cranny full of snacks. In any event, Leigh had been forced to circle back to shore early in the morning so they could grab breakfast from a diner in one of the smaller ports that opened in time to cater to the fisherman on their way out to sea.

They cruised at their reduced speed until they were close enough to Henrik's boat to call out, then Leigh cut the engine and allowed them to float the rest of the distance until she would be able to tie both boats together so they could board. As she maneuvered the ropes from their storage box, Leigh eyed the deck of the other boat with a growing tenseness in her belly. Despite the noise from the motor and the greeting she'd yelled, there was no sign of Henrik.

"Henrik?" Leigh cupped her hands around her mouth and directed her voice toward the opening to the hull where the sleeping cabins and eating area were likely to be. Still there was no answer. She scrambled aboard Henrik's boat, then put out a hand to help Amanda, who wasn't as sure-footed as Leigh was on the water, but was loathe to admit it. "I have a bad feeling about this," she said to Amanda when she'd steadied herself on the deck.

For once, Amanda looked inclined to agree. "Should we look downstairs?"

There were five steps leading down to the cabin, and as Leigh led the way, her knees threatened to give way with each step. Something was wrong. When she reached the bottom, she caught her first glimpse of exactly what. She gasped. "Oh god. Amanda, don't look!"

Seated at the table was Henrik, his eyes staring blankly ahead. His already red-tinged beard was dripping with blood. Something narrow and black protruded from his chest, with a dark stain forming a circle around it on his chest.

Not heeding her warning, Amanda came to a sudden halt against Leigh's rigid back and screamed.

The horror of Henrik's death was briefly overshadowed by the ringing in Leigh's ear. "Seriously,

Amanda? Not only is Henrik dead, but I've probably just gone deaf."

"Is he really dead?" These words came out in barely a whisper, and turning to face her, Leigh could see that Amanda was in shock.

"Yes, he really is." Her reply came gently, without a hint of mocking. "Why don't you stay where you are while I take a look?"

Nodding gratefully, Amanda sank onto the step behind her and watched as Leigh approached the body.

The closer she got, the more familiar the object in Henrik's chest appeared to be. Finally, when Leigh was an arms-length away, she realized why.

"Oh, shit. This is my knife."

Amanda pushed herself up weakly from the step and came to join her. "But, how?"

"He confiscated it from me last night when he tied me to the chair, and never bothered to give it back. With everything that went on, I'd forgotten."

Leigh looked at the hilt of her beloved ebony knife in distaste. She held her hand out to Amanda. "Give me your scarf."

Without questioning the order, Amanda removed the hideous scarf that had been part of her disguise and handed it over. Leigh wrapped it around her hand and curled her fingers around the knife, revulsion washing over her in a wave as she made contact with the delicate wooden handle.

"Are you going to pull it out?" Amanda sounded as repulsed by the prospect as Leigh felt.

Leigh shook her head. "No. It's in so deep I don't think I could, at least not without making a mess. I'm just wiping off the prints."

Amanda frowned. "But won't the police need those? Otherwise how will we figure out who killed him?"

Leigh laughed mirthlessly. "I think we all know who killed him, with or without the prints. But if mine are on there, I'd make an excellent scapegoat." She wiped the scarf up and down, though the knowledge that she'd handled the blade, too, pricked at her mind and amped up the tension. There was nothing she could do about that. Cleaning the blade was a lost cause. She unwrapped her hand from the scarf and stuffed it in her pocket.

"Now what do we do?" Amanda's eyes were wide and lost, and Leigh would've done anything to get smug Amanda back right then.

Leigh wrung her hands together, hoping a brilliant plan would come to her. Henrik had promised them answers but now they had only questions.

"Leigh, Henrik's finger has blood on it." Amanda had inched ever closer and was now as close to the body as Leigh.

Leigh gave her an indulgent look, this likely being her first dead body. "Honey, everything has blood on it. The stuff goes everywhere."

Amanda gave her a look that said she didn't appreciate the patronizing tone. "I'm not talking about everything, Leigh. I'm talking specifically about his right index finger. What if he tried to leave us a note?"

Leigh's nose wrinkled. "In his own blood? I'm fairly certain that only happens in movies."

"Fine, then let's look and when we don't find anything, you can laugh at me all the way to Stockholm."

In the end, it was Amanda who had the last laugh. Under the table, scrawled in his own lifeblood, Henrik had indeed left them a message:

Mulåsna
Vasa Museet
Tisdag, 18:45

"THE VASA MUSEUM," Leigh translated. "Tuesday at a quarter to seven in the evening."

"Nothing else, just a time and a place?" Amanda frowned, "What does that other word mean?"

"Mulåsna? It's Swedish for mule."

"Vasiliev's codename. What do you think it means, exactly?" Amanda asked.

"I'd assume a meeting, but I don't know for certain. We'll have to find out." Leigh took a deep breath, turning her back to the gruesome crime scene and putting the image of her slain mentor somewhere in the deep recesses of her mind for another time, sealing the lid to its box extra tight. Right now, they needed to get to Stockholm and find out what the hell a museum that housed a 17th century sunken ship had to do with Henrik, her mother, or the Russian mob.

Piece of cake. That's why they pay me the big bucks, right?

TWENTY-THREE

IT WAS early Sunday morning and the platform at Nynäshamn's train station was empty as Leigh checked the timetables for the next train to Stockholm. They'd narrowly missed the 6:49, and there wouldn't be another for an hour. She looked from her own rumpled t-shirt and shorts to Amanda's and sighed. They'd had to leave their bags behind at the hotel in Visby, as it had been too dangerous to return knowing that Vasiliev's men were closing in. Now they were without changes of clothing or toiletries, and almost out of money. They were also, thanks to their pre-dawn errand that morning, down one boat, the precious Pettersson motor yacht having been returned to her grandparents' backyard under cover of darkness.

They were in desperate need of a shower and a full eight hours of sleep, both of which awaited them at the agency safe house in Stockholm. They could've made it the night before, in fact, had it not been for Leigh's reticence toward having to explain herself to her grandfather face-to-face. Beside her, Amanda yawned loudly and stretched her back, looking impossibly weary, and despite the good reasons she'd had at the time, Leigh regretted the choice now. Amanda looked completely shell-shocked.

"It's just a little longer, Amanda," she said gently, hoping to give her companion some encouragement. Without anything in the way of creature comforts, it was about the only thing Leigh had to give. "The train will be here in an hour."

Amanda nodded, bleary eyed. "Can't we at least get something for breakfast?"

"When we get to Stockholm, I promise." Leigh felt a pang in her own stomach at the suggestion of food, but there was nothing to be done about it. "We don't have enough cash left to even split a cup of coffee. Obviously, credit cards are out to avoid anyone tracing our location. I was counting on Henrik to help replenish my stash of cash when we reached Gotland, but..." Needless to say, that hadn't worked out as planned.

"I thought you said you still had over a hundred and fifty left," Amanda said with a whimper.

"That was Swedish kronor, not dollars. Once I buy the train tickets, I'll be down to twelve kronor."

Amanda looked at her hopefully. "Well, how much is that in dollars?"

"About a buck."

Amanda's face fell instantly at this revelation. "I thought spies always had stacks of cash in vaults all over the place that they could access at a moment's notice, like, millions of dollars. Why have all of my movies lied to me?" She made a grumpy face. Then her eyes brightened she pointed to the edge of the platform. "Look! Isn't that Max?"

Leigh spun to look, and indeed the tall, skinny man who had just exited the yellow train station onto the platform was none other than Max Olson. He looked painfully out of place in the outdoors, his impossibly white skin made even more jarring by the black hoodie that he'd pulled up to cover his head. Leigh lifted her hand to wave to him, but there was no need. He had already spotted them and seemed to be approaching with singular purpose.

"Leigh, I thought I might find you here." Relief was evident on his face. "Hello, Amanda. It's good to see you again."

"You, too, Max," Amanda replied warmly.

But his appearance on the platform had raised a concern too pressing for Leigh to spend much time on pleasantries. "How did you know we were here, Max? Do you think anyone else knows?"

"I doubt it. I saw you taking the boat back. You passed my house on your way, and I assumed that's what you were doing. A train's the only reasonable option after that, unless you were planning on stealing their car, too."

"Really funny." Leigh shot him a look. "But what were you doing up so early?"

"I wasn't up early. I'm still up late from yesterday." Max shrugged. "I'm doing some security tests for a firm in Australia and it's got my internal clock flipped upside down. Come on. You have an hour until the next train, and we could all use some coffee."

"We're out of money," Amanda confessed with a pout.

"My treat. There's something I need to tell you about those files from Vasiliev's computer."

In the turmoil and confusion that had followed their discovery of Henrik's body, Leigh had scarcely spared a thought for the files that Amanda had managed to retrieve, and so the mention of them now sent a tingling down Leigh's spine. In the sudden rush of anticipation, it was agony to have to wait, but it wasn't until they'd walked a few blocks to a place that was serving breakfast, placed their order, and had been served, that they were able to talk.

"So, the files?" Leigh prompted after she'd shoveled a few bites of crispy waffle into her mouth and washed it down with strong coffee. The plate of heart-shaped waffles topped with whipped cream and a massive spoonful of cloudberry jam were to die for, but giving them the full appreciation they deserved would have to wait until she'd heard Max's news.

"Oh, yes." He wiped his mouth on the sleeve of his hoodie. "So, once Amanda uploaded everything to my account, I wanted to take a quick peek and see if I could get a better idea of what we were dealing with."

"You've already analyzed them?" Leigh looked at her friend admiringly, impressed with his speed, but he shook his head.

"No, there's too much for that right now. I was only looking to get a general idea of it, so I focused on a few spreadsheets. There were quite a few with lists of names alongside amounts of money."

"Members of Vasiliev's organization, maybe?" Leigh mused. "Although I'm not sure where the money is connected. We already knew about his money-laundering schemes, but it would be tracked through organizations, not individuals."

"What about gambling debts?" Amanda offered. "Maybe these were his records for some type of underground betting."

This time Leigh turned her admiration toward Amanda. "You know, that could be." Amanda beamed.

Max, however, seemed less than convinced. "Yeah, I thought of those things, too, but why would Vasiliev care so much if that got out? I mean, there wouldn't be anything there more incriminating than what they have on him already."

Leigh's spirits fell. "True. So, what's your guess?"

"Well," he responded, "I'm not sure exactly, but I

looked up some of the names, and that's where it got weird."

"Anybody famous?" Amanda asked.

Max tilted his hand back and forth. "That's the weird part. Five years ago, when that list was made? No. Not a single person on the lists would've been anyone of interest. But now? In the past year or so, more than half of them have emerged as candidates for positions in all levels of Swedish politics."

Leigh drew a breath as her nerves jangled. Given his ties to Russia and suspected sympathy for the KGB, Vasiliev and politics was not a good mix. "*Sverigedemokraterna?*" she guessed. It would make sense, as Henrik had mentioned the growing power of Vasiliev's alt-right connections.

"What's that?" Amanda asked.

"They're the Sweden Democrats," Max explained, "a very conservative, xenophobic political party that has become increasingly popular in the past few years. And their followers are notorious for falling for—what is it your president calls it? Fake news? Anything anti-Muslim, anti-immigrant."

"Anti-immigrant?" A deep line creased Amanda's forehead. She turned questioningly to Leigh. "But Vasiliev was involved with the foundation your mother worked for, and I thought they were supposed to help immigrants."

Leigh nodded, frowning as well. "They do. So, what is it? Maybe he doesn't see eye to eye with the rest of his alt-right buddies about the immigration issue, and he's funding candidates who do?"

Max shook his head. "That's where it gets even weirder. The candidates were spread out over all the major parties. There's no rhyme or reason to it. They have nothing in common. Different regions, different politics. The only thing that ties them all together is their names are on Vasiliev's list." He crammed a last bite of waffle into his mouth and stood. "Time to get you back to the station."

When they were back on the platform, Max reached into his wallet and pulled out a heaping wad of bills, stuffing them into Leigh's hand. "Here, I insist. Just in case you run into any more unexpected trouble."

Far from protesting, Leigh wanted to kiss her old friend for his generosity. She settled on a warm handshake, knowing that such a public display of affection would keep Max holed up in his house for weeks. "Thank you for all your help."

Max smiled sheepishly, and a little color made its way to his cheeks. "I'll keep working on it. Be careful."

Something about the whole situation with Vasiliev wasn't right, but it wasn't until they were settled into their seats, the train rattling its way toward Stockholm, that Leigh had a chance to broach the topic with Amanda.

"Why align himself with the alt-right?"

"You mean Vasiliev?" Amanda paused as she

mulled it over. "They're powerful, with groups all over the place. Maybe he knew they could get him out of jail."

It was plausible, but the whole thing still didn't sit right with Leigh. "Their anti-immigration stance is legendary. It doesn't fit with what I knew of him. He may be a lot of things, like a ruthless criminal and all around cunning bastard, but he wasn't like *that*. He wasn't a true believer of the alt-right."

"How can you be sure?"

Leigh couldn't. Like so many things with her, it was just a gut feeling, but she tried to put it into words. "Like, he supported Natasha's work with immigrants. That was sincere, I'm almost certain. Not to mention, he had no problem with her dating me, at least not that he ever let on. It doesn't fit the profile of someone with that type of ultra-conservative, nationalist leanings. And yet, Henrik said he had connections there, and according to what Max found, he has connections everywhere. But why? None of it makes sense."

Amanda nodded slowly. "Power, maybe, but he's not even putting his voice behind one party. You're right. It makes no sense."

Leigh continued to try to fit the pieces together the rest of the way to Stockholm, but it was no use. They simply refused to form a coherent picture. Her only hope now was to confirm once and for all that Vasiliev was the Mule, and discover what was so important about whatever his meeting was at the Vasa Museum on Tuesday evening- that Henrik was willing to write her a message about it in his last moments of life. If that didn't shed some light on what was going on with Vasiliev, Leigh feared the answers may have died with her mentor.

TWENTY-FOUR

LEIGH GROANED as she struggled to move her weary head in slow circles as they walked along the crowded Stockholm street to the safe house, her muscles after the abuse of so much travel having become resistant to the very concept of exercise. Everything was stiff. How her great-grandparents had managed to spend an entire summer sleeping on the narrow bunks of her family boat was beyond Leigh's imagination—though if Amanda's version of the story was correct, they'd been having too much sex to notice such minor discomfort. The mental image *that* conjured still made her shudder.

Leigh had not had the same set of romantic circumstances on her voyage, not by a long shot. The crick in her neck from the uncomfortable pillows was bad enough, but paled in comparison to the shear torture of spending three nights in a row in such close proximity to Amanda. Aside from their one encounter the night of the dance club, they'd gone the whole time without so much as brushing fingertips together, let alone a kiss or something more. Leigh knew where it would lead, and it was someplace she just couldn't go. A spy's life was a lonely one, and one that she had chosen, but the pain of restraint was excruciating. She was in desperate need of some space to herself, and a proper bed, and a good night's sleep to maintain that resolve.

The flat in Stockholm that served as a secure place for agents to stay when business brought them to the city did, indeed, have a bed. It was of the loft variety that was common in the city, where the living room furniture sat on the bare wooden floor and a ladder led to a platform high above, where the bed was situated. There was no safety railing, which was not a problem for Leigh who had no fear of heights, but the look Amanda had given it was dubious at best, and for a brief moment, Leigh entertained the idea that she might actually get her wish for a night alone.

In addition to the bed, the flat had another necessity, a shower, which proved to be the undoing of her wish. With an unlimited supply of hot water and an array of soaps and shampoos, plus a linen closet stocked with luxuriously thick towels and even a few terry cloth bathrobes like the ones handed out in five-star hotels, using it had been high on both Leigh's and Amanda's lists of priorities upon arrival. Though glorious while it lasted, it introduced a whole new set of unforeseen complications.

Upon inspection, the flat was found to be fully stocked with food and water and all the other comforts of home—pods for the coffee maker, tea bags, even a few pints of ice cream in the freezer. In fact, the only thing it lacked was clean clothing. This wouldn't have presented an issue for an agent arriving fresh from the airport with luggage in hand, but in Leigh and Amanda's case, their suitcases had been abandoned in the bedroom of a medieval hotel in Visby as they tried to stay one step ahead of Russian mobsters. This is why, when their showers were complete and they were both wrapped up in their robes and sipping their mugs of herbal tea in preparation for a restful sleep, they both realized somewhat simultaneously that they had nothing clean to wear to bed.

Leigh was the first to rise from the couch, cinching the belt of her robe tightly around her waist as she did, and giving a long look first to the ladder that led to the loft, then to Amanda, and finally to the couch that definitely did *not* fold out into another bed.

That she *wanted* to share the bed with Amanda wasn't in question. She ached with wanting it, and all that it would inevitably lead to. But she couldn't. Nothing had changed since that night on the boat, except that, if anything, all the risks had increased. Though it felt like a lull right now, Leigh knew it was merely the calm before the storm, and the storm on the horizon was a deadly one. They were still on the run, Amanda's life still in danger from Vasiliev, and all because of Leigh.

It was her fault Amanda was in the middle of this. No matter how badly she wished she could, Leigh couldn't let herself get too close, not with the chance that she would lose all perspective and start making mistakes. Her duty was to protect the innocent woman she'd dragged into this mess. Loving her would only put her in greater danger. She'd learned that lesson in the hardest possible way once before. She couldn't do it again.

Leigh focused on the floor, sizing up its potential as a sleeping surface. *With a few cushions and a blanket…*

"Nope," Amanda said flatly. "I'm not sleeping on the floor."

"I wasn't going to suggest—" Leigh started to protest, but of course it was impossible for her to get away with a lie like that. Amanda saw right through that type of thing, and had obviously caught her eyeing the empty space between the sofa and the television "I thought you didn't like heights," she insisted instead, changing strategy. She might be on the brink of falling helplessly in love with the woman, but that didn't mean she was willing to give up one perfect night of sleep without a fight.

"I don't like heights, but not so much I'm giving up my claim to the bed. And I'm not sleeping in my robe, either," Amanda added, beating her to the next suggestion. "It's really, really damp. And my clothing smells so bad I may have to put it out in the hall until I have the energy to wash it, so you can forget about that, too."

Leigh clamped her lips together, her final proposal nixed before she'd had a chance to say the words. "Fine. We're both adults. I'm sure we can come up with a sensible solution so we can both get some rest without tempting ourselves with anything we'd regret."

Amanda rolled her eyes. "*You'd* regret, you mean. But, whatever."

In the end, they agreed on each going up in their robes, one at a time, and settling in, far apart, on opposite sides of the bed. Only when the covers were pulled up to their chins, the bedside light turned off and blackout curtains closed against the eternal daylight outside, would either of them disrobe. It was a solid plan under the circumstances, but as Leigh drifted into a fitful sleep, her dreams made her restless and troubled despite the comfortable accommodations.

"Leigh? The bed's so high." Leigh distinctly heard Amanda whisper in her ear and snuggle up beside her, but when her eyes flew open, heart racing, Amanda was fast asleep on the other side of the bed and the voice nothing but a particularly vivid remnant of a dream.

Leigh closed her eyes again and felt an odd sensation in her limbs, almost like she was floating, as every part of her body rocked gently with the remembered movement of long days aboard a boat. She flitted in and out of consciousness, uncertain how much time had passed or exactly where she was, as images of sunlight sparkling on water filled her senses, and the imagined smell of strawberries teased her nose.

Despite being still in her bed, Leigh's body insisted it was in motion, the constant sense of swaying continuing until something like a weight seemed to settle on top of her, pressing her down into the rumpled sheets. "I still can't sleep," Amanda's voice whispered again, somewhere in the far corners of her mind. There was no escaping her. The woman whose nearness had tormented her for days now haunted her dreams.

But now they were back on the boat, back on the bunk with its red velvet cushions, and the taste of strawberries was strong on Leigh's lips as her mouth devoured Amanda's in a frenzy. In the dream, she didn't push her away. In the dream, Leigh was free to explore every inch of Amanda's mouth, to nip at her lip and swipe her tongue along her perfect, shining teeth without worrying about the dangers of getting in too deep. She pressed her mouth to Amanda's collarbone, savoring her taste, unabashed at leaving a pink, strawberry-shaped mark on the skin.

After an eternity, they broke from their kisses. Leigh tensed as Amanda's head dipped lower, the reflexes of that small part of her that even in her dreams knew she should stop. But as Amanda captured one swollen nipple with her lips, Leigh relaxed. Dreams had no consequences. She breathed in and out as Amanda's tongue trailed across her belly, letting her knees fall to each side as her head traveled lower still. Leigh's own breath came faster and shallower as Amanda's breath tickled the hair between her legs, and then her breathing stopped altogether momentarily as Amanda's tongue pressed into her, overwhelming her with the most pleasurable aching sensation that filled her completely.

Even as she dreamed it, Leigh was somehow conscious that it was the best dream she'd ever had, or probably ever would have. It was everything she could want—and everything she couldn't have—but here, she could. She gave herself completely to the fantasy, twining her fingers through the imaginary tendrils of Amanda's hair, immersed in an experience too sweet to exist in reality.

At last, they rested, their bodies folded together in an intricate origami. Amanda's head rested on Leigh's chest, the hair she'd run her fingers through with abandon spread out like a fan that tickled her chin and lips. She breathed in and held it, savoring the moment. "I love you," she whispered as she breathed out, because it was only a dream, and she could.

"I love you, too," came Amanda's breathy response, because in a dream it could happen no other way.

A SOUND somewhere in the apartment startled Leigh awake. The first thing she became aware of was the fact that Amanda's stark naked body was just as it had been in her dream, so completely entwined with hers that they might be mistaken for conjoined twins. Though the night had certainly been nothing but a fantasy, at least some part of it had merged with reality, and Leigh's head ached as it tried to sort out where fantasy had ended and reality begun.

She had little time to ponder what had or had not happened—whether there might have actually been a kiss, or whether one touch or another had been imagined or true—as the real shock hit just seconds later when she registered that Javier's face was peering at her over the platform of the loft bed. Though she might wish it with all her might, *that* was absolutely not a dream.

Her mouth flew open as she tried to outline for Javier the exact sequence of events that had led to her and Amanda being discovered in their current, indelicate position, but she only got as far as, "I can explain…" when Javier pressed his finger to his lips and shook his head.

"No need. I can see for myself."

With dawning mortification, Leigh realized exactly how true his statement was. There was almost nothing he *couldn't* see. In addition to unconsciously migrating into the compromising situation she and Amanda now found themselves in, they'd also managed to kick the covers and sheets clear off their bodies, leaving them completely on display. In a rush, Leigh made a grab for the top sheet. She succeeded instead in grasping a handful of Amanda's ass, which resulted in Amanda's eyes flying open in shock, fully awake.

"What the hell?"

"We have company."

Amanda screeched, and then accidentally clutched Leigh's breasts to cover in a fit of modesty, instead of her own.

"Why don't I just wait down below?" Javier suggested as his head dipped out of sight. Leigh could hear his laughter all the way down the ladder.

Wrapped tightly back in her robe, Leigh joined him on the main floor. "Why are you here?" she demanded. She wanted to place her hands on her hips for emphasis, but held back and continued to clutch the robe to her throat with one hand, knowing that if it fell open now, she'd die right there on the spot.

Javier's mouth muscles twitched wildly, but he managed not to smirk. "I got your message about Henrik, and I decided it was too dangerous for you to be here working alone."

"I'm not alone. Amanda's here."

"Yes, I saw that." The slightest snicker escaped. "But you know what I mean. You need backup, and I come bearing intel."

Amanda joined the two of them at the base of the ladder. "What kind of intel?" she asked, avoiding eye contact with either one of them.

"Have you found out anything about the Vasa Museum on Tuesday night?" Leigh prompted.

"As a matter of fact, I have." Javier produced a stack of documents with a flourish. "There's a fundraising gala that night. It's for some charity, the Foundation for Swedish Heritage. Do you know it?"

Beside her, Amanda drew a sharp breath, and Leigh's pulse quickened as she replied, "They work with immigrants. My mother worked there for years, and Vasiliev has ties to it, too. So, yes, I'm familiar with it."

Javier looked surprised by the news. "Most people I spoke with in D.C. seemed either to have never heard of it, or to have a vague sense that they do some good but they weren't sure what. However, a few years back some of our agencies found a disturbing trend with the foundation's research and policy papers."

"Leigh, remember what Henrik said?" Amanda grasped Leigh's arm as she spoke, and for just a moment, neither of them remembered to be embarrassed. "Do you think there's a connection?"

"The case studies," Leigh said, her eyes widening. "The ones that led to her calling Säpo in the first place."

"Yes, funny you should mention case studies," Javier continued, thumbing through his notes. "Several

US agencies and NGOs are questioning the validity of those. It was high profile a few years ago, although that's now somewhat suppressed with this new administration. The reports on it had been pulled from the various department websites. I had to go to the archives to find copies."

"And they're the ones holding a fundraising gala the day mentioned in Henrik's message." Leigh's expression was grim as she pondered the connection between her mother, the Foundation, and Vasiliev's files. She wasn't sure what to make of it yet, but she wasn't about to give up until she did. "So, what's the plan?"

"The two of us will go to the gala as guests."

"Excuse me?" Amanda crossed her arms, causing her robe to gape open to show an alarming amount of chest, and Leigh could feel her whole body hum in response though she immediately looked elsewhere. "What am I supposed to do?"

"Well, you're not going to the gala," Javier stated matter-of-factly.

"You're a civilian," Leigh added, still studying the coffee table.

"So, what, I should just sit in the apartment and watch TV?"

"Sure, why not?" Javier smiled and reached for the remote control, clicking the television on as if to demonstrate what a good choice it could be. "I'm sure there are plenty of things to watch."

He flipped the channels but stopped abruptly as Leigh's face appeared on the screen. Alongside it ran grainy footage of both Leigh and Amanda in one of their disguises, captured from a security camera at one of their stops. Leigh read the headline in Swedish and groaned.

Amanda looked stricken as they replayed the footage. "Leigh, what does it say?"

"Wanted in connection with the murder of a Säpo agent," Leigh translated flatly.

"Shit." Javier let out a breath. "Looks like you're out of the game, Leigh. And I've gotta run. I have a meeting at Säpo headquarters in an hour. I'll have them find someone to go with me to the gala. And I'll see if I can have them straighten out *that*," he promised, pointing to the screen. "And send over some clothing, too. Unless you ladies would prefer I didn't?"

Though he was trying to lighten the mood, Leigh nearly slammed the door on his rear end on the way out.

"Damn it!" Leigh fumed.

"Relax, Leigh. I think that was just a joke about the clothes."

"That's not why I'm upset. I can't believe I'm being benched!"

"Gee, it's no fun being left out, is it?" If Leigh had expected sympathy, she received little from Amanda on the issue.

Leigh settled herself onto the couch with a sigh,

feeling as if they'd gone over this before. "There's a difference. My job is to put myself on the line, in part to protect civilians like you so that you're not at risk."

"Well, maybe I don't mind the risk." Amanda's tone was earnest, her eyes pleading. "Maybe I want to take it."

"It's my job."

"Maybe I want it to be mine, too."

Leigh sighed again. They'd *definitely* had this conversation before. "We talked about this, Amanda. There are so many other things you could do."

"Yes, you explained that. But it hasn't changed my mind, Leigh. I've never felt like I had so much purpose before. How can I give that up? Besides, if I were an agent instead of a civilian, maybe this thing between us would have a better chance."

"This…thing?" Leigh's heart skittered erratically in her chest. "You mean, like dating, or something."

"Yes, or something. Not that we've been on an actual date, but whatever." Amanda's cheeks flushed but she pushed on. "The point is, I understand your concerns about being with a civilian—"

"Yeah," Leigh said with a snort, "they die."

"But, I thought if we were both agents—"

"An agent?" The word caused Leigh's panic to tick higher. "Amanda, do you know the only thing worse than an agent dating a civilian? An agent dating another agent!"

Amanda's eyes narrowed. "But, if you can't be with a civilian and you can't be with another agent—"

"Agents die, too," Leigh reasoned. "Look at Henrik."

"Everybody dies!" Amanda's eyes flashed. "Listen to me. If you can't be with a civilian and you can't be with another agent, who exactly does that leave, Leigh?"

"No one!" Leigh trembled in every fingertip and toe. "I thought I'd made that clear."

Tears welled in Amanda's eyes and her bottom lip trembled. "And I thought, when you said that you..."

She swallowed roughly and paused to take a deep breath. As she did, the top of her robe gaped and Leigh thought she caught a glimpse of a pink mark, roughly the shape of a strawberry, on her collarbone. Before Leigh could confirm it, Amanda had pulled the robe tightly across her chest. Still, it haunted her.

"Said what?" Leigh struggled to keep her body from shaking uncontrollably as she waited for the answer. "What did I say?"

But Amanda squared her shoulders and looked away. "Look, let's discuss it later. Right now, we have to figure out how we're getting into the gala."

"The gala?" Still shaken, Leigh struggled to switch gears. "We can't both go, and I don't just mean because you're a civilian."

"Then why?" Amanda's voice was disturbingly cold.

"Practically speaking? We'll have to fund this mission ourselves. Max only gave me enough money to cover one fancy dress. And since Max is *my* childhood friend, and *I* have the money, *I* get to decide who wears it." *So too bad for you.* Amazingly, though their unfinished conversation left her feeling unbearably punchy, she managed to keep the last part to herself, although it was strongly implied.

Amanda just smiled in amusement. "You're thinking about this all wrong. It's a party. They have caterers."

"So?"

"So, there are a ton of them and they don't wear fancy dresses, just uniforms."

"It'll never work. The catering company would know right away we didn't belong."

"Um, no," Amanda scoffed. "Not if Sweden's anything like back home. Those people are all temps. Trust me."

Leigh had the uncomfortable feeling that Amanda was onto something, so she resisted. "I don't know the first thing about catering."

"Well, I do. I've done it plenty of times. Haven't you at least ever had to go undercover as a waitress or a bartender?" Sullenly, Leigh nodded that she had. "Same thing. At least look to see who the caterer is and what the uniforms look like."

Leigh pulled out her phone and did a quick search. The museum contracted with a single caterer for all their events, and a quick look at the company's site showed a row of staff wearing simple black pants and shirts with black aprons and hats.

"Perfect!" Amanda clapped her hands together approvingly. "I don't know Swedish money, but I think Max gave us enough to rent two of those, don't you?"

Leigh hesitated and Amanda crossed her arms once more, this time exposing so much skin that Leigh had to look away entirely, lest she see the unmistakable strawberry mark and have to face for certain what now she only feared she had done.

"Look, I'll steal one if I have to," Amanda threatened. "I know you're going to find a way to go, and I'm not letting you go without me."

Leigh fumed silently, while Amanda chattered on about how to procure uniforms and blend in with the catering staff. She could still say no to Amanda and insist that she stay behind, handcuff her if she had to —though sadly the pink fuzzy cuffs had been left behind in the luggage—but she wouldn't. Eventually, Amanda would wear her down and she'd give in. Reaching for her phone once more, Leigh decided to spare them both the trouble and just give in now.

"Fine," she told Amanda, her voice grumpy but her heart growing lighter in spite of it all as a brilliant smile spread across Amanda's face. "I'll call around to some uniform rental places and see what I can find."

TWENTY-FIVE

IT WAS JUST BEFORE six o'clock on Tuesday evening as the first guests, dressed in their formal attire, filtered into the main entrance of the Vasa Museum. The Foundation for Swedish Heritage's fundraising gala was one of the highlights of the Stockholm social season, and a crowd had gathered outside to catch a glimpse of local celebrities as they arrived. Meanwhile, Leigh and Amanda stood near the service entrance, dressed in their catering uniforms, and away from the limelight.

"How does this look?" Leigh held out her arms, ready for inspection.

Amanda scanned Leigh's ensemble with an appraising eye, straightening out the bow on her full-length black apron and brushing a piece of lint from her crisp uniform shirt. The Bluetooth earpiece she wore was noticeable at the bottom of her right earlobe and Amanda fluffed the dark bobbed wig forward to conceal it. She gave a satisfied nod. "I think you're good to go. Is everything ready?"

Javier's contact at Säpo had procured a guest list for the evening, and as soon as they'd spotted Vasiliev's name on the major donor list, both Leigh and Amanda had felt certain that it confirmed him as the Mule. Javier had been more inclined to take a wait and see approach, pointing out several other people of interest among the guests, but Leigh and Amanda needed no convincing. Whatever was going to happen at 6:45 tonight, Vasiliev would be involved. Without the backing of her agency and with only limited funds consisting mainly of Max's money with just a little extra cash that Leigh had managed to convince Javier she might need for incidentals, Leigh had quickly improvised a plan that built on Amanda's initial suggestion of the catering disguise.

"Okay, here's the burner cell." Leigh pulled out one of three throwaway phones they'd purchased the day before and handed it to Amanda. "I've already installed the surveillance app and paired it with my earpiece. Once we're inside, I'll point out Vasiliev as soon as I spot him, then you look for an opportunity to slip the phone into his pocket. Are you sure you can handle it?"

Amanda's fingers tensed around the phone as the risk of what she was about to do hit her, but then dropped it into the front of her apron in a show of slightly more bravado than she felt. "No problem. I managed to take your wallet off you the other day, didn't I? And you didn't feel a thing."

"That's the only reason I'm even considering letting you do this," Leigh gave a slight shudder. "If Vasiliev catches you—"

"He won't. And if for some reason he looks like he might, I'll spill a tray of hors d'oeuvres down his front for a distraction." To gain the greatest access to the crowd, they'd both decided to grab silver trays and blend in with the staff serving hors d'oeuvres.

Leigh's horrified expression left little doubt how she felt about Amanda's improvisation. "You have the other phone, right? If anything happens and I'm not around, just slip away and send me a text." The corners of Leigh's mouth sank into a troubled frown. "I wish I knew exactly what was going on here tonight, so that we could do this some other way. I'm the one who should be doing all of this. You shouldn't even be here."

Amanda clasped Leigh's hand and gave it a squeeze. "I'll be okay. He has no idea who I am, so he's not going to suspect anything. You just keep out of sight, okay? We don't need Vasiliev catching you."

When Amanda thought about what would happen if Vasiliev recognized Leigh, it made her insides flip. The crowd at the cocktail hour would provide some cover, but the limited range of the Bluetooth device was a source of deep concern to Amanda. To keep it connected so that Leigh could listen in on Vasiliev's conversations, she'd need to stay within about thirty feet of the phone, or even less if he went behind a wall or heavy door. Though her disguise was as good as any Amanda had seen, being spotted was a real risk. She also knew that for the chance to figure out whatever intel Henrik had been onto before his death, Leigh was likely to risk far more than she should.

"Come on," Leigh said, straightening her back and squaring her soldiers like a soldier marching into battle. "Let's go."

They walked through the service entrance into the kitchen virtually unnoticed, as dozens of catering staff dressed in black uniforms identical to theirs, bustled around the steaming stovetops or heaped food onto platters. The first round of appetizers was on its way out the door, and it was easy enough for Leigh and Amanda to join the line of waitstaff in grabbing trays. When they were on the main floor, Amanda stopped and stared in disbelief.

The massive seventeenth-century warship, its heavily carved oak darkened with age and centuries spent underwater, stood hulking in the middle of the cavernous space. Its masts soared to a ceiling that was almost out of sight, it's keel nestled in a series of metal braces several stories below. From where she stood, Amanda had a perfect view of the beak-shaped bow that jutted out toward the clusters of tables where guests mingled and sipped their drinks. Most seemed unaffected to be in the presence of the four-hundred-year-old ship, but the sight of it filled Amanda with awe. Though Leigh had described it to her, it was much larger and more spectacular than she could've believed if she hadn't seen it herself.

"*Kom igen då. Folk väntar. Skynda dig!*"

She didn't know what had been said, but it hadn't been nice. Amanda stiffened, unsure what to do, as a Swedish-speaking voice barked in her ear. A man dressed in a catering uniform, but wearing a bow tie that seemed to designate some sort of authority, stepped around the spot where Amanda was frozen in place, looking irate.

"Bah! Another one who doesn't speak Swedish?" he muttered, this time in English. "I get so tired of all you eastern foreigners who only want to speak in English. I said get going. People are waiting!"

Amanda continued to stare in silence, struck dumb by the harshness in his tone. Considering they were at a benefit for an organization dedicated to serving immigrants and foreign workers, his attitude toward someone he assumed to be a recent immigrant seemed particularly out of place.

He rolled his eyes. "Please tell me you at least speak *English*?"

"Yes. Yes, a little," Amanda answered, affecting some vaguely foreign accent to her words. Thinking quickly, she'd surmised that foreign workers who were fluent in American English might be as thin on the ground among the serving staff as were fluent Swedish speakers. The last thing Amanda wanted was to call attention to herself by not seeming to be what he expected.

The supervisor shook his head in disgust. "Just get the food to the guests, all right? You think you can manage that?"

"Food on trays," Amanda said, milking the accent for all it was worth. "I bring now, yes?"

"Yes." With another roll of the eyes, he walked away.

"What the hell kind of an accent was that?" Leigh's voice was low in her ear as she came up behind Amanda, holding her own tray.

"A 'foreign' one." She used her free hand to trace air quotes. "He started talking to me in Swedish and when I didn't understand, I think he thought I was Eastern European. I had to think fast."

"Eastern European, huh?" Leigh chuckled, clearly amused. "It might not have been the best accent I've ever heard, but once again, I can't fault you for your instincts. If nothing else, you're good at thinking on your feet."

While Leigh melted into the crowd to search for Vasiliev, Amanda carried her tray around. Mostly the conversations were lost on her, but every so often she would come across a person speaking English and her ears would immediately perk up. As she approached one table, she heard a woman speaking to a man.

"It's quite a crisis, isn't it?" the woman said, using that overly important voice often reserved for stuffy cocktail party chatter. "Who knew that when Sweden opened its borders to so many refugees back in 2012, it would lead to this."

"Oh, I agree," the man said, reaching for a stuffed mushroom from Amanda's tray. "I fully supported it back then, but I'll admit I've begun to change my mind."

"You're not the only one," the woman said. "Have you read the Foundation's latest report?"

"I saw the draft. To be honest, that has had a lot to do with my change of heart. With all they've done for these immigrant communities, if even *they* see so little hope of integration, what chance is there?"

As she moved on to the next table, Amanda was reminded of the case studies, the one Henrik had said Leigh's mother was concerned about. Grossly misrepresenting data, he'd said. And Javier, too, had mentioned that the Foundation's reports had grown increasingly unreliable. And yet if these two guests were any indication, the average person on the street saw no reason to doubt the Foundation's findings as real. Amanda was still mulling over the implications of the conversation she'd overheard when Leigh appeared by her side.

"I found Vasiliev," she whispered, cupping her hand underneath Amanda's elbow and rotating her about twenty degrees to her left. "The large, balding man with the thick black mustache."

Amanda spotted a man matching Leigh's description standing several yards away, resting an elbow on a tall cocktail table. "In the blue jacket?" Leigh nodded. "Okay. I'm on it."

Palming the cell phone in her right hand, Amanda held the tray in her left as she approached the Russian crime boss. His bald head was so shiny that she could see the reflection of the lights on his scalp. Even so, it wasn't nearly as sweaty as the hand that held the phone. She tightened her grip and prayed it wouldn't slip.

"Hors d'oeuvres?" Though her heart threatened to beat itself out of her chest, she held the tray steady and waited as the Russian crime boss studied it with a frown.

"What is it?"

"Mushrooms." His nose wrinkled and she could tell that he was about to refuse. "I made them myself," she added coquettishly. His jacket pocket was out of reach and she needed to buy herself more time.

"Did you?" Vasiliev's eyes raked across her chest and down her body, and there was no doubt that he was less interested in her skills in the kitchen than in other rooms of the house, the bedroom in particular.

"Well, not really." Sizing him up quickly, she decided that the damsel in distress was her best approach. She batted her lashes and shifted closer, even though the thought of coming within fifty feet of the lecherous mobster filled her with revulsion. "The truth is, we get paid by the tray and my boss was very mean to me today and gave me the least popular choice. Who likes mushrooms, right? I'll be lucky to make enough to pay my rent."

"That's terrible! Point him out to me." The man's scowl was truly frightening and Amanda nearly took a step backward before she remembered her goal was to move closer, not farther away.

"No, no. I don't want him to get into too much trouble." Amanda pushed the tray a little closer, using the motion to position the hand with the phone just above his pocket. "But maybe you can take one, even if you don't eat it."

Vasiliev reached for the tray. "I'll take two." As he was distracted with selecting the mushrooms, Amanda let the phone drop. It slid into his jacket pocket with ease.

"Thank you!" Amanda lifted the tray casually and took a step away, stifling her urge to run as fast as she could. Before she could manage her escape, she felt the grip of strong fingers on her wrist. She spun back around to see Vasiliev patting the pocket where she'd just deposited the phone.

"Wait a moment." Amanda froze in fear, but then he moved to a different pocket before reaching inside. Still grasping her wrist, he flipped her hand over a banknote into her palm. "To make up for your boss."

She glanced at the bill uncertainly. Five hundred kronor. *Is that a lot?* It felt like a lot, but she couldn't remember. *It could be just a few bucks.* She hesitated, uncertain how grateful to appear.

"Maybe later on, I'll find you, see if you have any more mushrooms?"

This was not a man with an interest in mushrooms. *I guess it's a big enough tip that he thinks* that's *going to work.* She smiled as coyly as her inner revulsion would allow and slipped the tip into her pocket. "I'll be on the lookout for you, trust me." It was true, too. Just not in the way he hoped. If she saw him again, she might stab him.

Finally, free from the encounter, Amanda ditched her tray as soon as she could and went to the kitchen to find Leigh. Her body buzzed from a cocktail of adrenaline and pride. *I handled that like a pro!* She'd managed to pull off a textbook drop, even if she *had* been propositioned by a pervy Russian in the process. *Just another hazard of the job,* she reminded herself, as if she actually had the first clue what she was talking about. By the time she spotted Leigh, she was barely able to contain her cockiness. "Done. Your turn."

LEIGH CHECKED THE CLOCK. It was 6:42. Just three minutes to go until the time mentioned in Henrik's message, and nothing was out of the ordinary. On the other side of the room, Leigh could make out Javier and his date chatting with one of the persons of interest he had identified earlier from the guest list. His face was intense and he looked very pleased with himself over something, though when he'd seen Vasiliev earlier, he'd hardly said a word to him. *Damn it! Is it possible I guessed wrong?*

Then again, he might've just been gloating over the fact that, in addition to no doubt being a highly qualified member of law enforcement, his undercover Säpo agent date had the body of a supermodel and legs up to her chin. Leigh rolled her eyes. *Javi's a leg man, all right.* She was still positive Vasiliev was the Mule, even though, while most of the guests had begun making their way to their seats for dinner, he remained where Leigh had found him, lounging against the cocktail table and doing nothing. Sure, he chatted or shook hands as people went by, but he sought out no one in particular and did nothing of interest.

6:43.

Leigh's nerve endings burned from being on constant high alert. She checked the earpiece in her ear for the hundredth time. It was still working. From deep within Vasiliev's pocket, the phone's microphone was picking up every word, relaying it directly to her ear via the app she'd installed. When he spoke, she could hear his voice as clearly as if she were standing beside him, and anyone who spoke around him, too. She was ready, if he'd ever make a move.

6:44.

Testing the limits of her Bluetooth range, Leigh took several steps in the opposite direction of Vasiliev's table, counting each step as roughly a foot. At thirty-two steps, the sound became choppy. At thirty-four steps, it stopped. She took two steps back and could once again hear his voice. *Thirty-four feet - that's as far as I can go.*

The screech of a microphone being turned on filled the room, and immediately there was a drop in the volume of chatter as conversations were cut short. The last stragglers took their seats at the long banquet tables close to the stage. Leigh looked at the clock again. It was precisely 6:45 and the keynote speaker was at the podium, adjusting her notes and getting ready to begin.

Leigh's eyes darted to where Vasiliev had been standing. He was no longer there, but his assigned seat at the dinner table remained empty, too. As a woman's voice from the distant stage welcomed the guests, Leigh spotted the back of Vasiliev's bald head at the outskirts of the room. She moved a few steps in his direction, her heart picking up its pace as she closed the distance enough to hear a voice through her headset again, but it was not Vasiliev who spoke. It belonged to a man, and even after five years, Leigh couldn't help but recognize it.

"Anatoly!" The voice ringing in Leigh's ear belonged to Per Nilsson, the head of the Foundation for Swedish Heritage. They were not well acquainted, but the last time she'd heard that voice, it had been giving a eulogy at her mother's funeral. "It's good to see you free again, my friend."

"It's good to be back," Vasiliev replied warmly. From her vantage point, Leigh could just make out the two men shaking hands in the shadows. "And I appreciate you putting in a good word for me. It was crucial to the suspension of my sentence."

"Well, it was all true. No matter what else, there's no denying the dedication, not to mention money, that both you and your daughter gave the Foundation over the years."

Anger burned in Leigh's chest. The mere mention of Natasha, a woman who had worked so selflessly for the betterment of society, in the same sentence as her criminal father defiled her memory. So distracted was she by her sudden flare-up of emotions that she nearly missed the fact that the two men were on the move, only noticing when the earpiece cut out. They'd made it all the way to the staircase and were part way down to the museum's lower exhibit floor by the time she closed the gap enough to hear more.

"...the latest reports." Nilsson was speaking when Leigh regained audio. "I've highlighted key phrases for you to incorporate in the speech markups, along with some alternatives in case you want to change them based on affiliation."

"No." Vasiliev's tone was emphatic. "Using the

same phrases across party lines is vital to our success, and you need to be sure to promote consistency on your end, as well. When people hear something from one source, they may question the motive. When they hear it from multiple and opposing sources, they begin to see it as fact."

"I won't argue. Your country's use of *alternative facts* is nothing short of masterful."

Nilsson's wording gave Leigh pause. *Your country? He definitely isn't talking about Sweden.* It could only mean one thing—definitive proof that Anatoly Vasiliev was not just a mobster, but was actively working on behalf of Russia. *He's the Mule, all right. Moscow's Mule.* Judging by the direction of the conversation, the head of the Foundation for Swedish Heritage was in bed with the Kremlin, too. But for how long? *Was he already working with Russia during my mother's time?*

The sound of Vasiliev's chuckle, so close to her ear, made Leigh's skin crawl. "Yes. If only it were as easy here as it is in America."

"You're well ahead of schedule," Nilsson assured him, or at least Leigh was fairly certain those were his words. They'd reached the lower level of exhibit space and had disappeared behind a tall partition, which interfered with the sound and made it choppy.

Leigh surveyed the space with trepidation. Despite the partitions and the deep shadows they cast, the space was too wide open and well-lit to provide reliable cover. The safest course of action was to go upstairs, find Javier, and tell him everything she'd heard. He'd tear her limbs off her body for disobeying his orders, not to mention dragging Amanda into it, too, but after that, he and the Säpo supermodel could set up long-term surveillance on both Vasiliev and Nilsson.

Eventually, over the course of weeks or months, if not years, they'd get to the bottom of whatever these two traitors were cooking up. *Or, I can just take a few steps closer to the wall and find out right now.* Leigh took a deliberate step in the direction of the partition.

"We have fourteen of our people recently seated on county councils, and several more on board to run in the next election cycle." Vasiliev's voice once more filled her ears. "That's in addition to the members of Parliament, of course, who are well established now. I've heard one of them is likely to be named the next Minister of Culture. I'm certain that's due in large part to your influence."

"Getting one of our organization's loyal members as a Head of Ministry would be a major coup. Can you feel it, Anatoly? We're just a heartbeat away from Prime Minister."

Leigh shivered violently, her whole body nearly numb from the shock of what she'd overheard. *Exactly what is this organization of theirs?* Though he'd surely meant the word *coup* in terms of achieving a brilliant success, she couldn't help but conjure up images of the word's other meaning—a violent overthrow of the government. *Is that their ultimate goal, to take over the Swedish government?*

She was in over her head, and she knew it. What had started as a mid-level mobster with a personal grudge against her had turned into a potential plot to overthrow a major Western democracy. As Leigh crept through the shadows toward the stairs, preparing to find Javier and come clean, what she heard through her earpiece stopped her dead in her tracks.

"What the hell is this?" Vasiliev's booming voice sounded mostly puzzled, but with an underlying hint of his ever-present paranoia. "This isn't my phone."

TWENTY-SIX

SHIT. *He's found the phone that Amanda planted in his pocket.*

Leigh held her breath, crouching as if to become one with the shadow that was the only shield between her and discovery should the two men reemerge from behind the partition.

As if to confirm her suspicion, Vasiliev's next words rang out with the force of a canon. "Are you spying on me?"

He'd yelled it directly into the phone's mic so that it was all Leigh could do not to scream at the sudden and intense pain in her ear canal, even as his voice simultaneously echoed through the vast exhibit hall. Leigh grabbed the earpiece and yanked it from her ear before he had the chance to do it again.

"I'm sure it's nothing, Anatoly." Though she could no longer hear through the device, the men were close enough that Nilsson's muffled words filtered through the partition. "You probably just grabbed it by mistake."

"No!" Vasiliev was fuming, and Leigh could tell that his paranoia was gaining ground. "I know who it was. It was that slutty server with the mushrooms. I should have known she had a reason to get so close."

A soothing murmur was coming from Nilsson, but Leigh didn't even try to make out what he said. Her heart had stopped the moment Vasiliev mentioned the server. *Amanda.* He'd go after her without a second thought. Leigh reached for her phone to text her partner a warning, but her hands were so unsteady that she feared she would drop it and the noise would give her away. Instead, Leigh chose to reprimand herself silently. *You just can't help yourself, can you? You just keep putting the women you love in danger.*

"I gave you five hundred kronor, you bitch!" Vasiliev screamed. "Wait," he added, more quietly this time. "Did you hear that?"

Leigh was rocked by a sudden realization in that moment—and while perhaps it *should* have been the fact that she had just admitted to herself that she was in love with Amanda, in fact, that was *not* it at all. What she realized was that the volume of the sound coming through the earpiece that she still held pinched between her fingers had been so loud that it had vibrated her whole hand. In addition, it had emitted enough sound that it was possible Vasiliev had heard it from the other side of the partition, like a voice over a poor-quality speaker phone. He'd be sure to investigate. *In which case, I'm basically fucked.*

Nilsson said something too quiet to hear, and then Vasiliev spoke again. "I'm telling you, I heard my own voice somewhere in the room. I think she's in here right now, and I'm going to find her."

Without pausing for even a second to think things through and formulate some semblance of a plan, Leigh grasped the earpiece and chucked it as hard as she could toward the stairs. At least if he yelled into the phone again, the sound would come from as far away from her hiding place as possible. It was exactly what happened.

"There, did you hear it this time?" Vasiliev's agitation was mounting. "I think it came from over there."

Leigh shrank down even more, willing herself to become invisible as she heard the shuffling of feet and saw the men emerge into the open space of the hall. Adrenaline and relief caused her whole body to shake as she saw that they were both headed in the direction of the stairs.

"What's this?" His back to Leigh, Vasiliev crouched down over one of the stairs as if to pick something up.

He must have spotted the earpiece. Nilsson stood nearby, his body also angled in such a way that Leigh's hiding place remained secure, at least for the moment. She continued to watch, and as Vasiliev bent further, a tell-tale bulge at the back of his jacket announced the presence of a concealed weapon. Before either man had a chance to turn, Leigh darted behind the other side of the partition and out of sight.

Shit. He has a gun.

Leigh's breath came in short gulps and the sound of her heartbeat in her ears drummed out all other sound. The fact that a mob boss was carrying a gun would've been a given in the US, but this was Sweden. No one carried guns in Sweden, and as a result, Leigh hadn't prepared for the possibility. More importantly, she hadn't prepped Amanda for what to do if Vasiliev had a gun. Not that it mattered. Now that she knew, she didn't want Amanda anywhere close enough to the man for it to be an issue. She needed to get somewhere safer and warn Amanda.

"Calm down, Anatoly." Though she could no longer see them, the direction of the voices suggested they were still by the stairs. "Let's go back upstairs and look into it. Do you have any of your men here?"

Leigh froze. *His men.* Anatoly Vasiliev never went anywhere without his hired goons, but until that moment, they'd been nowhere to be seen and Leigh had dared to hope this was an exception to the rule. *Is it too much to hope for a break?* The feeling returned to her limbs when she heard him answer no.

"They wouldn't let them in without an invitation, and I didn't want to risk making a scene."

"That was wise," Nilsson assured him with the air of a man who knew the importance of not setting off any sparks in the presence of the Russian's short fuse. "The Foundation is handling security tonight, and my men can be trusted. Let's go talk with them and find out who this woman is."

As soon as she heard footsteps on the stairs, Leigh ran in the opposite direction, and almost immediately ran into a dead end. There was no exit in sight, just the giant warship towering above her. Maybe two stories up, light shone from the row of open hatches on the lower gun deck. They would have held cannons back in the day, but now were empty and formed a long line of narrow entrances to the ship, if only she could scale its hull. No one would think to look for her there, but without so much as a rope, and with a roomful of guests dining just one floor above her with a clear view of the ship, Leigh found it unlikely that she would succeed without getting caught. Giving up, she took a moment to send Amanda an urgent text to warn her that Vasiliev was on his way and on the hunt for her. There was no response.

Having given up on the possibility of accessing the interior of the ship, Leigh circled to the opposite side in search of an alternate staircase to the main floor. That's when she saw the scaffolding. The ship was a massive artifact and under constant conservation, and it appeared from the scaffolding and piles of tools that a portion of the exterior on the starboard side was currently undergoing renovation. The top of the scaffolding came within inches of an opening on the lower gun deck. Without a moment's hesitation, Leigh scurried up the scaffolding and shimmied through the opening.

She landed with a soft plop onto a canvas tarp that seemed to have been put in place to protect the delicate boards of the original deck. There were more modern tools inside. The space was brightly, almost garishly, lit by a series of fluorescent lights overhead that stood in sharp contrast to the ancient beams, and every so often, modern steel supports were visible, providing stability to the four-hundred-year-old vessel. Leigh looked around in awe. Ever since she'd first visited the ship as a teenager with her seafaring grandfather, she'd wondered what it would be like to stand inside. *And now here I am.*

Her moment of reverie was interrupted by an incoming text from Amanda.

VASILIEV SPOTTED. STAYING CLEAR NEAR BACK OF ROOM.

Leigh peeked through the open gun ports until she spotted a figure that looked like Amanda standing at the edge of the crowd, just ahead of the ship's stern. With a sigh of relief, Leigh acknowledged that Amanda was safe, at least for now. But with the Foundation's security guards on the lookout for them and Vasiliev still prowling the main floor, their best bet might be for them both to wait it out on the gun deck until the event was over and they could sneak out, even if it meant waiting until the museum reopened in the morning. Her phone buzzed again.

WHERE ARE YOU?

Leigh texted back: THE SHIP.

WHAT SHIP?

Despite the danger they were in, she couldn't help but find some humor in this. Clearly even Amanda didn't expect she'd do something as crazy as board the famous warship.

Leigh replied: THE VASA. COME AROUND TO THE STERN.

After sending the text, she watched for Amanda's reaction, chuckling as the woman's head suddenly popped up from the phone and swiveled toward the ship. Leigh scrambled up a nearby ladder to the upper gun deck and waited beside an opening that was eye level to the main floor, flanked on either side by almost life-sized carvings of men in seventeenth-century garb. Moments later, Amanda stood at the stern, out of view of the gala guests. Leigh waved and Amanda's jaw dropped as she finally seemed to comprehend exactly what Leigh had meant.

Leigh leaned forward as far as she was willing to risk and said in a harsh whisper, "Amanda, can you hear me?"

Amanda nodded, still looking dumbstruck. "Jesus Christ, Leigh!" she whispered back. "Are you trying to get arrested?"

"No, I'm trying not to get either of us caught.

Come on. There's scaffolding on the bottom floor. I'll meet you there and help you up."

Amanda shook her head. "No way. You must be joking."

Leigh thought back to what she'd overheard between Vasiliev and Nilsson and her expression grew grave. "Amanda, this is no joke. With what Vasiliev has in the works, he'd be more than happy to kill us both."

"You heard something? Was it about the reports?"

The reports? Leigh nearly laughed out loud. How she longed for the time when she had been naive enough to think this was just about some immigration reports. "It's so much bigger than that. This goes to the highest branches of government and involves politicians in every party. If what my gut tells me is true, they're planning some sort of silent coup."

The color drained from Amanda's face and her eyes grew impossibly wide and wild. "We have to get out of here. We need to tell someone!"

"We will. Don't worry," Leigh soothed. "As soon as it's safe. Now go find the scaffolding."

Amanda nodded and set off toward the stairs. Leigh had just taken a step toward the ladder to the lower gun deck when she heard-

"There's someone on the ship! I just saw a woman on the ship!"

Adrenaline pumping, Leigh tore back to the window. Amanda still stood on the top step, frozen in place as a growing commotion echoed from the guests.

From her vantage point, Leigh could also make out two security guards closing in on the staircase from the lower level. Amanda was seconds away from getting caught.

"Run!" Leigh screamed. "Find Javier!" Then she pulled her head back through the opening and toppled backward onto the rough wood plank floor. No longer able to see, she just prayed Amanda would, for once in her life, do as she was told without an argument.

Leigh could hear gasps from the crowd and the sound of heavy footsteps pounding on metal, causing the ship itself to vibrate. On the main level of the museum was a catwalk that led to the ship, with modern stairs providing access to the upper deck, and she felt certain that's where the sounds were coming from. *Is it security, or the police?* With police, she might have a chance to explain. With the Foundation's loyal security force, she might not.

The ceiling above her visibly bowed and swayed as at least one person, a large one by the sound of it, made contact with the deck at a spot just above her head. As the footsteps took off toward the bow, Leigh dashed toward the staircase at the stern that would take her to the upper deck. Whether police or security, she preferred not to take her chances with either while hidden in the belly of the ship. If she were out in the open, at least Javier might see her and come to her rescue, if only to kill her himself later on.

Leigh emerged onto the deck through one of two

domed doorways, shrouded by enough shadow that she wasn't yet visible to the crowd of gala attendees who gaped and pointed from the railing of the main floor. She surveyed the length of the ship and found that she was the only one there. Whoever had boarded was already on the lower deck, and had come alone.

Ahead of her, three towering masts seemed to scrape the ceiling, the rope rigging coming down taut on either side like the cables of a bridge. The light that filtered down through and around the ropes cast strange, dark shapes on the deck, distorting the carvings of faces that adorned the railings. For a moment the eeriness overwhelmed her, and Leigh had the impression of being surrounded not by carved faces but by ghosts. A chill ran through her.

Find the steps to the catwalk. Get off this ship and find Javier. Keep Amanda safe. She repeated her priorities over and over, silently, as she inched her way onto the deck. Haunted or not, it really made no difference. There was no time for dilly-dallying. She'd just spotted the metal steps beyond the first mast when the ruling figure of a man lumbered across the catwalk and into the light. Leigh froze. *Vasiliev.*

Even from that distance, Leigh could see that his face reflected the same shock at finding her there as she felt. As he worked out exactly who stood in front of him, Vasiliev's cheeks turned a mottled, angry red. "You!"

There was nothing left to do but turn and run back

down the stairs. Whoever waited for her on the lower deck, she was willing to take her chances. At least she wasn't to blame for *his* daughter's death. At least *he* didn't want to see her dead. The first inkling Leigh had that Vasiliev had drawn his gun was a deafening crack as the bullet smashed into the brittle old wood of the ship's arched doorframe.

There was another shot, and searing pain. Leigh clutched at her upper arm, stunned. She drew her hand away and found it stained dark red with blood. Time seemed to come to a standstill. As she swayed, impossibly unsteady on her feet at the top of the stairs, she saw Vasiliev closing in, fiddling with his gun, preparing to take aim. She heard footsteps below her, relentlessly approaching the base of the stairs. She swayed again, the edges of her vision turning black. Just before she faded out, she thought she saw a familiar face in the crowd, peering over the railing amidst the startled-looking crowd.

Natasha? Leigh gasped. *Am I about to die?* What other explanation could there be that that she'd come from beyond the grave to escort Leigh to paradise. Leigh stared at the apparition, frozen to the core. *Or is she here to accuse me of her death and damn me to hell?*

After what seemed an eternity, Leigh blinked, bringing the face into focus. The warmth rushed back to her extremities. *No, it's Amanda.* The Säpo agent who had accompanied Javier stood just behind. *Even if I die, she's safe.* But instead of relief, regret over keeping

Amanda at arm's length skewered her heart, making her double over as if in physical pain. *She'll be safe, but she'll never know what she meant to me.*

She was vaguely aware of stumbling backward, of her body teetering. At the same moment, a resounding crack exploded from Vasiliev's gun, and her muscles tensed as she awaited the impact of the shot. Instead she fell, and fell, and kept falling, surrounded only by darkness, and the look of shock on Amanda's face—and in her final moment of consciousness, she thought she detected just the vaguest whiff of a freshly baking strawberry pie.

JAVIER HAD BEEN STARING at her, unblinking, for so long that it was becoming unnerving.

Amanda tried again. "I said, Leigh's the one onboard the ship."

"I heard you the first time." At last, his eyelids fluttered closed, not in a normal blink, but in that way that says the person has become exasperated nearly to the point of it causing them physical pain. "What are you two even doing here? You were under strict orders to stay at the safe house."

"I know, but—"

"Do you realize that you're both still wanted in connection with Henrik's murder? Leigh's fingerprints were on the murder weapon! Technically, Agent

Berglund," he gestured to the tall blonde woman beside him, "should arrest you on the spot!"

"Javier, please." Amanda looked at him imploringly as she thought of Leigh trapped on that boat. "I know we shouldn't have done it, but Leigh had to. For Henrik. And it's turned out to be bigger than anyone thought. Please. You have to get her out of here before Vasiliev finds her."

Javier turned to Agent Berglund. "Ebba, do you think you can call in a team?"

The woman sighed and looked disapprovingly at Amanda. "A small one. So, this is your agent who's caused so much trouble?"

"No." Javier glanced away, looking embarrassed. "This is the civilian. My agent's the one on the ship. I'll go retrieve her now," he added with a sigh, and set off in the direction of the ship's catwalk. Moments later, he was on the upper deck and headed toward the bow and a set of stairs that led to the lower deck.

Seconds dragged on like hours as Agent Berglund placed a call to her team, when suddenly, a loud thud shook the room. Amanda wrenched her head toward the ship with a start, but could see nothing. There were gasps from guests in the crowd as someone exclaimed that they saw a gun. Though Amanda couldn't understand her words, at the mention of a weapon, Agent Berglund's demeanor took on an increased sense of urgency. Amanda's body tensed and her heart raced. She needed to get through the crowd to see what was going on.

She was only a few yards from the railing, but it felt like an eternity as she pushed past men in dinner jackets and women in gowns, seeking out a suitable vantage point. *Please let it be Javier. Please let it be him with the gun.* But as she reached the edge of the crowd and looked down onto the Vasa's upper deck, she saw, as if in slow motion, Vasiliev raising a handgun and taking aim. The crack of the shot seemed to split the very air around her in two. There was a shattering of wood and Leigh clutched her left arm with her right hand. Amanda stifled a cry as she strained to see more clearly. Had it been the bullet, or just a fragment of wood that had caused Leigh's injury? Whichever it was, when Leigh pulled her hand away, Amanda could make out the unmistakable crimson stain of blood.

Leigh stumbled backward and Amanda felt herself pulled forward as her heart wrenched inside her chest. She was leaning as far over the railing now as she could without tumbling over. A second shot rang out, and this time Amanda cried out as Leigh lost her footing again and looked like she was about to fall down the dark stairwell behind her. As Vasiliev advanced toward her injured partner, Amanda lost all sense of time or space.

He's going to kill her. There was a certainty to the thought that left no room for question. He would do it, and feel no remorse. *I can't lose her!* In her adamancy,

Amanda was every bit as determined to stop him, no matter what it took.

As he advanced toward Leigh's wobbling form, there was a brief moment where Amanda had a clear view of Vasiliev's broad chest, it's crisp white tuxedo shirt beckoning. Without a conscious thought, she reached onto the dinner table beside her and grasped a heavy, pointed steak knife from a place setting that had been left abandoned in the commotion.

What am I thinking? I don't know how to do this. I'm not a spy, I'm a temp!

But she'd done it once before by accident, and if she didn't manage to conjure that same luck now, Leigh would be dead. She could almost feel Leigh's arms around her as she tensed her muscles into position and threw, the dark studs on Vasiliev's shirt taking the place of rings on a paper target. She heard nothing as it hit, but a fraction of a second later saw the man who had tormented them and shot the woman she loved, grasp his chest and collapse onto the deck in a heap as a brilliant red circle blossomed across his shirt like a rose. When she looked back to the arched doorway, Leigh was gone.

Amanda stood numbly in place as the people around her began to move. She was vaguely aware of a female voice— maybe it belonged to Agent Berglund— alternating between Swedish and English, directing them to the exits. Instead, she pushed her way against the traffic toward the catwalk, the jabs and crushed toes from the crowd failing to even register. She had one goal, to board the ship and find Leigh.

With one foot on the catwalk, Amanda gained a better view. Down below, she caught a glimpse of Javier cradling Leigh, who seemed to be moving. *She's still alive!* Amanda's heart sang and her feet felt light as she raised the other foot onto the metal surface of the bridge that separated her from Leigh, but as she went to take a step, something dragged her back and down. In the panic of the crowd that surrounded her, Amanda felt the full force of Agent Berglund's scowling face.

"Oh, no you don't," the agent told her sternly. "You've caused enough trouble tonight, Ms. Princeton. You're coming with me."

Without allowing her so much as a backward glance, Agent Berglund snapped a handcuff to Amanda's wrist and dragged her out a back door, shoving her into a waiting van.

TWENTY-SEVEN

IT WAS cold in the room where they'd left her. Amanda shivered, the short sleeves of her caterer's uniform providing little warmth. There'd been no windows in the back of the van, and so she'd been limited to whatever she could glimpse out the front to provide clues to where she was being taken. Her ability to pick out landmarks had failed completely once they entered a long tunnel that led to their destination, wherever that was. Amanda wasn't certain, and no one had bothered to fill her in. She thought she was still in Stockholm, but couldn't be sure. Agent Berglund and someone else—the van driver, maybe—had escorted her from the van in an underground parking lot, down a plain white hallway lined with unmarked doors, and deposited her in the room to wait. That had been hours ago.

Am I under arrest? It was just one more question for

which no one had given her an answer. The room she now occupied wasn't a prison cell, exactly, but it wasn't a luxury hotel, either. For one thing, there were no windows. That fact, combined with the arrival by tunnel and the persistent chill, gave Amanda the impression of being deep underground in a secret lair. A secret lair that was modestly furnished with mid-range IKEA products—a bed, a desk, and a chair, all offering a pleasingly simple mix of comfort and style—which admittedly took away some of the mystique one usually associated with lairs.

But regardless of the bland comfort that surrounded her, Amanda's mental state was a blend of shock and terror. Every muscle was tensed and on high alert as she sat perched on the edge of the chair. The final moments at the Vasa Museum replayed again and again in her mind. The gunshot. The blood. The knife. *Is Vasiliev dead? Is Leigh?*

She hadn't seen Leigh since the glimpse she'd gotten before Agent Berglund whisked her away from the scene. Javier was nowhere to be found, either. She was an American woman traveling on a falsified passport, being held by Swedish special police, and the only two people who could vouch for her were missing, and one of them might be dead.

I'm completely screwed.

Unable to tolerate the cold any longer, Amanda kicked off her shoes and crawled under the covers on the bed. The thick duvet was unexpectedly cozy, and as her stiff muscles warmed and relaxed against the mattress, she soon succumbed to her exhaustion. She dozed fitfully, aware that time was passing, but having no idea how much. Her stomach rumbled, reminding her that she couldn't remember when she'd last eaten. Surely someone would come check on her soon and at least bring her something to eat, right?

Still wrapped in the duvet, Amanda sat up in bed but kept her eyes closed. She pictured a plate of meatballs and lingonberry jam, but the image soon dissolved into one of Leigh, smiling and laughing as her grandmother spooned gravy onto her plate at the farmhouse. *If she's dead, who will tell them?* Tears stung Amanda's eyes. Would they ever know, or would Leigh just seem to disappear without an explanation?

And what about me? Who will notice if I just disappear? She squeezed her eyes tighter and pulled the duvet close around her shoulders as a cold lump settled into the pit of her stomach. It would be so easy for her to disappear. Who would even notice?

There was Aunt Millie. Amanda's heart clenched to think of her elderly aunt all alone in a nursing home she didn't like, wondering why her niece had stopped dropping by. It killed her to imagine her aunt feeling abandoned and scared with no one to watch out for her. But with her memory, how long would it take for Aunt Millie to grow confused or forget? And if she did, would anyone else remember Amanda at all?

Sitting in her not-quite-prison-cell in god-knows-where, Amanda took stock of her life's accomplishments. At twenty-six years old, she had no close friends, no romantic relationship, no career aspirations—not even a steady job. Temps came and went and no one at the agency would question it if she simply never called to book another gig. It happened all the time. Hell, after skipping out of an assignment and running off to Stockholm without so much as a day's notice, she'd be lucky if they'd even hire her again. As for the old house in Ten Hills where she lived, it would sit empty, and eventually a neighbor would notice the uncut grass, but who would care? No one.

God, my life sucks.

Amanda had known she'd fallen a little behind where she'd wanted to be by this point. She'd have been the first to admit it if anyone asked, but until that moment, it had never felt so impossibly bleak. Perhaps it hit her even harder because since the moment she'd met Leigh, she'd felt so incredibly fulfilled for the first time in as long as she could remember. It had been hectic and unexpected, and sometimes terrifying, too, but ever since she'd answered that wrong number at the radio station, her life had, in many ways, become everything she'd always dreamed it could be.

For all its uncertainty and inconvenience, life on the run had been amazing. What she wouldn't give to be back on Leigh's grandfather's boat, pretending that Leigh's impressive nautical skills didn't get her all hot and bothered. Hell, she'd even settle for enduring the woman's terrible driving, bumping along a back road in the passenger seat of a rental car. Amanda smiled.

The unique pattern of bickering and banter they'd fallen into during their time together had been their way of channeling the constant current of electricity that flowed between them. It was probably the only thing that had allowed them to keep their hands off each other for as long as they had. And then, last night, they hadn't—and it had been glorious. *But then Leigh had gone and acted like none of it had mattered at all…*

Amanda pushed the duvet away from her, the ire she still felt over the incident raising her temperature more effectively than any blanket. She paced the room, the stomping of her feet bringing some satisfaction as she recalled how ready, almost eager, Leigh had been to dismiss everything between them, pretend like she'd never said she loved her, or heard Amanda say it in return. But she'd said it. They both had. As quickly as it had come, her anger evaporated and the pain of loss skewered her heart. Even when she was furious with her, there was no one she wanted more.

Will I ever have another chance with her, or is all that gone for good? At this point, given the uncertainty of her situation, she had to admit that she'd even settle for her old, sucky life back, but what she really wanted was the life she'd started living with Leigh. She stopped her pacing and sank back down into the bed, all the fight having gone out of her. No matter how this played out, that life was gone. For starters, Leigh might be dead, but even if she were still alive, she was a spy and Amanda was not. And even if she was, Leigh had made it perfectly clear that there would be no 'them'. So, the adventure was over, one way or the other and it couldn't get any worse.

Of course it can. Leigh might be dead and I might be going to the gulag, and then I'll have nothing at all to hope for ever again.

The door to her room opened and Agent Berglund came in, still resplendent in her shimmering evening dress, a thick file folder tucked under one arm and a general no-nonsense air about her despite her fancy attire. She was the picture of bureaucratic efficiency. She closed the door behind her and took a seat at the desk while Amanda remained on the bed, then opened her folder and read silently. Her expression gave nothing away.

Finally, Amanda couldn't wait any longer. "Has Leigh been taken to a hospital?" Agent Berglund remained stone-faced. "Is she dead?" Amanda struggled not to remember the extreme pallor of Leigh's face at the bottom of that stairwell. And the blood. How bad had the wound been? The first bullet seemed to have missed, shattering the wood instead of Leigh's body. But the second? Amanda had no idea where the second bullet had come to rest.

"Anatoly Vasiliev is dead," Agent Berglund announced, pointedly not answering the questions that troubled Amanda most.

This news caused trouble of its own. Amanda drew a quick breath. *Dead.* And she was responsible. "Then that's it? Am I under arrest for murder?"

"Murder?" Agent Berglund gave the faintest of laughs, but her amusement didn't stretch as far as her eyes, which were still cold and entirely without humor. "Which one? Seems to me I've got at least two dead bodies with your name all over them, and one of them a Säpo agent. Any more I should know about?"

Amanda frowned. "We had nothing to do with Henrik's death. I thought Javier was sorting that out."

This time, there was a spark in Agent Berglund's eyes as she spoke. "You Americans. Always thinking you can waltz into other countries and sort things out."

Amanda swallowed, her throat dry and rough. The woman didn't like her, or maybe it was just Americans in general that she despised. Either way, it didn't bode well for a timely release.

"You and your countrymen do have a way of wrapping things up tidily, though. I'll give you that." Whether she was sincere or sarcastic, it was impossible to tell. "We have one Russian mobster dead, and his gross misuse of the resources at the Foundation for Swedish Heritage has been exposed. The Foundation's director, Per Nilsson, will almost certainly be going to jail for quite some time."

Amanda waited for Agent Berglund to add more bullet points to her list. What about the misleading immigration reports? What about all that stuff concerning the government that Leigh had hinted at in the museum? Where was the deeper, more sinister plot just waiting to unfold? But Agent Berglund shut the file as if the case were closed. *Is she hiding something, covering it up? Or does she not know?*

"There's one more thing." Agent Berglund looked Amanda directly in the eyes and Amanda's breath caught. *There it is. Now she's getting to the rest.* "A laptop was just recovered from Vasiliev's home. An old one. We think you may know something about it?"

"A laptop?" Amanda's brain whirred. How much did they already know? "Yes, I'm familiar with the laptop. Leigh had turned it over to Henrik but it was missing when we discovered his body on the boat."

"And?" The thin veneer of Agent Berglund's patience was cracking to reveal the annoyance beneath.

Under the circumstances, Amanda figured it was she who had every right to be annoyed. She was being held with no explanation, without an update on Leigh's condition, and now this woman was hinting at —*what?* That Amanda was the one who was being the obstructionist? That Amanda was the one who had done something wrong?

Amanda bristled. "And? And I suppose since you found the laptop we turned over to Henrik in Vasiliev's possession, that's ample evidence that Vasiliev was responsible for Henrik's death. Not me, not Leigh." She drew a deep breath and glared, channeling the Amanda from some alternate universe who had gone to law school after all, and kicked ass while she was at it. "Furthermore, unless the laws in this country are very different than at home, what happened with Vasiliev at the museum was self-defense. So, when can I expect to be released?"

Agent Berglund blinked. "I meant, do you know anything about the contents? Did you manage to get it unlocked?" Whether she'd been impressed by Amanda's outburst or was seething over it remained a mystery.

Amanda hesitated, filled with a deep mistrust. Was it because the woman couldn't be trusted, or just because she was unfriendly? Amanda erred on the side of caution. "No, we have no idea."

"Very well. I'll leave it to the tech department to sort out."

Using brute force, if what Max had told them was correct. It was the first thing they would try. Would they realize the computer had a failsafe before they destroyed the hard drive? Should she tell Agent Berglund now?

"Well, good luck to them," Amanda replied with a pleasant smile. "I'm sure your Swedish hackers are up to the task." *Far be it from an office temp to tell the real spies how to do their jobs.*

"I'm sure they are." The pride in Agent Berglund's tone was the most emotion she'd shown throughout the entire interview. She rose from her chair and strode to the door. "Now if you'll follow me, Ms. Princeton?"

Hesitantly, Amanda swung one leg and then the other to the floor and rose from the bed. Her first impulse was to ask where she was being taken, but she refrained. It would be just one more question the icy agent would ignore. She followed Agent Berglund into the hallway and down past several identical doors until they stopped at one and the agent twisted the knob and ushered her inside. Amanda's heart leaped to see Javier, a little haggard but otherwise well, seated at a table within.

"Javier! How's Leigh?" Amanda's voice cracked, unable to keep back the flood of emotion at the prospect of finally hearing a truthful answer.

"In surgery, but the doctors are hopeful." His expression was grave but kind. "She has multiple shrapnel wounds from the wood, but only minor damage from the bullet. It went clean through so there was blood loss and tissue damage, but no broken bones."

"Can I see her?"

"I'm sorry, but no. She's in a secure facility and you lack the necessary clearance."

"Says the man who got me a real Swedish passport in under an hour," Amanda challenged, raising an eyebrow.

Javier shook his head. "Not this time. We've

already strained our relationship with Säpo enough for one mission."

"You really believe she'll be okay?" Amanda's voice was small, fearing the answer.

"She's a fighter. Also, much too ornery to die." Javier's face brightened considerably and Amanda couldn't help but chuckle. "But the best news," he continued, "is that now that Vasiliev is dead, the danger that prompted this whole misadventure is over."

Amanda frowned, sensing that there was something she was supposed to understand that eluded her. "Meaning?"

"Meaning, you can go home. And just in time, too. Your Aunt Millie's been kicking up a fuss, and I'm afraid she doesn't like me very much."

"You've met Aunt Millie?" Amanda asked, surprised.

"I went to her nursing home a few times undercover, pretending to be staff. When she asked about you, I'd tell her you'd just been by the day before and it must've slipped her mind, but she wouldn't buy it. Feisty lady."

Amanda nodded. "That she is."

"So," he said in a tone that indicated he was ready to wrap things up, "we've got you booked on a flight home tonight. It's on a commercial airline this time and not a private jet, but I got them to upgrade you to business class."

Amanda stared in shock. "I don't know what to say."

Javier waved his hand dismissively. "It's the least we could do."

"No," Amanda protested, "That's not what I meant." *What about Leigh? What about the government plot? What about the Foundation reports and Leigh's mother's murder?* "It can't really be over, just like that?"

"It really can," Javier assured her, as if that were a good thing. "The danger from Vasiliev was a personal grudge against Leigh. Even if his criminal organization carries on without him, they won't care about her or you. You're perfectly safe now."

"But...but, there's so much we don't know!" Amanda wrung her hands, agitation building. "What about what Henrik said about Leigh's mother having been murdered? It had to be Vasiliev behind it, right? Or maybe Nilsson. Could he have been the Mule?"

Javier shrugged. "One's dead and one is going to jail. Either way, as far you're concerned, it's over."

Amanda shook her head emphatically, unable to let it go. "What if it was someone else? What if there's more to this?"

Javier studied her intently, eyebrows raised admiringly. "I'm impressed with your tenacity. You don't give up, do you?"

"Not until the puzzle's solved." She lifted her chin proudly.

Javier looked thoughtfully at her for a few moments

longer, then he shook his head slowly. "But this isn't one of your puzzles. We can handle it from here."

"Right. Of course." Amanda's insides grew cold and she could feel her lips begin to tremble. He'd studied her for so long that she'd been nearly convinced he might suggest she come to work for the agency. Instead, she'd been dismissed.

"We appreciate all you've done, though," Javier added, perhaps sensing something about their conversation wasn't sitting well with her. "And you'll be paid for your time."

"I will?" She hadn't been expecting that, and the news acted as a beacon of hope even beyond the fact that her bills stood a chance of being paid, after all. *Maybe they'll want me as a contractor?*

"Yes, you will. You see, we hired you through your temp agency the morning the plane landed in Stockholm. Light office work. You'll be paid for all the time you've been here, and a few extra weeks for you to recover, too. Spend some time with your Aunt Millie and rest up. And we'll give you a glowing reference. In fact, I think that the temp agency will be very happy to have you back in the future, as soon as you decide to return." He smiled encouragingly, unaware that his words were breaking her heart. "Don't you worry. Everything's going to be exactly the way it was before. It'll be like all of this was just a dream."

TWENTY-EIGHT

BACK TO NORMAL, *Javier said. He sure wasn't joking. Bastard.*

Amanda sat on a chair in the sun-drenched courtyard of Aunt Millie's nursing home, her elderly aunt opposite her in a wheelchair with her legs draped in a crocheted blanket despite the blistering heat. Even in a tank top and shorts, sweat drenched Amanda's body in every conceivable nook and cranny. *Has it always been this hot in Baltimore?* The sea breeze off the Baltic seemed like a distant memory.

It had been three weeks since her return from Sweden, and life was back to normal, all right. *So fucking normal.* The first week had been the hardest, with news coverage on every channel teeming with reports of the huge scandal in Sweden. A mob boss linked to a prominent NGO. Money laundering, underworld dealings. Amanda had been glued to it at first, hoping to find out something she could use. But there'd been no mention of the types of political ties Leigh had hinted at, no new pieces to the puzzle. Did they not know, or were they just keeping it under wraps? She still had no idea.

And then there was having to see Leigh. Not the real Leigh, of course. Amanda increasingly was convinced that she'd never see Leigh again, which made it all the more painful to see the woman's picture splashed all over the news—the brave American agent who had killed Anatoly Vasiliev.

Bullshit. That was me. She'd stared at the television in utter shock when they'd first reported it that way, with no mention of Amanda's presence whatsoever. Her quick action and good aim had probably saved Leigh's life.

Yes, Leigh was still alive, not that anyone had bothered to keep Amanda in the loop. She'd found that out from the television, too, when Leigh's plane was given a hero's welcome as it touched down at Andrews Air Force Base. Somehow, she doubted her invitation to the homecoming celebration had just been misplaced in the mail.

"I don't know why the nurse makes me use a blanket," Aunt Millie muttered, breaking the silence.

Amanda looked up with a start, her mind a million miles away. "What was that, Aunt Millie?"

"The blanket. It's ninety degrees! And this wheelchair," she groused. "I'm perfectly capable of walking on my own two feet."

"They're just looking out for your well-being, Aunt Millie."

"They're incompetent. Like that Spanish nurse. I'm not sad to see that he's been let go."

"Who was that?" Amanda asked, not giving it her full attention. In the three weeks since her return, she'd heard every complaint under the sun at least twice.

"That one that kept telling me you'd just stopped by to visit, when I knew it wasn't true."

"Mm hm." She'd definitely heard this one before. "You don't think you might've forgotten?" Amanda didn't want to tell her aunt a lie directly, but saw no harm in sowing a few seeds of doubt.

Aunt Millie gave a loud *harrumph*. "How could you have just stopped by when you were in Sweden the whole time?"

Amanda sat bolt upright. *Now that's something new.* "I'm sorry? Why do you think I was in Sweden?"

"I saw your picture on the news."

Amanda's eyes grew wide as she recalled that her picture *had* been on the news, in connection with the murder of a Säpo agent. *Shit.* She laughed nervously. "And why was my picture on the news?"

Aunt Millie pursed her lips, looking stumped. "You know, I can't recall." Her eyes narrowed. "But don't you go thinking that proves I have Alzheimer's and should be in a place like this. It's just a little forgetfulness, is all."

Amanda sighed. *This again.* "Aunt Millie, you almost set fire to the house."

"I didn't!" Her aunt hesitated as if debating whether or not to reveal a secret. "Amanda, I passed out."

"What?" Amanda leaned toward her aunt, reaching out as if to feel her forehead for a fever. "Are you okay? Do you need to see a doctor?"

"I didn't pass out recently, dear," Millie explained. "I mean the day of the fire. I didn't forget about the chicken, at least not like you think. The truth is, Mrs. MacGregor came over from next door and we'd been hitting the gin."

"Gin?" Amanda's jaw dropped. "At that time of day?"

Millie set her jaw defensively. "See, that's why I didn't mention it before. I knew how it would look. I just didn't realize by not telling you, I'd end up someplace like this."

Amanda squeezed her eyes shut against the glare of the sun, and to tamp down her frustration. *Gin? Jesus.* "I just wanted you to be safe." She cringed at her own words. *I'm starting to sound like Leigh.*

Millie's eyes darted around the courtyard which was dotted with white-haired residents in wheelchairs. "This place is full of old people," she said in a loud whisper. "Let's go inside. They're giving me the creeps."

Amanda stood quickly, grateful for an excuse to get out of the heat. She seemed to have lost all tolerance for it in her brief time away. Millie moved as if to stand, but Amanda gently held her down with a hand on her shoulder. "You know the rules. You need to stay in the chair until you're inside."

The old woman pouted. "Fine, but I don't want you to do it. I want your friend the nurse."

"The nurse?" Amanda tried to puzzle out what she meant. "Javier?"

"Who?"

Before her aunt's revelation about the gin, Amanda would've chalked this up to forgetfulness, but instead she tried a description the woman was more likely to understand. "The Spanish nurse."

"No, no. Not that one. He's not here anymore." She fixed her niece with an impatient look. "Remember? I told you that. You really need to keep up."

Amanda's head was spinning from confusion. "I don't have any nurse friends, Aunt Millie."

"She's right there," Aunt Millie waved at a petite woman in scrubs who was making her way across the courtyard toward them. "Your friend from Sweden. Her picture's been all over the news for days."

Leigh? Confusion turned to shock as Amanda realized the nurse coming toward them was none other than Leigh—perpetually in disguise, but it was her.

"Can I help you get her inside?" Leigh asked, placing her hand on the handle of the wheelchair, no more than a hairbreadth from Amanda's. Instantly, Amanda could feel the invisible electric current arc between them. A rush of emotions overwhelmed her—elation, surprise, and joy, with some good old-fashioned lust thrown into the mix, too. Who but Leigh could look that good in scrubs? Especially for a woman who, by all rights, should have been dead.

"What, you just come waltzing back after no word for *weeks*?" Of all the emotions swirling around inside, peevishness was the one that won out when Amanda opened her mouth to speak. It was as if all the worry and doubt and grief since her return to the States coalesced into an unstoppable rage. *How dare Leigh put me through that!* "Where the hell have you been?"

"In a secret hospital in Stockholm," Leigh said blandly. "I was shot, remember?"

"Aren't you going to introduce me to your friend, dear?" Aunt Millie looked up expectantly from her chair as it rolled along.

"Of course. This is my Aunt Millie." Amanda's eyes formed narrow slits as she looked pointedly at Leigh. "I'd introduce you, but I don't even know your last name. How awkward."

"Bonde." Leigh paused. "Linnea Bonde."

"Oh, please, seriously?"

Leigh blinked innocently, but amusement danced in her eyes. "What?"

Amanda refused to be charmed. "Look, I can't believe you would pull that kind of crap with my aunt. That's even worse than Smith."

Leigh shrugged. "But it's true."

"Bullshit." Amanda snorted derisively. "I heard you say it to Henrik when we were in the ruins. Lundgren. So, I looked up the property record for your grandparents' cottage. Ulla and Olle Lundgren."

Leigh nodded approvingly as Amanda pronounced each name. "Hey, that was pretty good! Were you practicing?"

Amanda gritted her teeth, never in a million years willing to admit that indeed, she had been. "Point is, you don't trust or respect me enough to even be honest about your name."

They'd reached the small sitting room of Millie's suite, and Leigh stopped once they were inside, turning to face her full on. "Amanda, my mother's name was Lundgren. My father's name is Bonde."

"Right. James Bond?" Amanda rolled her eyes.

The corner of Leigh's mouth twitched. "No, Gregory Bonde, with an 'e'. He's a CPA in San Jose. You can look it up yourself. His photo is on the company website. I'm told the family resemblance is striking."

The ice inside her showed the first signs of melting as Amanda considered this revelation. "You're telling the truth?"

"The whole truth and nothing but." Leigh gazed

deep into her eyes, raising Amanda's internal temperature by several more degrees. The wall of ice was doomed. "You know what else is true? I missed this."

Leigh didn't need to define it further. Amanda knew what she meant by it, that back and forth banter that served as foreplay every time they were together. She swallowed hard, her throat feeling lumpy. "You did?"

"Oh, yeah."

"Me, too," Amanda said, her voice barely above a whisper.

Any trace of coldness was gone, replaced by burning fire as Leigh's mouth was on hers. The kiss could've lasted minutes or hours. Amanda had lost all track of time, lost herself to everything but Leigh, until a loud snore brought her back to the present. She pulled her head away, lips puffy and bruised, not that she was about to complain. She glanced to where Aunt Millie had dozed off in her wheelchair.

Leigh looked appraisingly at Millie, snoozing in her seat. "She doesn't have a roommate, does she?"

"No." Amanda's brow creased, uncertain why Leigh had asked.

"In that case, maybe she wouldn't notice if we just slipped into the bedroom, and..." She waggled her eyebrows.

Leigh stood so close that it felt like someone had lit a furnace on this hot summer day. Amanda longed to give in, but looked doubtfully at her aunt, recalling her suddenly keen sense of observation. "She'd notice."

Leigh skewed her mouth, unconvinced. "Not to be rude, but I thought she had dementia."

"Trust me, so did I." Amanda's eyes narrowed into slits. "It's probably not a good idea for us to get too physical, anyway. I believe someone told me that before. Oh, right. It was you."

"Yeah, I guess I did." Leigh hesitated, then took a small step away. "Well, then, we should get down to business. I came here to give you something."

She held out an envelope, and Amanda could see that it bore the logo of the temporary agency where she'd been employed. She reached for it with a sinking feeling in her chest. "What is it?"

"Go ahead and open it." She twisted her shirt between her fingers as Amanda took the envelope. "It's an offer of employment."

"It's from my old temp agency." Amanda blinked back the tears that had formed in the corners of her eyes. For one glorious moment, she'd seen Leigh and this letter, and thought everything was going to change, but it was all exactly the same.

"It is, but it's not."

Amanda's pulse quickened. "Meaning?"

"Meaning that the Agency has purchased the temp agency." Leigh gave a self-satisfied chuckle. "Not to brag, but it was kinda my idea. When we were investigating you, after that wrong number I dialed, the fact that you'd worked in so many places was a major red flag. It's brilliant, if I do say so myself."

"What's brilliant?" Amanda knew very well that the words 'temp' and 'brilliant' rarely went together.

"Amanda, don't you see? What better cover for gathering intelligence than being a temp. You can go anywhere!"

"So, you want me to be a temp?"

"Well, yes. In a way."

Amanda scanned the letter, and her mental gears began to click and whir when she reached the bottom and saw the signature of one Linnea Bonde. "This is signed by—"

"Me. I know," Leigh interrupted. "You may not have noticed, but my picture's been all over the news the last few weeks."

"Yeah," Amanda allowed a hint of sarcasm to seep into her tone. "You're that famous agent who single-handedly killed that Russian mobster with a knife, aren't you?"

"That cover story wasn't my doing." She said it earnestly, and her cheeks had turned a deep, embarrassed red. "But the agency can't exactly admit a civilian was caught up in all this."

"Uh huh." Amanda knew she was telling the truth, but didn't mind dragging out her groveling for just a few seconds more. "So now you're famous. Do you get a raise?"

"Here's the thing, being famous is great for normal people, but it's bad news for a secret agent."

Immediately, all teasing evaporated. Amanda reached out and grasped Leigh's hand in concern. "Leigh, are you being fired?"

"No," she answered, squeezing Amanda's hand in return, "Far from it. First, I'm going to be given a commendation for Vasiliev—one that should belong to you, by the way." She gave a modest shrug. "Sorry about that. But then I'm going to have to resign. I can't work as an undercover agent anymore with my face all over the place. I'll need to move on."

"Resign?" Despite Leigh's oddly singsong voice in delivering the news, Amanda's face crumpled. "Leigh, that's terrible!"

"Oh, I don't know. I think running a temp agency might be a great opportunity."

"Running a temp agency?" Amanda blinked.

"Absolutely! A whole agency of secret agents, and I'm the one in charge. Director! It says it right there, under my signature." Leigh clapped her hands as Amanda scanned the letter again. "It's my new cover, and one that I can carry on right out in the open, and where my sudden fame might actually be a boon."

"How so?"

"Because a temp agency run by a former secret agent is guaranteed to be discreet. We'll get all the top clients clamoring to try us out." Leigh smiled reassuringly. "It's a promotion, Amanda. I'm finally getting my own team!"

"But you don't know anything about temping."

"No, but my partner will."

"Your—?" Amanda raised her eyebrows, unable to complete the question.

"Partner." Leigh beamed.

"Partner." Amanda chewed her lip while she processed this new development. Just how deep did her change of heart go? "But I thought you worked alone. Isn't that what you told me? A spy's life is a lonely life, and you can't get close to anyone because everyone dies. What happened to that?"

"I almost died."

"It was a flesh wound." Amanda scoffed as she glanced at the small bandage that was still visible on Leigh's arm beneath her scrubs. "You were in the hospital less than three weeks."

"A minute ago, you acted like that was an eternity. Now it's not good enough?" Leigh gave a soft snort. "When Vasiliev pointed his gun at me, I thought I was going to die. Believe me, that was enough to regret certain things I may have said, or not said, or…" Amanda held her breath, waiting for Leigh to elaborate, but she only sniffed loudly and glanced away. "So, what do you say?"

"I…" Amanda pressed her lips together, wanting to believe her, but still cautious. "I really thought you just wanted me as a temp."

"I want you in all sorts of ways, Amanda." The passion burning in Leigh's eyes was hot enough to be felt from a block away.

"Oh, really?" Though it had quickened Amanda's pulse and set her body tingling, she wasn't about to let Leigh off the hook without establishing one vital point, no matter how smooth the line. "I know how you want me in bed. You've hardly kept that a secret. But what else? I don't just want sex, I want a relationship, too. What about a date? An actual date. Do you want *that*?"

"A date?" A slight look of panic crossed Leigh's eyes, but she managed to keep it in check. "I guess we could go on a date."

"Oh, you *guess*?" Amanda raised her eyebrow suspiciously. "Are you, or are you not, asking me on a date?"

Leigh fidgeted. "Well, uh, sure."

"What kind of date?" Amanda pressed, starting to find tormenting Leigh in this particular way even more enjoyable than usual.

"Dinner?"

Amanda considered. "I don't know. We've been for dinner."

Leigh frowned. "Coffee?"

"We've been for coffee, too."

Leigh nodded. "And the coffee was better in Sweden."

"Sex, too," Amanda added.

Leigh's brow creased and she bit her lip uncertainly. "We didn't have sex in Sweden."

"Huh." Amanda huffed. "You sure sound certain about that."

"Well, I—"

As Amanda took in the confused expression on Leigh's face, it dawned on her that she might not be pretending after all. *Could she have been drowsier that night at the safe house than I thought?*

"You know what? Never mind. What I *meant* is that we've already done all of the usual date things without them really being dates. Coffee. Dinner. I mean, even sex." Amanda shrugged. "I just pictured, especially with you being a bona fide secret agent and everything, that we'd do something different for our first real date, I guess."

"What, like scuba diving? Rappelling down a skyscraper? Trying to escape an ancient warship under a hail of bullets? Oh, that's right," Leigh said, cocking one eyebrow, "we did that last one already, too. Sorry, Amanda, but if you're going to be this picky about not doing a repeat date, I'm all out of options."

To anyone else, Leigh may have sounded like she was about to give up, but Amanda recognized the fire raging in her eyes. This was just the foreplay, and Amanda knew it. As much as she reveled in this back-and-forth between them, it was time to let Leigh have a victory so they could move this thing to the next level before they both expired from heat and longing.

Amanda shrugged. "A movie might be nice."

"A movie?" Leigh hesitated, as if not sure if she should trust the win. "There's an idea. I hear *Svärd och Sköld* is a good one. A real spy thriller. You like those, right?"

Leigh won that round fair and square, and Amanda rewarded her with a kiss. "It's a date." But as she thought about the phrase that had been Vasiliev's password, the weight of seriousness replaced her levity. "Are we ever going to tell them that we figured out the password and have the files?"

"We didn't figure it out." Leigh gazed at Amanda with a mix of wonder and admiration. "You did. And you were brilliant." She leaned in for a quick peck on the lips. "But as for telling, I don't know. Henrik died to discover the names on that laptop and what they meant. I'm not sure we know the half of it yet. I'd like to see the whole thing brought to light and the bad guys punished, but how?"

Amanda grew pensive, weighing the risks. "Given some of our own government's current Russian issues—"

"Exactly. I'm not sure if it's safe for anyone to know but us."

Amanda breathed in deeply. "Maybe we can work it out together, as part of the new venture we're partnering on?"

"I think this is the beginning of a beautiful friendship."

Amanda doubled over with laughter. "Was that supposed to be Humphrey Bogart?"

"What?" Leigh crossed her arms in front of her chest. "It's *Casablanca*. Forged documents, airplanes with fog—that movie has it all."

"The movie's great." Amanda was still chuckling. "But that impression is even worse than your Sean Connery, and frankly, I didn't think that was possible."

"Frankly my dear, I don't give a damn." Leigh waited a beat. "That was my Clark Gable."

"I know." Amanda grinned, and the effect it had on Leigh sent a thrill through her. "That one was pretty good."

All joking aside, Amanda agreed wholeheartedly with Leigh. They were at the beginning of a beautiful future, both in their professional partnership, and perhaps in their personal one, too. But the shadow cast from the list they'd recovered was long and dark. The danger they would unleash by following that lead was also just beginning, and neither of them could guess where it might take them in the end.

For a brief moment, a chill passed through her, but Amanda refused to succumb to worries that would keep for another day. Tonight, she had only one path she hoped to follow, one destination in mind, and she knew exactly how *that* one would end.

After saying goodnight to Aunt Millie, they hopped into the Mini and headed toward Amanda's house. Amanda drove, though whether she'd won the right through her insistence that she was the better driver, or whether Leigh had given in just because it was Amanda's car was an argument with no hope of resolution in sight.

What they could both agree on readily was that neither saw any reason to wait until after their official movie date to spend the night having sex. After all, they'd already done it before, but to paraphrase the motto of a certain very wise spy Amanda knew, why limit yourself to just once?

THANK YOU FOR READING!

Hi there!

Miranda here. I can't thank you enough for deciding to read my book today. I've always been a fan of spies on TV, whether it was Get Smart reruns, Scarecrow and Mrs. King as a kid, or, more recently, the likes of Alias and Chuck. My only regret, like Amanda's, was that the whole Russian spy trope of my youth seemed so out of place in the modern world that I wasn't sure how a spy caper would go over. Russians? That's so 1980s.

Then my country went and had an election, and I think we all know how that turned out. Unless you've been living in a cave since November 2016, in which case I applaud your foresight. OMG, y'all, there are Russians *everywhere*. Lesbian spies are our only hope.

When I started writing my first book, *Telling Lies Online*, as a project for NaNo (National Novel Writing Month) in 2015, I never imagined it would eventually lead to me making a living as a full time writer. It was a life-long dream of mine to do so, and I am so thankful to readers like you, because without you, I wouldn't be where I am today, doing what I love most.

I've written 0ver a dozen novels now, and I like to think I've learned a little more with each one. I continue to publish new books every year. Some are lighthearted, low-heat level romantic comedies. Others are sizzling, dramatic contemporary romances. I try to offer a little something for every reading mood.

I hope you'll sign up for my mailing list so we can keep in touch. You'll receive a free copy of *Telling Lies Online* for subscribing, and have the chance to participate in monthly sales and giveaways, plus find out when new books are on the way.

You'll also be the first to hear my behind the scenes stories, like the time I had a bottle of wine explode in my cupboard while doing research *Accidental Honeymoon*. Or the time I attended a paint and sip class in preparation for writing my medical age-gap romance, *Hearts in Motion*.

What can I say? This writing thing is *serious* business, that apparently often involves wine.

You'll also get updates on all the ways my two kittens,

the Sisters of Chaos, are helping me by sitting on my laptop or knocking my pens onto the floor. Wine and cats. What could be better, except maybe books?

Happy Reading!
    Miranda

ABOUT THE AUTHOR

Originally from southern California, Miranda now lives in New England and writes heartfelt romances and romantic comedies featuring witty and charmingly flawed women that you'll want to marry. Or just grab a coffee with, if that's more your thing. She spent way too many years in graduate school, worked in professional theater and film, and held temp jobs in just about every office building in downtown Boston.

To find out about her upcoming releases and take advantage of exclusive sales, be sure to sign up for her newsletter.

Let's be in touch!

mirandamacleod.com
miranda@mirandamacleod.com

Printed in Great Britain
by Amazon

57190243R00229